Bronze Miner

BRONZE MINER

BILL OVERMYER

iUniverse, Inc.
Bloomington

Bronze Miner

iUniverse books may be ordered through booksellers or by contacting:

iUniverse
1663 Liberty Drive
Bloomington, IN 47403
www.iuniverse.com
1-800-Authors (1-800-288-4677)

ISBN: 978-1-4620-6204-1 (sc)
ISBN: 978-1-4620-6205-8 (ebk)

Printed in the United States of America

iUniverse rev. date: 12/07/2011

THIS BOOK IS DEDICATED TO ALL MEN AND WOMEN WHO SERVE IN THE ARMED FORCES OF THE UNITED STATES OF AMERICA.

Acknowledgement

Permission to use the photograph of the mountain on the front cover has been provided by Larry Prosor. Larry is one of the best photographers in the world for photos of breathtaking natural wonders, competitive outdoor sports, and recreational activities. Refresh and renew your spirit of adventure on Larry's website. Check his Lake Tahoe Collection for action photos on outdoor activities from A to Z.

www.larryprosorphotos.com.

CHAPTER ONE

The morning sun lit up the window of Cheryl Pritchard's second floor efficiency apartment. The sunlight crept across the floor to the queen sized mattress, the old yellow sheets and the forest green dacron sleeping bag. Moments later Cheryl stirred. She was awake and gaining consciousness. She had put in five long days this week with extra hours at the foundry. She left the bed and moved to her window to see how much new snow was on the ground. Her latest distraction was telemark skiing and she planned to indulge herself today. Her gaze went to the world outside the window. Leadville was due for a warm March day. Last night's overcast left four inches of snow on the ground. She had fallen in bed fully clothed and she was grateful for the prospect of a few days off. She had been too tired to shower or change clothes. Her thick wool socks were still on her feet. They removed the sensation of the ice cold floor. She was relatively warm in a layer of long johns, a sweat shirt, and her jeans.

She gazed through her four by six foot window. The snow was glistening in the morning sun. All of the roof tops she could see were covered with snow. The cold winter was nearing an end and each day the icicles grew in length. Roof lines that saw a long period of sunshine during the day boasted some four foot icicles. A thin layer of small, cotton ball size clouds dotted the sky to the horizon. The snow covered mountain peaks seemed to tickle the bellies of the low lying clouds. Gray granite cliffs and large rock outcroppings stood out in contrast to the white snow. The snow covered forest skirted the mountain peaks. She could see the mine shaft head frames on Silver King Mountain. They had survived the 1880 silver mining era. The head frame held a large pulley and cable. It lowered cages filled with workers or equipment into the mine. Piles of tailings stood adjacent to the head frames. They were a testament to the monumental effort of miners and early mining machinery. Cheryl wondered if she could capture this vast majestic beauty on canvass.

She turned back to the room and walked past her easel and her large work table. A twenty two inch tall replica of a defiant miner stood at the end of the table. His arms were outstretched with a hammer in one hand and steel spike in the other. He ignored the up and coming artist as she walked past him. She stopped at a closet in the corner of the room. Her light blue foundry sweatshirt went in the dirty clothes pile. She picked out a beige sweater with alternating white, brown, and dark blue diagonal diamonds. The sweater was a one of a kind. She found it at Charlotte and Charlie's Second Hand Rose clothing store. It was so out of character that she gave Charlotte an extra two dollars. A cheap price tag on a garment was important when buying clothes for work and play. Taste was not always a requirement. Patterns and colors that clashed made for easy conversation. This sweater guaranteed Cheryl that her coworkers would razz her all day.

She picked up her hair brush off the work table. She passed it through her reddish brown hair. Cheryl required no mirror to tidy up. She was aware of her average looks and she was content with them. She did not have to see them in a mirror everyday. Ready to go at a moments notice was more important to her. She moved a couple of steps and sat on the bed by her hiking boots. The boots were found at the Second Hand Rose for pennies on the dollar. Cheryl laughed as she recalled finding just one boot. For the next half hour, she looked under piles of clothes upstairs and down for the second boot. Charlie finally found it in the garage on top of a basket of winter coats.

She effortlessly laced the eyelets and doubled tied the bows. She stood and stretched. She moved to her small bathroom and stepped in to brush her teeth and tidy up. She left the bathroom and walked through the small kitchen area to the TV table in the corner. She picked up enough chump change for coffee and donuts. She moved across the room to the front door. Her outdoor clothing and skis hung from wood pegs next to the door. She donned her light powder blue ski jacket. Her forest green knit hat had a three foot tail that served as a scarf. She slipped on her new water resistant down mittens. They were the only new item of clothing that she purchased this winter. Down or very good synthetic mittens are a mandatory item in the cold winter climate.

She stepped through the doorway onto a small deck. As she turned to lock the door she shouted to no one in particular, "I will be home by eleven!"

A straw broom greeted her. Cheryl swept the three inch accumulation off the deck and each stair. The temperature was now fifteen degrees at eight am with no wind. It might warm up enough today to consider Ski Cooper for a couple of runs on the telemark skis. At the bottom of the stairs of the one hundred twenty year old mining home, she looked over the building tops and church steeples of Leadville to Mount Massive and Mount Elbert on the west side of the valley.

Cheryl took in the reverence and majesty of the mountains and the early morning silence of the small town. The mountain ranges rose on both sides of Leadville and continued south to the six thousand foot Salida valley floor. The Arkansas River flows between them to provide summer recreation for rafters and fishermen. She watched the shadows of clouds move lazily down the sides of the snow covered mountains. She pulled a pair of sunglasses out of the zipper pocket inside her coat. She found them at Charlotte's Second hand Rose. The sunglasses had the fifties tail fin design.

Her trampoline was set up in the center of the small front yard. She jumped on it year round. Summersaults and back flips provided relaxation for her. She used the broom to sweep off the snow. "There you go, Tramp. Now you are ready for the sunshine! I will catch you on the bounce." The snow crunched under her boots as she walked to the snow covered 1977 Dodge Dart Swinger. The wheel wells and the grille were packed with snow. Cheryl made it over the pass last night before it was closed by the state patrol. She spoke to the Swinger. "Are you warm enough to start today?" She laughed. She thought she heard the car swear. The edge of a maroon blanket peeked out from under the partially open snow covered hood. It gave the appearance that the car had been tucked in for the night. A black extension cord ran from the garage to an electric heater on the engine block. Cheryl went around the car quickly with the broom to remove the snow. The Swinger was paid for and it was the only slice of Americana she owned.

Forget status, forget the artwork, and forget the foundry! It was time for doughnuts and coffee. She walked west on East Eleventh Street for the Davis Donut Shop. Splendid, absolutely splendid! Living in the mountains was wonderful no matter how cold it was. A little adversity helped one to appreciate the simple things in life. On the next block she approached Ignacio Mendoza's house. His sidewalks were clean. Cheryl could see Nash at the front door of his white doublewide modular home.

Occasionally, they car pooled to Minturn together to work at the Battle Mountain Bronze Art Foundry. He walked out to pick up a couple of logs for the wood stove.

She exhaled a frosty cloud of breath towards Nash. "Wa ta hey, Nash! How is Silvia and the gang?"

"Doing laundry and watching cartoons at the moment. I am ironing my work clothes."

"Everyone at the foundry will be grateful that you washed your clothes."

Nash walked out to the sidewalk, "You are quite the fashion statement with those sunglasses."

"Oh, yeah?"

"If you work on your statue today let me know. I need a ride. I need more overtime. Sylvia says it is okay for me to ride in with you and split the gas. She trusts you. I don't know why."

"Today I am going to play hooky. I need a change of scenery."

Nash replied, "In that case I will be at my brother's. The heating element is out on his water heater."

Cheryl gave Nash her best stern business deal look and she and shook her index finger at him. "Don't let him have it for free! Charge him top dollar Nash, top dollar!"

He laughed. "More than likely the best I will get from my own brother is an I.O.U. Enjoy your weekend, Cheryl."

"You do the same, Nash."

Cheryl continued down Eleventh Street. Only a few tire tracks were in the snow. She turned left at Poplar. She walked past Silver City Printing. An icicle stretched from the second floor roof half way down to the sidewalk. She turned right on Seventh Street. She passed the gift shop and Charlotte's Restaurant. At Harrison, she turned right and walked past the Rock Shop and the Golden Burro. She stopped at the front door of the Davis Donut Shop. Ann and Del Davis started the day for many people in Leadville. She kicked her boots against the concrete doorstep to knock off the snow. She pushed the door open to the jingle of sleigh bells on a leather strip nailed to the top of the door. She moved her five foot nine inch body through the door more like a construction worker than a lady. The unmistakable aroma of fresh donuts and coffee attacked her nostrils. Tables and chairs lined the walls and the large front window. She walked up to the antique glass pastry counter. There behind the counter in the middle of the kitchen amidst the donut making equipment was Ann and Del. Their morning had begun before five o'clock.

"Hello, Sunshine!" Del greeted her with a warm smile.

"How is Leadville's debutant artist?" asked Ann from the large double sink as she washed pots and pans.

Cheryl taunted, "I read your horoscope today, Ann! It says you will be cleaning up in the pastry business."

"Cheryl, come back here so I can hit you with this here rolling pin."

Del chuckled. "Ann might be making a killing in the business and the killing would be me! She could keep the profits all to herself."

Ann cast a sideways glance to both of them. "I am in a good mood today! I'm going to keep my present disposition and ignore both of you."

Del spoke in his matter of fact business voice. "Cheryl, when you sell that statue, Ann and I want to talk to you about a little business transaction."

"Del wants to sell the donut shop to you, the whole kit and caboodle."

Cheryl mocked, "Does that include the rights to all the doughnut holes?"

There was no immediate answer from Del. "Oh, no, no, no. The offer is much better than that. We are willing to sell you the whole building and business. There is an apartment upstairs that you could live in. There is all of the equipment and the standard box of donut recipes. Our secret recipe is a separate transaction with its own price tag."

Ann added, "You could put your sculpture in the window to lure customers inside. If no one bought it you could sell them a donut."

"That is a tasty idea. What is this rumor about you leaving Leadville?"

"Our daughter, Rhonda, is going to attend the School of Mines this coming fall. She will be a freshman," Ann beamed proudly.

"That is absolutely seismic!" remarked Cheryl. "I always wanted to be a geologist and go to the School of Mines. I grew up in Arvada about ten miles away. I always wanted to go for the big money in exploration, and now I'm a starving artist."

Ann put on her parent hat. "We understand that and we are worried about you. What are you going to do after the statue? We know you are a good painter. Does that market turn as big a dollar as the sculpture market?"

"Or the donut market?" jeered Del.

"It depends on how well you are known," said Cheryl. "Like your doughnut shop here. Nobody likes either of you so that is why you are not making any money."

"Watch it, young lady! I just might choke you with your knit hat." Del promised.

Ann laughed. "We thought you could have your studio upstairs. There is a living room, a bed room, a kitchen and a bath."

"What is the magic number?" Cheryl drummed her fingers on the glass counter top as she examined the specimens on the shelves below. She pointed at the Bavarian cream and held up two fingers. Del approached the counter and bagged two of them.

"One hundred thousand dollars minimum is what my wife is asking. Fifty thousand down. I would help you on the balance and carry a note for ten years at eight per cent."

"Is it too heavy to carry any further than ten years?" Cheryl feigned disappointment.

Del snorted, "I would not glaze over any of the details, Cheryl. You know that."

As if considering a complex business deal, Cheryl huffed, "Ha! One hundred thousand is a fair offer. At the moment, all I have for a down payment would be my sculpting tools and paint brushes. I could throw in my eye teeth as a sweetener!" Cheryl stood with her feet apart. "Maybe you would like this offer better, Mr. Davis." From the waist up she provocatively turned her shoulders to the right. She reached for the zipper on her jacket. She slowly pulled the zipper down and opened her coat so that Ann and Del could admire her new sweater.

"Ho, ho!" Ann and Del broke out laughing! "Cheryl! You could rob a bank in that outfit," roared Ann! "The tellers would be rolling on the floor for half an hour!"

"I can tell you like it. You are jealous, right?"

"Hu, hu! Devious people like you need sunglasses like those so you can hide amongst the innocent." Del snorted.

"I will bet that you've had no better offers in this town! What do you say, Del? What is it going to be?" Ann was still laughing at Cheryl as she moved up to the counter.

"It is gonna be my way or the highway, lady!" Del smacked the glass counter top with his hand. "It took me two lean years to get my wife trained and accustomed to this here routine."

Ann stopped at the counter next to Del. "Cheryl, you can't imagine the amount of verbal abuse he has given me."

Cheryl considered his behavior. "Your outburst suggests that I might not appreciate you as a collection agency, Mr. Davis. I'm not sure I could trust you as my banker."

Del feigned anger. "I will not allow you to insult us." He gestured towards the door. "You know where the door is!"

"Well then, I guess the only transaction we will be doing today will be for one of these tasty doughnuts." Cheryl pointed to the maple eclairs huddled together.

"How about a cup of our finest imported brew?" Ann asked.

"On the house?" Cheryl raised her eyebrows as if she was raising her stakes in a poker game. She held a thoughtful expression.

Del snorted and looked around the store. He shook his head and placed his hands on his hips. He gave Cheryl the evil eye for her benefit. He said sarcastically, "Well, I guess the floor could use some sweeping."

Ann nodded her head towards Del and warned Cheryl, "He is the same way when he is collecting money." Ann placed the bag of donuts and coffee on the brown plastic tray and added a napkin, creamer, and sugar. She took Cheryl's five dollar bill, passed the tray and mentioned, "That will be four hundred seventy one dollars. Be sure to check out the Herald Democrat today, sweetie. They ran an article on you. Nice picture!"

"It could have been better. My mom always wanted me to get my teeth straightened." Cheryl asked sincerely, "Where is the old antique cash register, the one almost as old as Del?"

"It just started falling apart. Like a lot of other things in this town." Ann and Del resumed their work. Cheryl made her way across the pine floor to the news stand by the front door. She picked up a Herald Democrat and then moved to a table by the window. Right of center on the front page was a picture of her. She stood beside a massive pile of clay that had been shaped by every muscle in her body into an eight foot tall turn of the century miner. The caption under the picture read, "Local artist wins competition." A small column underneath the caption offered further details.

It had been a close decision between Cheryl and an established artist who specialized in mining sculpture. The established artist's work was mostly 'still life.' To Cheryl 'still life' was about as exciting as a bust of a bureaucrat. Figuratively, a bust was dead. Cheryl favored motion artwork. Anything less was just scrap metal littering up the parks and sidewalks. She did not care for dull or boring sculpture.

Del gave her a chance to read the article. He bellowed from behind the counter, "From the looks of that photo, it seems to me that the mining museum and the taxpayers of Leadville got gypped if they paid more than a couple of dollars for that pile of clay."

Cheryl spit out a little bit of the donut and coffee in her mouth. The fallout stopped on the news paper article.

Ann shook her head side to side. "Forgive me, Cheryl. I am married to one of the worst excuses for a husband there ever was. I think he just proved that to you."

Cheryl looked their direction and pointed her index finger to Del. "There ain't gonna be no shop sale now, Del Davis! Never!" Cheryl hollered.

Ann and Dell were laughing. "We have to make our own fun around here. We like to tease you."

Cheryl relaxed. She finished the article and watched the town folk walking Harrison Avenue doing errands. A few tourists were window shopping. Old trucks with a snow plow were about in the morning hours clearing alleys and parking lots. It was a good part time income. SUVs passed by. Skis were strapped to the roof racks. Cheryl remembered a small pang of jealousy mixed with envy at such a sight in her past. Now she could share in the joy and fun that a day at the local ski area provided.

"Are you headed to the foundry today?" asked Ann.

"I am going to go to Ski Cooper today." Cheryl donned her three foot knit hat and smiled.

Del offered, "Don't break any bones. That statue ain't done yet!"

"I have decided to accept your generous offer on your shop, Mr. Davis. "I'll be back to finalize the deal when the mining museum cuts me a check." For the benefit of the customers just walking in, Cheryl yelled from the door, "Del, I wouldn't feed your lousy stinking donuts to a starving dog!"

She tucked the copy of the Herald Democrat under her arm. She noticed on the second page that the Tenth Mountain Division was having a reunion and barbeque today at Ski Cooper. She would certainly see Donald MacDonald and Greg Gutierrez. They were two of her staunch supporters and ardent admirers. Maybe she could scam a free lunch at the barbecue. Don and Greg were lecherous old brats disguised as bastions of Leadville society. They always made a fuss over her and she loved them dearly. They often feigned rivalry by vying for her every attention and need. "Your slightest wish is my greatest errand," Donald would say. Rascals of the best sort, mused Cheryl. She could imagine the conversation now. "Oh, Donald! Are you still cruising the town searching for young innocent women?"

Cheryl did some brief window shopping along Harrison. She slipped into Sayer Mckee drugstore for a few toiletries, two one hundred watt light bulbs, a box of colored pencils, and a large sketch pad. In ten minutes she was through the large beveled glass door and back outside. As Cheryl walked back to her apartment, she thought of the town's current situation. Six years ago the American Metals molybdenum mine north of town closed. Leadville's population at that time was close to six thousand. Three thousand people worked at the mine. Workers commuted from Colorado Springs and Pueblo to Leadville for a dangerous job with high wages. They rented motel rooms by the week. When the night shift went to work the day shift would go to sleep in the same room. Around the clock there was always someone sleeping in the room and someone working in the mine. Vacancies were scarce in Leadville and nearby towns.

The town now boasted a small population of two thousand six hundred. The active miners had left the state to continue mining in Arizona or Eloy, Nevada. They had families that required a pay check at the end of every month. Of the couple of thousand homes around Leadville proper one third of them were abandoned. Another third were rentals and the rest were owner occupied. There were a few gloom and doomers in Leadville who thought they were one or two years away from becoming a ghost town. This was the fate of the majority of small mining towns from coast to coast at the end of the 1800's.

Cheryl realized all of that was about to change. Leadville was already a bedroom community to half a dozen ski areas along the interstate. There was a genuine need for low price housing close to the ski areas. The economy was going to improve. Ski industry workers would be able to buy a home in Leadville and commute. Houses and rents were at an all time low.

Cheryl had been lucky to find a place after her breakup with Lou Pacheco. The relationship had finally dissolved. She was free and she sensed a new lease on life. The burden of a failing relationship was gone, and she was able to focus on her artwork. The bills would have to wait or go unpaid, and she chose not to care at this point. Cheryl was glad to be on her own again. In time she would find a companion. She walked uphill back to her apartment. The Silver King Loop and the snow covered Mosquito Pass filled the horizon in front of her. The pass might be open by the end of June. She opened the door of her car and sat on the cold seat. There had been mornings when the door was iced shut. On those days, if the tires had been low on air, then they would literally be frozen with flat spots. When the car rolled forward, the flat spots caused a noticeable bump until the tires warmed up and became flexible. Cheryl reminded herself that she needed to stay flexible.

The engine started from a light push of the pedal halfway to the floor, accompanied by the twist of the key. The fumes ignited. The bold six cylinder engine sucked air through the two hole carburetor. The engine idled roughly at first. As oil began to lubricate the cylinder walls the engine perked up and ran smoothly at a higher rpm. Another minute passed and Cheryl tapped the accelerator. The idle speed dropped and the engine held a smooth purr. "That's my baby! Good girl!" She disconnected the extension cord. She removed the blanket and closed the hood. She left the car and the heater running.

Inside in her apartment she dropped her morning shopping and donuts on the bed. She turned to the TV in the corner and pulled enough money out from under it for gas, a lift ticket, and ten extra dollars. She grabbed a plastic bag from under the kitchen sink. She opened the door of the forty year old Frigidair and she pulled out half a liter of OJ. She ripped off a couple of leaves from a head of lettuce and bagged them along with a good size lump of provolone cheese. She grabbed an avocado from the colander on the counter and tossed it in the sack along with a half of a loaf of rye bread. She added a knife from the counter drawer. As she went out the front door she stopped for her ski equipment. She locked the front door and returned to the Swinger. She stowed her gear in the back seat. Cheryl moved to the driver's seat and closed the door. She set the car in reverse and backed the green Swinger out to the street.

CHAPTER TWO

This winter ski season, Big John had left the metro area to find piece and solitude in the Rocky Mountains. He was hired at Ski Cooper to be a ski instructor. The management let John park his piggy back RV one hundred feet off to the side of the parking lot. The camper made for a very small living area, but it had all the comforts of home. Any port in a storm John always said. The ski area was generous enough to run a complementary power cord and telephone line out to the RV.

Big John made a controlled exit from his tight bunk area that extended over the cab of the truck. He stuck his feet into the cold foam of his moon boots and took two steps down the isle to the butane stove. He thumbed the gas control knob and struck a match to the burner. He set the coffee pot over the bright circle of blue flame and scratched various parts of his body through the light gray long johns. He yawned, stretched, and reached to open the small yellow window curtains behind the coffee pot. He needed to assess the current weather. There in front of his eyes a doe and fawn stared at him from beneath the five immense pine trees on the south side of his RV. "God's beautiful creatures! If I had a walk out patio door I'd jest pick you up and put you in the frying pan!" He was somewhat disappointed to see the new fallen snow. A gray wool ski mask was rolled up on his head. He pulled it off and ran a hand over the short snow white hair on his head and face. "So far no wind," he mused to himself. He thumbed up the thermostat dial ten degrees to sixty five.

During the war, John was in a search and rescue unit. It was a helicopter unit that operated on a Navy aircraft carrier. The SAR unit rescued pilots that ejected into the sea. They saved sailors from burning ships and they helped anyone who needed a fast way out of a bad situation. John had moved more than his fair share of pilots and troops out of harm's way. After the Navy he stayed with the guns and began a career in law enforcement.

His last assignment had been as a highway state patrol officer for the state of Colorado. He sat on the bench seat at the kitchen table and put on his knee brace. He adjusted the cloth material around the brace and hoped for comfortable wear. Today there would be no ski instruction. He had set himself up to be part of the entertainment for the Tenth Mountain Reunion. In fact, just before the noon time barbeque he was going to become the first person to parachute into Ski Cooper.

He pushed the sleeves of his long underwear up towards his elbows past the Neptune tattoo on his left forearm. It was still his favorite and a gift to himself on his eighteenth birthday when he was finally overseas. The right forearm sported a tattoo of a scantily clad woman in a short red dress. He always told the girls it was a picture of his "Momma." He thought about calling the airport. He decided not to. The new snow was light and the plane would be able to take off. There was no need to call the owner of the airplane. Al would call him if the jump was going to be cancelled. There was still one loose thread. It happened to be one person John could call any time night or day. "I think I will rattle Max's cage this morning."

The upside down chicken fought and squawked murder! Bloody murder! The six foot, fifty eight year old man, held the legs of the bird in his left hand. He walked with composure toward a tree stump. He slammed the bird on to the stump and pinned the legs of the chicken at the edge. The chicken flapped its wings and flopped all over the stump. Patricia Mason was nine years old. She had fetched her younger sister by sixteen months and her five year old brother Maxwell. They placed themselves around the stump to witness the sacrifice. Minutes ago Great Grandma Chasteen wisely told Patricia's mother and grand mother, "If the children are ever starving they need to know how to kill a chicken for food to stay alive. They should see it happen today."

The small rusty hatchet came out of the sky and thumped into the stump one eighth of an inch. The back of the chicken's neck was pinched underneath the hatchet. A dull axe was handy in these situations because it did not sink far into the stump. Max stared into the chicken's eyes and watched the mouth close and open as if it was gasping for air. There was no more "buc buc buc buwaahk" chicken talk. Grand Daddy Haehl easily pulled the hatchet up and delivered a timely and humane coup de grace. The second blow separated the head from the body. It proved to be easier this time because the chicken was not as lively as before. The tan man turned and walked back to the house still holding the chicken in his left hand and the hatchet in his right. He did not acknowledge the presence of the children. A little bit of blood was dripping out of the neck of the bird. Max stared at the head of the chicken at the foot of the stump. The empty eyes of the chicken returned his stare. Max was dumbstruck by the event.

Patti and Barbie were right behind their half indian grandfather. They went through the back door into the kitchen. Maxwell's sisters shut the back door before he could get there. He was sometimes easily forgotten in moments of excitement. Shaken by the actions of the last few minutes, he stumbled around the small white country farm house to the front door. He entered into the living room. He stared to the dining room where the women sat. Past the dining room in the kitchen the tall tan man dropped the chicken, feathers and all, into a pot on the stove. Max could see the feet sticking up and a few of the white feathers. Granddad said, "Ma, the chicken is in the pot." The ladies stared at little Max. Grammie Haehl said, "Well, I guess he might mind his Grandpa a little better now."

The phone began to ring. Max turned to the table in the living room and picked up the receiver. "Hello? Hello?" No one answered him. The phone was still ringing. His sisters ran into the room. They screamed, "Max put down the phone! Put down the phone!" Max was not allowed to talk on the phone. The blasted phone was still ringing. He rolled to the side of his bed. He swept his hand around the floor twice. He pushed himself up to his hands and knees and crawled towards the foot of the bed. The sleeping bag and blankets bunched up underneath him. His skin goose bumped in the cold air. The ringing was louder now. His objective was to disconnect the phone cord. Instead he pick up the receiver to stop the phone from ringing.

A deep gruff voice bellowed. "It's about damn time you picked up the phone!" Big John demanded, "What the hell are you doing?" as if it mattered a great deal. Max realized that communication between friends no matter what was said or how it was said was just as important as helping one another. Do not worry about misinterpretation. You can work that out later. Just keep talking. He liked to holler at his deaf buddy. He suspected that John had lost some of his hearing from riding in helicopters and practicing marksmanship at firing ranges during the war.

"Arrr, mate! I was just thinking about having a chicken burrito for breakfast. Want to join me? I can hardly hear you Big John! Turn up the volume on your hearing aid and your phone. Can you hear . . ."

John interrupted. "What's it like over at your place?" Big John liked to be in control. He liked to interrupt people to tell them what to do. It was one of the many tactics he employed to subdue people. The habit was left over from his days as a state trooper. Keep the suspect docile. There was no small talk unless it was Big John's.

Max left the bed sporting a pair of lemon yellow jockey shorts with a green mutant ninja turtle on the front of the briefs. He wisely wrapped the medium green sleeping bag around him. The floor numbed the bottoms of his feet. He padded to a six by two foot window that held original wavy lead glass. He returned to the phone on the bed. He got back under the covers and yelled into the phone, "It looks like the end for us John! We are surrounded by mountains!"

John guffawed. "Never surrender Max! What about the snow?"

"Oh, maybe a couple of inches of loose powder, not enough to stop us."

"I don't see why it would. It shouldn't be any problem. Meet me at the airport at ten thirty." John did not like to ask questions. He told people what to do. It made his life easier. If someone would disagree with him, then Big John just might shoot to kill.

"Sure, John. The white pants I bought at the Second Hand Rose don't fit."

"I've got you covered in style Max. Are you packed and in date?"

"Close enough. I packed the main last night. I'll close it up over morning coffee." He hollered the next thought into John's ear, "We should have a pretty good time today, you old pirate!"

"Man, oh, man. We are going to have some fun today!"

"By the way John, thanks for asking me along for the fun. And don't worry, if you pay me one hundred dollars I will let you land first!"

John lowered his volume as if he was discussing some confidential information. "I have a pro rating. I can land as close to the crowd as I want. How about you?"

"I have a D license. I'll have to land about seventy five yards form the crowd."

"One hundred yards," John corrected.

"Big deal. By the way, how much are you going to pay me?"

"You ain't getting a dime mister!"

"What? You mean I am going to perform this death defying feat for nothing?"

"Let's put it this way Max. If you are willing to die on this jump I will pay you one hundred dollars."

Max replied thoughtfully, "Damn, I got a ton of debt John. Let me think it over."

"Har, har, har. See you at the airport." John hung up the phone.

Max thought about the clothing for the jump as he made up his bed. The clothes might be a problem. He did not know if they would fit like a glove or if they would be loose and in the way of the parachute gear. He would worry about that later. He had an extra hour on his hands and breakfast would be a plus. He would need something in his stomach to throw up if the jump went wrong. It was time to dress. He stepped into a pair of loose fitting jeans and his black moon boots. He found a fresh T shirt and covered that with the same sweater and sweatshirt he had worn yesterday.

Max walked the length of the narrow second floor hallway past three bedrooms and a bathroom to the back stairs. Just as the stairway reached the bottom, two triangular steps allowed one to turn right into the kitchen. Without fail he hit his head against the top of the low door frame. He reminded himself that he needed to paint the last two steps a different color. A six by six foot window opened up the back wall of the house and allowed the sun access to the kitchen. The magnificent view was south down the valley. His parachute lay on the white vinyl floor beside a yellow metal patio table.

Max was moving fast now with the help of modern convenience. All the coffee pot required was a flick of the switch. The coffee had been loaded last night. He left the kitchen and walked into the small dining area. Across the room on the left, he took the narrow hallway that bypassed the living room. It ran beside the main stairway to the front door. He stopped at the furnace closet under the stairway. The fire code specifications required a minimum thickness of one inch of sheet rock. Supposedly this would hold back a good furnace fire for two or three minutes. Max had one and a half inches of sheet rock. He turned the thermostat to seventy degrees.

He was remodeling the one hundred and twenty year old house under a homeowners permit. He opened the front door and walked outside to start the car. A white 1967 Mercury Meteor with a red roof and red interior greeted him. It held a Ford 283 cubic inch V8. Compared to the price of a new car the Meteor was free. He had paid all of $550 dollars for it. In protest of the high price of gasoline, Max super glued a rubber toy triceratops on the front of the hood. Thankfully, the door of the Mercury was not frozen shut. The engine turned over and he adjusted the heater.

Max returned to the kitchen and knelt beside his parachute. Four flaps of the parachute tray covered the main canopy bag, and held it in the container. To close the four flaps over the parachute, he passed a shoestring through the one inch diameter loop attached to the top edge of the bottom flap. He then passed both ends of the string through the grommet hole on each of the remaining three flaps. He pulled the shoestring until the loop popped through the top grommet. This closed the flaps over the parachute and held it in the container. Max placed a two inch metal pin through the loop above the last grommet. The pin is attached to a flat ribbon one inch wide and six feet in length. The ribbon connects the main canopy and the pilot chute. The pin holds the parachute secure in the container during freefall. The pilot chute is two feet in diameter and it has the shape of a round parachute. When the pilot chute is opened in freefall it is like a kite in a windstorm. It pulls the locking pin out of the cord loop. The container flaps open and the parachute is pulled out. *Who would want to do something like that?* Max folded the pilot chute. He secured it and the excess ribbon in a pocket on the right leg strap.

He rose to pour a cup of coffee. He found a bottle of aspirin on the counter. He took one aspirin and put two in his pocket. After a sip, he sat down to ponder the events of the day. A beautiful day of skiing, celebration, and barbeque was underway. He was mentally prepared for the demo. He wished he could put a shot of whiskey in his coffee. He dared not. Things would happen soon enough. The organizers of the reunion had asked the jumpers to wear a white parka and pants. This was the winter outfit of the Tenth Mountain Division when in snow country. Max factored in the outfit and visualized the jump. His heart rate and blood pressure increased slightly. His armpits moistened. A bulky outfit would be a problem. Especially one he had never worn on a jump.

The best solution was to exclude any questionable variable from the very beginning. On his first day as a student, Max was taught to never change any aspect of the skydive, without additional ground training with the new change. "Any aspect" referred to gear, clothing, the type of aircraft and the planned exit. To ease his worry he made a mental note to practice the jump on the ground while wearing the outfit. Deliberation and rehearsal on the ground often reveal a problem that might arise during the actual performance. The isolated problem could be dealt with on the ground. A solution could be provided. There was no time to deal with a problem in freefall. All he really had to do was keep his hand on the pilot chute handle as he left the aircraft. That would solve his minor dilemma.

He picked up the parachute and walked out of the kitchen into the dining room. He took the narrow hallway beside the second floor stairway. He turned the thermostat down to fifty five degrees and continued to the front door. He set the parachute by the ski equipment that hung from the pegs on the wall by the door. He donned a mid thigh down coat. It was like being in a sleeping bag with arm sleeves and a hood attached. He grabbed a straw broom by the front door and swept the loose powder from the small front deck. He cleared a path to the street and pushed the snow off the Meteor. He was thinking about how good the breakfast burrito at the Golden Burro would taste. Would he order chicken or sausage? He returned to the house to stow the broom and pick up his gear. The rig fit nicely on the back seat. The car sported a manual transmission with four speeds forward. He found reverse and carefully backed the car onto the street. New snow tires were on the back rims. He looked out over the hood at the triceratops. Max used it for aiming and he pointed the prehistoric monster down the street. He rolled down hill past Danny Duran's place and on to the Golden Burro.

CHAPTER THREE

Nash Mendoza was pulling tree bark cuts off his trailer. He had been to the mill a day ago. His timing had been good. He was able to fill his flat trailer full of unwanted bark cuts for a few dollars. He stacked the cuts by the side of his house. He would cut them to wood stove size another day. Nash saw the Swinger approach and he moved to the curb to flag Cheryl down.

"Looks like you are gonna save some money on your heat bill, Nash. How did your laundry come out? Any fading at all? Did the colors all run together?"

"Wha ta hey, Cheryl. Yes. We bought an earth stove out of the classifieds. It's a real beauty. I've got enough wood here for two homes. I have been thinking that I might be able to sell some to you. Maybe we can work a deal."

Cheryl never wondered why men were always trying to work a deal with her. She already knew. "That would be great! First I need a fireplace. That could be costly."

Nash produced a sly, devilish grin along with a wink of his eye that Cheryl had seen twenty times at the foundry. "No problem Cheryl! You be my wench for the rest of the winter and I can set you up."

She looked at him quizzically for a moment and said, "You think you can keep Sylvia and an extra wench warm for the rest of the winter? Isn't that double duty?"

"You just say the word and your heat bills are going to be less than $5.00 a month."

"I want to believe it, but it's too good to be true. No deal, Nash!"

Nash glanced at the ski equipment in the back seat. "It don't look like we are going to car pool today. It looks to me as if you are fixin' to play hooky."

"I need a day off. I am pretty much a physical wreck. My hands are so cramped from pushing and pinching clay that I can't hold a wash cloth to shower off the foundry stench."

"Boo hoo. Go find the hot tub over at the high school community center."

"That is a good idea. I may take you along to handle the massage work."

"No problem girlfriend. We will do the art work some other weekend."

"I tell you what, Nash. When I am rich and famous and I have a fast street hot rod, I'll come back and talk to you about all this."

"And what will you talk about Cheryl?"

"I'll leave rubber in front of your house."

Cheryl mashed the pedal to the floor and the Swinger lurched forward in a semi flooded state. She turned right and headed north on Poplar to US Highway 24. She checked the fuel gage as she approached Starvin' Marvin's Amoco station. Whoops! Unless she bought some gas she would be coasting downhill on her return to Leadville. She saw Buddy at the door and pulled into the station without slowing down. She mashed the break pedal as she neared the pumps. The tires screeched and the Swinger rocked to a stop. Marvin looked out from under a hood in the service bay through the bay door windows. Cheryl coyly rolled down her window and batted her big light brown eyes at Buddy as he approached her car. She hollered in her southern accent, "Say, Boy! Would you be a de uh and put twenty dollars of regular in my tank for me?"

"Lady, I would rather put one hundred dollars worth into your tank." Buddy eyed her with a wink and a nod. Cheryl returned a disapproving shake of her head. "I can't help it Miss Cheryl. I ain't never gonna be nuthin' but a man around you. Never nuthin' less. That's all I am and that's all I know how to be. Can I get you anything else, Miss Cheryl? If you been drivin' the way you wuz when you come in here you probly gonna need some new tires. Now that I have a close look at your tires, you are definitely in need of some new mud and snows."

She laughed openly at Buddy. "Buddy, you know I cain't be marryin' no poor blue collar mechanic."

Buddy stamped his foot and hollered. "I ain't po, Miss Cheryl!"

She held fast. "Buddy! I have to find a man of money and culture. Money and refinement. Money and . . ."

Marvin's eyes lit up as he stopped beside Buddy. He had left the broken water pump on the vehicle he was servicing in the garage to greet Cheryl. Sometimes it was just impossible to be less than a friendly retailer. "Miss Cheryl, you really ought to bring this baby in some afternoon so I can get my instruments on her and tweak her a little bit."

She eyed Marvin suspiciously. "You know you big greasy mechanics make me just a little week in the knees what with all that slippery tweakin' and everything."

They had a good laugh. Buddy shut off the pump nozzle and placed it in the cradle. He replaced the gas cap. "Half the town is at the pancake breakfast and when are you gonna finish that statue?"

"I don't know. I'm running away today. Cheryl paused a moment and then relented. "A little more clay work. Not much. I think the plaster mold will be on at the end of the week"

"Good!" Buddy smiled, "The whole town is waiting to see it."

Marvin asked, "Where's that fancy hat of yours?" He was referring to her trade mark brown felt hat with a wide bill like the flappers wore in the 20's. It sported an attractive bow on it. It looked like a pony express riders hat with the bill folded up in front.

"It's back at the house. It is a little too cold for it today. Today is going to be a ski day and I am fired up for a day off."

"We're fired up for a year off." Marvin quipped. "We just changed tires on every vehicle in town in the last two weeks."

She handed over a twenty. "I need two new ones on the back. Can you fix me up?"

"Sure. Drop the car off and drop the keys in the mail slot."

"Alright, I will. Thanks guys!"

Cheryl turned onto the highway and drove past the bowling alley, the small drive in liquor store, and the Silver King Inn. She passed the dentist office and Ken's Lumber. She turned left on US Highway 24 and Minturn. She followed the winding two lane road until she passed the Cavalli Ranch. There the road began the gentle rise of turns and switchbacks through the pine forest and up the mountainside to Tennessee Pass and Ski Cooper. So far the road was snow packed and sanded. At the summit, the road would be snow packed with some icy spots. She was eager to get on her skis. This would be her fourth day on the telemarks and she was improving. Just the thought of finally getting to the ski slopes was beginning to excite her. What a wonderful day it was going to be. She relaxed and began to reminisce.

Cheryl had worked for the Robertson's almost two years. She was learning the ins and outs of casting bronze. She was an accomplished metal chaser. She could smooth coarse welds with a large fifteen pound electric hand grinder. She could match fine surface detail with a hand dremel. Her eye was calibrated for perfection in texture and detail. Her taste and touch were extraordinary.

She possessed a willed determination and work ethic similar to her grandfather's. Her grandfather had been her pal and confidant through a lot of lonely years from the seventh grade to high school graduation. He was a welder during his enlistment. He repaired DC 3s while he was stationed in Korea. Dad told her a few stories about the damaged planes his unit repaired, just so the pilots could take them on one more mission. He also told her of the bodies that were pulled from the planes and how the space they occupied was cleaned out with the local fire hose before the next gunner or radio man would occupy the spot.

He felt years spent in school perfecting A B C's was a total waste of time. *One should learn as many jobs and develop as many skills as possible. One will never lack for work or a pay check.* That was her grandfather's motto. He taught Cheryl how to weld when she was twelve years old, and he was immensely proud of his grand daughter. She learned both rod and tig welding.

Dad had an uncanny mind and eye. He gave her hands on experience in conceptualization. They would raid the local salvage yard. They collected metal gears, springs, rods and pipes in a fifty five gallon drum. Cheryl remembered the day he dumped the barrel close to the garage. Dad said, "Imagine something unique. Conceive something totally different and bring life to it. Create it. If you have a need for a thing you do not have, then invent it and make it yourself." She learned to use the tools and the work bench vice in the garage. She learned to use her hands. Sometimes she would let them go as if they possessed minds of their own. She and Dad would take turns piecing the junk together into shapes of animals, humans or any object they could imagine. Cheryl never tired of transforming metal junk into a sculpture. Soon she would be welding her own statue. Unbelievable! *Thanks, Dad!*

She was a sophomore in Arvada High School by the time her step father, Hal, arrived. Hal and Marilyn's early friendship developed into a working relationship in residential drywall, and the partnership eventually led to marriage. Cheryl worked right along with her mother and Hal during her high school summers. After she graduated she worked with them full time for a year. The ability to depend on herself to pay the bills was her first priority. It allowed her freedom of choice and not dependence or servitude on someone whom she might later wish to avoid. A married relationship was the last thing on her mind. She was not willing to put complete trust and confidence or dependence on someone to support her at this point in her life. Hal and Marilyn paid handsomely. Cheryl socked the money away to a bank account. This was much better than working for the "other man" as Dad would say. She signed up to attend a few classes at the Rocky Mountain Art Institute in Aurora. Art was her only choice.

The sculptures most students created for course assignments were cast at a small foundry in Aurora. Cheryl had taken hers to a foundry in Boulder. She met a resident named Goodman. Her work was just beginning to be recognized on a national level. Cheryl also met Frank Weir, a high falutin' sculptor. There she was. Fresh out of school looking for work and she was lucky enough to rub elbows with some big shots of the sculpture world.

Cheryl made many trips to the foundry when she only needed a few. She watched the employees work. She liked to visit with them during break time. She would ask them questions about their jobs and their personal art works in the making at home. All of them had home studios in a garage or a bedroom. Some workers boasted of studios in their apartment living room. One of the older employees bought a two bedroom house. She made the entire house a studio while she lived in an apartment. One worker rented a barn from a local farmer just outside of town. Work areas included patios and back yards. A couch in the living room was a convenient place to rest or sleep. A decent bathroom was necessary. A cook stove and refrigerator were great but not required.

It was in this setting that one of those once in a lifetime events took place. Mary Robertson, a partner at the foundry had her eye on Cheryl. Mary recognized that the young gal had quite a bit to offer. She liked everything about Cheryl from her mental frame of mind and abilities to her work ethic. She knew Cheryl would fit in without any problems. She might be slow at first, but all that would change very quickly. Great strides are quickly made when one nurtures talent and allows it free rein to run its course.

Cheryl recalled the sad day she cleaned out her locker at the foundry. From out of nowhere Bob Robertson casually stepped up beside her.

He spoke evenly. "Mary and I want you to join us for lunch about two o'clock this afternoon. Meet us over at the Green Parrot Restaurant in Louisville and don't be late. Tell no one."

They ordered sandwiches and thick cream soups. Bob Robertson said with a hint of disappointment, "Well, Cheryl I have not slept at all for the past week. My wife has been nagging me night and day." Mary recoiled slightly and gave Bob a stern look.

"Ordinarily we hire experienced workers and pay them as little as possible. I finally relented to my wife that we would hire you as long as you would work for free."

Cheryl was not amused. Mary cocked her head and said with a slight smile, "Oh, right!"

Bob gave Mary a stern look to remind her that he was conducting the conversation. "We believe you possess extraordinary talent and ability. We think you are capable of great things. We want to hire you to work with us on a long term basis."

Cheryl was floored. She couldn't believe her ears. Sometimes we take for granted the sum total of the talents we have developed over time.

The Robertson's were silently waiting for an answer. Bob asked evenly, "What do you say Cheryl?"

"Yes! I want to work for you. That is what I want to do!"

Mary gave Cheryl an honest assessment. "We need your help on the bronze finish work. After a couple of months you can work in some other areas. Bob and I will pay your salary."

"Does that mean I will be working as your associate, or on a contract basis?" Cheryl shook her head. "I don't understand."

Bob explained. "Our partner does not want to hire anyone. He is pretty grouchy. Mary and I are going to pay you out of our pockets. At best it will be part time right now."

Mary interrupted, "He has bad social skills. He has grown children, but they don't want to work with him. He may resent when you begin to work. We will tell him that you are our personal assistant. Hourly wage will be seven and a half dollars."

Cheryl repressed a smile. She had yet to be overworked and underpaid. She did feel that the Robertson's were genuinely appreciative of her skills and she was eager for the opportunity. She wrote down her cell phone and home phone number on a napkin and passed it to Mary. "I really appreciate this. It is just what I have been looking for." They left the restuarant and bid goodbye to one another. Cheryl was beaming as she recalled the meeting. Mary informed her that Bob had found a building suitable for a foundry in Minturn. Everything would be in place in a couple of weeks. Minturn! Could Cheryl manage to find a place to live in the mountains? She was overwhelmed. A job she loved and in the mountains to boot!

The right rear tire of the Swinger spun free and the back end slid out to the right. The hood of her car pointed slightly across the yellow center line. The tire found traction and the car began to take Cheryl and her ski equipment to the yellow no passing line. Given sufficient velocity and mass she might successfully launch through the snow bank and out into the air beyond the edge of the road. Her eyes widened. She tightened her grip and corrected the direction. The hood moved back slowly to the center of her lane. Both tires spun free. Cheryl lightly backed off the accelerator until the tires found traction. She was close to the ditch on her side. She made one more gentle correction with the steering wheel. Wet, hard packed snow and ice with scattered sand was the current road forecast. She chided herself for daydreaming. She moved ahead at a slower speed. She let her muscles relax. She began to breathe again. The sudden twinge of fear began to dissipate. She was warm from the daydream and a bit of moisture was in her eyes.

CHAPTER FOUR

In ten minutes the Golden Burro sausage breakfast burrito was gone and Max was on his way. He left a generous tip for the waitress and decided to pick up a half a dozen donuts next door at the Davis Donut shop. Max avoided the main streets. He drove west across town on Seventh. Roads in the small town were not really big enough to accommodate the tourist traffic. He passed Donald MacDonald's house. Donald was the current President of the Rocky Mountain Chapter of former members of the Tenth Mountain Division. His house sat on the crest of a hill on Seventh Street. The home made "4 Sale" sign was still in the front yard. Max hoped that Mac would sell the house to him.

He turned left and drove to the south side of Leadville. He saw the sign that boasted the "Highest Airport in the Continental U.S." Max turned onto a narrow two lane asphalt road. The road rose to a plateau large enough to accommodate an airfield. He turned right to a snow covered gravel road. He rolled fast enough so the car would not get stuck in the snow. A small clearing appeared. There were two cars in the parking lot. A couple of fresh tire tracks continued on through the trees to the runway and the hangers. He drove out of the forest that bordered the field. The airport view opened up to snow covered Mount Massive and Mount Elbert. The town and any other signs of life were hidden below the plateau.

Max slowed the car until it stopped. He sat in awe of the surroundings. He was happy living in the mountains as opposed to a metropolitan area. Every once in a while a moment would catch him off guard. When it did, he would sit and let a tear fill his eye. Max began to reminisce. His parents had provided for his childhood sufficiently, and like most parents they wanted their children to stay close to home. Max was not interested in living under a microscope. His parents were total meddlers. They had even selected a girl for him to marry.

Max took to the world of fun, travel, and adventure. On his eighteenth birthday he enlisted for army airborne training and he promised his mother that she could go with him. The benefits and the pay were too good to pass up. Medical benefits were for life. Education would be paid for. He would be able to stay in the guard or the reserve and possibly retire in twenty years. If he lost his life in combat, then he would never have anything to worry about. The benefactor of his insurance policy would inherit a tidy sum of money. That would make someone happy, and that was part of the deal. Max was going to make his own decisions in his lifetime.

He finished college on the GI Bill, His first job was working as a clerk for an electric co op utility in the mountains. If he had just sat still for one more year he could have been the junior assistant accountant. Back home his uncle waved an indecent amount of salary under his nose. Max packed his bags and moved back east of the Mississippi where he had grown up. His uncle had patented a one of a kind foundry exhaust system. Uncle Jim needed manufacturing help. None of the relatives would work for him. The new found success was having an adverse effect on Uncle Jim's personality and his people skills. Max's visit to Indianapolis lasted for sixty days. During those sixty days, he relived a couple of insufferable days of his youth. The disgust that he held for family resurfaced with a vengeance. It also clarified a certainty in his future. If he walked away from this opportunity, then he would be poor for the rest of his life.

Max was wise enough to realize that he was happy to some degree struggling on his own. The stock market crashed and he rushed back to Denver. He took a crash course to pass a test so he could work as a securities salesman. In his first year as a stockbroker, he bought as much disaster as he could buy. After all it is not a matter of buying low and selling high. It is a matter of whether or not you have the nerve to buy disaster. He secured enough reward from the effort to be somewhat independent and do as he pleased. A parachute center forty miles from town kept him entertained on the weekends. Enough reminiscing!

He eyed the main office for signs of activity. The wind sock was pointed at the ground. He turned his attention to the county maintenance hangar in front of him and two other hangers to the left. He saw John's white pick up truck parked beside the last hangar to the left.

Max entered the hangar as John and Al removed the passenger door and the passenger seat from the plane.

"Thanks for the doughnuts Max. The outfit is in my gear bag."

Max donned the baggy parka and pants. He did not like the fit.

John was dressed to the nines. His outfit was tailored and he had his good conduct medal pinned to his parka.

"Going to geek a few cameras today, John?"

"We are waiting on you, Max."

Al hooked the tow bar to the front wheel. "Help me push it out so we can start the engine."

John and Max leaned on the wing struts of the airplane. Al pulled the tow bar and guided the plane over snow covered gravel a short distance to the asphalt pathway. Al climbed in the plane. He set the choke and throttle. He pressed the starter button. Click click click chum chum duhm duhm **chu chu chu braaapppp**! The propeller snapped at the cold air and pushed it back along the sides of the fuselage. Al put his foot on the brake pedal. The engine was alive! The adrenaline began to flow. Hearts and minds a fire. The excitement picked up. No one in the world can start an aircraft of any kind without that happening. Max was not comfortable. Things were moving fast and he was unsettled. A nagging notion remained in the back of his mind about the clothing. He sensed a fleeting notion not to go. He reasoned to himself. *Just hold on to the pilot chute handle when you exit the aircraft.* Relax and enjoy!

John and Max checked each others gear and exchanged pleasantries. Max figured they were about to play out a dramatic conversation of "who gets the last word" as they boarded the Cessna. By this time Big John was salivating like a rabid dog. They hollered at one another over the engine noise.

"Max, they want the parka hoods up when we land!"

"I guess I will be out of costume."

"Just put the hood up before you are about to land. Comprendo, my friend?"

"Thanks for including me on this jump. This is going to be one of those memorable ones!"

"Hop in back Max! Let's get going!"

"I know this means a lot to you John! Thank you for inviting me along and sharing this moment. Not many skydivers would share an opportunity like this."

John was running out of patience and he realized Max was messing with him. "I just thought you could use some time away from the houses and some fun for a change. Now quit horsing around and get in."

The 182 Cessna taxied down to the end of the snow covered runway. There was enough adrenaline flowing to keep them warm during the taxi. The mini adventure was underway. They all shared the usual second thoughts. Would the engine quit at one thousand feet or before? How would the jump go? Would they be killed for any reason? The thoughts dwindled as fast as they were considered. There were smiles all around for the joy of flying and the incredible mountain panoramas that surrounded them. Max and John put their helmets on. Big John's altimeter was on his chest strap. Max had a new wrist mount altimeter. They were zeroed out at nine thousand. The plane altimeter read nine thousand feet. They adjusted their postures for comfort. The back seat in the plane put Max's head into the roof. The seat was a block of ice. He was barely on the edge of the seat because of his parachute. He turned sideways so he could actually be on the seat and look out the window.

Al executed a slow controlled turn at the end of the runway. The Cessna pointed north into the wind. They might fly over town. Anything was possible with Al. He ran up the engine idle to test both magnetos. Everything was AOK. Al loved to fly. He had left his family at an early age to join the Army. After six months he had completed basic and advanced infantry training. With the money he saved he took flying lessons at the Army base. Most military bases have a runway and at least one single engine plane tied down somewhere. All he had to do was pay for the pilot instruction. It was an inexpensive way to get a license. He learned to fly in a De Havilland. It was a large, single engine plane that the administration used to ferry mail and small cargo to other bases. No one in Al's family had ever flown a plane. In their mind his ability to fly lowered their opinion of their son. He was crazy and irresponsible. Alan continued to get the licenses needed to obtain a commercial pilot license. Instrument rating. Multi engine rating. Retractable wheel rating. After four years in the army he had the GI Bill. He attended a flying school to fulfill his goal of becoming a commercial airline pilot. His brothers and sisters back home were swallowed up by their jobs and mediocrity.

Al had met the most incredible people in his life while he was in the military. They made him laugh. They made him cry. They helped him to carry on. They worked on his intestinal fortitude. They ate Thanksgiving dinners at the dining facility. There were no more holidays with a bunch of disapproving relatives who could solve the problems of the world by flapping their lips. His service gave him incentive to look down the road and plan ahead. Al thought of these things before he was about to fly. He was doing what he wanted. He was a Certified FAA Pilot Instructor by the time he was twenty six and a licensed airframe and power plant mechanic. He was certified to work on the engine. He bought a plane instead of a house. It was free and clear by the time he was twenty eight. He made money as an instructor. He loved his plane and he loved his licenses. Alan looked around him. He stared down the runway. This was it. This was his destiny. He was doing what he loved. His buddies were calling him. His buddies! *These were not the people his parents wanted him to play with.*

"Hey! Dipshit! What the hell are you doing? Get this shit box moving!" He scanned the instrument panel and the gages one more time. Everything was a go. His buddies were one step closer to their demo jump. One short flight to stupidity! Alan now had the honor to show his friends a good time. He smiled and eased the throttle out. The plane lurched in place in response to the increased throttle. He released the breaks. The Cessna sped forward and kicked up the loose snow. He slowly pulled the throttle until it was almost all the way out. The small craft lifted smoothly off the runway at the hands of the veteran. Al did a sharp bank to the left that squashed their butts to the floor. He headed straight for the forest and skimmed the tree tops. John and Max cursed him mightily. Al's mouth opened in a satisfied smile and he belly laughed. He hollered, "Call me names, will ya? That will teach you not to call me names!" Al would show his buddies a good time. He planned to scare the piss out of them.

CHAPTER FIVE

The entrance to the ski area was upon her in no time. Cheryl managed to collect her wits and slow down enough to make the turn without sliding off the road. Her car fishtailed slightly. She continued on through the entrance to the parking lot. She parked her car and put her leggings on. She stuck her hands into an absolutely awesome pair of warm skin tight, cross country ski gloves. The name was Swank. They were originally developed by NASA clothing experts. She had just enough money diverted from partially paid bills to pay for a lift ticket and the barbecue. She fastened her fanny pack around her waist. It held some power bars, a knife, and first aid items. One never knew when one might need a band aid for a cut or scrape. She picked up her skis and walked to the ticket window. She purchased her lift ticket and barbecue ticket from the attendant and walked to the front of the lodge to face the ski runs. She sat on a wood bench beside the patio for ten minutes and checked out the area, the day, and the people.

The lodge was aesthetically nestled in the large pines below two mountain peaks. The snow covered forest rose another fifteen hundred feet to timberline. The huge mountain peaks were bright white. Gray granite rock cliffs dotted the mountainside and forest. A large snow cat ferried skiers to the enormous open area above timberline. Cheryl thought her eagle eye detected some misting of snow on some of the rock cliffs. Moisture came to her eyes for the second time. What a great place to live. She wondered if someday if she might have one or two small children learning to ski here. It was mid morning. Volunteers young and old cleared the large wood picnic tables. Just an hour earlier, tasty pancakes and maple syrup had quickly disappeared into hungry mouths. Everyone was skiing on the mountain now. The lift was about fifty yards away, and at the moment, the lift line was empty. She readied herself for the telemark effort. She should be able to get three runs in before the barbeque. She retied her boots tightly. She stepped into her cross country bindings and shuffled slowly to the lift line. A friend and co worker yelled to her and Cheryl stopped to wait for him. Charlie sped downhill towards his objective. He leaned back and shifted his weight to the inside edge of his ski for a fast hockey stop beside her. He splashed snow over her skis and boots.

"Yoda says it is better to be confident and look downhill than to watch your skis and ski slowly." Charlie wrinkled his face.

"You certainly look like Yoda this morning. Up late last night were you?"

Charlie lived just outside of Leadville in a small subdivision named String Town. He worked at the foundry with Cheryl and on the weekends he worked as a lift operator at Copper Mountain. "Hey, you old granny! You should talk! I remember the beat up, run down wench I saw at the foundry Friday."

"Charlie, let's get in line." They shuffled slowly towards a small group of skiers who were waiting in the lift line.

"You looked refreshed."

"I got ten hours of sleep. Some well deserved sleep."

"Everyone we know is here today. I am going to draw this gathering out to a full day of fun." He was scamming. He liked being around Cheryl. He hoped someday they would be more than friends. He would see more of Cheryl today if he invited her to an event rather than ask her out and be turned down. He plotted like a tactician. "Maybe we could get a pool tournament going. If you go to the tournament, a couple of your friends might turn up. Then again, you might bump into some local talent like me."

She laughed at his choice of words. "There is the bowling alley. I like the Pac Woman game there."

"Okay, great!" Charlie was a quick wit. He was fun to be with. He was cool and calm. "Let me make a run with you so I can check out your telemark form."

"Sure thing, Charlie." Cheryl liked the quality time she felt with him. "We can make a couple of runs."

They rode the chair together and they talked about work at the foundry and their friends. The lift followed the trees between two ski runs, and up the hill to the mid mountain off ramp. Charlie looked at Cheryl's high forehead and her thick reddish brown hair. The beautiful eyebrows arched over the light brown eyes. Her lips were medium size.

She was attractive. Enticing. She was an outdoor girl. She was a terrific friend and fellow artist.

"I heard you called it quits with your man. I know you don't want to talk about it, but Lou is not taking the break up lightly."

"Ya know, it really isn't going to bother me. He moved on. It's over. The physical part of the relation slowed down. He started going over to one of his friend's house. Single mom. Older woman. We just distanced ourselves from one another. I figured it might be time to go."

"Atta girl! Good to get it off your chest. Good for you!"

"I found the apartment by accident. The landlady had a sign in the window. She didn't have enough money for an ad in the paper. The house is up on east Eleventh."

"Hey, that is a pretty decent view over there on East Eleventh." Charlie spoke as if they were standing in her front yard.

"It is a great view once you are out in the yard."

"Well, all of Leadville is like that."

"I do have one window with a view, but you are not going to get to see it just yet. I don't want to rush into another relationship. Right now I'm enjoying the escape, and the sculpture project is taking up all of my extra time anyway."

"Did I tell you I won the lotto?"

Cheryl laughed. "I would invite you up if you won the lotto, Charlie. You would need someone to share all of that money with."

Charlie shifted and turned a little so he did not have to break his neck to see her face. He took off a glove and ran a hand over the thick brown hair that ended halfway down his neck. He peered at Cheryl with his dark brown eyes and heavy brows. He whispered softly, "It's all about the money isn't it?"

"Don't Charlie."

"Lighten up, for Pete's sake! I don't want to marry you! I just want some wild twenty four hour uninhibited sex!"

Cheryl laughed and played along. "And here I was about to trust you and invite you over. You men are all alike.

"Just put me in the list of your potential playmates. I will always be waiting for you, Cheryl. Did you hit the trampoline this morning?"

"Nah. I thought about it. I concentrated on getting to the lift line this morning. I have a little bit of energy for the runs we are about to take."

They checked for clothing connected to the lift chair as they approached the unloading ramp. Charlie burst out laughing. "I got a hanger the other day on S Lift. The bottom of his big jacket caught on the chair. He was leaning out to ski down the ramp. The chair pulled him around the ramp and back down hill. He bumped his head a couple of times. He was semi conscious. I got the lift shut down just as he started downhill. He was about ten feet off the ground connected to the chair by his coat. One ski was still on. I could have made ten thousand dollars on the Funny Home Video show."

"You should have let him finish his ride."

"I got a ladder to him before he broke free. That's dangerous stuff trying to get someone down. If they break free they might land on you."

They left the chair and the off loading ramp. They raced across the level area to the trails on the back side of the mid mountain ramp. The back area offered more intermediate runs and some tree skiing. Cheryl easily led him. With equal ease Charlie skied behind her and took in the scenery. They stopped at the top of the run to admire the panorama and to decide which run to take down the hill.

"You are getting better on those skinny skis."

"I was just going to say that you have lost a lot of your youth and strength."

They made two intermediate runs together skiing leisurely. Cheryl started slowly and worked her way up until she was totally focused and everything flowed together as it should. Charlie relaxed and took a break from his usual fast pace. For fun he began to critique her form.

"Here we are on the slopes of Ski Cooper with the lovely artist, Cheryl Pritchard. She is currently holds third place in cross country ballet. Her next feat will be a full forward gainer with a double twist. Here is the ramp and . . . she missed it!" Charlie deliberately skied across her path in front of her to try to throw off her timing.

Cheryl gasped and yelled, "I know a sports announcer who is going to be hospitalized from a ski pole injury, if he keeps messin' with me!"

They took the lift back to mid mountain. They agreed to meet later at the barbecue. Charlie headed for a couple of steep runs to kick up the snow. Cheryl skied across mid mountain to the intermediate run in front of the lodge. Her ability was improving. She was more responsive and in better control on quick turns. Her thighs and hips were feeling the burn from the fun. "A good time to head for the lodge," she thought to herself.

About half way down the run she stopped. Just a few yards in front of her was a crowd of skiers of all ages. They were family descendants of members of the Tenth Mountain Association. About twenty yards to their front was a group of thirty white haired men dressed in snow white ski parkas preparing for their ski demo.

The members of the Tenth stood together dressed in their original parkas and ski pants. As teenagers many of them grew up and learned how to ski in the New England states. They conversed among themselves as they did when they were overseas decades ago during the Italian Campaign. The Italian Alps would be the same environment as they were in today. They stood here now just as they stood together in that part of the world in the early 1940's. They were laughing and sharing longtime friendship. They were comrades against the elements and against the enemy. Now their bodies were older and the skin more wrinkled, but their eyes and conversation remained as bright as ever. They were happy to be alive and to share one another's friendship. Many were animated and joking as they chose up sides for their ski run. "Mac Donald have you sharpened your old rusty edges? I don't want you falling down and sliding into me as you did last year," quipped Greg Gutierrez.

"It wasn't me. It was your imagination that made you fall down, Greg. You were scared!"

A somber moment fell among them. They grouped tightly together around one member for a call of inspiration. In silence, with heads bowed, a voice was heard. "Heavenly Father, we will never forget what happened and what we endured. We will never forget our buddies and our friends who did not make it back. We will always remain steadfast with what we do in life, and we will share our experience and knowledge with those who have not yet made the journey. Help us to overcome all obstacles and fears in our futures. Help us to keep wisdom close and to cherish our lives, our wives, our sons, and our daughters. Help us to live everyday the best we can, and to keep your thoughts in our hearts and minds. We ask this in the name of your Son, our Saviour, Jesus Christ." There had been no movement in the group. Without a cue, the members left the group two at a time to ski downhill to the patio.

They skied one behind the other in two parallel lines ten yards apart. As they approached the lower part of the run the two lines seemed to merge. They were interlocked in S turns. The group of descendants and relatives began to follow them down the hill hollering and whistling.

Cheryl pointed her telemarks down hill and joined the group. Video cameras followed behind them down the slope to the patio in front of the lodge. Cameras and cheers greeted the Tenth members as they approached the patio. Close to the patio, the two lines of the Tenth separated and the lead skier of each line skied to a stop at opposite ends of the patio. The rest of the members filled in the gap towards the center. The line grew from two to thirty. When all were stopped they removed their goggles and hoods and bowed theatrically to the shouts and cheers of the crowd. The members of the Tenth removed their skis and joined their loved ones on the patio. The celebration was underway.

The smell of the barbecue was an irresistible lure. The grills were blazing. The food was piled high in anticipation of the rush. Early birds were getting their food and saving places at the tables for others. The deck was a swarm of activity. Hungry skiers began to pick up paper plates. The snow birds and squirrels darted in for some human food as if they were part of the festivities. Skis were stuck vertically into the snow everywhere. Cheryl was looking for a place to park her skis and enter the foray. She spied Donald MacDonald bent over reaching for his boot buckles. She skied up behind him. Greg Gutierrez was out of his skis and crawling over to Mac on his hands and knees.

"Yes Master MacDonald! Let your humble steward unlace your boots for you, lest you injure your back."

"Stay back, you ingrate, or I'll have the warden hand you ten lashes! Now fetch me my beer!" Don finally got one boot free of the binding and knelt to free the other boot.

Cheryl spoke loudly to the back of their heads, "I am looking for a handsome rogue to escort me to the barbecue."

Greg interjected. "I will escort the fair maiden"

Mac interrupted, "Be gone and out of my affairs you townie!" cried Mac. "Come with me my sweet and I will promote you to kitchen wench!"

"That sounds like a demotion to me."

Greg reasoned, "Cheryl, why do you continue to hang around this lowlife loser?"

Mac retorted, "Back you humbug! This chamber wench belongs to me!"

Cheryl swept her arm in an arch towards both of their faces. "On second thought, I shall be charmed to attend the barbecue with both of you oafs! Perhaps after viewing your table manners, I will finally be able to cast the undesirable one aside. Now which one of you is going to pay for my barbeque ticket?"

Greg and Mac hollered simultaneously as they pointed at one another. "He is!" They laughed and moved to the food line. It was all there. Chicken, turkey, pork ribs, beef ribs, hot dogs, steaks, potatoes, mixed vegetables, potato salad, sloppy joes, cold slaw, sour kraut and corn on the cob. Nobody seemed to know where the corn on the cob came from. Desserts were in abundance. The picnic tables were five to a row, and five rows on the patio. Each table could seat ten people. The grills and serving tables were along the edge perpendicular to the lodge. Fifty gallon plastic garbage cans were placed on the corners of the patio. Some were full of ice and mixed brands of beer and wine. Empty garbage cans stood by to accept trash. The members of the Tenth and their families sat at the tables closest to the food. They were surrounded by their relatives and workers from the hospital and the ski areas.

Charlie Hall was one of the early ones through the food line. He left the food line and sat down with Alison MacDonald and her husband, Andy, a master chef. He fed the masses everyday at the Copper Mountain Base Lodge. Alison saved places for her father and Greg. Barry Bounds and his wife joined the table. Charlie made himself comfortable. He dug into the au gratin potatoes and the bratwurst. He breathed in the wonderful smells of the barbeque. He opened a can of Pabst Blue Ribbon. He took a swig and admired the red white and blue can. He watched for his coworkers and friends. He waved at Marty Williams and his sister Kim.

"We're holding a seat for you three. Hurry up!" Alison yelled to her father and Greg.

"Alright! Alright! It just doesn't get any better than this," Mac offered to Greg and Cheryl.

"Barbeques are a big weakness with me," admitted Cheryl. "I sure am glad I showed up today."

Mac whispered, "After this we shall retreat to my living room and my warm fireplace. Once there, I will tell you of my weakness." Cheryl was eying a well done hamburger and a chicken leg. She decided she could bend her vegetarian diet today and asked for the chicken.

Everyone took in the scenery and the friendship. Ski Cooper was proud to sponsor the reunion. Cheryl looked around. There were tourists on vacation. There was a man with his leg in a cast who looked amazingly like Cliff Robertson. He was sitting with a man whose face she could not place unless he was from the society section of the Denver Post. The cancer donor? There were local merchants and their sons and daughters. There were workers from the city and county administrations. There were retail shop workers and utility company workers. It seemed as if everyone she had met or seen at least one time in Leadville was here at Ski Cooper today. The man who owned the bowling alley was leaning against the lodge smoking a cigarette. He was enjoying the festivities as much as everyone else. There were hospital workers and a few miners from the Black Cloud Gold Mine. There were former miners from the Climax mine. All were grateful to be away from work and out from under the microscope. The skiers from Leadville were always anxious to spend a day on the runs with their families and their friends.

CHAPTER SIX

The solemn mood changed to a festive one for the members of the Tenth. Everyone was taking in the scenery and the barbecue in a relaxed easy going manner. Everyone enjoyed being among friends in a well behaved neighborhood crowd. Some were scanning the peaks and rock outcroppings for the walls of ice and snow built up by the winter wind. They witnessed an ice wall over hang when it broke loose. The overhang dropped three hundred feet straight down, and crashed into the snow below. An avalanche began and continued to make its way down hill before it slowed to a stop at the tree line. The sound of the avalanche rumbled into the ski area a minute later. Inhibitions began to diminish after a couple of beers or wines. The time and confines of the habitual work day world had slipped away. The beauty and the joy of the outdoor mountain day emerged and won the greater influence in the psyche. The day was a warm, heartfelt occasion in the great outdoors. Of course the semi professional drinkers were way ahead in spirit if not intoxication and so were a few of the extroverts. Cheryl caught a few glances from the crowd. She was proud to be sitting between Don and Greg. Donald MacDonald jumped to his feet to toast the crowd.

"Bring me your burdens! Tell me of your sorrows and troubles lads and lassies! You all should be ashamed of yourselves, all of you poor lambykins who feel sorry for yourselves. You live in one of the most beautiful settings in the world. Did you ever stop and wonder what you would do to survive if you were here in Leadville one hundred years ago? You stout lads young and old alike would be laboring in the mines! You would have the prickly dust in your lungs that would shorten your life, or you might break your back!" He turned to one of the hospital tables. His arm and hand tracked a sweeping motion towards them. Mac pointed his "ruler of the moment" index finger at them. In a tone of condemnation he blared, "And you ladies!

What would you be doing? Ha! Pray tell!" Donald leered convincingly at them, heavy eyebrows furrowed. "You would all be down in the cribs at the Past Time Saloon, waiting for your dirty miner to share sin with him and take his money!" Cheryl saw glares and looks of shock on the faces of the hospital workers.

Guffaws and boos surfaced from the tables. A chorus of rejection arose from the nurse's table. "You louse!" "Die you creep!" "Pervert!"

Linda Kay was never one to be shy. She spat out, "MacDonald! I'll have you know a few of us are doing that bad thing on the side right now, but yew should mind yer own business, you pitiful meddler!"

Mac recovered in his practiced manner of charm. With a broad smile and lust in his heart and eyes, he dared Linda to divulge the names. "And which ones might they be?" roared McDonald. "Tell me now, Linda Kay!" Gasps of air and more guffaws were heard among the tables.

Linda Kay spoke to Mac as if he was a child. "Donald, why don't you move a little closer to our table? We want to talk with you."

"Isn't Mac the sweetest man you have ever known?" Elaine hollered over the comments. She wore a sling for her left arm due to a shoulder injury.

"Yes, a real teddy bear," chimed Kelly.

"He says the kindest things!" yelled Alison.

Once on a roll Mac rarely retreated. "Elaine! Elaine! It is so good to see such a charming, intelligent woman. It looks like you have had an argument with one of your boyfriends."

"Sorry, Mac! You have been replaced!"

"Hey! Who invited you MacDonald? You lecherous old geezer!" Donald was chuckling as he returned to his seat.

Mike Coles yelled across the isle, "Charlie! Is your bump arm still sore?"

"Sure is Mike! So is Marty's. I bumped every chair yesterday. It was more than twenty five hundred."

"I got some lingering tendonitis." Mike was bragging. "I don't see Dave Peterson here. He claims he couldn't lift his arm!"

"Oh! That was from the beer party afterward at the B Lift Pub!"

Barry threw in, "He wasn't the only one."

Andy stood up for himself, "That's what I feel like after lifting the big pots and food containers all day in the kitchen."

Mac addressed Cheryl, "Well, Cheryl. How is your sculpture coming along?"

"I will be honest with you. It hurts to hold this plastic knife and fork. My fore arms are sore from pushing and shaping a couple of hundred pounds of clay for three months. The ligaments in my fingers are so stiff it feels as if they are just going to snap off. Would you be a dear and cut my chicken for me." Don and Greg laughed. "And then, as if that's not enough, I have to help my parents drywall on the weekends." Sympathetic aaawwws filled the air. Cheryl raised her small glass of wine to the table. "Drywall made me what I am today!"

After the food had been consumed, people began to converse across the isles. All of a sudden everyone wanted to talk to someone at a different table. Sue Coles hollered over to Cheryl, "I saw your picture in the paper." Sue, a single mom with three out of control children was a little bit jealous of single adults with uncomplicated lives. Like most parents, Sue was not ready to give up her children to be single again. She actually preferred the "Mom" role. She continued with the slap down, "It looks a lot better than you do in real life."

"Ooooh! Ooooh!" Oooohs from the tables. The hospital tables were catching fire from the liquid refreshments.

Charlie wanted to get in on the act. "Hey Patti! Is it possible for a theoretical mathematician or a lift operator to fall in love with a clinical psychologist?"

Patti laughed. "Charlie! Nice try! I think the used car sales lady will make you happy. I wish to remain unencumbered."

Charlie looked at Marty. "Am I wearing a sign that says leprosy or something?"

A few of the hospital workers began to collect money and serve beer and wine from cardboard boxes. It helped to keep the isles clear and the spirits flowing. Like vendors at a ball game they would yell "Beer here!" amid the cries of "Nurse!" and "Oh, Doctor!"

"We are trying to get y'all drunk. Maybe a couple of you will ski into the trees and require our services at the hospital. We have too many empty beds now!"

"What is wrong with you? We just got rid of all of those victims from the forty car pile up on Vail Pass! What a pain in the ass those people were!"

"Most of them were from out of state. They couldn't even breathe up here at ten thousand feet. Who lets these people fly in here anyway?"

"You know I have always said they should have to pass a written test before they can buy a lift ticket."

Conversations flowed and ebbed. Talk at one table shifted to legalized low stakes gambling.

"Rumor has it there are over two hundred contracts to sell real estate in this town. They all have a conditional paragraph that says, 'Given that legalized gambling is passed by the voters of Leadville, we agree to purchase for x amount of dollars!'"

"Hey! There was a group of foreigners wearing turbans. They were at the Silver King Inn talking with the manager. They wanted to buy the hotel!"

"I don't think any thieving foreigners should be allowed to buy anything in Lake County. We ought to have that as a county rule."

"The townsfolk want to keep their stores and put a few slots in them. That is what a lot of them envisioned."

"Patti McMahon wanted gambling. She was all for it. She invited the building department over to her place one afternoon to talk about the possibilities."

"Patti wanted a couple of slot machines in the forward bar area, and about twenty in the dance hall area. That was all! She wanted to keep the Silver Dollar just as it is! The building inspectors and the building department told her that the building could not handle two or three hundred people under the new code."

"Aw, don't sugar coat it! They told her that her building was substandard. They said she couldn't open up the second floor for business. They were telling her that her building could not handle three hundred people day after day."

"Now these bureaucrats are talking big buildings. Bigger than anything we got except the high school and the hospital."

"The building department started issuing statements and memorandums to store owners to comply with new building codes for increased service capacity in restrooms."

"They should put it all down by Granite. There are no buildings there. They could start from scratch. Build streets, sewers, and new subdivisions. Then this old part could be a historic area."

"Yew mean a hysterical area."

"The new building code states that new construction has to have a certain number of commodes per so many people."

"Yew mean a shitter?"

"You need a floor straight and stout enough for a small herd of buffalo. It's all oversized design! Basically, they are requiring new construction. They tell you how many front and back double doors you have to have."

"How many fire extinguishers and all."

"Yep! It yer government to help and protect you. Never mind if you were first and should have rights."

"They told Patti she would have to build a whole new building from scratch."

"Just for twenty slots?"

"Yep."

"You know what she did next? She threw them out of the Dollar!"

"No!"

"By God, she did! They had not been inside more than thirty minutes and she took their beers."

"She didn't give 'em their money back neither! Told 'em to get out or she would call the sheriff!"

"Well the rumors are flying. Cripple Creek is gonna vote theirs in before Victor and Cripple Creek turn into a ghost town."

"Central City is gonna get gambling. It is right next to Denver."

"That's a fact."

"We gots families in this town before anyone else ever got here and they don't bother to ask us anything. They just do what ever they want."

"The Fathers dun come up with a new plan. They want to put it down West Third Street. All new building construction. They envision a whole new West Third Street."

"It's all houses."

"Go figure."

"All brand spankin' new buildings. More concrete poured in one year than what has been poured in the last forty years."

"I'll bet they are raising their salaries already, in anticipation of a large increase in sales tax revenue! You know what I'm talking about?"

"I know that building inspector. Another failed business owner."

"A Man's gotta feed his family."

"He's been on Third Street the last two weeks. One family moved out."

"These homes are grandfathered."

"Not anymore. That inspector marked one of them uninhabitable. Foundation not structurally sound."

"This new school of thought is causing a lot of unnecessary pain and heart burn, but it is the only way you can get things to change."

"You mean it is okay to mess up a couple of hundred people's lives and dreams just to build a new gambling town? You mean it's okay to enforce the new building codes on the old homes here in Leadville or declare them no good and tear them all down?"

"Nah, they will get good money for their houses."

"You can't sell one after it has been targeted."

"Can't get anyone to buy a home that needs a new foundation, unless you sell it at half of its value or less."

"If you can't hang in there financially, you have to give it all up and get out."

"You mean go bankrupt?"

"Nope. There is another way. It's what they did in Oklahoma when oil went down to eleven dollars a barrel last time. You just pack up and move out of town."

"No shit?"

"They left their cars and boats in the driveway. They turned off their utilities, locked up the house and moved. They left all the mortgage payments and never went back. The lines were too long to wait around for bankruptcy!"

"What I don't understand is, if they bring in gambling, who is gonna lose the money?"

"See that gambling thing. I never could understand. Who is gonna come up here to Leadville to gamble? It is a risk to drive the highways."

"Oh, boy, they would start construction for four lanes between here and I 70 on both roads going north out of town."

"Maybe it was gonna be tied in with the new airport."

"Fly into Leadville to Gamble? Ha!"

"Ain't gonna be no new airport!"

"No, sir! We don't need a new two mile runway bringing in all of the fricking tourist of the world to Leadville! There is a two mile runway at Buena Vista thirty miles south of here. Is that too far from the frickin' ski areas for the rich people of the world?"

"Do you really care if people from other countries get to ski here or not?"

"Hell no!"

"You better believe it. The ski areas are big time world resorts now."

"Hey did you see that editorial in the Democrat? A lot of replies in the letters to the editor about the superfund cleanup site."

"What about the super fund mine clean up?"

"All of those tunnels connect into that Yak Tunnel. Robert Jones says that huge plug will hold for now, but in five or ten years it will be leaking contamination again. He says that tunnel will be backed up like a New York City storm sewer."

"One editorial said that anybody protesting the airport should be careful about walking across the street in downtown Leadville cause they might get run over!"

"I saw that one. The guy was mad cause his kid wanted to become an aircraft mechanic and they had to travel all the way to Buena Vista to go to the school."

"Waaaaaa!"

CHAPTER SEVEN

A sense of awareness was heightened among the pilot and the two skydivers. The jump was on schedule. Half of the sky was decorated with small fluffy clouds that were moving west to east about two thousand feet above the peaks. Relative winds were on and off at ten miles per hour. The plane gained six hundred feet in altitude by the time it was over the north end of town, yet the ground was three hundred feet below them. Al followed the two lane highway to Ski Cooper. Max was staring out the window straight into the side of the mountain. The snow covered trees were about too hundred feet away. His stomach was leaking a little extra acid. He realized Al was going to stay three hundred feet above the trees the entire way to the ski area. Max accepted this fact to subdue his nervous discomfort. He thought that Al must be extremely confident of the plane's mechanical condition. Why should I sit here and be quiet about it all? Why not have some fun? Max had stayed quiet as a child because he was ordered to do so. After four years in the army he learned to voice his displeasure on purpose just at the wrong time. It always brought a few forlorn looks and some inappropriate laughter. Someone would always add a wise comment. Max was not a bully but he usually got his way if he deemed it necessary. He figured out what he was going to say and gave it a ten count.

He yelled over the roar of the engine to Al. "What the hell are you doing, Big Al?"

Al slowly turned his head with a disconcerting wrinkle of his brow and mouth. The cat had the mouse. He shot Max a look of disapproval. As if the answer was an inconvenience, he stated blandly, "I am climbing the thermals and flying the plane! What does it look like to you?"

"You are joking, you big elephant!" Max insisted, "You are crazy! There are no thermals off that cold mountain! I think your mind is frozen!"

The corners of Big John's mouth spread out towards the sides of his face. "Max! You are losing it!"

Al almost broke into a laugh, but he kept a serious face, and played the highly insulted role. It was working. He had gotten to one of them. He would terrorize them until they left his plane, and they would never forget this gut retching climb to altitude. Al bounced back as if irritated. He gave Max the elementary qualifications statement, "You are no pilot! How the hell would you know?"

"Christ on a crutch! I need a dull, peaceful, mediocre ride! You are trying to traumatize me!"

"What are you talking about? This is nice and peaceful." Al rebuked, "You are hysterical. Get a hold of yourself!" He yelled to John. "John! Check Max for shock"

Big John had closed his eyes. He was meditating like a Tibetan Monk. He ignored everything. He was on a higher plateau now. His demo would soon be realized. Maybe he was visualizing his photo finish in front of the crowd. Max was happy for him. Max wished he could sit by the heater and catch a few winks. The only thing for Max on this ride was going to be the three hundred feet of fright and a frozen pair of buns. The shivering would continue after he got out of the plane. He would be shivering after he landed on the ground. He would still be shivering tonight in the hot shower he was going to take, if he made back to the house. He wished that he had turned on the hot water heater before he left for the airport. You just can't think of everything. Then it occurred to Max that he was in automatic shiver mode. He willed himself to stop. This jump is not over yet. Catch your breath. Get your wits about you. In a lower volume Max announced, "Hey! I'm boiling back here! Can you turn the damned heater off?"

A smile formed slowly across Big John's barbaric face. His eyes opened. He laughed with glee!

"You burnin' up, Max?" Big Al hollered. "You jes got to collect yourself once in awhile! Don't hold nothing back now, yah hear? Don't be a weenie! You got to toughen up son."

Collect yourself. Yeah, right. The petrifying view of the treetops and rock outcroppings warmed him with fear. Max stared at the floor and the back of the pilot seat. The slope of the rear window roof line forced his head straight down. He had to put his ear on his shoulder to be able to see straight ahead or out the window. The propeller blasted the cold air through the open door to him. His butt was frozen. The big brothers laughed at him. It angered him. They still had a long way to go. All he could do now was try to survive the freezer. Why worry? Everything was in its place. There was orderliness. John and Max began to think about the actual jump. John closed his eyes again and smiled. He anticipated the jump into the ski area in front of all of his buddies and friends. Max didn't know a soul there except for Mac and Greg and his ski buddies.

Lunacy of the highest order! They were about five minutes from the ski area. The sky was somewhat gray in the west. The cloud ceiling was just above the peaks now. It was lower. They felt a gust of wind over twenty miles an hour. It was a long steady one. It pushed the plane sideways before Al could get a good correction on the rudder. Max willed his stomach not to sink. It seemed as if someone balled his stomach up and threw it into a bottomless pit. Everyone was thinking the same thought. Al turned the plane west into the wind to avoid being pushed into the mountain. They would gain more altitude. They would have a more expansive view on approach to the ski area when they turned around to go back. The clouds looked greater in number and a little more threatening for some reason. The bright sunlight was gone. Maybe that was because the plane was just underneath the clouds. Suddenly they were flying through a slight snow shower.

"Good thing you guys are dressed for the snow!" yelled Al.

Max got his eye on the plane altimeter gage and found his wrist mount altimeter reading to be two hundred feet lower. No big deal. He mentally began to prepare for exit. His mind took over his feelings. His concentration on how to save himself filled his consciousness. The wind blasted the big fluffy flakes through the door and Max soon had a light coat of snow on his outfit.

Big John laughed as he hurled the first insult at the snow covered figure in front of him. "Hey, Max! Where did you park the sleigh and the reindeer?"

"Ha, ha! Ha, ha, ha! Yeah!" Big Al laughed. "Did you bring us any presents?"

"I've got one for you, Big Alan. I'm going to give it to you after the jump."

"Max, you kind of look like Frosty the Snowman."

"And you kind of look like Mr. Potato Head," Max shot back. The engine began to reach its performance limit. The engine was no longer excited about gaining any more altitude. At this point the climbing was much slower. Inevitably, Al yelled, "We are not going to get much more altitude. If I keep trying, we will run out of fuel. Someone needs to get out." John was still seated. Al's statement had registered with both jumpers. "I put in the minimum amount of fuel to keep the weight down, you guys know that! Now do something!" It didn't seem like too much to ask, although their present elevation was just above the base lodge. Damn it! Was that the first mistake? How many mistakes had they made up to now?

"Max, you need to get out first. I need more altitude."

"Oh, yeah. Spare me! How considerate of you!"

The barbecue crowd was suddenly interrupted by the engine noise of a plane moving one hundred ten miles an hour through the air. The aircraft passed directly over the crowd at fifty feet above the tree tops.

Seth and Angie said in unison, "Someone is looking out of the plane!" Indeed the head and shoulders of one of the passengers could be seen outside of the airplane. The figure was silhouetted by the overhead wing. Max looked down at the throng of people on the lodge patio. A few of them returned his wide eyed stare and waved. His face and body were frozen with fear. Now would be a good time to relax and toss that Golden Burro burrito. The Colorado and Tenth Mountain flags were sticking straight out to the right. Max estimated one hundred fifty feet. No time to be scared. Just like waking up in the morning. A second thought passed through his mind. "Lord, I hate hot shot pilots."

Angie Coles yelled with delight. "Wow, Mom! Did you see that?"

"Pretty low I'd say," commented Greg. Someone in the crowd yelled, "Big John has arrived!"

The crowds' interest went back to conversation, food, and alcohol. The squirrels and snowbirds dared to get closer to the food.

Max was in a delayed state of shock. It would all add up later. Calm down. Fear and shakes would have to wait because conscious thought is the only hope to get through this jump without injury. Max reasoned to himself. The flag was sticking out to the right. They were upwind all ready. Half the problem was solved. The snow was moving past the plane from nose to tail. There was not enough altitude. Max looked at his altimeter. It registered a hair under ten thousand feet. The plane altimeter was two hundred feet higher. Great. He knew Al was flying compass now because Al could not see the ground. Max guessed that he might have a thousand to twelve hundred feet if the plane kept climbing. He looked out the door back to the lodge to plan a jump run line up. He saw the ski runs and the lodge. They were a mile away. The lodge must be under nine thousand. He looked at the forest about five hundred feet below the plane. A snow cat was moving up a wide trail hauling skiers to the open bowl above tree line for some powder skiing. Max forced himself to look for detail. The trees were smaller along the trail and thinned out compared to the thick trees around the runs. The sun was blocked. The light was flat. The landscape was one dimensional.

A small cloud suddenly engulfed the plane and spit it out. Max pulled his frozen face back inside. His mind was thinking calmly. It was a requirement when the action began and he was good at it. What did he just see? Something about that snow cat. There was a fenced in equipment yard with trucks and snowmobiles behind the snow cat. The trail was too wide. Max willed himself to recall. The trucks and shed and the snow cat were small. Or were they big? His face went back outside. From the distance he could barely see the see the trail. He put a calculating eye on the distant lodge. The lodge was perched in a clearing on a ridge of the mountain. The snow cat trail was a fire break in the forest of trees. It took a couple of seconds for the perspective to kick in. The trees, what about the trees? They were thinned out. They looked as if they were balanced on top of each other. They were on top of each other! It is a ravine. Sure it is! How deep? Six or seven trees times sixty feet. The bottom of the ravine might be over four hundred feet lower than the trees.

The plane was passing to the left of the peak area. Al had increased their altitude. It was time to go back. He rudder kicked the plane around to keep from losing altitude. Max tightened his leg straps and checked his handles. Everything was good. He squared himself to the doorway for the exit. Wait a minute. The snow was blowing from nose to tail! Did the wind change? If the wind changed he would never get close to the lodge. Wait! The snow falls straight down. The plane moves through the snow. It is the forward speed of the aircraft that that creates the illusion of the snow moving from nose to tail. The flag is right! The wind did not change direction. *Wake up, Max! Where are you now?* This is jump run! Out of nowhere, he recalled John's words. "If you are going to bounce, then bounce on the patio in front of the guests and give them a thrill. I'll give you a hundred dollars." Now all Max had to do was squeeze past John to the door.

The ravine would be the exit point. It was his only safety net. Max allowed himself to gain one hair of confidence. His heart and mind warmed a little. If his main canopy malfunctioned, there would be enough room for a reserve ride into the ravine. Who cares about the lodge? The patrons at the barbeque would not even miss him. The small safety cushion brought a little warmth to his frozen body. If the canopy opened high enough above the ridge line, then he could try for the lodge. He put his gloved hands on each side of the door. His right foot was on the edge. He looked outside the plane. The approach was questionable. What existed was a dog leg to the left against a crosswind from the right. He pulled his head back inside. "Right, right!" Al gave Max a large correction. Damn! It does not matter now. We are near. His goggles were fogged. He took them off. He didn't need them. Completion rather than perfection was all that mattered.

Now it was Al's turn to lose it. "Christ on a crutch! Get out of the airplane! I don't have any fuel!"

John watched the wind whip at the baggy parka. Max would grip the handle wouldn't he? He knew what to do. John took a breath to yell the warning, but Max was gone.

He was alive and over the ravine! His head was back and his belly button was forward in a hard arch. His hands were at his shoulders and his elbows were in at his sides. The heels of his feet were on his butt. The sound of the plane engine dopplered away from him. All was quiet. He did not move a muscle. He tucked his chin to his chest. His eyeballs rolled down until the iris was at the bottom of the socket. He had five to seven seconds to get a chute open. He was obviously outside the USPA altitude safety envelope.

He realized that he should have held on to the pilot chute as he left the airplane. He dropped his right hand down to the leg strap to grab the pilot chute. All his hand found was baggy parka material. His hand returned to his shoulder. He tried a second time. The wind began to pull at the loose parka. The parka was now his body bag. He bent at the waist and made a visual search. What a mess! Both his hands shot to his hip to grab the material and pin it to his stomach. His body began to roll. He saw the leg strap and got his hand on it. He pulled more parka out of the way. Wah lah! The fingers on his right hand closed around the handle. He was so excited he pulled the pilot chute half way out of the pouch. *Not time yet!*

Max was on his back in an awkward position. He lost his count. Screw it! He pulled the pilot chute and threw it behind his back as he continued to roll to his right, just like on the floor at home. Nothing happened. He was picking up speed and loosing precious altitude. Open! Open! Max mentally disassociated himself from his dilemma. He ignored the view. He had panicked. He threw the pilot chute too soon. He went on his left side and pulled his arms and knees in towards his stomach. He needed speed and he was going to have a look at his gear. He felt a light tug on the back of his container. The pilot chute pulled the pin out of the locking loop. The container flaps would open and the pilot chute would continue to pull the suspension lines tight. The chute would pop out of the little bag that held it neatly folded and the canopy would open. He looked up. His blood turned cold and his heart skipped a beat. His gear was just falling right along with him. He estimated he was at sixty miles an hour. The pilot chute was fully open. The parachute bag and the suspension lines were flailing about.

He needed a canopy now. His hands went to his chest. The thumb and fingers of his right hand closed in a death grip around the red cloth covered handle on the right side of the harness. The red cut away handle would disconnect the main canopy. The thumb and fingers of his left hand closed in a death grip on the metal reserve parachute handle on the left side of the harness. The metal handle would open his reserve parachute. It would require five hundred feet of altitude for the reserve canopy to fully inflate. The suspension lines were tight. He rotated his right fist and peeled open half of the red velcro cut away handle from the harness. He had to make a dead reckoning with the ground to decide if it was time to take the reserve ride to live. Without moving a muscle in his body he turned his chin to his left shoulder. Tears filled his eyes from the wind blast. He squinted at the ground. He was low. He had five seconds or so to live. He calculated one thousand feet to the bottom of the ravine and less than three seconds to get the cutaway for the reserve.

The canopy snapped open. Max was jerked straight up to a standing position by the sudden stop. The leg straps dug into his crotch. His head wanted to keep falling at eighty miles an hour but it stopped when his chin hit his chest. The riser smacked the left side of his helmet. A white light flickered behind his eyes from the impact. The riser spun the helmet on his head one quarter of a turn. His nose stopped the helmet from turning any further. He was alive! He carefully replaced the handles. A taste of blood reminded him that he had bit the inside of his cheek. He shook the cobwebs and bad endings out of his head. He released the canopy steering toggles from the keepers. Always one to pay his respects any time any where, Max was never shy about praying or talking to the Lord. He looked up at the beautiful blue and gray canopy and yelled at the top of his lungs, "Thank you Jesus!" The nylon parachute was running with the wind at forty miles an hour to the lodge. He estimated that he was sixty feet above the trees as he passed over the ridge of the ravine. The terrain dropped seven hundred feet over the next half mile to the lodge. The lodge seemed distant and cold, but Max knew that it was alive and vibrant. He felt wonderful. He wondered to himself why he had not tossed his breakfast burrito. He must have shivered it off in the plane.

Seth Coles kept one eye on the airplane as he continued eating. "Hey! Someone fell out of the plane!" He pointed to the plane. No one paid any attention. Seth watched the body in the air. The chute opened. "Look! There is a parachute way over there!" Sue and Mike looked for the parachute. "Good grief! There it is Mike. Way over there."

Max checked his canopy for rips and tears. His present course would carry him into the parking lot to crash against the parked cars. Maybe he could stay on the roofs and the hoods and off the windshields. He was scared. He thought of the hot coco and the cold beer and the sloppy joes. Now he was properly motivated. Next he had to get the upper hand on this landing. He could land the canopy safely in the high wind. He needed to pay attention to the trees.

When the wind rushes over a forest of tree tops into an open field, it rolls down to the ground like a wave crashing on the beach. He had to be careful when he got to the ski run. The vortex would collapse his canopy and throw him to the ground. He had to stay away from the trees. He could only loose altitude in the middle of the ski run. He desperately needed altitude. As he neared the lodge the mid mountain ramp was above him to the left. It occurred to him that he should go as high up the run as possible. He needed to angle uphill and get to the center of the ski run. That would give him altitude, and at that point, he could land or figure an approach to the lodge.

Seth and Angie watched the wind blow Max from the treetops out over the ski slope. He was one hundred feet in the air. It was still downhill to the lodge for about one hundred fifty yards with a forty yard drop. He had to turn before he got to the lift and trees on the other side. In the middle of the ski run, Max pumped the left toggle gently four times and turned his canopy uphill. The wind picked up and blew him sideways to the big steel chair lift cables. His back was to the lodge. The view of the canopy from the deck did not look promising. The jumper and his canopy had disaster written all over it. The crowd had doubts about a happy landing.

Greg spoke to Mac and Cheryl, "I used to think John had it all under control, but it looks as if this might be the day that everything goes wrong."

Kelly, a physical therapist at the hospital, was thinking she may have another accident victim to work with. She said in her favorite hillbilly monotone with no hint of excitement, "Look girls. That man is going to crash into the trees or hit the lift line."

"Maybe you can help him learn to walk again," Beth added. They laughed together with several nurses and maintenance men.

Max spit down towards an empty lift chair thirty feet below. He knew the spit would miss the chair. He wondered if he would. It scared him. The wind took the blob straight to the tree line on his right. Now he knew the wind line for certain. He was trying to remain calm but his nerves were on edge. Stay with! Don't quit! Don't close your eyes! Land your stinking canopy! He looked left where he needed to be. He was on the high side of the run, and just then, the wind stopped. He said good bye to the bad landing below him and turned his canopy to the center of the run. As the slope ran downhill away from his feet he gained twenty feet in altitude. The new perspective refreshed him. Another little cushion. He allowed himself one hair of confidence. A bowl of hamburger chili and a beer would be good right now.

The lodge was downhill to the left one hundred twenty some yards. Now all he had to do was get his feet on the ground. The surface was constantly falling downhill away from his feet. It was elusive. Would the surface hold him? His feet touched the surface as if he was ice skating downhill. He was a nervous wreck. A foot in the snow would snap his lower leg bone and ankle. He flared the canopy to stop. He held the toggles at his waist until his butt was on the ground and sliding with his legs out in front. The crowd was on its feet and laughing. He could see people at the barbeque stand up to have a clear view of him sitting on his ass. The patio seemed distant as if he was dreaming. Mentally, he was still focused on his feet watching the ground move underneath them. It was over. Breathe Max, breathe! Get a hot dog. No applause today for you. No one was impressed, but they were having a good laugh! Max was happy for them and for himself. The yelling seemed louder now.

He was on the ground. The air was warm. He would have another beautiful day in the mountains. The hell with a stand up landing. He could wiggle his toes and nothing was broken. A smile of relief was on his face. He was safe. Lordy! Max had just lived through one of the dumbest things he ever did. The worst skydive of his life.

He got to his hands and knees as children skied up to him and over his canopy. He yelled at them through his quivering lips. "Get off my canopy!" Max stood. The snow pack held his weight. Maybe he did not have to land on his ass after all. His legs were involuntarily wobbling. His nerves were racked and jittery from the cold and fear. He was drained and had genuinely been scared more than once. A ski patrolman stopped just above the canopy to divert ski traffic. He was sharing the laugh.

"It is solid enough to hold you here," he smiled knowingly. "I'll bet you wish you knew that earlier. I actually saw your feet sliding across the surface for about twenty yards I guess. You did the right thing. It never hurts to be safe."

Max started laughing. "Damn! Everybody's laughing! You would think I fell on my ass or something!"

"I would guess that it is barbeque time for you."

"Definitely. All food items need to be inspected." Max released the clasp on the chin strap. He took of his helmet and laid it on the ground. "I am beginning to thaw out. It is actually warm today."

The patrolman instructed Max to move to the edge of the run and walk down. The patrolman yelled at a group skiing down on them, "Hey! Go around!"

Max neatly daisy chained the suspension lines and gathered up his canopy. He walked across the slope and downhill. He stopped about twenty yards to the side of the patio. He could get lost in the crowd because everyone would be watching John. The squall winds had passed through. All was calm except for his frayed nerves. Big John would have a picture perfect jump. The far away drone of the plane engine had everyone's ears and eyes searching the sky over the top of the ski run. A few moments after most people had located the airplane, all video cameras waited for John to jump. He dove out of the Cessna when he was directly over the off loading ramp at mid mountain. He left the aircraft in a perfect arch. After he picked up some speed, he knocked out a back flip. When he recovered he deployed his pilot chute. His canopy fully deployed five hundred feet in the air above and to the side of the operator lift shack at Midway. Ever the showman, John proceeded to do some lazy turns in the sky from one side of the slope to the other. He did this much to the delight of the crowd, all the way down the slope to the lodge, where he made a picture perfect landing. As he descended the final three feet, a video camera moved forward and up into his face. The crowd was hollering for him. Every video camera was on him. His tailored parka gleamed brightly in the sun. He appeared rugged and saintly at the same time.

Suitably impressed, Max went inside to the basement level of the lodge and stowed his gear in one of the convenient lockers. Unheralded and unnoticed he melted into the crowd and slipped into the food line. He actually preferred it that way. Some people have such desire to be noticed that they insist on making a scene. So far, no one recognized him as the buffoon that fell on his ass. That would be the way everyone remembered him.

Sue's brother yelled at her. "Sue! Max Mason!" He pointed towards Max. Sue had a warm spot in her heart for the guy. She looked in disbelief trying to disguise any feeling for the bloke. She was happy to see him and he was going to get a warm greeting.

In her typical persona, she remarked to her brother and for all else to hear, "Well, that jerk! Do you believe it? He didn't tell me!"

Max found a cheeseburger and a bowl of hamburger chili in the food line. He turned to look for a place at the tables. Mike Coles jumped up and waved him over. "You are sitting over here, Mason!"

Cheryl watched the modest man scoot sideways along her table.

Max addressed the table, "Hi, Charlie, Barry, Marty. Alison, it looks like Andy has been beating you with the big kitchen spoons again."

"Mason you are so rude. I did not get my make up on today." Alison grinned.

Max first met this group six months ago when Copper Mountain held a hiring seminar. They had all helped him at the mountain and in the community. He felt more attachment for these people than he had felt about his entire family.

"Alison, I hope your daddy hasn't caused you anymore embarrassment" She laughed with her mouthful of food.

Max turned to Mac. "Your Honor, Greg, always a pleasure. I'm looking for the luau with the dancing girls." He eyed the new arrival. "Greg, aren't you robbing the cradle here? Who is your new hostage?"

Greg answered, "I am concerned about your landing. I am worried that you might have suffered a concussion when you fell on your ass." The table laughed.

"Yes! I do it better than anyone! I bet you and Mac laughed the loudest. I am here to bring a little sunshine and laughter into your dull pitiful lives. What complaints have you now?"

Mac yelled, "You are a failure, just as your father said you would be!"

"It's all true. It couldn't be any other way. Only enough room for one jerk in our family." Max smiled evenly at MacDonald and nodded.

A moment later, Cheryl asked, "You know that man, Mac?"

"Yes. He doesn't know it yet, but I am going to sell my house to him."

Sue gave Max the ultimatum. "Get over here Mason! Right now!" Max put his head down as a child in trouble. He swayed back and forth and dragged his feet as he made his way over to Mike and Sue. They stood so he could get his feet over the bench and under the table to sit down. Max saw her move to him. He placed his plate on the table and Sue pinned his arms with a big hug.

"Don't stop. That feels good. Squeeze me harder please, Doctor Sue. I have much pain." Sue's hand went for his crotch. "Ooops! Not the bratwurst, honey! We are in public." He looked at her short styled curly black hair, the vibrant, brown eyes, the mischievous grin, and the few wrinkles on her forehead that the kids and financial stress had given her. Intricate bulky ear rings were hanging from her dainty ear lobes. "Like them?"

"I like everything on you that shakes."

"You wonderful idiot!" Her eyes were wide and she had a smile to match. She gave Max a big kiss on the mouth. "You are so thoughtful, Max! And such a flirt! You have been hiding from me. You know I will have to spank you if you have no excuse."

"There is no life when you are a working stiff. There is no time."

"There is when we can play with the stiff. I should make you pay for this hug."

"Name your price. I will gladly pay. I would like to buy ten on payday."

Max sat between Angie and Sue. He looked at Mike. A big smile and a thumbs up were in full view. Max got two legs under the table and sat on the bench. Sue shoved his tray of food to him. "Not too much variety there. But I would never question your motives. Enjoy Max."

Angie smiled to him. "Max! That skydive was awesome. Will you teach me to skydive?"

"I will, but don't tell Sue. I don't think she is quite ready to hear that." Mike hoped that Max would spend the day with the family. The kids loved to beat on him and Sue appreciated him.

Seth Coles chimed in. "I want to be a pilot! Was that you who stuck your head out the door when the plane flew over?"

Max felt his stomach flip flop and squeeze out another drop of acid as he recalled the view of the patio. It was indelibly etched in the terror compartment in his brain. "Yes. I wanted to see if I was high enough to jump."

"That would have been cool if you jumped then."

"Seth, there were a couple of people who wanted me to do that. Maybe next time. You never know." Seth laughed at him. "It is good to see you, Seth. Maybe someday I will get to watch you and your mother jump."

Sue offered, "Oh, no you don't! I'll get you a beer Max. I'm surprised you don't have one."

"Thank you, Doctor Coles."

"You do not have to call me Doctor until I am examining you."

"I am due for a check up this week."

Seth and Angie looked at each other with grins on their faces. Angie removed Max's knit hat and placed it on top of her head.

CHAPTER EIGHT

Charlie spoke to his friends at the table. "I think it would be fun if the hospital workers and ski lift operators went skiing together in two or three large groups."

Alison agreed. "I was thinking the same thing."

Barry nodded. "That is a good idea, Charlie."

Charlie excused himself. "I am going to the other tables to find more skiers." He rose with his plastic utensils and paper plate. He hit the garbage cans to do his part on filling them up. He returned to the hospital workers table and suggested, "It looks like you might be finished here and headed back to the slopes. I thought I would invite you ladies to ski with the lift operators. After that, we can retire to the bowling alley and the bars of Leadville for an elimination pool tournament!"

A chorus of answers greeted him. Beth spoke first. "Not all of us are ladies, Charlie."

"We are sultry nurses of the night shift crew."

"Sorry, Charlie! Only the best tuna for sultry nurses!"

"Please feel free to crash into a tree! Then we can wrap you in bandages and fix you up with a catheter. Beth specializes in catheters. You like Beth don't you, Charlie?"

"I thought I did. I'll think it over. That is really the only offer I have had in the last three or four weeks." Undeterred, Charlie added, "How much is a check up?"

A voice rose from the maintenance and admin tables, "Charlie, we will ski with you so we can keep an eye on our women." This comment resulted in a chorus of denunciations of proprietary rights between the tables.

Elaine chimed in. "You have no special designs on us just because you work at the hospital."

Charlie tried one more time. "Hey! We all have different schedules. We never get to do anything together. Today would be perfect."

"You are not the only one who feels that way!" hollered Linda Kay. "Any group is a good group to ski with. Your worst day on the mountain is better than your best day at work!"

"It is unanimous! We have agreed!" announced Beth. "The hospital workers are going to host another evening barbeque! And we are proud of it. Bring your own drink specials! We are going to take this joy and warmth to Linda Kay's house tonight!" A look of puzzlement crossed Linda Kay's face and then laughter. "Show up this evening at seven thirty for you early birds. Eight is the formal start. Bring your own booze. Bring your own steak if you want meat. We will keep the grill running. We are passing the hat right now to collect for food, soft drinks, and propane. The left over money goes in the cookie jar for the next barbecue on the Fourth of July. We are talking about these four tables right here. That is about forty. If you want to help out, show up at six thirty at the earliest!"

It was unanimous. "We love you Linda Kay!"

"Let's all go skiing!"

"Take your burdens and your grief and your unhappy miserable selves to the mountains!" boomed MacDonald. He rose for one more toast."

"One more toast, toastmaster!"

"Easy ladies! There is enough of me for all of you, just be understanding. Please if you will just cooperate and form a line."

Mac toasted the crowd "To your lives! Your health! Your family, your friends, and good living habits!"

The hospital workers departed the tables and attacked the trash cans. The group moved to don their equipment and ride up the lift together.

"Max! Come on!" Charlie shouted. "Ride up with me!"

"Charlie, I have to warn you. It's my third day on the snow board."

"Thanks for the warning. I want to watch you fall. I need someone to keep me in laughs and you've been doing a great job today!" They grabbed their gear and joined the herd headed for the lift.

The two skiers in front of them caught their chair. Charlie let Max move first to the "Stand Here" marker to catch the next chair. Both skiers looked over their outside shoulder and sat down as the chair moved up fast behind them. Charlie stuck his poles under his leg and they both got comfortable.

"Charlie, I will probably fall. I'm just letting you know in advance."

"Hey, man. That is why I wanted to ride up with you. Don't you get it? My stomach hurts from laughing so much when you fell on your ass! Everyone was laughing."

Max quipped, "I only heard one or two people laugh."

"It has been a good day for everyone." They watched young boys and girls chasing each other over small jumps on the packed trails through the trees off to the right.

"Are we going to have children skiing in wolf packs like these, Charlie?"

"I know you are just a tad late, Max. I don't think it is going to happen for me."

"Are we too smart or too dumb?"

"You might be right. Anyway it sounds better than saying, "What female in her right mind wants to marry a homeless person."

"I feel the same way. We do not have to worry about it today."

"Do you have any summer employment lined up?"

"I hear that jobs are scarce. Most of the ski employees we know are going to apply for unemployment. I will apply for work to as many places as I can. Hopefully, something will turn up."

"Well. I can tell you are not looking for the big bucks or chasing the money anymore."

"No, I am not. I have chased my dream to this location. Hopefully, I can keep the houses rented. They should cover living expenses."

Charlie confided to Max. "I am going to work for the Forest Service. Another summer of fighting fires. I may get picked up full time this year. I'm about due." Charlie added, "I've been working part time at an art foundry. They will need someone when I leave. Max, you should go over there and apply for work! Go over and meet the people. They are super! You would really like them. It is a great experience and this will be the only chance that you will ever have in your life. You should take this time to experience it. The pay might not be as good as construction, but you would not have to drive all the way to the interstate. Do you have any foundry experience?"

"I worked with a sheet metal company before."

"Good. I will let them know you have done some work for a sheet metal company, and that you do construction work also. When can you get over there? The sooner the better." Charlie let him think about it for a moment.

Max replied, "You know, now that I think about it, I have Monday and Tuesday off. Okay, Charlie. I will do it. Yes. I will catch up with you Wednesday and let you know how it went. When are you leaving?"

"Probably at the end of next week. Brother Max, I am glad that you are going to check it out. It has been a terrific ski season. No bad skier accidents. We could be closing on one right now though." They neared the off ramp. They both swept their hands around the edges of their coats to make certain they would not catch on the chair. Charlie lifted his leg to retrieve his ski poles. He deadpanned, "I'll go to the left. You go to the right where the ice is."

"Good plan. What ice?"

The lift operator was standing at the side of the lift shack on the ramp. Charlie signaled him to slow the lift down. Fresh out of training the operator starred at the thumbs down sign that Charlie gave him. The new lift operator was oblivious to the signal. He did not slow the lift. Max got a good start. He was up and slightly forward, but he had no momentum. The hard snow on the ramp checked the edge of the snowboard. Max was unable to slide down to the right, away from the chair traffic. The chair made contact with his back and pushed him forward on to his face. He got to his hands and knees and hopped with his board behind him like a frightened rabbit to the side of the ramp. The skiers in the next chair managed to ski around him.

Charlie howled. "What did I tell you Max! Ha, ha, ha! Thanks, Max! What a sport! I have never seen you biff an easy one! You have not failed to disappoint today."

"Let's time out a couple of minutes."

"Why can't every weekend be like this? Ski with the nurses and complain to each other."

"That sounds like a good life." Max stepped into the board bindings again. "Charlie I can't keep up with you."

"Okay, you are on your own. We will have to ski at Copper this week. The season is about over." Charlie skied off to catch up with the crowd. Thirty five people decided how to divide up into four groups. They had to chose from two expert runs, an open tree run, and two intermediate runs.

Cheryl could not match the speed of the group on her telemarks. She skied behind them and caught them at the bottom of the run. It was fun to watch everyone having a good time. She needed to widen her circle of friends and this group was fun to be with. They skied the same runs with one another for an hour. Two thirty arrived and people began to think about things left undone back at the house. Cheryl left the group after two runs. She was tired of the difficult runs. It was time to call it a day and she skied back to the lodge.

Max had enough. Falling down was not going to improve his skill. He had hoped for an easy transition. He discovered that the stance for a snowboard was totally different from the skis. He was tired. He would come back another day. The snowboarders have a saying about how long it takes to learn. "Three days or three hundred falls. Whichever comes first." Max decided he would give it two hours at a time and as many days as it required. He stared up at the blue sky and the small cumulous clouds over head. He relaxed. He could fall asleep right here. Three hours of crawling on his hands and knees was good exercise. He was making progress, but not as fast as he had hoped. This would be the last run. He stared down the forgiving main run. Most of the moguls had been cleared off by the trail grooming crew.

Cheryl skied down the off ramp at mid mountain. She skied thirty yards across the broad hill to the main run. She stopped for a breather and looked down to find the path she was going to ski. She noticed a snowboarder in her way. The boarder moved slow and wobbled. He was obviously a beginner. He made an attempt to turn and he made an attempt to stop. He lost his balance and fell down. Cheryl skied down to him and stopped behind him. As a courtesy, most skiers would ask if the other was hurt. She felt an impulse to converse. She recognized the snowboarder from the barbeque and cajoled, "Why are you torturing yourself? You should quit before you kill yourself, and sell that board for firewood."

The snowboarder emitted a heavy sigh. He was on his back, the board was uphill. He drew his knees up to his chest. He let his feet and the board pass over his head. Now he was face down and his feet were downhill. He lifted the board with his legs and kicked the nose of the board to the open side of the run. He rolled his upper torso as he did so. Like a bar patron with one too many he attempted to stand up. His eyes saw his assailant and he lost his balance. The board moved. He sat down into the snow.

"See how easy it is? As soon as I get down the hill I promise to give your suggestion serious consideration." Max looked up at the pretty woman. "I am not doing this because I like to crawl around on my hands and knees.

I am snowboarding to learn something new." He smiled at her. "Although I suppose I might crawl around on my hands and knees for the right person." She registered no expression. He repositioned the board slightly and slowly righted himself. He looked over his shoulder to talk to her. Max thought to himself. She is attractive. Cheryl's high forehead rose straight up off the remarkable reddish brown eyebrows to her outlandish green knit hat. Shoulder length hair fell out from underneath. Her light brown eyes sparkled in the sunshine. From the cheekbones her face narrowed to a full feminine jaw. Shapely medium lips. A medium size and slender nose. A good looking woman. Set yourself up for some conversation. "Standing up is difficult. Other than that they say snowboarding is more fun than skiing."

Cheryl smiled. "They say the same thing about telemark skiing."

Max was thinking desperately of something to say. "Did you ski over here to see if I am hurt?"

Cheryl answered, "No, I skied over here to see if you want to race downhill."

"That is not a smile on your face! That is a smirk! I think you stopped here to laugh at a person with lesser skills than yourself."

"That is right. So what?" Cheryl could picture his falls. She laughed openly. "I grew up with a younger brother. I encouraged him to try outrageous things all the time. The results were sometimes comical."

"I see. I grew up with two older sisters. They used me for entertainment on a daily basis. Sometimes they would sit on my chest and drool onto my face."

"Perhaps your sisters were too kind to you." Cheryl made a brief inventory of him. Salt and pepper hair. Standard military moustache. Tall. Pretty much a square face. A not too prominent nose, rounded no point. Not a jutting jaw but a thick neck. Nice lips. He seemed slender and muscular. Difficult to tell in the bulky clothing. She took him in visually. A pair of dark blue eyes you could dive into. He was as they say "easy on the eyes." She found herself slightly intrigued with him and she wanted to learn more about him. She asked, "What are you thinking?"

"Mercy! I could use a couple of hot toddies right now before I answer your open question, but I will give it my best shot. I was just thinking that you need to give all of your worldly possessions to me so you can concentrate more on your telemark. There is a lot of room for improvement."

Cheryl sneered. "You don't have to be rude. You have not seen me ski. Unlike you I am on my feet one hundred percent of the time. I never fall. You are a deceitful person and you do not tell the truth."

"Big deal! Is someone keeping score? You made fun of my snowboarding ability. I am thinking that you owe me the winning numbers to the lottery."

"Your ability deserves criticism. A penny for your thoughts."

Max groaned. "I wish I had one billion pennies! Do you have any other questions while you are digging? You should be an interrogator."

"Let's keep it civilized, if you please. What would you do with a billion pennies?"

"I would let you have as many pennies as you could physically carry. Would you care for a list of my worldly desires and possessions? That might cut down the number of questions you need to ask."

"You seem to be somewhat generous."

"I try to help others. You know. Friendly, courteous, kind and trustworthy. A good boy scout. Pillar of the community. A humanitarian. Are you a jet setter? Do you like to snowmobile?"

"I never have. I bet it would be fun." Cheryl wanted to see how he responded to irritation. Her mother had taught her that a derogatory remark or a burr under the saddle would sometimes elicit an interesting response. The response may not lead to a good character assessment, but it was cheap entertainment. "Did your old girlfriend kick you to the curb?"

"What? Wait a minute. I prefer to stay in the introduction zone." I am not ready to talk about strained personal relationships present or past. You can have delightful conversation if you stay in a neutral zone. Conversations can actually continue for years before you ever learn anything about the other person. You have chosen to move on to a new level here. Obviously, nothing is sacred to you and you have no respect or consideration for the feelings of others. By the way, I shot my old girlfriend."

Cheryl looked across the ski area below them and to the mountains on the other side of the valley. "Beautiful isn't it?"

"Yes. Today has helped me get away from my problems for a little while."

"Would you care to elaborate on that?"

"I am remodeling an old house. I need to complete the work and rent the house before the bank takes it away from me. And you?"

"Alright, I have a statue problem. I do not have the materials to complete the job. I have not received the customary up front partial payment. I have been working for the last five months on my own time before and after work. It took over my life and my weekends. The telemarks have allowed me an escape. It is good exercise and a welcome change of scenery."

Max offered, "I will bet that your mental spring is wound pretty tight. One of these days it is going to snap! Deadlines that involve money and hard work are full of stress. I am learning to snowboard for another reason. I become complacent with what I accomplish. I tell myself that it was easy and that I could do it all again. Learning something new reminds me of how much work it takes to reach a goal."

"Oh! I see. You are an analyst! Maybe you should be a professor." Cheryl calculated, "You do not know how to stay happy or content. Just gazing at this magnificent scenery is good for a start. It is quite relaxing. It is so immense. I think of my life now as a working vacation."

"I like that! Live in the mountains to play. Work just enough to cover expenses. I guess that is one way to look at the situation."

Cheryl wanted to ski. She cut him off. "I want to make a couple of more runs here while you work your way down the run. Let's hold that thought and ski, Mr. Wobbley. We can compare thoughts later. Otherwise we will be here all night."

"I love to camp out!"

Cheryl started down hill slowly using exaggerated movements. She made certain to set a good edge before she added her body weight. She shook momentarily as she felt herself go off balance. Her arms and poles went out to her sides. She fell back into the rhythm. Her long green knit hat flew behind her and floated away from her turns. As she picked up speed Max taunted her.

"Get the flow going! That's right, baby!" Max shouted. "Go with the flow, baby! That's right!" Cheryl looked uphill at Max on her next traverse. She gave him an angry stare. He chuckled and continued to watch. She had everything synchronized. She focused her concentration as she began to study the slope and path out in front of her. She picked up speed and felt a corresponding increase in excitement. She glanced down the run and planned her moves well ahead so she could ski faster without losing control to a surprise mogul or turn. She deliberately increased her angle of attack on the smaller moguls as the run leveled out. Cheryl reached the bottom of the run exhilarated. She looked back uphill for Max. She could not spot him. Let's see. He should be the one on his hands and knees. There. That's him rolling! Ha! She waved at him and motioned she would get back on the lift for another run. He waved back. She rode up the lift by herself and absorbed the views of the snow covered forest. She returned to the edge of the run and located Max half way down the hill. She figured he might make a play for her now. Most men would. She decided to encourage him to join the festivities in Leadville. She soon caught up with him.

Sometimes love is a question that someone else decides for us. Don't stop talking. Get a phone number. Max was glad to see her. "Thank you for your company and for returning." Max suddenly seemed unenthusiastic. "There is something else that would take your mind off your work besides telemark skiing."

Cheryl braced herself mentally. "Oh, and what would that be?"

"Would you like to go for an airplane ride tomorrow?"

"An airplane ride? Around here? Where do you get one of those?"

"I am going to the Fort Collins Airport tomorrow. A large aircraft is here for the weekend. It is an old DC 3."

Cheryl decided to ding him again. "A Gooney Bird?" She watched his face as a school teacher watches and errant third grader. "My grand father welded on them when he was in the during his enlistment. He taught me how to weld. It comes in handy at work." She caught a slight reflexive eye reaction. She saw him register the thought. His mouth turned into a slight smile. He was pleased.

"It will really get your mind off everything. Believe me, this will do it. A friend called me last night. They know that I might show up because the big plane is so much fun. You get to jump with more people. Like group skiing today." He continued unemotionally. "There will be at least ten women there who skydive. You might find them interesting to talk to. Think about it. Ten dollars. A free airplane ride along the side of the mountains. You get to watch the skydivers. The scenery and experience is entertaining." Max casually glanced at her expression to see if he could read anything. Cheryl registered no reaction and no comment.

"You don't have to ride in the airplane if you do not want to." He paused then added, "I would never call you a chicken." Max added with a grin. "On my word of honor."

Cheryl laughed and choked at the same time. "You? Your word? What would you know about honor?" She thought about stabbing him with her telemark pole. "I see how you manipulate. Now you have me on a dare! That is so childish."

Max gave Cheryl his best wrinkled up little boy face. He made an annoying chicken imitation. "Buc buc buuu wwaaahhkkkk"

"Ha, you are childish and immature." What was he up to? This invitation raised suspicion. Cheryl expected they would go their separate ways after skiing. She wanted this encounter to come to an end. "I was kind of planning on going to Linda Kay's. Why are you telling me all of this?"

Max relented. "Oh, I shouldn't have mentioned it." He was defeated. "I should never have brought the subject up. I thought you might want to extend your vacation for one more day. No big deal. Well, time to go to town and play some pool, I guess." His enthusiasm waned intentionally to get her defensive barriers out of the way. It had saved him so much time and false involvement with women in the past. He did not bother to spend his time stalking or trying to romance someone who was not attracted to him in the first place. It would be her decision.

Cheryl smelled something amiss. This guy is really sneaky. "This would be strictly platonic." Max nodded his head vigorously. Cheryl suppressed a slight smile. "Well, I'm not sure. Is that all you have going on?"

"They make a big party out of it. It is a big reunion. Lots of jumpers. Probably all one hundred and fifty in Colorado will be there at the same time. I get to see buddies I haven't seen for a year or two. You get to ride in the plane along with the skydivers. You can watch them through the window or door when it is time for them to jump out. You don't have to jump out though. Observers are not allowed to jump. At that point you can chicken out. Buuuwwwaaaakkk."

"Ah! Your true character emerges. You are repeating yourself. Most men are not capable of an intelligent conversation of much more than a minute or so. That is a fact." Cheryl gave a cynical sneer. Not quite a laugh. He was starting to torment her. He certainly could be annoying.

Max pressed on a couple more points. "Actually they won't let you jump out. Some observers feel compelled to follow the jumpers. There have been studies done. Maybe you could volunteer for the study. It is so unrealistic. It is like being in a dream. They make you wear a seat belt while you are in the plane just in case you might be suicidal or become delusional. I know that starving artists with big hearts often give into the pressures of life at an early age. Well, I guess I've talked enough about it. You are more than welcome to visit. We could leave in an hour. Tonight you would have your own room or a couch in the living room along with two other girls. No pressure. We would have two hours of driving out of the way and a fresh start in the morning. A penny for your thoughts."

"Give me just a minute. I need to tighten my boot." As Cheryl knelt to retie her boot strings a plethora of thoughts crowded her mind. She reasoned them out fast. Men had tried to steal her away for a weekend before. They made false promises and plans and then changed everything at the last minute. They did not get to the ATM. They lost the check book. The friend called and said he was flying to the Bahamas next weekend, not this weekend. They had fantastic plans to soften the victim up and keep her overnight at their crib. She had to lose them, and call a cab. A parachute center certainly was a strange suggestion. Are you going to take this old fart up on these cheap dares? She had been through this before. She had taken dares before. Some work out, some don't. But it is nice to help one another. Maybe he could be just a good friend. You can never have too many good friends. Just be yourself. Keep your distance. There are a bundle of "ifs" here, and there is also the art festival. Cheryl wanted to go to the art festival in Loveland. She should tell him. His reaction might reveal something. She decided to push Max one more time. What fun to annoy him. He seems non threatening, but you never know.

"Well, time to go to the Past Time and play some pool. Ready?"

Cheryl admonished him. "I'll let you know when I'm ready. You just keep testing and pushing, in kind of a nagging way."

"Hey! That is my line."

"You said earlier, 'There really isn't anyone you can trust in the world.' Remember?" She looked at this new stranger.

"You are assuming that I have ill conceived plans or desires for you?"

"Why should I want an old man anyway?"

Max knew that the rebuke would be part of your common and ordinary conversation so he countered with a statement. "I can push a marble a mile with my tongue, while I crawl on my stomach."

Cheryl snorted and laughed all at the same time. She turned her head to avoid hitting him. "You are quite finished now, I take it? May I please continue?" She looked at him as if he just finished last in the crawling home drunk contest and was knocking at the front door.

"Hey! You are looking at me like I am a disgusting drunk crawling home."

"Pay attention, Max. Stop the distraction routine." A smile uncrossed her lips.

"Yes, let's keep it formal."

Cheryl straightened her shoulders for the delivery. "Alright Max. Here is one for you. Listen closely. This is an offer of consideration for you. The Loveland Art Festival is this weekend. It is an exhibit of national scope and all of the exhibits are quality artwork."

"Really?"

"You could help me out here. I could use a lift to Loveland. My car is on the fritz. It is too risky to take. I need some new snow ties and I never really know if my beater is going to make it. If it snows, I won't make the passes without tire chains. I am tired of strapping them on. You could take me to the festival and go on up to Fort Collins."

"There might be enough time to do both." Max offered without a stutter or a blink. "I would like to see the Art Show."

Cheryl continued, "You can stay at your friend's house if you like or we can stay at my mom's place. They want to go to the art show. There is an outside chance you could sleep with my fourteen year old sister. I think she is still a virgin. Your second option is to sleep with my mom and step dad. Your last option is to sleep on the couch. You can not sleep with me. We could go to both events because the Fort Collins airport is only fifteen minutes away. Don't take too long to decide, Max. I just told you the truth."

"Don't you trust me?"

"You do have a sense of humor. I'll give you that. Do you see anything humorous about me? You see me laughing about this, Max?"

"It's a deal. Let's go pack."

"I would like to ski one more run. We have time."

Max remembered, "My car is at the Leadville Airport."

"I can give you a lift. I'm in the very back of the lot. A green Dodge Swinger," Cheryl stated proudly. "You can't miss it."

"A Dodge Swinger? I think I am jealous," Max smiled thinly. "This is the last run for me. I have to turn in the board and get my things out of a locker. I will meet you in the parking lot."

"Don't hurt yourself. I need your car remember? Focus on that, Max."

He watched her and lectured himself. This might turn out to be the best weekend I have had for some stretch of time. Be serious on the jumping. Stay unaffected but engaging on the girl stuff. Shouldn't be any problem. Then everything became perfectly clear to Max. He was at a ski area. He was supposed to be enjoying himself. Life goes on. Cheryl was already at the bottom of the run. Max went to work and fell the rest of the way down the hill.

CHAPTER NINE

Cheryl was able to by pass the lodge and make it to the parking lot. She removed the skis and walked to the car. She reached into a small pocket on her jacket for the key. She started the car and checked the heater setting. She opened the trunk and the doors and they stowed their gear. When they were seated, she left the lot and they coasted back to Leadville. At the airport, Max changed to his car and Cheryl followed him to a two story house at 407 East Fifth Street. It appeared to be twenty five feet wide and fifty feet long. It appeared to be uninhabited.

"What is the stripe down the side of the house for?" asked Cheryl.

"The previous owner had planned to cut the house in half and make two rentals on the same lot. It would not have been easy to move. Now promise me you won't be jealous of my personal possessions."

"Oh, but I am. I know someone who had a 1967 Mercury Meteor just like yours. He got it running the summer before his senior year. Then the bastard dated Angie Owens and I never saw him again."

Max turned his head to her and smiled. "Good one! Get that one out of your system."

Cheryl was astonished. Her eyes were wide open in disbelief of what she said. "I apologize. I do not know where that came from."

"No problem. People have always confided in me. I do not know why. Do you wish you married your high school sweetheart?"

"I might answer that another day." Cheryl looked around. The front yard was small. "You could build a nice size deck here and have a barbeque grill and a couple of lounge chairs. You have a good view of Mount Massive. That would give you some quality time and you might have trouble keeping me away."

"Oh, thank you for sharing that with me. Come inside and see where Mongo lives. You have to give me a minute's head start so I can hide the fruit cake. I am not ready to share my fruit cake yet."

"Wait a minute! I'm will not walk into any double personality here. That is the true mark of a serial killer. I will not take one more step. Who is Mongo?"

"When my sisty uglers were playing castle princess, or Cinderella, they would say to me, 'Monster, I command you to go!' Hence the name, Mongo."

Mentally Cheryl recoiled. "It seems innocent enough, but evil traits can be developed from early childhood experiences."

"You never know. This could be the week I go over the edge. It could be the week that I stop stalking and start hacking."

"Get on with it Max." He opened the door and she led the way inside. Just in front of them a simple wood banister rose with the stairs to the second floor. She appraised the banister. "Elegance in simplicity." Max wanted to kiss her. Cheryl shivered. She expected some warmth in the house. "You manage your heat bills like most of the people in Leadville. There isn't any heat. Do you sleep in your work clothes to stay warm?"

"Sometimes I just lie down tools in hand and go to sleep wherever I can."

"Oh, sure, give me a break!" Cheryl noted the paint scheme to be a light institutional green. She added, "From the little I know about you the paint scheme fits you perfectly. This is the color used in a lot of mental institutions. You really need some work on your feng shui. Mind if I have a look around while you pack?"

"If you make it back to the kitchen there is a small stairway up to the second floor. I will know if you steal anything."

Max went up to his bedroom. He used a pillow case to collect a change of clothes for the next day. In the bathroom he added an electric shaver, a tooth brush, tooth paste, deodorant, a towel, and a washcloth.

Cheryl walked into the spacious living room which sported an attractive bay window. The house had settled evenly around the main support beam that ran the length of the original house. The center of the floor was high. The floor boards were pulled up in the living room. Floor joists rested over an eight by twelve inch main floor support. She noticed that the beam rested on pine tree stumps. The roots were still in the ground. New blocks of wood, to be used as new supports waited close by. The beam would drop if the tree stumps were removed. The floor would be level on the new supports. The settling had of course caused the mortared walls to crack in some spots and pop out from the lathe board. Areas of loose plaster had been removed and replaced with pieces of drywall. The surface in need of repair would be covered and smoothed over with drywall mud. This guy is pretty good. He leveled the floor. She moved into a small room just before the dining room. There was a smaller hole in the floor with the same conditions.

Cheryl moved into the added on structure. The ceilings were two feet lower in the addition. Lumber must have been expensive or heat bills must have gone up. The kitchen sported a large window with a view. A worn out counter and cabinets ran the length of the wall on the right side. On the left side the kitchen door opened to the back yard. In the back left corner was a small door to enter the stair well. She did not even realize there was a stairway. A small closet door opened for storage space under the stairs. 407 was not the quality of a new home, but hey, for the right price, it was a decent mountain getaway or art studio. *Why did I say art studio?*

"Pardon me for yelling. I am up here in the bathroom." Cheryl climbed the narrow passage. She walked the narrow hallway to the bathroom. A one by three foot vertical window looked out to Mount Massive. "Let me guess. The bath tub goes by the window. What do you do for electricity?"

"All I really have is forty watts coming in."

"Is it a construction hook up?"

"How would you know?"

She looked at the cardboard boxes of bottles on the floor. "Mom and Dad do drywall."

"Hey, I could use some guidance."

Cheryl helped herself to two perfume bottles.

"They are from the old outhouse and the crawl space under the house. Can you date them?"

"I shan't tell if I find something rare. I might offer you a pittance for these two."

"Not for sale."

"I have a secret place where I dig for bottles. The empty lot next door to you looks promising."

"The lot next door belongs to someone else. The tavern on the lot burned down. Rumor has it that this house served as an after hours club.

It is reported that this place was full of whisky and sin. That is why I bought it. It fits my personality."

"You must have got a good price for the house. Spoiled rich people would drive right past this place with their nose turned up."

"Ah, the plot thickens. There was no for sale sign. I went straight to the county clerk at zoning and found the owner's contact information."

"The house is a construction zone. Why don't you take just one room at a time? That way you would have a couple of nice rooms to relax in while you work on the house."

Max soured with the remark and was offended by the suggestion. "Okay, time to go! That is exactly why I never let anyone in here. Everyone makes the same stupid suggestions."

"Ohhhhhhh. Sensitive are we?"

"I do have one room that I relax in. You haven't seen my bedroom yet. Cheryl followed Max to the front bedroom."

She looked into his bedroom from the doorway. A huge four poster bed took up almost half of the room. The slope of the ceiling began on the outside wall about five feet above the floor. Max had added some space saving shelves and closets underneath the slope. Light blue curtains from the Second Hand Rose covered the closet spaces. There were two windows open to the north. "There were no closets in these early homes, huh?"

"No, they had big, fashionable chests, and drawers like you have."

"Down, Mongo, down! Obviously this endeavor is hanging over your head. It explains some of your unusual behavior today. I imagine your tiny brain is being squashed like a turnip under an elephant's foot." Max laughed and she gave him a playful hug.

"Stick with it, Max. You got a good thing here. Actually I wish it was mine. I would gut it. I would tear all the walls out and make it an art studio! Who messed up the wall over there with those cabinets and shelves?"

"Very funny," countered Max. "You really can't appreciate them until you are inside the room relaxing on the bed!" He pushed her playfully into the room. "How about a real hug this time and then we can test the mattress springs!"

"That might destroy your mattress."

"Then how about a romp on the . . ."

"No!" Cheryl laughed and they briefly had a playful push and shove match towards the bed. Max momentarily had both her wrists in his grasp. She was strong.

"Max we need a time out here. I want you to be nice. Don't destroy all of the points you made today with a hasty innuendo that will not be satisfying for either of us."

Max blurted, "I have been nice to you long enough! It's sickening! You have the only two points I want. Now it is time for a passionate kiss, my love." Max playfully puffed his lips out in a disgusting display. Cheryl squealed! He tried to steal a quick kiss. It bounced off the side of her nose.

"Ohhh! How dare you!" She moved her hands in a large circle between them and turned her wrists to break his grasp.

"You were lucky! I was aiming for your lips! My poisonous saliva would have paralyzed you had you swallowed any of it! Then I could ravage your lifeless body." Cheryl swung at his nose. "Oh, I see! You have your principles, do you? Let's throw them away, my little butterfly!" He grabbed her wrists again.

"What fun would it be to ravage a lifeless body? I take it you haven't been getting any lately? I said down, Mongo! I knew you were a stalker! I should add that you are not co operating at this moment and that your personality rating has fallen into negative territory. It is much worse than President Obama's. I knew you could not keep up your disguise as a good guy for very long." She broke his grip again. "Let's go!"

"You are afraid you will melt like butter in my hands."

"I am afraid of going to jail for pushing you out of your second floor window."

"You think you can take me?"

They noisily dashed down the stairs. They got to the first floor and Cheryl spun to Max. Cheryl offered, "I'll make you a deal, Max. I feel sorry for you and your pathetic efforts. Why don't you gut this place? Knock all the walls out. I'll put all my artwork in here. After I have sold everything, I will let you have the house back. That is the best offer you are going to get from me today."

Max opened the front door for her. "I knew it! You are a taker aren't you? You're the kind of woman who would bleed a man dry and say 'Honey, you never really did anything for me.' I think you were right when you told me just a little while ago that you can not trust anyone in the world anymore. Well paybacks are hell! It's your turn, Cheryl. Let's go to your hovel and see what you have."

Max followed Cheryl to East Eleventh. She parked the Swinger in the usual spot. She grabbed her skis and poles. "You have to wait here Max. You are not allowed at the moment."

"Hey! What is with this inequality? I let you demonize my place and criticize my hard work."

"Shut up, Max. You are growing tiresome. Wait in the car for me." She was up the stairs and in the apartment in no time. She put the skis in the corner. She picked up the usual bath accessories. She grabbed a light blue cotton jean skirt and a long sleeve, light blue blouse with oversized billowy sleeves. She picked two scarves, two long necklace beads, and two hair clasps. Cheryl grabbed the rest of her cash from under the TV set in the corner. She checked to make certain the stove was off and the refrigerator was on. She threw everything in a heavy cotton carry all bag with two big pull straps. She used it for hauling small art tools and just about anything else. She shouldered her backpack and was back outside in less than ten minutes.

Cheryl found Max bouncing on her trampoline. She set her belongings in the back seat of the car. His back was to her and he did not see the four quick snowballs she packed together with her bare hands. He had gained enough composure to knock out one lousy back flip. It took a few bounces to get the stomach centered again. It was very relaxing at the peak of the jump without earth's gravity. Cheryl appeared annoyed. "Get off my tramp!"

Max spun around to face her, "What did you call me?"

"I said tramp!" Now using a sarcastic tone she added, "I see you do things without asking permission."

He continued to spin in a circle as he bounced. "I figured it was your landlady's. I know a poor starving artist does have the money to buy such an exotic toy." He faced her again with a silly grin and prepared to do a back flip. He took a large bounce. The snowball from nowhere whizzed past his left ear just as he peaked in height. The close proximity and the hiss of the projectile broke his concentration. Max landed on his butt and bounced back to his feet. He spoke defiantly. "I see that you are a lousy shot. It follows that I do not fear your order to cease and desist. Nor will I honor it. You are nothing but an anarchist. You are a common proactive meddler and you better not break anything on my classic car." Max took a slow deliberate bounce. He believed another snowball to be forthcoming. He taunted Cheryl as he had taunted his older sisters by making faces and deer antlers with his hands and thumbs.

"Oh, that one is good enough to break a cheap camera." She held a snowball in her hand. She hoped to raise some fear into him. *Just need timing and one more bounce.* Both were enjoying the moment.

Max went into his spaceship comedy relief act. In a high nasal voice he said, "Intruder alert, Captain! All hands prepare for missile attack. Prepare for counter missile strike." Then he made the submarine diving noise, "Nerrr, nerrr, nerrr! Force field engaged, Captain."

Cheryl was delighted. "Oh, you are so full of bullshit today! Good for you!" The second snowball was headed straight for his chest as he bounced up. His trained eye calculated the speed and trajectory of the coming missile strike. Cheryl had burned one in on him. He quickly extended his arm, open palm out, as if to catch the snowball. The ball exploded into a small snow shower on impact. "Incoming missile destroyed. No collateral damage." His hand stung as if the skin was peeled off the fingers of his hand. He was relaxed and having fun. He barely saw the rapid, successful launch of another snowball. Max took for granted that it would go over his head and he actually bounced up into the trajectory. The missile was perfectly timed and Cheryl's third snowball hit him in his left eye. His glasses flew off his face and landed in the snow behind him.

Cheryl hooted. "Hoo, hooo, ha, ha, ha, ha!" She couldn't stop laughing. Her knees buckled and she put a hand on the snowy ground. She belly laughed and gasped for breath. She pointed a finger at Max as the spasm shook her.

A flash of bright white light filled his left eye. His normal vision had been replaced with a large painful whiteout. The haze of the white cloud lingered. She damn near knocked my head off! I think I need it examined. I let it hit me. Cheryl was still whooping it up. Max reeled from the pain. He completely underestimated her ability. "Tracking radar disabled, Captain." He was still bouncing on the trampoline but not as high as before. The defiance was gone and rage took its place. "Oh, yes, you look splendid just spazzing away there! You have all the grace of a hyena. Have you ever seen one of those?"

Cheryl fell to the snow and rolled. "Ha, ha, ha!"

"I see how you really feel. You really have little concern for life or damaging someone's eyesight." He did a couple of victory spins to the left. "I must warn you Princess Leia. If you do not sign the peace treaty and submit to our terms we will annihilate your people and your planet. Surrender now! By the way, did you just have an orgasm?"

Cheryl hesitated a half second and then began to cough. "Oh, ohho, ho, ha, ha, oh, boy!"

His eye throbbed with pain. The skin around his eyeball stung and his eye lid held some melting ice. "That does it! I don't like you anymore."

Max wanted to charge her and push her in the snow. He got off the trampoline. It was over. He avoided the typical revenge reaction. "I give up. Help me find my glasses."

Cheryl stayed cautious for a sudden surprise attack. She admonished him. "That will teach you to mind your manners. They flew over towards the street."

"You snickered when you said that."

She watched him search for a few seconds. She was still laughing. Cheryl walked around to the other side of the trampoline and reached down for the glasses. She threw Max another barb. "Oh, Max, I was wrong! Here they are over here." She handed the glasses to him.

"Did you know that you snort through your nose when you laugh? That is not very lady like."

"Gosh, Max! That must have really hurt. She looked at the short length brown and gray hair. She looked at the dark blue eyes without the glasses. He looked younger. The upset look of disapproval on his features made Cheryl want to laugh again. "That's it? You are just going to let me win?"

Max was furious. He repressed all desire to throttle her. "You won fair and square, Cheryl. I could have ducked, but I dismissed your throw as a probable miss. I attempted to look fearless for your amusement."

"That's what made me laugh. You bounced up into it. Are you angry?"

"No. It is the verbal abuse. The verbal abuse and humiliation cut worse than the pain." Max had an idea that it was not over.

"Gosh, Max! Can you see out of that eye yet? Maybe you better not go to Fort Collins." She could see the steam coming out of his ears. He moved slowly and acted as if nothing had happened. "It looks like that eye is swelling shut. Can you see to drive? Does it still hurt? It looks like you are going to have one of them there shiners. Is that what you call them, sweetie pie?"

Max decided to play along as if he was okay. "There are two white spots now. No, three. And I am not your sweetie pie. I have one good eye and a splitting eye ache. Why don't you drive?"

"Alright, I will drive. No problem." She checked the mailbox and pulled out three envelopes.

Cheryl laughed again. She was having fun. She was going to take him for a ride in his own car. They closed the doors. Her foot found the clutch. She barely pressed it in as she turned the key. The engine purred. She palmed the small cue ball on the chrome shift. She found reverse and waited for one car to pass them. She backed out to the street. She pointed the rubber hood ornament down the road. They rolled effortlessly downhill. She skipped second and went for third as if she had been driving the car all her life.

"Be careful! Fourth gear might make you orgasm! Honey! Watch out for the stop sign!"

"Where? It's two blocks down!"

"Your driving scares me." Max paused. "I guess you have subjected me to too much trauma today. I can't handle any more. You, you have broken down my resistance."

"We need to stop at Marvin's for gas." Cheryl pulled in at Starving Marvin's. Buddy eyed the rubber triceratops on the hood. He peered through the windshield to Max and said, "I always wondered what kind of hood ornament a skydiver who falls on his ass would have on his car."

Max offered. "It's bad mojo on you if you stare at it, Buddy."

Buddy turned to Cheryl. "Watch this man, Miss Cheryl. He is a boozer and a vagrant. He has been living in abandoned property." She handed twenty dollars to Buddy. He offered the latest forecast, "Snow the rest of the day but no serious accumulation. See you next time"

They passed the strip mall on the north side of town and Cheryl turned right on 24 East to Fremont pass and Copper Mountain. Occasionally, she broke out laughing. Max decided to play dumb and ask her what she was laughing about. He asked the question in a soft voice with all the words running together. "Honey, what was it you were laughing about back at your house? What was so funny?"

"Nothing, honey." She looked at him and burst out laughing. She howled. They went on down the road arguing about whose car was better.

Max was overdue for a rebound. "I am quite confident that you have never driven a high performance sports car."

Cheryl looked at him eyes a blaze and answered, "Why, no. I have not. What would that be like? Are you going to tell me?"

"So how does this car handle for you? I might add you are doing an adequate job for your first time."

"This? You are telling me this piece of junk is a high performance sports car? It may be a light car with a V8 in, it and it sure is fun to drive, but it is not a sports car."

"I think it is a two eighty three cubic inch."

"Oh! You are so knowledgeable on trivia!"

"You know the tail lights are really unique. Those red cones are one of a kind. The only other cars that have the same kind of tail lights are the '59 Cadillac and the '58 Imperial."

"I am so impressed, Max. So this is a sports car and a luxury car."

"That's right, baby. I thought you might be. I know you are jealous of my hood ornament."

Max decided to be nosey and opened the bill from Public Service of Colorado. Cheryl protested. "Don't you dare! It is none of your business!"

He whistled softly. "You owe Pubic Service Four hundred and twenty seven dollars."

She gasped, "You lie! I just sent in a check for two hundred."

"Nice rebound. I imagine them cold hearted bastards at Public Service will be shutting your heat off come Monday, Miss Cheryl. I could make you a small loan for half of the amount. The interest is pretty high though."

Cheryl probably would have cried any other day but today. "Piss on them. I will gut the walls of the apartment and burn the wood in my oven."

"That's the spirit! Well said!"

Her disappointment was evident. Before her anger could fester Max blurted out, "That must be the bill for the whole house. Let the landlady pay for it. Don't let it bother you. I know a neat house you can move into, and the rent is only two hundred a month, and that includes the utilities."

"Are you serious? Where is this place?"

"Your roommate is only slightly neurotic. I could put in a good word for you if you treat me right."

"Max, why do you say the stupid things you do? I swear. Most people would think you are retarded."

"I have a really good answer for that one. A lot of people in the world build themselves up by tearing someone else down. I do just the opposite of that. I make people laugh. I guess I would rather be laughed at for saying stupid things, than have a friend never talk to me again because I accidentally said something offensive. Do you want me to tell you what my views are on every little thing, and how everyone else is wrong? Or do you want me to make you laugh so you forget your worries and have a good time?"

"Max, how did you let that philosophy stick on you? Is it from the education system? Did you have to repeat a couple of the elementary grades?"

"See, you are doing the same thing. Good one. Ho, ho!"

"Are you any fun to be with when you are serious?"

"Maybe tomorrow will tell."

"Are you going to show off?"

"There will be plenty of people there who will show off for you."

CHAPTER TEN

The driveway was open and waiting for her. She parked there to draw a rude comment from Hal. Max pleaded to Cheryl. "Let's not say anything about skydiving, okay? I don't want to have to defend myself."

"Say please. I suppose it would be best to concentrate on the art exhibit. That might be a good idea."

They grabbed their things and walked up the driveway. The yard was early xeriscape. There was one large busted wagon wheel, a broken rusty spade, an old wood bucket, and a few small oak bushes. Cheryl's mother opened the front door walked out to them. "Out sneaking around as usual, Cheryl? What did you drag home this time?"

"Now remember what I told you," Cheryl talked loud enough for her mother to hear. "Mom doesn't take kindly to strangers."

Max decided to go first and lay his best honed social skills on the folks for the rest of the evening. "What happened, Miss Marilyn? Looks like your wagon wheel broke and the billy goats ate up all of your grass. Looks like nothing works around here. Did your neighbors heave this trash over the fence?"

Marilyn gave him a quizzical look with brown eyes and a smile pleasant enough to stare at. Light brown hair in one loose braid fell half way down her back. There was a freckle here and there on her face.

Cheryl gave her a hug. She whispered, "This one deserves a chance, Ma, and he is fun to pick on."

Marilyn peered at Max as if he was ill. "The last boy Cheryl brought home was one of those mamby pamby artsy fartsy wierdos."

Cheryl whispered to Max. "Marilyn doesn't keep score. She stays ahead."

At the same time Max said, "Cheryl, your mom is full of hard looks. She scares me. Is she psycho?"

Cheryl scratched her left eye and nodded toward Max.

"Would you like me to dot your right eye so they are both puffy and red? Cheryl, are you going to introduce me to this live one? If he isn't more sophisticated than the last bozo you brought home, don't bother."

"Mom, meet Max." Cheryl turned to Max. "Don't get your hopes up." She gave him a second to defend himself.

"Hello, Marilyn, pleased to meet you. My, what a lovely home you have here."

Marilyn guessed. "Been skiing today huh? Glad you broke away from that statue long enough to have some fun." She led them up the winding xeriscape walk past the broken wagon wheel and an old barrel to the front door. Marilyn had worked two summers getting the yard in shape.

"It sure looks like somebody ran off with your covered wagon and left this broke wood wagon wheel."

They entered the house. On the left a posh sofa faced an immense surround sound entertainment center on the far wall. Hal looked over the back of the sofa to check the commotion at the door. "What are you two dry walls hags draggin' in here? Fresh road kill?" He paused the movie. "How come you women are always dragging strangers into my house?"

Max stepped down and walked to the sofa. Hal's hand was a regular vice grip. He had light blue eyes and short thinning blond hair. No hint of a smile. He was lean, trim, mean, and muscular. Hal and Max were close to the same age.

"Max, meet my husband Hal."

"Hello Hal! Nice to meet you. Cheryl says you are a one man construction company."

Hal corrected gruffly, "Drywall! Drywall made me what I am today!" Hal decided he would let Max live a couple of hours.

"What are you watching?"

"Black Hawk Down."

"That is a nice relaxing movie. Your house is beautiful. How long have you been renting?"

Hal's ears perked up. Marilyn nodded with a sneer. She was keeping score.

"You girls keep an eye on this here fella. He looks like the kind of man who would steal a blind beggar's money."

"Please excuse me. It looks like I am going to take the home tour here."

It was a multi level, multi functional house, with an innovative floor plan. Straight ahead was the kitchen and dining room in a shared space. A door way had been knocked through the back wall of the dining room. An enclosed circular porch for overflow dinning was being constructed on the outside of the house. Large plastic sheeting covered the entrance to shield the house from the construction dust and dirt.

Cheryl whispered to Max, "See how the plastic keeps the dirt and dust from getting all over the house?"

"The place is elegant, Marilyn. And your full plastic curtains are beautiful."

Marilyn gave him a stern look and said, "That's one. Could you turn a little bit to the left? I need a better angle at your right eye."

At the kitchen four wide steps led down to a walk out patio. The steps turned again and led to the lower level. Marilyn spoke causally, "Max, there is a place for you to sleep downstairs. You can curl up next to the water heater in the storage room. That should be warm enough for you. But by all means feel free to sleep outside or in your car."

"That certainly is generous of you, Marilyn, but Cheryl told me I could sleep with her sister, Tara." Marilyn's eyes widened. Her mouth opened and drew a sharp breath. Cheryl chuckled and kicked Max in the calf. Marilyn was not a premarital sex enthusiast. She cast an evil look at Cheryl and then she led them past the steps and down the hallway to the garage. Max was jealous as soon as the door opened. A fifteen year old faded red and black Dodge Power Wagon was waiting for work. Everything in the garage had a place. There was maximum utilization of space. A table saw and miter were at the end of a large work bench on the back wall. Four large cabinets were on the wall above the bench. Every tool imaginable for carpentry, plumbing, and electrical work was present. Paint, texture, and drywall materials were neatly stored underneath the work bench. A large eight drawer box full of brass fittings sat on top. Fifteen sheets of four by eight foot dry wall stood vertical against the wall by the garage door. Tall closets lined the far wall. Ladders and two ten speed bicycles hung from the ceiling. A white economy pick up truck was parked next to the Dodge.

Max questioned, "It doesn't look like you have any leggos in here."

"The leggos are in the front room coat closet," chuckled Marilyn.

Max went on, "Millions of things and each in its own special place. This is truly the sign of a workaholic." He felt more questions were necessary.

"How do you remember where everything is? How many times do you forget where you put something? What is the hardest thing to find?"

Hal appeared at the doorway.

"Hal doesn't allow us to put anything away. He has given us assigned spaces where we can help put things away."

Hal interrupted in a booming voice, "Hal does all the loading and unloading. The hags are too tired by the end of the day."

Max suppressed a chuckle. "Incredible. Anyone who can organize so much stuff into one place, so that you can not see half of it, is probably in need of a vacation at the Institute for Better Mental Health."

Cheryl and Marilyn admitted that they could only find half of the stuff Hal needed or asked for. They returned to the living room. Max calmly made a low volume protest against a tour of the upstairs level.

In her bedroom on the second floor, Tara sat at her desk doing homework. "Hello Miss Potato Butt! Hi four eyes! Are you going to fall in love with my egomaniac sister? I always try to drive away all the jerks she dates. An old fart like you should be easy to run off. Cheryl tells me all of my boy friends stink. You wear glasses. Do you study? Are you halfway intelligent?"

"My, what a charming little girl."

Cheryl offered. "Max, meet Tara, my half step sister. She possesses entirely no coordination at all. She is cute in an unsophisticated and elementary way."

Tara countered, "Max, I have to live in her shadow."

They looked quickly at the other two bedrooms. Hal and Marilyn's connected to a bathroom and a balcony.

"Marilyn, this is a beautiful house with an innovative floor plan. I am totally jealous. Home design certainly has changed for the better."

It was close to dinner time. Hal fired up the outdoor grill. Cheryl was anxious to visit her favorite carry out restaurant for egg rolls.

"Max and I are going to pick up a DVD. Is anyone hungry for egg rolls?"

They returned safely with the videos, and a large bag of egg rolls, to a dining table with burgers piled on one plate. There was lettuce with slices of different colored things for the vegetarians, potato salad, milk, and pineapple juice. They fixed their plates and moved to the entertainment center. Hal loaded "Always" into the DVD player. Everyone sat in the living room, to eat and watch the movie.

Once the food was devoured Max moved around the room and collected the plates. He set them on the dining table to move to the kitchen sink. The women eyed him suspiciously but no one said anything. "Don't worry. I want to do my part. You enjoy the show and I will clean up the dishes. I can still see the movie." The Pritchard's were watching him more than the movie. He opened all the overhead cabinets and the drawers until he found the tupperware and the clear plastic wrap.

"Oh, my, everything is stored nice and orderly! That's a surprise!" Max sealed the leftovers in tupperware and left them by the refrigerator. He plugged the left half of the double sink and ran the water. He found drying towels, and dish detergent in the cabinet below.

"Well, he may have one good trait after all, Mom. It is nice to watch the movie instead of clearing the table and doing the dishes."

Max began to scrap the plates and pre wash the dishes. "Before I really get started, I guess I better ask you ladies about any silly little kitchen rules you might have. Do you have any rules I should know about?" Max stared evenly at Marilyn and Cheryl. "You know what I'm talking about, little do and do nots. The last thing I want to do is break some little silly rule like, which way you stack the dishes in the dishwasher." Cheryl and Marilyn eye checked each other. "I mean it really doesn't matter, does it? If they do not come out clean you just put the dirty ones back in and run them again, don't you? It isn't like you should get so mad that you want to kill somebody, is it?" Max held a large cutting knife in his hand. He turned it over and over so it flashed in the light.

"Cheryl, I don't think a man his age would have the know how to operate the new dish washer we have. Do you?"

Max continued. "Tell you what. I'm gonna go ahead and just mess this up all by myself. I don't need no help from no wimmen folk. Ewwwee! Damn! This dish rag smells like someone used it to clean an elephant's butt! Same with these sponges! I guess I'll just throw them in this here beater dishwasher along with the dishes. I'm not breaking any sanitation rules, am I?"

The girls conspired. "We better go put an eye on what he is doing," said Cheryl. They moved silently to the kitchen. Max saw their reflection in the window above the sink. He was rinsing and loading a few dishes in the washer. He worried aloud. "Oh, oh, here they come. Jest like two black wider spiders with pink hour glasses on theys tummies. They's gonna crush my head with their powerful mandibles and suck my brains out. Then they are gonna drag my husk over to their fresh lait eggs so their young will have something to eat when they hatch." Max turned to face Cheryl and Marilyn. The spiders were eight feet away. "Oh, woe is me!" He bent to load another couple of plates in the bottom rack.

Cheryl seemed concerned. "Did that snowball knock a screw loose in your head? It seems your thinkin' is messed up."

"Now don't be afraid," cautioned Marilyn. "Cheryl and I are going to help you." Marilyn moved in on his left and Cheryl moved in on his right. Max was the only one who knew what was going to happen next. He thought they would attack him if he turned his back. So he did. He turned to the sink. Both of his hands opened the water faucet handles.

"Cheryl, I will hold him while you slap some sense in him." Marilyn took the step into Max's personal space and threw her arm around his neck. With an amazing speed that required no thinking, his right hand grabbed the water spray nozzle faster than you can say "Oh shit!" It was backward in his hand.

Marilyn saw Max lift the handle in the air. She gasped. He squeezed the handle and the water shot out over his shoulder. Marilyn blocked the spray with her face. She shrieked and loosened her grip on Max. Cheryl stepped back. Max spun in the loose grip and continued the spray assault. The nozzle moved closer to the victim and danced high in the air.

"Get him, Cheryl! Get the sprayer! Hit him!" Marilyn was not a woman to quit because she was wet. The damage was done. She stepped behind him and got her arm around his neck as he glanced to Cheryl. Cheryl's eyes were wide and her mouth was open because she wanted to laugh at Marilyn. She hesitated just a half second. It was long enough time for Max to launch an ear to ear grin and turn the spray nozzle in her direction. Marilyn tightened her arm around his neck.

"Ack! Ack! I can't breath! No fair! That's a choke hold! Careful there's water on the floor! Don't slip!" Max held the sprayer over his head and sprayed down over towards his back soaking Marilyn's blouse. Max hollered, "Who is the next kitchen victim!" At the same time he grabbed Cheryl's sweater and pulled her to his side. Cheryl saw the sprayer turn in her direction.

"Remember all those nasty things you said to me today at your trampoline? Well, it is payback time!" Max hollered, "My name is Cinderfella! My name is Cinderfella!" Max knew Marilyn had enough time to put a good move on him. She surprised him again. She kicked him hard in the butt two times. "Ow! Ow! Penalty! Penalty!"

The spray hit Cheryl in her right shoulder and was immediately redirected to one long continuous blast in the face. She couldn't believe Max was soaking her. She doubled her fists and boxed the sides of his face. Her right vibran sole connected on his shinbone. "Ow! Damn it!" He wisely moved both feet to different places several times to dodge more kicks. Hal yelled enthusiastically, "Kick that haggard old man again, Cheryl. I thought I taught you better!"

"Oh, oh, they are trying to steal my magic wand! Illegal holds. Illegal hits! They are cheating. Cheating!"

Hal and Tara had been watching the melee from the living room. Hal was guffawing pretty good. Max was tired and out of breath. He had not felt this good for a long time. He could not overpower them now. It was time to move on to a new plan. Things can change fast in battle. Cheryl recovered and instantly smacked her open palm into his forehead two times. He turned fast to the sink and her third smack hit Marilyn square on her right cheek.

Max said, "Good shot, Cheryl!"

She was surprised and embarrassed to hit her mother. Caught off guard but never at a loss for words Marilyn scolded, "You are supposed to be hitting him!" The black widows ripped the sprayer out of his hands. Max turned to the sink and closed the faucets. He left his hands on the taps. They girls were eager for revenge. They pinned him to the sink.

Max howled, "Score two big ones for the old fart in the top of the first inning!" Hal and Tara were still laughing. Revenge was near. Cheryl and Marilyn got an idea at the same time. They both reached for glasses and filled them from water in the sink. They dumped the water on his head. Marilyn splashed water and soaked his mid section. The girls laughed hysterically.

"That's it Ma! Pour water on him until he wilts and shrivels up!"

Eventually, Max was receiving more than his share of water and moved away from them. They stood in a triangle laughing and smiling. A time out was called.

"Hey, you clowns missed the best part of the movie!" Hal rejected the video and walked into the kitchen to get morning coffee ready. "Out of my way!"

Max grabbed two kitchen towels and began to wipe up the floor before anyone slipped. "They are pretty quick for decrepit old drywall hags."

Hal volunteered, "I have to work tomorrow. We are behind on the drywall. We pick up the materials at Home Depot and get to the job site before the morning traffic even begins. If you and Cheryl want to help you are welcome." Hal immediately reminded his audience "There is no need for monetary compensation. You receive much more real value with the spiritual cleansing of the soul and your sinful subconscious. An honest career in drywall will do that for you."

"Awww! That means I have to go!" sniffed Marilyn. "I thought we were going to the festival." Marilyn suggested, "Why don't we work until noon and then head up to the festival? Afterward we could put in a couple of more hours."

"That sounds good, but you better not try to talk me out of work after the festival. How about we meet at Denny's for breakfast tomorrow around seven?"

"That sounds good," Cheryl put her arms around Hal and gave him a playful peck and bite on his cheek.

"Watch it home girl!" Hal and Marilyn retired to claim the master bedroom on the second floor.

Max volunteered to sleep on the sofa. Cheryl was cleaning up in the bath on the lower level and was going to sleep there. The lights were out and she left the downstairs bedroom to watch the last part of "Always" with Max on the sofa under a warm blanket. The volume was so low they could barely hear the sound. Hal had turned the thermostat down. A slight chill existed in the house. They watched the end of the movie and fell asleep fully clothed.

CHAPTER ELEVEN

His sisty uglers argued for the piano. Patti got to play first because she was oldest and biggest. Patti played for thirty minutes. Barbara got to play second. She played for about twenty minutes and then left to see what her sister was doing in another room. The little four year old boy would spy on his older sisters to see how they opened the dust cover. One day he was big enough to climb the bench. The bench tipped back and forth. He pulled himself on top without falling over. The key board cover was heavier than he thought. He placed both hands against the cover. He could see the white keys underneath. The cover was up and he pushed it back. Now the white and black keys were his. He smacked both hands again and again on the keys. Loud discordant noise was heard in the kitchen. He heard his mother tell his sisters, "Go get Max off the piano." He moved his hands left and right to make the sound harmonious. They would be upon him soon. He could hear their feet. They were coming after him now. Max pounded the keys furiously. He didn't care what it sounded like. He wanted to play the piano. He knew he could do it!

Their hands were upon him. One sister on each side, as always. They pulled at his arms and legs. They yelled, "Mother doesn't want you to play the piano." They were not allowed to say "Mommy." "Mommy" was demeaning. Maxwell fell backward. There was a big white light when Maxwell's little noggin bounced off the hard wood floor. His vision was blurred and out of focus. Maxwell began to scream. His sisty uglers told him to stop crying, and then, they ran away. He could not hear anything. His head was ringing. Martha picked him up and pampered him until he stopped crying. "You are too little to play the piano." He sobbed and fought for his breath. He could not breath. He was gagging.

Cheryl was awake before Max. He was on his side. His face was buried in the back of the sofa. Occasionally he would draw a loud snore followed by a short one. Cheryl had her arm on his side. She gently cut off his breath with the palm of her hand several times. She was playing with him and trying to stop the snoring. "Max! Wake up." Cheryl finally covered his mouth. He woke gasping for air.

At five fifteen the smell of rich coffee enveloped the first level of the house. Hal had already filled his mug. The last bit of water was gurgling through the automatic to announce that the pot was full of high octane brew. Hal was up and moving in socks, light blue jeans and white work shirt. He started the truck and returned to the kitchen. Cheryl stuck her finger in Max's ear and was poking her fingers about him to find a ticklish spot. Max rolled over. He pinched her boob. "Ouch!" yelped Cheryl. She slapped him. He pressed his woody against her. There was no harm. Nothing was going to happen with the family in close proximity.

"Down, boy!"

Max whispered lazily in her ear, "Come on, baby. Squeeze my sausage."

Cheryl whispered right back to him, "I didn't know old coots like you could get a woody. How is your eye this morning, baby? Does it still hurt?" Cheryl bumped his eye area with her head.

"Owww! Keep that up and I will have to find a nurse to take care of me."

"You had no volunteers yesterday."

Max wanted to attack her with his hands. He wanted to squeeze every bump viscously to produce a yelp. He envisioned ripping her clothes off. Max let the thought escape faster than it arrived. He braced his back to the couch and pushed Cheryl slowly to the edge. He allowed her adequate time to struggle. "This is my roost," he proclaimed. Cheryl fell to the floor.

"Your roost?" She got up and started putting her heel to his ribs and legs.

"Hey, are you trying to rupture my kidney?"

Marilyn left the stairway for the kitchen. In passing she remarked, "Are we a little feisty this morning?" She examined leftovers in the refrigerator and added them to the cooler on the counter. "Oh honey, isn't that sweet? That reminds me of the time I put my heel on your instep!"

"Dumb love!" offered Hal from the hallway. "Are you two gonna get married?"

Max rolled to the floor and tried to pin Cheryl's feet together. Oblivious to looks of disapproval Max offered, "Are you kidding? Getting married is like asking a man to be a virgin for the rest of his life!"

Disgusted, Hal announced, "We are leaving for the Home Depot. We should be at Denny's before seven thirty if you two can get your shit together."

"My goodness! Thank you for the invitation, sir."

"You pay for your own meal." Hal announced seriously, "Somebody better get this piece of shit Ford out of the driveway before I call the wrecker to tow it away."

Cheryl changed to a mid thigh, light blue skirt and blouse. She added a narrow white belt. She came out to the car with her carry all bag in one hand and her light blue ski jacket in the other. She put the bag in the back and slid behind the wheel. They were at Loveland by fifteen minutes to ten. She parked the car. She combed her hair. She added a white visor and sunglasses.

Some exhibits were beginning to open. There were six large tents. Two were open for view. Cheryl moved quickly through the open exhibits. She talked with several people she knew. A new foundry in Aurora opened. So and so went back east. Frank Weir won the Cherry Creek commission with three chrome cranes. Cheryl brought her friends up to date where she was living and working. Max followed her everywhere. There was straw art, wood art, oil paintings, water color, pencil, crayon, wood sculpture, glass sculpture, bronze sculpture, alabaster, paper art, metal art, cloth art, and leather art. There was an abundance of art made out of every material one could imagine.

An hour and a half later, Cheryl agreed to go to the parachute center. Max could have wandered another hour. Back at the car she stepped into a pair of blue jeans. She pulled the waist of the jeans up underneath her skirt. Max happened to see what transpired. He did not look away. The skirt came up at her sides as she pulled up her jeans. Cheryl sported light beige panties. Max was blinded for a half a second. That half second seemed to etch into the frontal lobe of his brain next to the barbeque flags. Max had a lost, dumbfounded look about him.

"Is something amiss? What is wrong? Have you never seen a pair of blue jeans?"

"It is nice to stare at what goes inside them once in awhile."

"You should go swimming more often."

"Want to go to the beach?"

"Go to the beach. Catch some sun and some Asti Spumonte. Then we could have an awkward moment back at some cheap, sleazy hotel because you are low on cash? Her tone lowered. "Sorry, Max. Not my idea of a mini vacation. You have been confined to the mountains too long."

"I suppose you are right."

"I hope your eye is better. It is your turn to drive. I want to enjoy the scenery for awhile."

"Thanks for changing your clothes."

"Forget it, Max." Cheryl changed the blouse to a sweater on a remote section of the road to the interstate. The light beige brassiere was all business and amply filled.

Max suffered on. "I think I am going to paint 407 light beige. Frisco Paints has a couple of five gallon buckets for half price."

"Go for it."

They arrived at the Loveland Fort Collins Airport just before noon. They drove past a four by six foot sign at the entrance to the airport. Sky's West Parachute Center advertised the drop zone. Someone spray painted "Go in here" and a directional arrow at the bottom of the sign. One three story building dominated the unsold three acre lots in the industrial park. The paved parking lot close to the hangar was full. Max eased the car into the open field overflow lot. They were one hundred yards from the hangar. Between the two parking lots was a landing area for the jumpers. The land on the far side of the hangar held a two mile asphalt runway. They left the front seat of the car for the warm bright afternoon of the airfield. They stared at the DC 3, as it roared into the air against the snow capped mountain range. Sunlight flashed off the shiny aluminum skin. They walked for the manifest booth and the gear rental on the second floor of the hangar. Upstairs they found out there were nine open slots on the next load. Cheryl signed her name and wrote "observer."

"Whatever you do get this lady on the load and put me with the group of eight."

The young manifest lady replied, "No problem. Got you covered, Max. Load six. Are you back for good?"

"Just visiting for the day."

Between the hanger and the next building was a small grassy area full of skydivers packing their parachutes. On the asphalt close by was a barbeque concession stand on wheels. A sign on the canvass awning advertised "Hawt Dawgs." No price list could be seen. It was manned by CJ Shanaberger and Suzy Dishroon. Both wore sleeveless tee shirts, gym shorts, and tennis shoes. Regular babes as beautiful as the day. Neither one had any love for Max. They eyed Cheryl conspicuously. They had their tough girl faces on. Suzy drew first blood with her free and fast communication skills. "Nice eye liner you got today, Max. You steal it from your friend?"

"Not exactly. She applied it." The women drew a slow breath.

"How much for a hot dog? The works."

C. J. blurted, "Ten dollars for you. One dollar fifty for the lady."

Max pleaded. "Listen. I need to talk to manifest about an open check. Would you two girls run a tab for me?"

Suzy exploded. "Step aside buddy! You are holdin' up the line! We have cash paying customers behind you."

Cheryl pulled a thin money clip out of her back pocket. She put $10.00 on the counter. "Two dogs with the works. Hold the spit. They better be hot."

CJ and Suzy looked at each other. Then they got busy with the wrappers, mustard, ketchup, pickle, and the hot frankfurters.

Suzy looked up. "What would you like to drink?"

Knowing that alcohol is not allowed anywhere near parachutes while the DZ is open, Max volunteered, "Whiskey."

Cheryl offered, "Two Sprites."

CJ placed the papered franks on the counter. "Are you baby sitting Max for the day?" She did not wait for an answer. "We feel for you. You can come back anytime as long as you leave him in the car."

"Keep the change."

Max suggested, "Let's go to the landing area and watch the skydivers land."

CJ hollered at their backs. "Most of the women are on this run."

Cheryl heard laughter and soft conversation as they walked away.

Max talked loud enough for the girls to hear. "Couple of hard cases, eh mate?"

"You called them girls to piss them off, didn't you?"

"They made fun of my sore eye."

"Don't you ever call me a girl, Max, or I will dot the other one." They walked back to the car. Thirty outdoor camping tents and five RV's made up the transient housing complex next to the landing area. A small red and white stripe canvas shade screen on six poles invited Max to pack his chute. Together they opened the doors to the back seat. She grabbed her ski jacket and cross country gloves. He grabbed his gear bag that held his parachute and warm clothing. They could hear the engines of the plane overhead. Cheryl opened the hot dogs. He spread his light blue and gray canopy on the packing mat in the shade of the sun screen. He began to pack his parachute.

Cheryl listened to his request. "You can do me a big favor. When the jumpers land, ask one of the women to help you get suited up for an observer ride on load number six. Please? I have a few things to do. I have to pack, and then I have to find the group I jump with and practice the skydive. That will take me an hour all together.

Cheryl found herself a little bit annoyed. "Oh, sure thing, Max. Do you want me to do anything else? Do you need your teeth whitened?" She was slightly angered at him. She let him talk her into this and now some mixed emotions were beginning to surface. The request seemed to rub her the wrong way. She was worried about being stuck in this place for the afternoon, when she should be working with her parents or at the art festival with them. "I should not have come here. I should not have gone along with this." She was sulking. "Are you going to dump me off here, Max? Is that it? You secretly want to leave me stranded at this place? Is this what you do best? Lure young single women to parachute centers and then abandon them?"

Was she mad or was she messing? "I wouldn't say that you were young."

"Okay, Mason! Just wait. You are going to get yours!"

"Cheryl, please. I will be with you all the time. You are going to have a nice day. The women are great. You already have two new friends. Why don't you make about ten more? Please don't turn on me. When the jumpers land here in five minutes, get one of the women to help you. It is not an inconvenience to anyone. Tell them you are manifested for an observer ride on load number six. It is about an hour or so away. Tell them you need to find some gear to rent. Believe it or not the two things I have to do will take an hour." Max pulled the slider down to the risers and made a four line check.

"Can you see the plane? It will be about as big as a fly. Can you see it?" Max continued to fold his canopy.

Cheryl heard the drone of the engines. She searched the sky and caught the reflection of sun off the metal of the plane. It was just a speck in the sky about the size of a fly underneath the crowded puffy clouds. "Got it!"

"Keep your eye on it. You will see a small dot separate from the plane. It will be the jumpers. Watch them all the way to the ground. They are about two miles up. They will have a minute of free fall."

The sun illuminated the aircraft. Cheryl saw a spot about as large as a small gnat separate from the outline of the plane. The engine RPM drop finally reached the ground. "The plane slows down to about ninety miles an hour so the jumpers can exit without being turned upside down or sideways from the wind blast."

The gnat began to grow to the size of a dime. A nickel. The jumpers moved a short distance apart. "It looks like there are fifteen jumpers." They moved back together again. The size of a quarter.

"They are really moving!"

The group formation had increased to the size of a ping pong ball. She could see tiny bodies and arms and legs. The jumpers quickly moved away from one another as each one searched for space to open a parachute. The circle exploded to the size of tennis ball. "Wow!"

"They move away from each other to avoid canopy collisions. The jumpers could run into each other and get tangled up."

Cheryl watched a canopy open about three thousand feet above the ground. Two other skydivers streaked past the stationary jumper like two speeding drivers flying past a parked state trooper. "Wow! I don't believe it! You can see how fast they are falling! Eeuuuwweee! Hot damn!"

Somewhat disenchanted by the choice of words from this perfect stranger, Max asked, "Gosh, Cheryl. Where did you learn to talk like that?"

"Oh, the parents at Bobby's little league games." The canopies were getting larger. Cheryl could hear laughter and shouting. The canopies flew past them with the wind to the southeast. Max S folded his canopy into the canopy bag. Cheryl tried to separate the men from the women. Size was her only clue. The canopies gathered momentarily before they turned back into the wind toward the landing area. They flew forward into the breeze much slower. As a jumper prepared to land Cheryl watched the hands go to the hips. The back edge of the rectangular canopy pointed down like a wing flap on an airplane. The jumper rocked forward of the canopy, as if he jumped out of a swing on a play ground.

Cheryl was intently focused on the action in front of her. Max stood beside her. "That was the brake. It slows the canopy forward speed, so you can get your feet on the ground. That is Pam in the pink jump suit. Mia is in earth tones. Liz is the one in gray." Just then Max saw someone cut in front of Karen. "Oh! Here comes Karen in the blue jumpsuit and canopy. She has been working on her landing." Max anticipated what was about to happen. Karen at the last second swerved to avoid a collision. An unwanted admirer intentionally cut in front of her. She got her hands to her waist too late. She only got half of a brake. She burned in on her hands and knees and rolled over. She just kind of sat there in the dirt for a minute. She shook her head. Max knew she was taking inventory. She was wiggling toes and bending her neck and shoulders and her knees and elbows to check for any injury.

"Alright, Cheryl, go get her! Talk to Karen! It looks like she is waiting for someone to help her. Tell her it looks like she is going to need a new jumpsuit pretty soon. Hang in there, Sugar! It is like your first day on telemark skis. You are going to have a good time once you get past the uncertainty and begin to understand the drama."

Karen's group had picked up their canopies and they were walking back to the parachute loft. She was yelling at one of the jumpers ahead of her. "Mitch Arnold! You just pulled your last stupid trick! You idiot! You are out of here! I am going to turn you in!"

Cheryl caught up with Karen. "Hello, Karen?" Karen thought she heard a voice behind her. Cheryl asked a second time. "Karen, would you help me find some gear for an observer jump?"

Karen thought to herself, "Just when you least expect it. Just like finding gold. Impression and consideration are everything right now. Slow down." Karen's light blue eyes sparkled. She stopped in her tracks and turned to greet the person behind her with a genuine heartfelt smile. She mustered just the right amount of enthusiasm.

"I am Karen. What is your name?"

"Cheryl."

Karen's brow wrinkled with concern. In a totally calm voice she asked, "Cheryl, did I hear you right? You need to find a canopy for an observer jump?"

"Yes!"

Karen chuckled softly. She shook her head from side to side. She looked at Cheryl with a grin. She quickly spit out the words, "Are you crazy?" Cheryl recoiled somewhat. "You can have an observer ride, but we can't let you have an observer jump!" Karen laughed mildly at her own joke, but kept the angelic look on her face.

A moment passed. Cheryl offered, "I like to ski. Some people think that is crazy. Other than that I have never done anything out of the ordinary."

Karen smiled and answered calmly. "We usually don't let observers jump without a couple of lessons first." Karen suppressed a laugh and turned on the smile. It fit beautifully in her round face with the small dainty nose and short, light brown hair. Her teeth were perfectly aligned straight up and down. Her appearance was that of a strong healthy woman.

Cheryl said with a smile, "My only hobby right now is sewing. It looks like you could use a new jump suit. I could make one for you."

"You can do that for a reasonable price?" Karen laughed. She smelled an accomplice. She turned her volume up a notch. "I see. Are you out here with anybody Cheryl?"

"I hate to tell you this. I am out here with a real whiner. He talked me into this. Truthfully, I am not certain that I trust him. I really need your help."

"Who is it?"

"Max Mason."

"Oh, my gawd!" Karen started laughing. "Don't take offense, Cheryl. Where is he?" They turned to see Max on his knees stuffing the bagged parachute into the container. Sweat was pouring from his face. Karen winked at Cheryl, "Pardon me a second. I have some words of encouragement for Max." She took two steps around Cheryl towards Max and hollered, "Hey! Four eyes! Your glasses are crooked! One of your lips looks bigger than the other." Max gave an acknowledged shake of his fist and repressed flipping a finger.

He answered, "I can't hear you!"

Karen turned back to Cheryl. "We were side by side docking at the same time on a formation when he slipped under me. We funneled. It's like a summersault down a playground slide together, if you can imagine such a thing. My foot hit him in the face and bent his glasses a little." Karen knew better than to tell Cheryl that her foot actually broke his glasses and bloodied his nose. Karen willed herself not to laugh out loud. She realized Cheryl was going to need faith in Max to help her make it through student training. With a wide open, loving smile on her face she again turned back to him. "It's good to see you on your knees again, Max!"

Max retorted, "What dumpster did you find your jumpsuit in? I've seen better looking cleaning rags." Max continued to close the parachute into the container.

Karen noted a look of disbelief on Cheryl's face. "Pardon me, Cheryl. The guy is a sweet heart. You don't know what you got. Trust me. I just couldn't resist. Max has been gone for quite awhile. Let's get to the loft." They turned and walked to the hangar.

"Let's see, you are going to need at least a large women's harness. A large medium men's will do, if you keep the leg straps loose. Your boobs are big. I bet your boyfriend likes those beauties! Cheryl did not know whether to laugh or flush. You will definitely need a waist strap and a high chest strap." They walked toward the hangar.

Karen added, "Today it won't matter though. You will have to wear a seat belt in the plane and you will not be jumping." *No shit! Cheryl said to herself.* "I will get you a window seat as close to the door as possible. What ever you do, don't jump out of the plane! Resist the urge! This is not a fairy land and you can not fly! Well, not yet anyway. You have to stay in the plane and ride it back down to the ground. Believe it or not some people feel a strong urge to follow the jumpers and go out the door. It has happened before. Today it is best if you stay inside the plane and watch what is going on. Maybe some day you will do the jump. Who knows?"

"I will try to restrain myself."

Karen noticed Cheryl was developing a case of the jitters. It was probably due to the ridiculous proposal of this entire afternoon. She waited for a response from her.

"I am just tagging along today. Kind of like a dare, but I always wanted to see a parachute center."

Karen volunteered, "I know what you mean. It is better to check out a place like this with someone you know.

"Exactly."

"Let's go to the manifest. The gear is up there on the second floor. This is gonna happen fast, Cheryl. Don't quit on me and don't get discouraged! You are going to get the royal treatment today! Let's get moving and keep the blood and deep breaths flowing. Trust me!" She winked at Cheryl. They both laughed. "It will all be worth while. Don't worry. I will give you a chance to back out at the last minute. You can always scratch your observer ride for any reason at all. No stress! Is that alright with you?"

"Gotcha, Karen."

"Atta girl!"

The DC 3 taxied slowly to the packing area beside the loft. The two engines were slowly winding down with a sound Cheryl had never heard before. The DC 3 seemed immense now beside the smaller single engine planes tied down along the tarmac. The airplane had simple elegant lines. The nose was high in the air and the tail rested on one back wheel. She detected movement and saw two heads behind the windows in the pilot cabin. She studied the spatial relations and imagined two bodies in chairs crammed together just above the nose of the aircraft.

Karen stuffed her chute in her gear bag to protect the fabric from the sun's ultra violet radiation. "Let's go inside and find some gear for you. You need to fill out a waiver."

"A waiver? What is a waiver?"

"It's a statement that you will not sue the DZ if you bump your head in the plane or trip and fall down in the parking lot. They need your address and phone number."

This was all new, very entertaining, and a little bit scary. They made their way upstairs to the gear rental area next to the manifest counter. The gear was hanging on pegs along one wall. Along the other wall was a three and a half foot wide counter that ran for thirty feet. Karen opened two wide doors under the counter and began to pull out some observer rigs.

"That is a pretty nice counter top. Do you guys eat here?"

Karen chuckled and kept digging. "That's a good one. We pack reserve parachutes on the counter."

"Reserve parachutes?"

"If canopy number one doesn't work out, then you open canopy number two, the reserve parachute. Trust me! Reserve parachutes are a good thing. I have too many boyfriends to leave this world anytime to soon!" Karen found two rigs for Cheryl to try on. "Here, try this one."

Cheryl slipped her arms through the men's medium harness and buckled the leg straps. "Now exhale all your air and I will pull the chest strap." Karen tightened the chest strap maybe two inches too tight.

"Eeeyowww! That's not funny!" Cheryl's face flushed. She snapped out of her dread mode. The chest strap fastened dead center right across her breasts. Her heart rate was up. She felt a tweak of, what was that? Excitement? Fear? Nerves? Stomach tension? Adrenalin? It was the same feeling of dread she experienced when she stood at the top of an intermediate ski slope the first time.

"That was a cheap trick to take your mind off of things and get you angry. Come on, Cheryl! Don't get moody on me! You have got to talk to me and we have to get this done. Keep smiling and keep your good disposition. There is just a half hour left before the fun starts."

"This one is kind of tight."

"Kind of . . . ?"

"That's right! Let me try on the women's large." Cheryl repeated the motions and this time the chest strap fastened above her bosom. The harness was comfortable.

"If you ever buy any gear save yourself some money and buy used gear. It takes a while to figure out what you really need. What ever you get, it would not hurt to have a high chest strap. You should have a waist strap added."

"Why the alterations?"

Karen whispered softly to her so no one would hear. "When the parachute opens it will pull the harness off your body unless you have your straps buckled. Now you know. Think about it later."

"Oh, that's a good reason. This one fits fine."

"That is the whole purpose of trying on two. You discover that each one may be a little bit different. This one is good for you. It is only for an observer ride, right? The main thing is to relax and enjoy your self. Now, let's grab our stuff and head for the plane for some practice. There are a couple of things you need to be briefed on about inflight emergencies."

"Inflight emergencies?" Cheryl raised her voice.

"That's right, and we are not talking about going to the bathroom."

Karen stared at her seriously and said, "Cheryl don't tell me Max left you in the dark on all of this." She added with a big smile and a wink. "He must not think very much of you," They both laughed. "Come on. Let's go have some fun. Were big girls now, right?"

"Right! What a day this is going be."

"That's the spirit! And if any thing goes wrong, remember that it is always Max's fault. Always tell him that, okay?"

"Ha! Sure thing Karen. You can count on it!"

They left the hangar in great strides. Mike hailed Karen. "I packed your chute!"

Karen nodded and smiled. "Did you put a good snivel in it? Mike is one of the AFF instructors." They walked across the tarmac where the DC 3 was waiting for them. The aircraft grew in size as they approached. It was all shiny metal. The wing tips were orange. Cheryl was hot. All the juices were flowing. She pinched herself on the arm. This was not a dream.

"The name of this plane is Agent Orange. Two ex Gulf war vets are trying to get it paid off. They haul fish out of Seattle and Alaska so it has an odor of fine dining to it."

Close to the tail of the aircraft was an open door large enough to stand in. Cheryl and Karen climbed the wooden steps and passed through the door into the aircraft. The floor angled up to the cockpit. The plane was completely striped of any items but low grade hallway carpet and a snake colony of seat belts bolted to the floor.

"Where are all the seats?"

"Skydivers are tough on furniture. It just doesn't fit in the scenario. You will see."

They had time. Karen explained an emergency exit. "For any number of reasons it might be best to leave the air plane if you want to watch the sun rise tomorrow. The plane might run out of fuel. An engine might quit. The controls might deteriorate. The hydraulics might malfunction. If it happens, you need to leave the plane with only three things on your mind. Thumb and fingers tight around the handle. A hard arch, belly button forward and head back. A three second count." Karen helped position Cheryl to the correct posture.

"I can't see where I am going."

"Get used to it. You have moments like that when you skydive. Count to three. Arch thousand, two thousand, three thousand. You have to clear the plane before you pull the handle. You will feel off balance because your feet will not be on the ground. The wind blast will cause you to tumble or summersault. If you do not pull, you will pick up speed and spin faster. You may have a bad opening if you wait. If you have suspension lines around you, then it is up to you to get untangled." She handed Cheryl a pocket knife. "This is for your jeans pocket in case you have to cut a line or two." She moved Cheryl to the door. "Hold on to the handle. You have to hold on to that handle like you are strangling your red headed step brother. Alright. Now, climb down the steps, and count at the same time. When you get on the ground, hit your hard arch and pretend to pull, but do not pull the handle this time, okay? Take your time. Don't trip or fall. Did you sign that waiver?" They laughed and counted together as Cheryl stepped down. "Arch thousand, two thousand, pull thousand!" Cheryl reached the ground. She slowly let her head go back and moved her belly button forward as she arched her back.

"Feel the arch, feel the arch! Real good job, Cheryl. Perfect. What ever you do, pull time is pull time." The loud speaker announced a ten minute call for load number six.

"Practice that text book arch, Cheryl. If you actually go out the door, have your hand on the handle! If your rig is loose, the handle will never be in the same place and remember, even if you summersault or spin, pull the handle on three thousand. Get your chute open."

Max returned to the packing area to look for three jumpers manifested on the same load. He saw Brice Buches and Pam Knutsen packing their chutes. Max looked around again. Jeff Luchsinger, Dave Anderson, Brian Cowell, Mike Hayden, everyone was close by. There was one more skid to grease. He walked over to Rick Eddy and told him that a pretty female, last seen with Karen, was looking for a tandem jump. He then walked back to Jeff to get ready for their jump.

Brice spoke to Max. "We are trying to put a tube dive together. No one seems to be enthused about it."

Jeff Luchsinger pleaded to nearby jumpers who were packing their parachutes or just waiting for their turn to jump. "Come on! We need one or two more people for a tube dive! Who wants to go? Come on! Let's do a tube dive!" Not everyone thought it was a good idea. Jeff was a relatively new jumper with an incredible amount of enthusiasm. He wanted to make his first tube dive today. At the top of his lungs he spoke to the nearby folks with a little more enthusiasm. "What in the world is wrong with you goofy chickens? You can do your pitiful three ways and four ways next weekend in a teeny weenie plane."

"Somebody might hit the door"

"I like my bone alignment the way it is, and I am definitely not up for a funnel today."

Jeff replied, "Oh, no! He put the mojo on us!"

Steve Harrell, and Dave Anderson were manifested with a group that wouldn't leave for another hour. They were packed and agreed to go on the tube dive. "We will go with you. Let's have some fun! Eight jumpers is a good number for a tube dive from a large plane with a good size door."

Although it was spring on the ground it would be cold at altitude. Cheryl was wearing her light blue ski jacket, cross country ski gloves, her green knit hat, and a red protect helmet. The green tail of her hat was wrapped around her neck. Karen told her, "Now there is no need to be nervous. We are just going to take a little airplane ride up to twelve thousand five hundred feet. Your lip is quivering Cheryl. Are we a little nervous?"

Cheryl replied as evenly as possible. "Tell you what Karen. You are a great hostess and all that. I just need to release a little nervous tension. Step a little closer so I can throw up all over you."

"Why me? Why not Max?" Cheryl eyed him suspiciously. He looked too complacent. Karen winked and made an imperceptible nod toward Max.

Cheryl challenged Max. "You didn't tell me I had to wear a parachute!" He was caught off guard. He had to remain neutral. Max wanted to grab Cheryl by the helmet and put a dozen wet sloppy kisses on her but settled for the next best thing.

"Oh, Honey! I am certain I must have mentioned it at some point." He gave Karen the once over and the evil eye. "She was a nice girl before she met you." He had a good idea that Karen was behind this sudden change in Cheryl's demeanor. "Is someone intentionally giving you bad advice, honey?"

"What is up with this honey bullshit? Is this National Honey Week or something?" asked Cheryl.

Karen whispered loud enough for him to hear. "Isn't Max a champ? You sure picked yourself a good one. Stick with me, Cheryl. Your old friend Karen is looking out for you. You can forget about Max now. I gave your phone number to a couple of the good looking single guys and a married one."

A slight smile appeared on his face. Everything was going to work out. "Don't waste a brain bucket on her, Karen. There is nothing there to protect." They laughed. What a beautiful day.

Cheryl stepped behind the groups to relax and watch the jumpers practice. They had their jumpsuits and parachutes on. A variety of color was everywhere. A few sported knit hats and neck mufflers. They stood in groups. Each group walked through the maneuvers and the docks that they would make on the freefall. Maneuvers in the air? Are you kidding me? It was good to practice on the ground. There would be no time to practice during the freefall. Everyone had to memorize the movements.

Karen, in a group of twelve jumpers, stood in the exit door of the aircraft. Three jumpers stepped outside of the plane onto a foot bar attached to the fuselage behind the door. They held on to a metal hand bar. Cheryl stared in disbelief. It soon became clear that these folks made serious plans for the brief time they would spend in the air together. They practiced the exit from the plane. They discussed break off altitude and they even checked each others gear to make certain there were no twisted leg straps or misrouted pilot chute ribbons. They checked the container pin to ensure the locking loops were tight and that the pins were seated.

Cheryl sat close to the door and she faced the tail of the aircraft. When the engines turned over, Karen calmly told her, "If you are feeling okay after the last group goes out, you can lie on your stomach and stick your head out the door. See if you can pick out the formation. Remember, you have to stay inside the plane."

"That shouldn't be a problem."

"I told the copilot that you would help her replace the door. She will be looking for you." Karen explained to Cheryl that once the plane was above one thousand feet that she could remove the seat belt and turn to look out the window. The left engine fired up.

"Okay, Cheryl, I know you are good to go. You have a good time. Just one more thing"

"What now?"

"Don't piss your pants!" For a fraction of a second Cheryl looked mildly offended. Then she laughed. The right engine whined and the propeller turned slowly. A cloud of white smoke rose from the exhaust. Cheryl stared at the smoke and thought about the in flight emergency exit. Her stomach tightened. A sour bile began to drip in the upper part of her abdomen. She willed herself to do the exit if she had to. She accepted the emergency procedures. Now maybe she could enjoy the flight instead of worrying about a scary "what if scenario." She would get out of the plane if there was an emergency.

As the engines revved up the jumpers for the tube dive climbed aboard and walked up to the pilot cabin. Max blew her a kiss and tapped her helmet as he passed. They turned to face the tail of the plane and sat down. A second group climbed aboard, and Karen's group was last. They sat around Cheryl. Karen and a jumper from her group replaced the wood door from the inside and secured it as the plane taxied out to the runway. She sat down in front of Cheryl and fastened her seat belt. The DC 3 flew down the runway. The tail lifted from the ground. Cheryl tensed as she felt the plane move. It made her a little nervous but she noticed no one else paid any attention. From the window, she watched the plane leave the runway and begin a gentle climb.

It was high noon and clouds were in the sky above the mountains. Cheryl looked at the range of snow covered peaks and promised herself that it was only an observer ride. That everything would be alright. That it was a good deal. A ten dollar observer ride. Relax. Enjoy. The climb to jump altitude was twenty minutes. Cheryl watched the jumper beside her turn slightly to tighten his straps. In an unexpected deft motion he put a quick kiss on her. There were some snickers among the jumpers. It was custom to kiss first time observers and jumpers of the opposite persuasion. The ride to altitude was over and "jump run" was called. Cheryl watched Karen and Mike open the door. They looked for the airport. Karen passed a hand signal to the cockpit. Heading corrections were relayed to the pilot. The plane turned in response. Karen's group was lined up single file to the door. The plane speed was reduced to give the jumpers an easy exit against the rushing wind. The spot was made. Not to waste a second the floaters were quickly outside and holding on to the cold surface of the bar. Cheryl looked through the window at the big happy smile on Mike Unruh's face. One loud shout from the last jumper in line. "Hot!" Everyone shouted the count down "Ready! Set! Go!"

The ten jumpers that were lined up, raced out the door in the blink of an eye. The plane was empty. The jumpers were gone. Cheryl felt her stomach twist at the thought of running through the door. The tail of the plane bucked from the sudden loss of weight. Her stomach contracted again, and her heart and mind felt hollow and empty, as if death had opened a door and personally beckoned her. She knew the jumpers were dead. You can not jump out of an airplane two miles in the air and live. Everyone knows that. A cold chill of revulsion filled her body. The engine roared in her ears. She was numb with fear. Her mind was assaulted with conflicting emotions. Logic was nowhere to be found. Her body would scatter like a watermelon when she hit the ground. Was the engine going to explode next? She was almost frozen with fright. Before her mind could wander any further a new group of jumpers moved to the exit door. Cheryl began to recover from the point of no return. She became engrossed in their actions. No wasted movement and no wasted time. In an instant, the second group was gone. Again, the plane was empty. Was this is the moment some observers had said to themselves, "Well, everyone else has gone, I might as well." or "Hey! Wait for me?" Without any training they would hop out the door on their own accord. Certainly, there were some fatalities.

She was on her knees against the wall and she stared at the empty door. She collected her composure and tried to push the fear back. It was too easy for Brice Buches to sneak up on her. He applied a wet slimy kiss on her cheek. His attempt to fondle her breast was blocked by her arms. He went to the door. It was time for the tube dive. He stood in the doorway and laughed at the cold blast of air and what they were about to do. Max sat down behind and put his legs through Brice's. Brice reached down and grabbed Max's leg straps. Max reclined awkwardly to the floor. His parachute was somewhat in the way. The other jumpers, squashed like sardines, stood over him and behind Brice. They took grips on each others leg straps as if they were bags of money from a bank vault. Brice was gently pushed head down and partially out the door. The wind tore at his goggles. Max gripped the leg straps of the last person and shouted, "Hot!" In unison the jumpers continued the count down. "Ready! Set! Go!" There was one massive push through the doorway. Feet shuffled faster than a homeless person moving up to the soup line. The last jumpers were literally pulled through the door by the weight of the jumpers outside of the plane, and the gravity of the situation. Miraculously, no one was pulled into the side of the door for a concussion or a dislocation of shoulder bone.

Cheryl dropped from her hands and knees to her stomach as the tail of the plane bucked upward from the loss of two thousand pounds. She stuck her head out the door into a blast of cold wind. There was no way to describe the feeling. Like an animal her eyes detected the skydivers falling on their side against the background of small clouds and the green surface of the earth two miles below. She could physically feel a tug or pull to join them. They had left her behind. She belonged with them. Her breathing stopped. She willed it to continue. She experienced a sensory overload. It was hypnotic and powerful. Her vision and rational thought had been assaulted.

The tube was in slow motion going over on its side as they left the aircraft. Ooooohhh! The first rotation was slow and the jumpers readied themselves. The speed picked up dramatically halfway through the second rotation. The formation snapped suddenly to a purely vertical descent.

The jumpers were hysterical. Each jumper looked at the big grins across the tube. Crazy screams were heard. They had pulled it off. They struggled to keep the tube tight. The spin accelerated. They held the grips tight as the tube rotated towards the earth, faster than a speeding ferris wheel, at one hundred fifty miles an hour.

Jeff's head was turning from side to side. It was obvious he was distressed. His eyes were rolling. His cheeks were puffing out like he was taking a roadside sobriety test. The big soda he chugged before he got on the plane was chemically reacting to the barbecue sauce on the cheeseburger he polished off twenty minutes ago. The big soda was an accessory to the crime. Max watched Jeff's stomach give a convincing contraction that launched a torrent of hot puke directly toward Max. He blocked the projectile stream of vomit with his goggles and jumpsuit. He caught the added benefit of the acrid smell. Eeeuuuuuwww. Max felt his waistline squeeze out a contraction of sympathy in response to the visual recognition. He fought back the reflexive urge to puke. It might start a chain reaction. First he was mad. Then he was insulted. A second later he was laughing. Max couldn't help but laugh. He had to log this jump. How dare Jeff puke on me!

A second maneuver had been planned. It would be an easy transition to a round formation. On a shake signal everyone would release the right grip. This would put every jumper face to earth with a hand hold on the leg strap of the jumper in front of him. Wa lah! An instant eight way doughnut! But even the best laid plans go astray. Not all jumpers released at the same time. The holds and the tube broke apart. Some anxiety arose as the bodies collected into a funnel. Feet, arms, heads, and bodies were seemingly in a vortex like water going down a drain. Slide away! Slide away! Some jumpers put their arms to their side and straightened their legs to move forward. Some lifted their heads as high as they could with arms out in front to slide backwards. A few moved to the side by shoving an arm and leg on one side of the body straight out while pulling the other side in to the body. Everyone moved to get out of the funnel. No one was anxious to be knocked unconscious or have a parachute open on a falling jumper. The jumpers tracked away from the funnel and canopies opened between four thousand and twenty five hundred feet. Max spotted Jeff as they escaped. They opened at the same altitude. They laughed and hollered at each other during the canopy ride. They were close enough to one another to do a side by side canopy formation, but they lacked the necessary focus at the time. Most of the jumpers were still laughing after they landed. All agreed to stop at Bev's Pizza Bar after the day's festivities.

Cheryl pushed herself upright. She was scared to be so close to the door. *But I have a parachute. It's ok!* It felt strange to be kneeling in the open door of an airplane two miles above ground. Mentally and visually she had been outside the plane behind the last group. *I can do it too!* She felt someone kick her foot.

"Hey! Help me put this door up! That chauvinist pig always sends me back to do it!" Cheryl complied. It was good to get away from the door for awhile. Let the fear of the unknown go away. "My name is Carla. Welcome to the sky! Is this your first observer ride?" Cheryl nodded her head. They covered the doorway to fun with a home made wood door. Carla secured it with a two by four. Cheryl finally felt safe.

"Come on up front and I will introduce you to Carl, my husband. We will see if you have pilot ability in your brain and blood." She motioned for Cheryl to sit in her seat. "Put your toes very lightly on the bottom of the pedals. Hold the control wheel and wrestle with it if you want. If my dirt bag husband gives you any lip, I'll back hand him."

A dog tired, dog face pilot bellowed at them. "Aaahh, honey!"

Cheryl grabbed the controls and could feel some resistance. Carl gradually released his grip on his control wheel.

"Whoa!" Cheryl felt a lot of tugs from different directions all of a sudden from a strong gust of wind. She felt the right foot pedal move as the pilot pressed a little bit of rudder correction.

Carla shouted to Cheryl above the engine noise. "I'm not trying to brag or anything. This is what we do for a living. Last month we lost an engine. It simply wore out."

Cheryl gave the seat back to Carla. She knelt behind the two seats and leaned forward to watch them fly the plane. They showed her how to do tail turns and wing turns. Cheryl liked the banked aileron turns. The landing was more exciting than any rollercoaster ride she had ever been on. Eventually, the DC 3 rolled up to the tie downs by the parachute loft. She thanked the pilots and walked to the tail of the plane. Would her knees ever stop shaking? A tall brown hair handsome man set the wood steps, and helped her down from the door.

"Hi, Cheryl! My name is Rick Eddy." Her eyes took in some movie star material. "Lew Wenzel and I run this drop zone. We have enough time to get a tandem jump in by three if you feel you are ready."

"Oh? What is a tandem jump?"

"One harness and one parachute for two jumpers. I do all the work." He had to fight the urge to lick his lips in front of her.

Cheryl confided to Rick, "I just had quite a shock." She hesitated. "I am scared. I know that. I need a little time to recover."

Rick acknowledged her appraisal. "Well said. We are all scared. It comes and goes. We may appear calm but there are always a few jitters hanging around close by in all of us. Are you drained? Do you have any energy left?"

"I might be able to recuperate. I don't know."

"Tell you what. We can rehearse the process on the ground and check the gear. Then you can decide if you are up for it. You can always cancel and come back next weekend. It is quite a sensory overload if you are not prepared. On a tandem jump I do all the work. You relax and take in the sights and sounds."

Carla yelled from the door. "Watch that man, Cheryl! He will try to fondle you!"

Rick did not flinch or laugh. "Please call me Rick. We are professionals. This is not child's play here."

She recalled the terrifying feeling of "What was on the other side of the door?" What was the attraction? What was it like to fall to the earth at one hundred miles an hour? What was it like to ride a canopy a quarter of a mile above the earth or higher? Cheryl decided to find out. She bit her lip.

"Okay, Rick! You are on! Let's get it over! Let's rehearse."

"You are of great spirit, Cheryl. Welcome to Sky's West! We can always put it on the shelf and continue next week. Just say the word." She signed up for the tandem jump. She vowed to make the transition through the heart of fear and the door of no return.

It was three thirty by the time the Meteor left the parking lot. It would be a long drive with three mountain passes ahead of them. An hour to Golden and just over two hours to Leadville barring any road delay. Three hours on the road should put them close to Leadville by eight o'clock. They both thought of the day and talked about everything that happened. The art festival and the DZ. They talked about her work and the foundry. Cheryl mentioned that she would attend a mining convention in San

Francisco in a couple of weeks. The mining museum was going to have her replica on display and she was invited to attend the convention.

"So you are off to San Francisco! Now you will come back as Miss High Class. All stuck up and everything."

"Something wrong with that?"

"Nothing."

"I am going to scout the Second Hand Rose for some old beat up bib overalls. I am thinking that a ragged flannel shirt and a hard hat would complete the outfit. I have a friend who would let me take a genuine carbide lamp, but I worry that something might happen to it. A little coal dust for make up would be charming don't you think?"

"Like you just walked out of the mine?"

"Purtyest thing to ever step out of the mine."

"Who could resist buying your replica?"

They arranged to trade cars on Monday. Max would leave the Swinger at Starvin Marvin's for the snow tire change. Cheryl stopped in front of 407 and gave him her spare car key. He pulled his gear out of the car and turned back to her. "Good night, Cheryl. Thank you for sharing your day with me. Be sure to check under your bed for the boogeyman."

She turned to Max and said, "That was the worst weekend I ever had in my life! I am never going anywhere with you again!"

Without stopping or looking back Max hollered, "I'm glad you had a good time! See you later! Don't wait too long to call me."

Cheryl parked the Meteor in her driveway. She grabbed the carry all bag with the extra clothes. She took a moment to hook up the heater for her Swinger. No use in taking any chances. She walked into her apartment and flipped on the lights. She turned for the bag on the porch. She sat on the edge of her bed to take off her tennis shoes. She ran the events of the weekend through her mind. Barbeque. Water fight. Art festival. Parachute jump. She turned to the replica and said, "You will never guess what I did this weekend!"

Max left his gear bag downstairs. He let his mind drift back to the horrible jump Saturday. He thought of all the fun he had today. An old fart with a young aspiring artist and a good looking one at that. Quite a contrast. He decided to remember the tube dive and forget about the demo. He thought about the weekend. Everything worked out good. What will be will be.

CHAPTER TWELVE

Monday, Cheryl was back at the foundry. She wore jeans and the weird diamond pattern sweater that she wore Saturday. A navy blue bandanna with a white line pattern covered her hair. Nash approached her full of vigor and Monday morning curiosity. She looked distant or in thought. Maybe she did not get enough sleep.

"Wha ta hey, Cheryl! How was your weekend? Are you all rested up and ready for work?" She looked at Nash and began to pull her mind out of her thought process to answer him. "Am I asking too many questions?"

"All is well, Nash. How about you? Glad to see that you made it into work today. We can use the extra help!"

"Oh, are you the new manager now?"

"I know you require leadership and guidance, Nash."

"No one bosses me, Cheryl. I had better clue you in."

"Really? I think Silvia might have something to say about that."

"I got the wood cut. How much do you want?"

"Did it take a lot of beer? Did you cut off any hands or feet?"

"Why must you always torment me, Cheryl? Here I am trying to be good to you."

"Because we always torment one another for fun."

"Alright then, it's my turn. I had time to play some pool with my brother Sunday. Greg Guiterrez was there and he said that the barbeque at Ski cooper was a good day for everyone. There were a lot of parties afterwards. The bars in town were full of celebration."

Well, here we go a bunch of meddlers. "Yes, it was a good day! Got on the old telemarks and skied my cares away. I am well rested and ready for another week."

"Greg said someone saw a stranger get in your car when you left the ski area."

"Just playing the good Samaritan, Nash. Someone needed a ride to the bowling alley."

"We couldn't find you Sunday. We were wondering if you were going to make it to work today."

Meddlers.

"I decided to help out on the drywall in Arvada, Nash. Just a little bit homesick."

"Ok, Cheryl. I won't press you. I will get the details from you sooner or later. You must really like that sweater. You wore it Saturday. Were you too busy to change clothes this week end? You ought to change clothes tomorrow. You are starting to smell like a homeless person. Is that the only sweater you have now?"

All morning Cheryl was cleaning up the girl on the swing. She was smoothing out the skin of the face and working on the detail of the eyes, ears, and nose to make them sharp and appear more life like. Small air bubbles showed in the hair. The ceramic shell for the dress had chipped and flaked a little during the hot metal pour into the shell. Bits of the ceramic were on the surface and a couple of pebble size blobs of metal were in the dress. Perhaps the slurry had not been mixed well enough before the wax was dipped in the slurry. Maybe the slurry recipe was not quite exact. She would remove these unwanted interruptions in surface contour and texture. She would chase them away as she worked on the metal surface with the tools she had available. Cheryl used anything from the electric fifteen pound hand grinder to a hand held dremel. She had a variety of bits to choose from when she used the dremel.

The area from hair and scalp detail to polished skin required a change from a cutting or grooving bit to a smooth stone that would polish the surface rather than groove it or cut it. Bits used for surface texture effects vary from smooth to coarse. The metal bits are used to cut and carve. The foundry provided most of the costly bits. Cheryl was good at smoothing and removing any irregular spots without detracting from the appearance of the bronze surface. She decided to change bits to a fine stone, a polishing stone. Occasionally, a section had to be scrapped if there was too much ceramic contamination in the surface. Cheryl thought the girl on a swing should be wearing a pair of jeans and not a dress. She did enjoy working on the face. She made the features smooth as a mirror, clean and crisp. A small hole existed at the edge of the dress and her leg. Cheryl pulled the dolly over to the welder. She would have a chance to do a little verbal fencing with Marty.

"How is it going handsome? You all finished up for the day or are you just taking a break?" She fished in the scrap barrel for a small piece of bronze to fill the hole.

He leered in her direction and laughed. "Your insinuations are not insulting to me. I am just taking a breather little girl."

"Sometimes your breathers are pretty long. You look distant and confused this morning."

"Whoa, whoa, stop right there. I am not going to let you tell me that I look terrible and perplexed. Last time I was really mad when you said that and you promised never to go there again. I worked all weekend. Where were you?"

"Just trying to push you a little closer to the edge to find out how you handle yourself. I do remember the last time I said that. You were really angry and you didn't talk to me for three or four days. That was like a vacation for me. You had me worried though. But now we are good friends, huh Marty? We are passed all the ill feelings, huh?"

He smiled. "Yes, we are. You make me laugh and keep my spirits up most of the time. After two years of verbal fencing we are pretty good friends."

"Oh, whenever you are in a good mood I suppose we are. When you feel like it, I guess. So be a good co worker and tell me what is eating on you."

"Is it that obvious?"

The welding area was Marty's domain. Occasionally, Cheryl liked to remind him that she was an accomplished welder.

"My wife is hounding me night and day about going back to Sacremento to spend Easter vacation with her relatives."

Cheryl turned her head towards him. "Oh, no! The whole famn damily? Aren't we religious enough here in the mountains?"

"I told her no. There was no way I could leave because of all the work here."

She crossed the neutral line. "That is rich! You gave her those three little words, 'No you can't.'" She mimicked his wide eyed look of shock. "If you ever told your wife no, I think she might divorce you." They were both surprised at her truthful remark.

Then Marty laughed at her mimic of his shock. "Your face. That was the best one this month."

"Well, I ain't finished. You should be the guest speaker at church on Easter Sunday. Your sermon could be, 'The evils of giving in to relatives.'" Cheryl continued. "Now repeat after me. Honey, you are going to Easter in Vail."

"She will kill me."

"That's what I thought. The thought of divorce is scary, huh? Now we are finished with your dilemma. We both know you are going to California."

"I'm going to have to work night and day for the next month with all the work we have."

"Tell you what, Marty. Take off and go to Sacramento for Easter! The eggs are bigger there. Everything is bigger and better there, except the women. I will cover for you. I will perform only quality welding on your precious statues." She thought she detected a flinch. "You go steal some eggs from the little ones at the egg hunt. Think of all the home videos you will be in."

"I keep forgetting that your grandfather taught you how to weld way back when,"

"Thanks, Marty. You're a swell boss. Mind if I use the welder for a minute?"

"I am counting it down now. I might be generous and give you some extra seconds."

"Like I said. You and your daddy think welding is for men. You are old fashioned and set in your ways. Both of you have some potential though." Cheryl filled the hole on the leg and dress and continued the conversation. "I'm going to go ahead and weld the miner together. Will it be alright with you if I use the equipment? I'll pay you back for the rod I use when the mining museum sends the big check."

"So, Cheryl, if you contribute to the welding, are you going to ask for a pay increase?"

"Oh, no! Heavens, no! You pay me too much already."

"You are right. I need to talk with Mom and Dad today."

"Good man, Marty. You have restored my faith in you. When do I get my certificate for chasing a mile of bronze?"

After lunch the rest of the day was a blur.

Cheryl chased surface texture all day with only two breaks. When the day was over, she made her way to the break room to retrieve the usual veggie sandwich. She held back some energy today so she could work through the night. She was fired up to get her project moving forward. The clay monster had come to a standstill. She had to determine how the completion of her project was going to come about. She was determined to get it resolved. She had been thinking about it on and off during the day when she finally admitted to herself that she had no plan. She had to get it all written down. If she wrote everything down she would have an easy reference guide to solve her problems and voice her opinions in a professional manner. There were too many variables from no materials or time, to money, and now Marty's Easter vacation.

She pulled the plastic bag from the refrigerator and headed for her locker. Her mind was racing. She would list calendar time, process time, materials, and money. Maybe she would include a list for shortcuts if any were available. She found the spiral note book and her tape measure in her locker. She walked to the shell room. It would be easy work to leave the head and hat all in one great big piece. Would it fit in the slurry tub? There was only one way to find out.

Cheryl walked to the shell room. She would measure the tub and the distance to the shaft so she wouldn't make any section too big for the tub. She reached into her pocket for the tape measure. The motor shaft entered the bottom center of the tub through a water tight seal. One long blade similar to a lawnmower was on the end of the shaft and close to the bottom of the tub. She wrote the dimensions in the notebook. Thirty six inches across and thirty inches deep, minus three for the blade, and one or two at the top edge of the tub. The slurry would only be twenty four to twenty seven inches deep. She looked at the shells hanging from the racks and she realized that she had to allow for the sprue cups. Well, that settled the issue. It would not fit in the tub. She walked back to the classroom where her clay monster was being held captive. She realized that her next goal was to get this project through the door and out to the pouring area.

Cheryl climbed the scaffold. She measured across the brim. It was two inches too wide. And from the collar bone to the top of the hat, four inches too long. She climbed down and opened her notebook. She wrote down the four problems confronting her. Three projects were going to be pushed through the foundry in the next month and a half. The mining museum had not paid the customary fifty percent upfront cost of the statue. There was currently a shortage of materials. Her obsession with perfection was holding her back. She would deal with perfection tonight. If she did not, then she would never get this project out on the foundry floor. Time had made the decision for her. She was bound and determined to get the miner in a suit of plaster by the end of this week.

She wanted her first sculpture to be perfect. Flawless and innovative! Nothing less than a masterpiece. She looked at the statue. To hell with perfection! She would hit the areas of most importance tomorrow. She wrote down "correct muscle definition in the left arm. Eyes okay. Face not too bad. Work on nose and moustache" The go to hell hat was not quite right. Moustache? Max had a moustache. She added to her list, "Wrinkles in the work pants. The knees. The suspenders." Man, oh man. They needed something. She wrote down "Suspender edge needs definition." She had to get an edge on the suspenders otherwise they would not be visible.

Cheryl thought forward through the next steps of the production process. There was a way she could speed up the completion of the statue. She would send the easiest sections through the ceramic shell room first. The base of the statue was mine floor rubble on which the miner stood. The base would be fast work in welding and chasing. Not much surface detail to worry about there. She was going to push the base and the legs through first. That would give her more time to work on the difficult and time consuming sections. She wrote a reminder in her notebook to tell Molly and Mary her new plan. Why wait until all the sections were waxed before sending them all at once to the shell room? She could get about half the miner through all of the processes and welded in a short period of time, while the other pieces eventually caught up. It would work. She wrote it down and drew a star by it.

She had to prioritize. What was not finished would remain undone. She would allow herself only one more night to worry about any more sculpting. She would pick only the glaring errors that she could correct in one night, and that would be the end of it. She would latex the miner Wednesday. She wrote in her notebook, "The latex goes on Wednesday." There! It was written down! It was going to happen. She could feel a mental and physical release of pent up emotions. Her endeavor would become fun again.

Now she had to come up with an idea for the hat dilemma. She quickly sketched the head face and shoulders in the notebook and added some written notes. She would think about how to cut the head and hat down to two or three pieces another day. All of a sudden it became clear to her that she should just cut the bill of the hat off all the way around. She may as well cut the crown of the hat off. She exaggerated the neck to include a shoulder to shoulder horizontal cut at the collar bones, and an equal distance down the back, say just above the shoulder blades. This resulted in a nice large oval. Kind of like the collar outline of a boat neck shirt. With the persuasion of a hammer and a pry bar, the sections would line up easily. There would be plenty of room in the slurry tub for the neck and head sections.

Now she had to deal with her deadline. If she came in early and stayed late, the waxes could take as long as twenty days. It took twenty to thirty minutes for the hard wax to melt so you could brush it on the latex molds. That meant her first thirty minutes in the morning would be down time. That was not good. It would not even be worth the effort to come in an hour early. She would have to wax during lunch and after work. She would have to ask Molly for help. Molly lived close by in Redcliff. She could come in an hour and a half early and start the wax pots. Cheryl would pay for her help. Molly would agree. Her husband worked construction and this old recession was really dragging on. They could use the extra money.

What was next? Let's see. The ceramic shell room. That was out of her realm. After the shell room was the wax melt furnace. It was half an hour to melt four or five shells. The problem was, there would be about four hundred shells to go through the furnace, when the push was on. Then the metal pour. This afternoon she had estimated there would be thirty sections to her statue. It would take three days to pour the sections. But then again, there would be four hundred shells to be poured. Who was going to pay for all of the electricity to melt the metal? Then what? Sandblasting. A minute or two for each section. First you had to knock the ceramic shell off what was now a piece of metal. She could do all thirty sections in less than two hours, unless they were out of blasting sand. More electricity to run the sandblaster. Man, oh, man. The cost of making statues just keeps going up and up!

She summarized. It would be more than one week for the waxes. More than one week for the shell room. The wax melt would be less than a week. The chasing and welding would be more than a week. The metal pour was difficult to assess. There would be two other statues going through the process at the same time. Cheryl had doubts that her statue would have priority. There was only one plausible assumption she could make. She had to push her thirty sections through the entire process and ride herd on the project. She would have to be tactful and diplomatic, but she could not give in to bottlenecks.

She felt better already. What else, what else? There were a couple of things. She had to get a dollar figure to Rob Gage and the museum. He was waiting on an invoice from the foundry. It should request fifty per cent of sale price up front with the balance due on delivery. Those were the terms that she had been promised. Maybe Sandy at the mining museum could help her. What was the phone number? Then there was the patina and the installation. The marble base for her statue was not yet at the museum. That would be something that she would have to look into. Cheryl estimated that she had six weeks left. If anymore projects show up her miner would not make the deadline. It was obvious she was out of time. It was obvious she had no money in her hand.

There was one other thing that she had to take care of. She picked up her notebook. She went to her locker and fished her checkbook out of her carry all bag. She had written Karen's number down in the checkbook. She went to the front office area. The Robertson's must have gone to the local taco shop for dinner. She grabbed the phone and dialed Karen's number. "Hello, Karen!" Her sudden excitement diminished when she heard a recorded message. "Please leave your number and a short message."

Disappointment surfaced. It was proof that she did have a new distraction. Was it something that she really wanted to do? Or was she just trying to run away from her deadline? After the beep, she spoke rapidly, "970 428 6773. This is Cheryl, your observer ride yesterday. Call me within the next hour. Let the phone ring for twenty seconds and call back if I don't answer. I'm working late in a big foundry and no one else is here. It might be a minute before I recognize the ring. Thank you." She felt better. She had initiated the call. She should have left a calm message in so many words that she wanted to enroll in the AFF class. She would have all week to get enrolled in the AFF program. She could call the parachute center or Rick Eddy. At least she got it out of her system. Maybe now she could focus on her work this week.

She photocopied all of her notebook. She walked out from behind the counter to return to her miner. The phone rang. She ran back around the counter and answered on the third ring. She did not realize that she shouted into the receiver, "Hello!"

"Is this a big foundry?"

"Yes!"

"Is there an observer ride there?"

Cheryl recognized Karen's voice as if they were still bullshitting Sunday afternoon. "Can you get me in the accelerated freefall class this weekend?" There was a long silence on the other end of the line, as Karen counted to five, while she took another bite of her apple.

"The AFF class? I don't know? Who is this?"

"I am the woman who is going to murder you."

Karen replied calmly, "There is no call to go flying off the handle here, girl! It is a little early in your career to resort to murder! You are just experiencing a small anxiety attack. Hmmm, I will make this as fast and as brief as possible. Would you answer the following questions please?"

Cheryl giggled. Karen was good. "Okay, I am listening!"

"Are day dreams of your observer ride and tandem jump interfering with the thought process required for your daily work routine? Are you having flights of fancy with life and death situations? Have you pictured your tandem jump over and over in your mind? Are you reaching for your cutaway handle in your dreams? Are you currently taking any over the counter or prescription medication? Are you going to ask a circus clown to marry you? Are you willing to freely admit yourself for treatment? If you do not admit yourself for treatment, then we can not help you. You will receive no further information or attention from us."

Cheryl laughed, "Yes to all questions!"

"We do have more than our fare share of fun. It sometimes results in anxiety, and a loss of direction or purpose that can lead to joblessness. Are you willing to expose yourself to these dangers?"

"Make me laugh! Your warnings do not scare me. I ain't skeert!"

"That's the spirit because it is a brand new problem, and it just doesn't fit in anywhere in your life. You could forget about the whole thing and drop it right now. That way you will not have to deal with it. But there is nothing in your past that you can compare to yesterday, is there?

"I never had so much fun in one day for a couple of years. I have a big project going and I am uncertain if I can meet the deadline. I can not concentrate and I can not get piece of mind. And right now all I want to do is sign up for the AFF class this weekend. I have to get this skydiving thing out of my system one way or another so I can get back to my normal routine."

"We have to have our priorities in order, you know."

"It is all I have been thinking about all day. I am trying to get motivated on my project, and I can't figure out when I'm gonna get the time to jump! It is ridiculous! I am having uncontrollable anxiety attacks!"

"Cheryl, I think you can do it. Did that tandem jump light a fire under you?"

"Yes it did."

"Did you say, 'Thank you, Jesus,' after your canopy opened?"

"I could hear Rick laughing!" snorted Cheryl.

"Rick is pretty smooth isn't he?"

"Don't start!"

"Good for you, Cheryl! You focus on being a student first. Everything else has to wait except of course your work for a living. That has to be first. Don't enter the skydiving world just to hope it will change your life. Desire and performance change lives, not distractions. The DZ is as good a soap as you will ever see on TV. We call it 'As the Prop Turns' and it happens at the drop zone just like it happens in high school, college, or your place of employment. It is our own little soap opera. You can ruin your chances for skydiving in your first month. Be a good girl. Stay away from the boys. Jump for a year. You will be way ahead of the game and still have a great recreational activity that will burn off excess fat and keep you young at heart and skinny. Now, you better sit down and brace yourself, because I have to tell you the truth, and it is better if I don't hold back."

"Go ahead."

"You are normal! We skydivers pay hell trying to get through a normal work week and get a few jumps on the weekend. We learn how to cut a lot of corners. The biggest one is utilization of time because you don't have any. You can lose a whole weekend waiting for the clouds to part, and the plane engines to work, and other jumpers to be with you to share a jump. You suddenly find out that you are falling behind in your real life. Just like any recreation activity, you have to do a lot of extra things during the week, so you can pursue your weekend hobby. The lucky ones are the ones that make the transition to a parachute center life and can financially sustain themselves. Some work part time twenty hours or so during the week to keep the wolves away. They make the transition. The recreation becomes the career or job style."

"Just like my rich Uncle Ben's boat dock."

"Now write this down."

"Ready."

"Class starts at seven. Bring your own food and soda or tea. No alcoholic beverages or drugs. Are you taking any prescriptions, or anything stronger than aspirin?"

"No."

"We break at ten for twenty minutes. Lunch is high noon. It will be a half hour. At twelve thirty, you will ground drill until you are just about ready to puke. At one o'clock, you will dress rehearse. The plane is not always on the ground for practice, so we use an old wreck behind the hangar. Plan on spending a lot of time in it. Bring a turtleneck and warm gloves you can pick up a pencil with. Bring at least two hundred fifty dollars cash, check, or credit card. We have been asking five hundred up front for the first two dives. I can loan you the difference or I will get Rick to go along with a tab." She paused. "Cheryl, we have talked about you. We want to give you every chance to make it through AFF. It is seven jumps if you don't mess up. Have things been pretty rough today?"

"Actually I am in a really good mood now that I have signed up for the class."

"Good. You are a winner, Cheryl. Never forget that. This Saturday will be even better than last weekend. Take at least one night this week and run everything through your mind. I don't want to run up our phone bills so we have to save all the talking for the DZ. Write your questions down. Everything. We are going to put you on a new plateau where you can see the finish line for yourself. You are going to move beyond everything that happened last Sunday. **You** have to be ready for **us**, Cheryl. If you are mentally and physically focused, then we will take care of everything else. **Do not** show up without rehearsing your ground drills at home. We will be able to tell, and you will receive no further preferential treatment."

"I get the picture. I will see you six damn thirty Saturday morning."

There were voices and the front doors to the foundry opened and closed. Marty was the first through the door. "Hi, Cheryl. We are back."

"How was the hot taco sauce Marty?" She threw out a neutral question to let him open his thoughts.

"It was good! So was the pow wow." He moved past her, anxious to get on with his chores and to get home. "I have to do an inventory back here on the materials. We have to get the old projects out of here and the new ones in." He moved on to the foundry floor. Mary and Bob walked into the office where they shed their winter coats. They were deeply in love. The Robertson's were committed to one another. They took turns being either the leader or the pin cushion. Constant watch and care for the other, yet plenty of room for each to run free. That was how they survived the storms and squabbles of life. They talked about problems together. Then they put them on the back burner for a day or two. After a couple of days a solution between the two of them would be agreed to. Mary had gone out of her way to chase him down. She had to chase the women away as well. They married young before he went over seas to Vietnam with the Marines. They were both free spirits.

Bob hailed Cheryl and he set a bag of burritos on the counter. "We were talking about you at the Minturn Ranchero!"

"About how awfully thin and weak I look? Did you figure out that I could probably eat a half a dozen bean burritos in a minute?" You could never get mad at the Robertson's. They were as resilient and elastic as the super balls. They could bounce back under any circumstances and beyond.

Mary spoke up, "I knew you could eat a bag and a half of them to maintain your girlish figure. I made Bob buy them, so help yourself."

"Thank you. I can eat two of them on the way home."

Bob jumped in, "I wasn't going to spring for them, but Mary reminded me of all the work around here that needs to be done. We figure we need to keep you strong and well fed to get it all finished!"

"It is wonderful that someone is concerned about me."

"We didn't want anyone in Leadville to see you looting the dumpsters behind the restaurants for scraps of leftovers."

"It has been awhile since pay day."

Mary inquired, "What are you going to do with that miner? Are you getting anything done with him?"

"I need to get him into a body cast and hopefully that will happen this week." They laughed. Cheryl thought, God bless the Robertson's. They have their own worries and here they are watching out for me, just when I had abandoned all hope.

"We are low on slurry and I don't have any money. I have to resolve the check crisis from the mining museum. The only thing they have shared with me is a tap dance. I thought they were going to send a check two weeks ago. Rob Gage made it sound that way. He gave me no further details. He probably is using the lack of an invoice as an excuse."

Mary laughed. "Yes that is how you postpone payments in the make believe world. There are many common excuses. Oh! We thought you were going to send us an invoice. You did not. We are so busy around here. If you did send one I haven't seen it yet. Is it on the way? Well, we have to vote on it. We forgot all about it! I have a new accountant. She might have misplaced it. I'll check with the payables department on the second floor." They shared some laughter and then they stared at Bob with big smiles. They were waiting to hear how he was going to save the day.

"Yes. I have big patches of skin peeled away from both ear areas and some minor first degree burns on my face from Mary's dinner inquisition. We do have slow pay right now on the bronco, the girl on the swing, and Casey. One for the swing is in the mail. Mary has ordered me to phone duty tomorrow. We will institute a new program to be held every Tuesday. We are going to call it dialing for dollars. On Thursday I will make follow up calls."

Mary read Cheryl's look of concern and added, "The slurry was supposed to be here Friday. I literally ordered a ton of it."

"I had no idea. The finances are none of my business."

Bob offered. "We decided at the taco house that I am going to have to go to the bank tomorrow for a bridge loan on the statues if we do not come up with something."

"Mary offered. "I will make the invoice for the museum tomorrow. Cheryl, I have a couple of thoughts on your miner that I want to run past you. It will only take a minute."

Bob jumped in. "Mary did not want me to say anything, but she thinks the suspenders need work, and she has some questions about the hat. There! I said it for both of you. Kill me not tonight. Curse me not tomorrow."

Both women stared at him and laughed. Cheryl handed her notebook to Mary. "That is exactly as I have it in the notebook here. Bob was never a shy one was he Mary?"

"Hardly." Mary looked at the notes. "Good work Cheryl. We are with you on this project. The waters are a little stirred right now. Nice work and organization on your notes here." She pointed with pencil at the hat in Cheryl's sketch. "Hmmmm, cut the bill all the way around and cut the crown off. That will take some extra welding."

"You are right. It will make for more welding and chasing, but three sections is the only way to fit the bill in the tub. I am ready to drive back to Leadville." She stuffed the notebook back in her pack. "The long road to my bedroom is calling me."

"Watch for the deer! The deer are back on the road just past the Red Cliff bridge, in that short down hill section. Get going, now."

"Goodnight, Mary, and thank you."

CHAPTER THIRTEEN

The car radiator heated up going over Tennessee pass. Cheryl coasted down the switchbacks to Leadville and the temperature reading dropped. Max was at 407 East Fifth Street. He was working on the hump in the living room floor. He used a floor jack to raise the beam just enough to cut the pine tree stumps. The new wood supports were in place. The beam would drop to the new supports and the floor would be level. Two of the floor joists were cracked. He bolted a large flat metal plate across the fractures in the floor joists. Three other joists were compressed over the main beam but not fractured or cracked. The wood after one hundred and twenty years was still fresh and strong.

Cheryl parked in front of the small front yard and pulled the hood latch handle. She could see through the large bay window into the living room. It was nine o'clock. Max was knees first in the hole. Mr. Duran and Herman Hauser were standing over him. Would they approve of his work? Herman was supportive, but being an old mining union man he was still skeptical of work performed by someone who was not licensed or certified. He was interested in Max's solution as there was a spot in his house across the street that had bowed up from settling.

Herman excused himself. "Well, it looks like you have company. I am going back to the house." He said hello to Cheryl as she walked into the entry way. She wanted to kiss Max right there in the living room. It would have to wait for another day. They were still holding back. Intimacy was not yet in the cards. Max wanted to give her a long hot kiss that might take all night. Cheryl smiled and gave Mr. Duran a quick kiss on the cheek.

"Hi, Mr. Duran! How is Danny?"

"He is staying busy. He is working on a guard rail for the state highway. Still no money for the payroll. You know how it goes."

"Afraid so! So much for government work. She looked down at Max. "On your knees again, huh?"

He suppressed a grin. "Careful, honey. We have company."

"Danny Duran lives catty corner to you. He is a certified welder and very accomplished. He has every tool you can imagine. If you need to borrow, just ask him. He will help you."

"He has already made the offer, what a terrific neighbor. And his father has been cutting off my square corners, so I will be a well rounded gringo. Right Mr. Duran?"

Mr. Duran laughed. "Max, I will see you tomorrow. I have to be going now." He left the house to cross the street in the light evening snow.

"Max, the car overheated. It is the thermostat. Let's do it now. I left the hood open for you. If you have a socket wrench for me, I will take off the two bolts."

"The tools and a flashlight are in the five gallon bucket. I could use a full time mechanic. How much do you charge?"

"I might cut you a good deal. Do you have any gasket material?"

Max thought for a moment. "There is a milk carton in the refrigerator." He tore the top third of the milk carton away. He stopped in the living room on the way outside to pick up a buck knife and a utility knife from the tool bucket.

The radiator hissed as Cheryl used a heavy glove to relieve the pressure. "You still have some water in there." She had the metal elbow off the engine block. She pried out the thermostat with a screw driver.

"My you waste no time at all."

"I have done this more than once. No rest for the poor." Max shaped a piece of the heavy wax paper close to the size of the gasket. He cut a hole in the center and handed it to Cheryl.

"I coasted down the pass and the engine cooled. It heated up again just before I got to town."

"Thanks for saving my car. I will get a bucket of water."

She grabbed the buck knife and scrapped the old gasket from the engine block. Max returned with the water for the radiator. "One stegosaurus foot needs to be glued again. She is dancing on your hood and she might get away."

Max said with a warm smile. "I don't have enough money to pay you. I'm certain you are expensive. Could I barter with a couple of kisses?"

"Ha! Max, you have to get to the foundry tomorrow. The word on Charlie's vacancy is getting out. They will hire someone by Wednesday. I might take a few of those kisses in lieu of payment, though. Let me think it over. Did you pick up the car today? It was not at Marvin's when I drove by.

"Yes, it is at your apartment. Here is your spare key. I will drop you off at your place."

At home, early Tuesday morning in Minturn, Colorado, Bob Robertson was up early. It was time for a conversation. He quietly went downstairs to the kitchen. It was five thirty am when he called Wes Culpepper in Fort Worth. Wes picked up the phone on the fifth ring. "Culpepper."

"Wes, this is Bob Robertson. Mary and I are out of money. You must send us fifty per cent as stipulated in the contract, immediately."

"Ouch! That hurts this early in the morning. Have we been sharing mental telepathy?"

"We can't go any further with your statue, Wes. We have fronted the materials and the work for you. Your sculpture is waiting for your approval and you have put us off two times already."

"You have no reason to believe me, but I have been very busy. I have just finished two exhibits. Los Angeles and Phoenix have taken more time than I had to give."

"You have put us off for too long, Wes. Because of you we have no money for our overall operations. Did you hear me? We have no money."

Wes replied, "The State Fair has not sent their partial payment to me. They have been working with a Fort Worth bank. The bank said they could help when the Fair Board was within thirty days of receipt of funds. The Fair also has donations and pledges although I do not know how much."

"You know, Wes, there are lots of donations and pledges, but it is never enough. There are many senior citizens and homeless people who are neglected and dying. There is a lot of pain and suffering in the world. Corporations are going bankrupt. So, after you have finished crying, you need to wire funds to our bank account. Is anyone receptive to a bridge loan for you?" Bob paused to let Wes talk.

"I have approached three banks here in Fort Worth. They seem amicable. Give me a couple of hours to call around this morning and I will call you back before nine."

"Wes, I want you to know that I have been forced to look for a bridge loan just to stay in business, and it is because of you. You have failed to send the money for materials and Mary's time on your project. Just so we understand each other. Wire the money first. Do not bother to make the trip without the money. If we do not have money from you in forty eight hours, I will rent a bobcat, and Mary and I will push your dime store pony to the truck dock."

"Ouch! Bob, please don't do that."

Later that morning Mary and Bob sat in the office behind the receptionist counter. She faced Bob across the table. She poured them both a cup of coffee. "You know when we left Boulder we said we were not going to let this happen to us." Bob stared into Mary's brown eyes and smiled as if he could never be upset by anything. "And here we are with the same old problems! Dialing for dollars and asking for partial payments. Isn't life exciting?"

Bob hesitated in mid gulp on a partial choke. "We get to do everything ourselves!"

"Our accountant must have one hundred resumes for a part time assistant."

"Maybe he went to the temp agency and struck out with the first assistant he picked."

Mary laughed. "To tell you the truth I did not get back with him Friday. I would bet that he has not hired anyone yet."

"Didn't he say he was going to handle collections for us?"

"You know how it is. People mean well, but they just do not have the time, or they lie to you. Take your pick. Any luck with Wes Culpepper?"

"I left a message on his answering machine last night. He left a message with us that some of his work is on display at a local gallery. I called him three hours ago before I left the house. I caught him at home."

"I heard you go down the stairs. Any good news?"

"I let him know that we have stopped work on his statue and that we could go no further. That was the first thing I told him. He said he would call back by nine."

"Damn, Honey! I wish you would have told me. Sometimes I like to watch you whip the bear's ass. Are your going to the bank this morning?"

"I am. I have an hour or two. I will stop at the accountant's office and pick up the financial statements. I plan on going to First National in Avon and Commercial Bank in Leadville. I should be back by three."

They drank their coffee and looked at one another with understanding amidst the money troubles.

Mary spoke first. "Okay, Robert Robinson. Let me tell you something. I did over hear you talking with Wes this morning"

"And?" Bob projected a blank look, not even a raised eyebrow or one forehead wrinkle.

"It reminded me of that brave young Marine, Lance Corporal Robertson, a good looking cuss. I heard you mention the part about the bobcat. Would you really do that?"

"If you did not have so much work on it, I would push that pile of clay off the truck dock."

"I want to share something with you, dear. After your shower, when you are home tonight, I plan to ride you like a dime store pony."

A fine spray of coffee passed Bob's lips before he closed them tight. The stomach muscle spasm brought both of his feet off the floor and a couple of drops of hot coffee shot out of his nose. Mary leaned to the left and threw her hands up. Bob deftly managed to hold his cup level and not much coffee was spilled. He managed to say, "Treat the girl right and she will never forget. That is what Pop used to tell me. It's none of my business, but I hope you put me away dry. I catch cold easily."

Cheryl had just passed by the office to the front door to look for Molly's car. She overheard the pony part of the conversation and quickly escaped undetected with a big wide grin. Molly Musser walked through the front door of the foundry. She saw Bob and Mary in the small office. A pot of coffee and a legal pad were on the desk along with a pack of cigarettes and an ash tray. Molly waived and smiled, "Sic 'em, Bob" and she continued at a fast clip after Cheryl.

Mary's eyes sparkled. "We should be able to get Casey out within two weeks, a week from Thursday."

"Casey at the bat. I told them we just finished packing it for the transport carrier and that they would pay the freight bill. I gave them the wire number for the bank. I am holding my breath on that one. The wire may hit tomorrow. The newspaper boy. They should have a few shekels in the bank. Then there is the mining museum."

Mary spoke up. "I have the invoice right here, all nice and neat."

"I have a call in for the Shepherd Girl. There was an answering machine. I left a message. I am thinking about registered mail and an invoice. I have to error on the side of safety."

The phone rang. They both reached for it and Mary answered. "Battle Mountain Bronze." Bob and Mary laughed. "That Molly. A regular good luck charm."

"Mary, Wes Culpepper. The bank in Fort Worth is going to help. Their loan committee meets Thursday. I have been told the loan would go through. Funds would not be wired to your bank until next Monday or Tuesday. They need your wire transfer number. The state fair has a modest amount of donations. About two thousand dollars. I will bring that with me."

"Here is Bob."

"Wes! Are you coming up to do the final critique?"

"Yes, Bob. I might make it there by Friday."

"Fine. We will see you this weekend."

Mary dialed the mining museum. "Sandy, this is Mary from Battle Mountain Bronze. Cheryl is going to slip an invoice through your door this evening. Do you have a drop box or will it fit under the door?"

"Hi, Mary. We do have a drop box on the employee side entrance. We close at four. Just a minute, Rob wants to talk to you."

"Mary, the board wants me to visit the foundry and inspect the sculpture before they issue a check."

"There is nothing to see, Rob. We have been waiting for you for the past month. The sculpting is finished. The molds have been taken. They are sitting on shelves in the wax department to be processed. We can not go any further until we have your fifty percent of the contract agreement."

The better part of Rob Gage's life had been spent underground in the Climax Mine. He made it to superintendent. As a young electrician he had the misfortune to touch a loose electrical wire as he was standing in a puddle of water. Rob lived to tell about it. The angle that he preferred to use was that God had saved him because the Devil did not want receivership. Rob Gage stared at one of the most beautiful mining related artworks that he had ever seen in his lifetime. The twenty two inch replica of the "Single Jacker" submitted for competition by Cheryl Pritchard was on the file cabinet next to his oak desk. Rob was retired and fortunate to have a job in Leadville. He loved his job. It was payback time for the round the clock work he put in one mile below the surface of the world for the last twenty years. He solicited donations from mining executives and corporations, and he handled all of the correspondence. He got to meet with everyone whose efforts transformed the old high school into the mining museum.

He stared at the replica and rocked back in the old wood swivel captain chair. He barked into the phone, "Well, I guess I will have to take the blame. How soon do you pour?"

"Thank you, Rob. We will pour the middle or the end of May. You should plan on a visit then. I'll have Sandy mark your calendar."

"I will forward what you have told me to the board. I will send fifty percent of the total proposed amount on Monday."

"We are not going any further until we have payment in the bank. There are payrolls and materials you know."

"Send Sandy the particulars."

Mary replied, "You won't be sorry, Rob. The mining museum is getting a sweetheart deal on a beautiful bronze." Mary copied the bank wire number on the invoice for the mining museum. She added a note. Sandy, please mark Rob's appointment book to visit Battle Mountain the second week in May and check with us for the particular day.

Bob mused, "What other projects are there to line up?"

"There are two, the kids with the water hose and the prairie people."

Bob, "Wouldn't you just know it. The insurance company has yet to pay up for their statue. Oh! There may be two new ones, the Tenth Mountain and a big one called in yesterday."

"What is it?"

"The jazz quartet plus a singer, five big pieces and a piano."

"Why didn't you tell me?"

"I thought you liked surprises."

"Okay, enough of this. I need to get back on the bronco. Can I fire the accountant today? We can not wait for him anymore."

"Let Marty do it." Bob donned his coat and left for the accountant's office.

On her way to the bronco, Mary turned into the wax room. Cheryl and Molly acknowledged her. "Cheryl, you didn't think we were going to have this much fun, did you?"

"Hal says you got to do what ever it takes. If you get worked into a jam, then you got to work yourself out. Plenty of scammers and irresponsible people will help you into a jam, but no one will help you get out of it."

"I have the museum invoice. Would you drop it in the mail slot at the employee parking lot?"

"Mary, you can count on it. Thank you."

Tuesday morning Max headed for gas, a doughnut, and the county paper at the nearest convenience store. He sat in a small plastic booth with a yellow table and opened the help wanted section. He had been watching the local papers in three counties to find a job. He did it religiously every week. Let's see, the bookkeeper position was open again at the Managers. Must be something going on in the accounting section there. There were a couple of driving jobs. The waste treatment plant in Frisco was looking for another operator. Personal secretary was needed for GMAC and Associates, the third time in as many months. Welders, plumbers, and electricians were needed for construction work. A small news blurb on the second page revealed that process chemicals were stolen from the waste treatment plant in Summit County.

Max finished his doughnut and left for Donald MacDonald's house. He parked on Spruce Street and walked into the snow covered alley that passed between the back yards of Seventh and Eighth. He passed the Ten Ecke's house. He walked around a black BMW on the car port and stepped through a three foot black iron gate. He entered Mac's back yard. Nikita, a Russian Gray, danced past on the shoveled snow path with a mouse stuck on his incisor. The house was situated on a hill three blocks west and above downtown Leadville.

As he reached the side porch he could see part of the view straight down the Arkansas River Valley. To the east rose the Silver King Loop and Mosquito Pass. The side porch was thirty feet higher than the downtown Leadville roof tops. On the west was Mount Massive and Elbert. South of Elbert for sixty miles all the way to Salida, the Collegiate Peaks guard the west side of the Arkansas River. The river rolls past the Independence Pass road to Aspen. At Salida, the Arkansas River rolls out of the mountains and east across the lower part of the state. It passes through several states on its way to the Mississippi. This was a view to live for. Max would probably kill for it depending on the circumstances. He entered the side porch and pounded as hard as he could on the back kitchen door. "AT Barf agent! Come out with your hands up!"

There was a delayed pause. "Come on in, Dipshit!"

The kitchen door opened with a large squeak.

"Massa need a little oil on these hinge!"

"Nonsense! Best and cheapest burglar alarm I ever had after the dog died and Big Goofy left."

"You mean after he ran away." Max loved to set Mac up, and Mac loved to knock Max down.

"Don't interrupt me! Grab two Ribbons out of the refrigerator on your way to the living room!"

"Okay, Mac." Max opened the refrigerator and picked up two PBRs off the top shelf. He mimicked Mac's statement in a surly monotone. "Get two Ribbons and take them to the living room, uh huh, uh huh." Max took great delight in playing the dumb oaf. This was nothing knew to him. As a young boy it had given his father heartburn and driven him to dislike his son. His biological father had constantly reminded the wavering lad that upper class people do not act in a clownish manner. Max worked his way to the living room. A young attractive Asian lady was sitting on the sofa along the west wall. She was organizing papers that were scattered on the sofa and on the floor in front of her.

"Pop those beers open without delay, boy!" Max did so and handed a beer to a domineering, take no prisoners man, who was front and center of the huge bay window in the living room. Mac was sixty five and he had made the decision to retire and downsize. He turned toward Max. "Short and to the point, I have good news for you! Max kept a startled look and suppressed a smile. Crystal and her husband want to stay in Grand Junction. Alison and Andy are planning to live on Fourth Street. That means Alison will move out of my second home on Sixth."

"So?"

"So, Mr. Smart Ass, I plan to move into my house on Sixth Street, and I am going to sell this one to you for the agreed amount to pad my retirement account. This house is now for sale to you!" A genuine smile appeared on Max's face. "I already called my attorney Neil Reynolds. He wants you to stop by his office Thursday to sign a couple of legal papers. He is on the second floor in the old Iron Horse building. I told him five thousand down as we agreed. Congratulations!" They bent their elbows and drank. After a good chug and a large robust gasp, Mac continued. "We are having a beer to celebrate! Cheers!" They bent the elbows and drank again. "How about a toast to congratulate you on your jump?" They bent their elbows and drank. "And your landing on your ass in front of the reunion Saturday!" They bent their elbows again. "That was quite spectacular. Were you paid for your effort?"

"Believe me. I was honored and happy to do it for nothing." His stomach growled as he recalled a frightfully close encounter with certain pain. He felt a slight shiver on his spine and one of his knees seemed to weaken as if it was going to give out. People always want to gossip if you are paid anything more than a dime. "I was to be paid one hundred dollars, but that stingy bastard kept all the money!"

"We told him not to pay you because you fell. Cheers!" They chugged and gasped again.

Max continued, "I am glad it pleased you, and I did it for the sheer glory of the reunion."

"Har, haw, haw!"

Jennifer placed Mac's memoirs and memos to the Tenth Mountain Association into her brief case. She put on her black winter coat. She had to return to work in Vail and she would ride with Max. "I'm ready to go anytime you are."

"The truck keys are on the peg by the kitchen door. I do not want to be disturbed this afternoon. Take them with you. Catch up with me tomorrow, and may God speed."

They bid good bye to Mac and left for West Vail. They arrived at her office near the Vail Bank building after a quick trip of one hour and twenty five minutes. She gave him a wave good bye and headed for the front door of her office. It was almost twelve noon. It was time to visit Charlie at the foundry. Max hoped to catch him at lunch time. In Minturn, he turned off the two lane highway and drove through the stand of pine trees to the former middle school parking lot. He walked through the front glass door into the lobby area. A lady sat at a desk behind the counter in the lobby. She peered through her reading glasses at the papers about her. Mary rose from the desk and entered a small windowed office behind her. She placed the papers in a basket on the desk. She returned to the counter and said with a cheerful smile, "Welcome to Battle Mountain Bronze. How can I help you?"

"I was hoping to talk with Charlie Hall and I would like to apply for any job that might be available. I have a resume and I have time to fill out an application. My name is Max Mason."

"Oh, Yes! Charlie is not here today. He mentioned your name." She reached under the counter and produced a pen and generic application. Max passed his resume to her. "My husband will be here soon and he will have ten or fifteen minutes to talk with you." She looked at Max to read his face. He was actually listening. Mary continued, "Do you have foundry experience? Are you an art major?"

"Sheet metal work and rod welding." Max had an answer for everything when he needed one, even if it was contrived. "Thank you for the form. I can fill it out now."

"Fine. Please excuse me. I have some calls to make." Max moved to the end of the counter and ripped through the application. Ten minutes later the glass door opened and Bob walked into the lobby. He spotted Mary and stepped into the office.

"Bank of Avon said they would cover us on a line of credit. The interest will eat up any profit, but at least we have an alternative if we do not receive payment from anyone soon." Bob spoke softly. "Has anyone called back?"

"One."

"Did you get through to the sheriff's office?"

"Yes. He just called back. He's had some minor arrests. Two were for resisting arrest. All related to traffic offenses. You know how they like to leave open bleeding wounds on every record they possibly can."

"Tell me about it. I remember verbally confronting one or two dull police officers myself."

"Apparently he is allergic to law enforcement. You got five seconds to make up our minds. Your call, dear. I think he is just another runaway from the big city and has no particular line of work at the moment. Molly knows a friend of his. He was doing bookkeeping and income taxes in Summit County before he moved to Leadville."

"Am I supposed to say something? I don't know squat about accountants except that they never finish the work you ask for. None of them stay in the mountains longer than three years."

"Yes, dear. Just like everyone else."

"Maybe it took him ten years to figure out where he might be happy."

Mary continued. "He lived in Glenwood Springs. The girl at Holy Cross told me he has a good work ethic and that he is a decent person. They really like him. I think he is back to the mountains because the rent is low in Leadville compared to the metro area and Summit County. The great outdoors is where he likes to be. He has a car that is running."

"That would be great for the car pools. What is he doing besides the ski area?"

"He is remodeling two abandoned homes that he bought in Leadville. It looks like he is one of those guys that can handle lots of different jobs. He has five unrelated jobs on his resume."

"Maybe he has been fired from two or three of them."

"Well, that is possible."

"He has definitely started over more times than we have. That's what worries me."

"That is going back a bit, dear. Would you rather have two cheap youngsters?"

"Nope."

"Maybe he would be receptive to part time work while you check him out."

Bob walked out of the small office and approached Max. He smiled. "I have five or ten minutes with nothing to do. Would you like to see what we do here?"

"You bet, Mr. Robertson!"

"Let's take the five minute tour. Call me Bob."

"You bet, Mr. Robertson." Max mentally kicked his brain into gear. It was dragging. Time to wake up. Do not miss a beat. *You are going to be hired or fired on this tour.*

"No I don't bet, but some folks are trying to get legalized gambling voted into Minturn or Edwards for the Vail tourists."

Max suppressed laughter. "Seems minimum stakes gambling is going to be the buzz word of the year."

A large window revealed the inside of the wax room. "This is the wax room. There is Molly. Mountain Molly! The best wax technician in the nation. If anyone makes her mad or drives her away I will kill them. We will stop here on the way back. Molly has a lot of say in what goes on around here. I respect her judgment." An attractive lady of medium height stood behind a large work table. The pot in front of her was full of melted wax. She dipped a brush in the pot and applied the liquid wax to the latex impression in the plaster mold. Curls of black hair were dancing about her head. She wore a white apron over a navy blue dress covered with small flowers. She looked like she was dressed more for a kitchen than a foundry. The room was a library of shelves and plaster molds. Molly was giving Bob the "Better come talk to me eye." She was definitely concentrating on the subliminal communication and her work. Obviously, they had something to talk about. "Just a minute." Bob stuck his head in the door. "Give me until tomorrow afternoon, okay?"

Molly offered no answer. She spoke as if she might have been calling a bluff. "I need to talk with you."

"Materials should be here tomorrow."

"Thank you. Stop in again soon as you can."

Bob turned back to Max. "Let's go next door to the shell room." They walked to the first door after the wax room. He said loudly to no one and everyone, "Deadlines! The whole world is on back order!" Max wisely offered no comment. The most obvious feature of the shell room was the metal pipe racks for the ceramic shells. The shells were hooked to the racks like clothing on a hanger. Each rack was thirty feet long and four feet off the ground. The bars were an inch and a half in diameter. Max new it was gas line pipe put together with elbow and tee fittings. There were seven racks about four feet apart. Enough room for two hundred forty shells or approximately eight statues of thirty pieces each.

"Molly has lived here all her life. You can't find anyone better." Max followed Bob to the slurry tub just inside the door. They were standing between the slurry tub and the rows of pipe. "We make the liquid ceramic here. The dry ingredients are mixed in the bowl over there." Bob pointed at a large floor mixer that you might see in a bread factory.

"The mix is transferred to this slurry tub and we add the secret ingredient of water. This foot pedal floor switch turns the blade in the bottom of the tub. Step gently on the switch." The potion began to swirl. The texture reminded Max of cream of wheat breakfast cereal.

"I'm getting hungry, Bob. It looks like cream of wheat."

Bob stared at Max with a questioning disbelief. "One more interruption and the tour will be over." He continued. "Once a wax is ready, Molly attaches a hook and a sprue cup. It is called spruing." He continued, "If the wax is small, then it requires seven coats. Medium size waxes require nine coats. We put eleven coats on the large ones depending on shapes and angles. The large ones are closest to the slurry tub. The small pieces go in back and they take about four hours to dry. These big ones in front have twelve coats on them. They take about seven hours to dry. There are seven racks and they correspond to the number of coats the wax has received. If a wax gets eight coats it goes back on the first rack. Row two would be coat number nine. The waxes are dipped for thirty seconds and then they go back to the rack. New waxes are delicate. Mix the slurry and then take your foot off the pedal. Wait for the mixture to stop swirling. Do that for the first three coats."

"Let's check your touch for a minute." Bob nodded at the large ceramic in front of them. It would fill up the whole tub. "Pick this one up without breaking it. Use both hands on the hook." Max did so. "Good. Now carry it over to the slurry tub. Good. Now clear the edge of the tub and center the shell before you lower it. Leave the blade off so you do not chip or crack the ceramic. Good. Now slowly lower it until the slurry is up to the top of the cup. We pour the metal into the cup. Okay, if the tub is not deep enough then you have to splash the slurry up on the dry ceramic all the way up to the top edge of the cup. That is what the rubber gloves are for, if you want to use them. Always coat the entire wax from the bottom to the top of the sprue cup every time." Bob grunted. "Good! Now count to sixty." A pained look grew on Max's face as he looked at Mr. Robertson.

"Just kidding, ha! Boy, you should have seen the look on your face! Ha! I guess the headaches of foundry life have made me a touch sadistic. Count to thirty. If you even bump the tub or the propeller, the shell will crack. If there is a crack in the shell, the hot liquid bronze will leak out of the shell onto the foundry floor during the pour.

Twenty eight, twenty nine, thirty. You are not even breathing hard, Max. That is good. Thank God there are still a few places in the world for us men. This is a strong man's job. Women tend to drop these big ones. It is even funny when two of them try to carry one large piece with ten coats of ceramic. When we lose a piece it has to be redone. That can set us back production wise. How is your back these days?"

"Fine. No problems. I am on the lean side, but I still work out occasionally."

"Ready? Now lift that shell straight up in the air and return it to the next rack. We try to keep all the pieces of each statute together in one row. Invariably they get mixed up a little bit. What do you think? Can you handle a row at a time or two or three rows if you have to?"

"No problem, Mr. Robertson."

"The racks hold two hundred and forty shells. Could you dip them all without stopping?"

Max calculated. "Let's see. Two hundred forty minutes divided by sixty minutes in an hour is four hours, for a minute dip on each shell. Two hours for a thirty second dip. Add in walking back and forth and you have two and a half hours to three hours. Four to seven hours to dry depending on size. After four hours the small waxes can be dipped again so they might possibly get two coats in one day and possibly the large ones can be dipped again at the end of the day. Let's see, two hundred forty minutes times two is four hundred eighty and there are four hundred eighty minutes in an eight hour day. Yes, I can, Mr. Robertson."

"Good! Did you have a math tutor?" Max laughed. "We are running out of time already. Let's move on." There were several large floor fans and an open door in the back of the room. "We try to keep the air circulating. With the moisture from the snow melt it takes longer to dry the shells. In the summer all the doors and the windows are open. Bring your mosquito repellent. Otherwise they might hospitalize you. I've got about two minutes to show you the rest of the place." They walked out into the hall. There were two life size bronze statues in the hallway. One was a girl on a swing and the other a newspaper delivery boy throwing a rolled up newspaper. They walked down to the end of the wide main hallway to a T intersection, and straight across into the foundry floor. The large room had once been a gymnasium and assembly area for the middle school. Bob continued. "Max, I'll be honest with you. Charlie did a little bit of everything. He was willing to be flexible and help in any area. If you work here you will only spend half of your time in the shell room. When Charlie finished a job he found the next chore to work on. He was not a character to hide from work or cheat on his hours. If he was finished for the day and could not find something to do, or someone who needed a hand, then he would clock out. Can you be trusted to do that?"

"Rest assured, Mr. Robertson. Charlie and I share that same trait."

"The gym was converted by the vocational auto shop program when they owned the building." Max took in the view. On the left and the right were two large canvass partitions that divided the foundry floor into three long rectangular areas. The area in the middle was the widest. The areas on each side were half as wide. Tables and benches lined the partitions on the left and right. Tools waited tirelessly on the table for the true craftsman who required their function. Together they would create a masterpiece one slice, one cut or one nick at a time.

A statue lay on its side in the middle of the foundry floor. It appeared to be a man. Marty Robertson, Cheryl and Nash were there working together. There she was in her element. She wore a blue bandanna around her head and a thin, faded blue denim jacket to protect her from the hot sparks. A plastic face shield was strapped to her head and gloves were on her hands. Max could see fire in her eyes. No smile right at the moment. They were surrounded by works in progress. A large gray clay statue of a man and a woman with a small child stood in front of them by the partition. It looked to be ten feet in height. Two partial bronze sculptures were close by. Cheryl worked the fifteen pound two handed grinder. The large grinder made quick work of smoothing down the welds. Sparks were flying everywhere. Care was required as the coarse disc easily cut into the bronze metal surface. Cheryl made a sweep along a weld and asked Marty, "What were you thinking about when you welded this together, Marty?"

"It was three in the morning. I should have gone home. It is sloppy, but I knew you could handle it."

"Geeze, Marty, thanks a billion! I appreciate the quality of your work. It is good job security for me."

"You did not work this weekend. Were you trying to run away from us?"

"You don't know for certain and I am not going to tell you."

"There is no reason to be so nasty. You should be all nice and cheery today."

"Oh I am! I love it on days when people tell me what I should be." The plastic face guard did not hide her eyes. He could tell that she was laughing, by the wrinkle in the corner of her eye.

"Are you okay today Cheryl?"

"Oh no you don't. Don't go there, Marty. Don't pretend you care about me when you really don't. You are just prodding me for any information that I might accidentally divulge to you. Information that would be advantageous to you.

"What on earth are you talking about?"

"You pretend to be concerned about problems people have. Your real intention is to find out what troubles they have so you can take advantage of that person. Then you can steal something from them. You are a scammer, nothing more."

Marty threw his head back and laughed. "That is rich! Nash, did you hear that?"

"Cheryl and I worked it out yesterday."

"Ganging up on me again . . ."

Cheryl interrupted. "I am not finished yet! Let's say that I told you I hated my car and was tired of it. You would offer me one hundred dollars for it and turn around and sell it for two hundred fifty. In reality you are just meddling in my business. You are trying to discover anything that you might find useful, that you can use for your own benefit. You are pretty smooth, but in reality you are just a thief and a scammer! Am I right Nash?"

"Whoa! Whoa now! You are all wound up today."

"Did Bob and Mary adopt you? I can't believe you are made of the same genetic material."

"Okay, that's it! Don't go there! Don't cross the line."

"Nash dared me to say it."

"I will get you for that last remark. What did you do this weekend?"

"Oh, things were kind of up in the air. I went to Ski Cooper. I am improving. Saturday night I went down to the front range and visited Mom and Dad. Sunday we attended the art festival in Loveland."

"You're kidding! You lucky devil. I wanted to go! Now I am depressed and can not work. You have to take over."

"Nash offered, "No problem, Marty, but the pay will be time and a half."

"How was the festival?"

"Fascinating as always. But you probably didn't miss anything there. There were works that you might not have been able to comprehend. Kind of over your head, you know."

"Are you trying to insult me or hurt my feelings?"

Nash spoke up again. "I don't think that is possible."

Cheryl was making a large sweep along the leg. She saw Mr. Robertson. She pointed the grinder towards him in the air and pressed the trigger as if to say, "I am waving at you." At that instant, Max recalled the pain in his left eye from her snowball. The wheel shrilled from a high tone to a slow low growl that echoed inside the statue. She guided the grinder on a long weld down the statue. A shower of sparks flew out in an arc, four feet from the grinder.

"That girl has an incredible range of abilities," Bob remarked. "Behind this curtain on the right is the pouring furnace. Let's walk over and take a quick look. Thank God the auto shop left us a dandy overhead boom and crane. We use it for the furnace and pouring operation. They moved to the curtain and looked behind it. A small Inductotherm furnace was close to the back wall. The ladle used to pour the hot metal into the molds hung from the crane. A gray clay sculpture of a ten foot tall bucking bronco and wild eyed rider bore down on them.

"Moose and Gary work with the furnace and the pour, and I mix the bronze and help them. The mix is a coveted family recipe." They retraced their steps to the main door. "Behind the other partition is a storage area for material. The sandblaster, and the wax melt furnace are overthere. They walked to the sandblaster. Max saw the materials storage, fifty five gallon drums of copper, mica, silica, and forty five pound bags of slurry mix. "There are a couple of classrooms once you get to the back hallway behind the sand blaster and the truck dock. There is an injection mold machine in one of them." They walked toward the back corner. Just past the sandblaster was a two door exit into the last classroom hallway. Inside the hallway on the left was a two door exit to the side parking lot. "This is also a fire exit. The door alarm still works, but it is turned off at the moment. It is on at night time. You always have to use the front door at night. Never use the side doors. The doors at the end of this hallway are fire exit only." The classrooms were on the right. On the way to the first classroom window Max felt he detected a very slight uneven walk in his potential employer.

"You have a slight limp."

"From a bullet while I was finding cover."

Max leveled evenly, "Was that here at the foundry? I have a right to know."

"Ha! No. It was overseas."

Max looked into the window of the first small classroom. A huge green mound of clay occupied most of the space. He slowed down and they stopped for a moment. His eyes focused for recognition. It was a huge clay sculpture of a man in motion. Mr. Robertson stared into his eyes. Max could not hold back. "Wow! There is a lot of power in that sculpture!"

Bob searched the reaction on his face. Bob replied as if he was bored with the beauty that surrounded him everyday. "Yes there is. This is Cheryl Pritchard's creation for the mining museum. What do you think?"

"What a concept! Very powerful. I have never seen anything like it." Bob liked the respect that he witnessed and he almost hired Max on the spot. *Well, he passed the second test.* They walked on to a small room, two doors down.

"This is it. We have an injection mold machine in here. Right now we have an order for this leaf pattern. These individual squares with the leaf pattern will be part of a metal fence for a driveway and entrance gate."

"Fancy!"

"Do you have any experience with injection molding?"

Max replied, "I wish I could say yes."

Bob went quickly through the steps. Max caught on to it but could not recall the last step at the end of the process. "Good enough. The first one hundred are the most difficult. Do you think you can do this?"

"Yes."

"Can you stand here all day in this room and make a million of these one after another? I mean all day, piece after piece, minute after minute, hour after hour. Tell me right now. Do not lie because I have to have someone who has the ability to cope mentally with this task. This is what you are going to be doing when you are finished in the shell room. The last two people quit before they made it through their first week."

"Not a problem. It will give me some extra time to study up on my analytical chemistry and calculus."

Bob Robertson had nothing to lose except another potential smart assed employee. He looked at Max and furrowed his brow. "Remember what I told you about jokes around here? I am serious! We get some real off the wall applicants and some who really do not care about anything. That attitude is contagious and I have no need for it. I am an engineer by education and my wife and I are the team that makes this endeavor work. I need only good workers with a good conscience. Charlie Hall spoiled us. He is an art lover and he always stayed busy for us. He didn't sit on his ass. If Charlie ran out of work he found me. He would even notify me an hour before he ran out of work. The repetition of the injection mold piece work did not bother him. Some people find it boring. I am not taking anything away from construction workers. The last one here was decent but he was could not stand the boredom of this machine."

"Fair enough."

"We are short handed right now. It is hard to keep part time workers. We have orders coming in for next month, and right now I am barely making payroll. I can not afford to hire someone ill suited for the job, or someone who will leave after one week. I . . ."

Max interjected, "Mr. Robertson, for the last six months the ski area paid me once a month. At this moment I would not need a paycheck for three weeks at the earliest. I will give you the first week free. I want to work here. I have never seen so much creativity in one place in all my life. The sculptures are incredible. I can run the mold machine all day. I can wait patiently for the wax to harden in the mold." They stepped out of the mold room and walked back to the side entrance. Outside Bob lit a cigarette. He offered one to Max who declined.

"Alright. I am going to hire you on one condition. If I am not satisfied with your performance and the quality of your work after one short week, then you leave the foundry. No questions asked. I want you to work for a week on a trail basis. I need to find out for certain if you can do the job." Bob paused. "Why haven't you found a job?"

"The area is new to me. I have no connections. Charlie gave me a big break and told me about this opportunity. I do not know where to go to walk into a job. I cannot build a business in bookkeeping or accounting because Leadville is quite a drive from the available market. It worked in Summit County. I was doing okay, but the houses are too expensive for me to qualify for a loan."

"And why not construction?"

"Construction is about the only thing I can walk into. The disadvantage for me is the one hour and thirty minute drive to the job sites on the interstate."

The five minute tour had turned into a fast grueling twenty minutes. "Max, let's give it a try. Let me ask you a couple of questions. You were an accountant. What do you do for slow pay?"

"You must promise not to reveal this answer to anyone. It is highly classified."

"How so?"

"Instead of the usual over due notice and a fourth or fifth invoice I would send a 'Deepest Sympathy' card with the invoice. The kind used for tragedy or illness. I would write 'We can no longer provide you with our services. Your account has been terminated and turned over to a collection agency. Make no mention at all of a chance to bring the account current. It must appear that this final course of action is in place." Max saw disbelief register in Bob's eyes. "There are two ways to collect. For thirty five dollars I would file a summons and complaint at the courthouse. I would list the allegations and file it pro se. You can always get an attorney later, if you need to. The court sets a date and the sheriff will deliver the summons, all for less than one hundred dollars."

"No way."

"It will have a sobering effect on the client, and it will let him know that he needs to move you up on the payables list. It forces them to acknowledge you, and at least get a partial payment to you. You need to have a signed contract. You will have a difficult time in court with just an invoice, but an invoice is considered a legal document of a verbal contract or a written one. There may be ten others on his slow pay list. Your client may be past forty five days due on all of his payable accounts. The downside is that the summons can create uncontrollable rage. The beauty of it is two fold. The action has been taken, and you can always drop it later."

"It gives you leverage," Bob remarked.

"If everything falls apart and you find out they really do not care, then you will be thirty days ahead. If you win the case, then you can turn them over to a collection agency."

"That would prove to be a festering wound."

"Yes, sir! No hard feelings, right? That is what they always say to me when a renter moves out in the middle of the night. They could not pay and had no intention to pay."

"The sympathy card could be mistaken as a joke. Don't some people just laugh at you?"

"Sure they do. Some call right away to say they passed it around the company for grins and giggles. If they fail to realize that you are serious you will be more inclined to use the summons."

Bob smiled. "I don't think it is very professional, but it might be fun to try."

"If you do win in court, then you are entitled to keep the work and the molds as your collateral for payment. It is really an inconvenience for them."

"Without the molds they could not go to another foundry. What if they need more time to get the money?"

"Simple. At the court hearing you can request a continuance, but you should call in, and let the court know what is going on ahead of time. It is a courtesy. They have lots of cases to try and they will cooperate with you. If your client gives you a partial payment, you can ask for a continuance of thirty days. It seems cruel, but it forces their hand. All of a sudden they are on the phone talking to you instead of showing you their recorded message machine. That is always a great feeling for me."

"But what about the bad feelings?"

"Well, you get to make the call. It is up to you whether to pursue or not. Let the client's actions and promises determine your direction. I detest people who kiss up to me for my service and my work, especially when they had no intention to pay in the first place. The downside is a ruined relationship and a morning or afternoon in court. But it forces their hand to do something. A collection agency can rain on them everyday, and your client will have difficulty borrowing money or entering into any agreements with a bad credit rating. It will follow them everywhere."

"Okay, Max. We will have plenty of waxes for you to dip in a week. I will call you to let you know what day."

Max gave a slight hint of a smile. "Terrific. Thank you, Bob."

Tuesday night Cheryl had her miner lit up with halogens. Imperfections were captured and revealed in the intense light. Cheryl was not going to trust her memory tonight. Her notebook was open. She referred to her ideas and thoughts from the night before. She needed to correct muscle definition in the right arm. The suspenders lacked definition. She began to work on the nose and the moustache again.

Mary entered the room. "Did you have to make him so big?" Cheryl gave Mary an odd look. "I think the first time there is a big temptation to make a large statue. Do you want to do King Kong next?"

Cheryl laughed. "No."

"How are your fingers and forearms coming along? Is there much pain?"

"None. I deny you the pleasure of goading me. If you lean a little closer I can pay you back for those nasty remarks with a quick cut to your jugular with my scalpel." Cheryl and Mary were all over the clay with their sculpting tools under the flood lights.

"Ah! It is so much easier to share opinions and let a few things slide when two people get together. A little reinforcement and a second view point helps." Mary had an idea to pronounce the suspenders. "The suspenders are thick enough, but there are some spots where they do not stand out from the shirt." One of her sculpting tools used for definition was a triangular loop at the end of a water color paint brush handle. With the help of a pair of pliers, Mary squeezed one corner to a ten degree angle. "This is a great aid in definition." Mary demonstrated the clean cut on a brick of clay to Cheryl's delight. The loop sliced into the surface at an angle. She moved the loop along the edge of a suspender. It worked. The contrast was clearly more visible. "Now, the edge is separated from the shirt." Mary put her pliers to work and made a loop for Cheryl to use.

Cheryl went back to the front of the statue while Mary worked the back. Together they raced along the edge of the suspenders.

"Thank you for your assurances on material and your help today."

"You are welcome. The first statue is never the way you want it. You just have to get it done."

"Remember the Green Parrot restaurant?"

"I do. How could I forget? We snagged you that day before you could get away. I think about what you are doing now with this project, and it just amazes me."

"You were going to enter the contest, am I right?"

"Nash had told me about the contest. I had a couple of ideas, but nothing compared to what you have here. I should tell you, Cheryl. I have harbored jealousy and envy in my heart and mind for the last thirty days. Tonight is as good a night as any to do you in, then I can take credit for your hard work. We plan to shove your body into the furnace so you will become one with your statue!"

"Eeeeek!"

Mary clutched her scalpel and pointed it at Cheryl. "I will have all of the proceeds to myself," she cackled like a witch on Halloween. "What say you now, Cinderella?"

"I can not allow that grasshopper! You can not get me now with only one stab in the dark." They laughed.

"There are people who sham and scam. Hal and Marilyn have them on their heels all the time, but I never thought that you would stoop to that level, Mary."

"No, I am happy for you and I am proud of you. You are tremendous. I am working on that beloved bucking bronco. I had no time to give. The mining museum would have to wait a year if I was selected. I could go so far as to say that I am jealous, but to tell you the truth, your idea is better. And besides, I could not have accepted the terms of price."

Cheryl exclaimed, "See? That was hateful."

"I have an idea for a small bronze that I might present to the gift shop, but they have plenty of contributors right now. Maybe in a year or two. Right now I am stuck with a rodeo clown who is too lazy or too busy to get up here and finish his project."

"How is your buckin' bronco? Have you finished the buckin' work yet?"

"You can't hurt my feelings. Everyone has teased me about the bronco."

"We all know the work is perfect in your eye now. There is nothing more you can do. Is the man ever going to show up?"

"Yes, he is supposed to be here the end of this week."

"Excellent!"

"Now, back to your sculpture. I am here for your moral support. Let's talk about that. You never finish the first life size sculpture mentally. It will haunt you the rest of your life."

"I am going to have good memories of this one. It will be a good haunt."

"It will be a welcomed haunt just to get it over. Incidentally, Nash calls your work the incredible hulk. Do you have a name for the miner yet? Is it Quasimodo?" Mary caught Cheryl by surprise.

She answered, "Cletus."

Mary howled. "Wait till I tell Bob!"

"Oh no!"

"I think your miner is excellent as it is. You are wise to make this cut off. You have to throw your hands up and say, enough! If you do not, then you will have a constant source of mental irritation that will drain you emotionally. If you lose interest, then everything becomes a burden."

"Does it give you a little mental instability?" Cheryl asked with a smirk.

"I think it can. Bob certainly seems that way sometimes." They laughed. "Please don't tell him I said that."

"I think I understand you a little better now, Mary."

"Some people welcome distraction just to have their mind on something else and off the objective. Then they do not have to confront the stress of the deadlines and the completion."

"I think I am going to put a condom on Cletus tomorrow." They laughed.

"Good for you! That's when you want to start is it? Sometime tomorrow? Alright, we will do it together. Cheryl, you have been pretty fired up lately. You seem to have hit a powerful stride."

"I'm all worked up and tired of looking at the green clay. I want to get the cast on him."

"It is exciting to move on to another stage."

"That's right!

"Push on. Time to go!"

Cheryl looked Mary in the eye and said evenly, “Hey, Mary! Did you whip that dime store pony last night?” At first Mary tried to hide her look of surprise. Cheryl laughed. “I was close to the office yesterday morning and I over heard you talking to Bob. I covered my mouth and ran so you wouldn’t hear me laughing! It was just before Molly walked in.”

“I see. Well, since you caught me, I will let you in on a little secret. I spur him gently. I don’t like to beat my animals.”

“Ha, ha, ha! Giddy up, Silver!”

“I am laughing to hard to work on this clay any longer. Let’s put the big guy away for the night.”

“We will put the trojan on him tomorrow.”

“Okay. I’m leaving now. Get the shims and the brushes and everything ready. We will start bright and early.”

“Thanks again, Mary. I will return the scaffold tonight.”

“No need to. Let’s start on Quasimodo first thing in the morning. We can do the prairie people in the afternoon. I might even come in early.”

“That would be terrific. Thank you, Mary.” Cheryl finished her last touch ups just after midnight. She locked the door to the miner and walked to the break area. She turned down the thermostat. She went to the utility closet and found her sleeping bag. The mattress that leaned against the wall was pulled to the floor. By the time she was prone, she was wrapped in her sleeping bag, and she was falling asleep.

CHAPTER FOURTEEN

Mary arrived at the foundry early and went straight to the miner room. Cheryl had collected all of the shims and brushes she could find. "After we finish up the miner, I am going to borrow you to help me shim the prairie people. Is that alright with you, Cheryl?"

"You know it is. Lordy, that will really get things moving around here."

"Well, let's get started."

They collaborated on the most advantageous places to section the miner. Mary shared her insights with Cheryl. Good planning led to correct fit, correct alignment, and easy welding and chasing. If possible, the shims would be placed in areas of less detail. This would make it easier to chase the weld marks away without marring any surface detail. Once on the scaffolding they stared at the miner's hat. "Wow, Cheryl, how did you ever support the bill of this hat?"

"It is actually three pieces of sheet metal. They are all the same size and they are welded to a metal head support."

"Then it is stout enough. That pretty much settles the question of how to section this rascal. Just separate the bill from the crown and cut the bill in three pieces." They shimmed the top of the bill right along the crown of the hat, and the bottom of the bill was shimmed where it met the miner's head. They divided the bill into three sections. The shims had to be placed gently or they would mar the clay surface. The mar would leave an unwanted blemish or mark in the latex impression, and ultimately, the surface of the metal.

"It looks good. Let's get after it." Mary looked at Cheryl. She was silent for awhile. "Have you made some new friends Cheryl? In the past couple of weeks you have said some things that have startled me a little bit."

I am beginning to speak out now. I do not always choose the right words to express my feelings. I will get better though. I am tired of holding things back and holding things in. So, now I just kind of blurt my feelings out."

"Oh, you will eventually acquire that skill of interacting without offending someone. Do you feel any better after you state your case or your cause?"

"That's right. Maybe this place is the reason I have changed."

Mary threw her head back and belly laughed. "I know what you mean! And you never used to say 'That's right.' either. You have to change to protect your heart and mind."

"I was at a rowdy barbeque at Ski Cooper last weekend. There were a lot of crazy people there. Some old feelings and attitudes resurfaced. Abruptness. Offending people on purpose and making them feel ridiculous. And you have to consider that I have been in hibernation for six months while working on this miner. I have not had a whole lot of the normal social contact with anyone, and it has pushed me close to the edge." Mary was laughing now. "I have lost my social skills and graces."

"But in your conversations, are you intentionally bursting bubbles?"

"Oh, I have always done that. I just never did it in front of you and Bob. You are picking on me now. Will this inquisition continue?"

"Anything for a laugh. You used to remain silent on some things, and not reveal your point of view."

"If you don't state your views, it leaves too much unresolved emotional conflict all pent up inside."

"The emotional baggage gives you added stress, and big zits break out on your face. Am I right?"

"Bingo!"

"See, there! You never said bingo before. You have new lingo."

"Well, Miss manners. I guess I just keep growing up and acting like most adults. Are you are worried about my moral fiber slipping into decay?"

"Well, you should try to hang onto some of your good character."

"Yes, but sometimes good character eventually erodes."

"When the light goes out?" They laughed.

Bob stuck his head in the classroom. "Hey! Wes is going to be here Friday afternoon. Are you going to work on the bronco?"

"You know, Bob, I am not going to spend any more time on the bronco. I have nothing more to do on the bronco, my love. I have picked nits off it for the last five days. He will change a few things anyway and that will irritate me. I am venting now, ahead of time. When Wes is here, I will be all nice and cheery and I won't have to tell him to kiss my ass when he starts redoing all of my work." Mary looked at Cheryl. "Did I say that right?"

Cheryl had her nose buried into her elbow to hide her face. "That's right, that's right!"

"You can't be serious."

"That bronco will not be ready until Wes is finished. We need to get ahead of the game here. It will be better if we get Cletus and the prairie people ready for the wax room."

"Good thinking, dear." Bob hesitated. "Cletus?" They laughed.

Mary stated clearly, "Honey, after we shim this miner we are going to shim the prairie people. Then after that is over we are going to put the condom on the miner."

Cheryl laughed.

"Gosh, dear, you really know how to get a man all excited."

"We will launch three statues into the wax room at one time, and we will all be in there for two weeks, until we drive Molly crazy."

"It can not be helped."

"Now, darling, do you have anymore questions for me?"

"What has got into you women? You got a bug in your navel?"

"I tell you what. If Wes gives you a line that he really needs two people because two people would save time, then you are going to be the one holding the scalpel, not me."

"Let me see if I understand you. Maybe I should sculpt his jugular?"

"Get the money first."

Cheryl opened up. "See? You try to choose the right words, but there is always clarification required. You have to clarify what you said, or explain what you meant to say, because it did not come out right."

"Two random statements are floating around in the air and they never get connected until additional thoughts are received to tie the conversation neatly together."

"That way everyone has to perk up and pay attention."

"You go girl!"

"Are you girls on the sauce? Have you been nipping?" Bob looked deep in thought. He was trying to assess the atmosphere. "Alright. After your foray here, Casey and the prairie people are the priority."

"Not a problem. We will put some slave time in today. Right now, we are going to give to the miner. The creative juices are flowing and I like to be where the action is. Besides, you need some time off for those spur marks to heal." Cheryl laughed. It was one of the few times she ever witnessed Bob flush. His smile seemed to wrinkle. Bob was not certain if Cheryl had been clued in.

"You two girls are a bad influence on one another. From now on you are not allowed to work together. Mary, I will pay you back for talking openly about our private lives." He turned and hurried back to the foundry floor.

Mary and Cheryl laughed. They were undeterred.

"Mary, you were just a loose cannon back there, and you talk about me!"

"You are family now, Cheryl. No need to hide things from you."

"And you were just talking about my new conversational skills. I guess stress and deadlines are the cause for our new methods of communication."

"I like that analogy."

They had shimmed right down the side of the miner from the shoulders down to the waist. They finished the boots and the base just before lunch time. The big green miner was gone. Now there was a big green pincushion. Cheryl snapped a few pictures for her scrap book. They moved the scaffolding and the materials to the prairie people in the middle section of the foundry floor. When the scaffold and everything was ready to go, they broke for lunch. By the end of the day the man woman and child were sufficiently shimmed. Time had flown by. Tomorrow they would latex the miner and the prairie people.

The next morning they loaded three buckets of latex and their supplies on a floor dolly in the shell room and moved it all to the miner room. The women lifted a latex bucket to the top of the scaffold. They wore disposable latex gloves. Once again they were looking down at the miner's hat. The lid of the latex bucket was pried open, and the latex was scooped into two aluminum bread pans. The bread pans were easy to hold while leaning and stretching. The latex had to be applied without causing any damage to the surface of the clay. It had to fit like a layer of skin and over the shims. Great care was taken not to trap any air bubbles between the latex and the clay. Any trapped air would be filled with metal during the pour. The result would be visible bumps on the surface of the metal. The bumps would have to be removed. The latex work was slow and tedious. They gently pressed the latex into place and they spread it one section at a time with the brushes.

"Does the pain ever leave your hands, Cheryl?"

"Only when my heart and mind is open to my work."

"Only then do you learn to love the pain because you love the work that you do."

"It's all mental. That's what Hal says. If your heart and mind are in it one hundred percent, then pain and suffering is accepted and tolerated."

"If you are only in it fifty to eighty percent of the time, then slovenly work begins to appear. This eventually leads to unhappiness and a bad state of karma."

"Ya think? Max says he wants to be a burden on society when he grows up."

"Ha! I'm glad Charlie sent him. It is a relief to know we may have another Charlie."

"I think Charlie and Max are pretty much alike."

"Do you know anything at all about Max?"

"I just met him through Charlie."

"I left a Summit Daily by your locker. There is a letter to the editor you should read."

"Oh, yeah? Are you going to keep me in suspense?"

"Well partly. Some disgruntled artist criticized the ultra modern sculpture proposed for the city park."

"The one in Frisco?"

"Yes. It compared the sculpture to the hood ornament on a 1937 Packard. It rambled on about the goddess that holds the wheel out in front of her gowned body."

"Ha! It really is just another chrome pretzel. I saw a picture of it in the Summit News. Who is the critic?"

"It's Charlie! He said the statue would be suitable for any automotive junk yard, but not suitable for the great outdoors."

"I thought it was as beautiful as a quarter mile of cloth across a beach or river on a windless day."

"Aren't those pathetic?"

"I always wondered how an artist could conceive such an idea."

"Too many chemicals in the laundry detergent." They laughed.

They had covered the miner from the hat down past the outstretched arms. They ran out of latex, and had to open the second bucket. When the second bucket was empty, they were down to the knees. It was time to take the scaffold down and move it outside of the room, to get it out of the way. They could finish the rest of the work while they were standing. They filled their pans again and resumed the latex work. When the miner was finished, Cheryl captured the event with a few photos. They broke for sandwiches and refreshments.

At Mary's request, Mark and Moose moved the scaffolding to the prairie people and returned to the miner room to collect brushes and the floor dolly. Mark cleaned out the pans to get rid of hardened bits of latex. He washed the brushes. Moose moved three buckets of latex out to the sculpture of the prairie people. Everything was ready for the women when they returned from lunch. They placed a bucket on the scaffolding along with the brushes and donned their disposable gloves. Just as with the miner, Mary took one side and Cheryl took the other.

"Gosh, Mary, I was hoping to have the plaster on by Friday."

"Oh, oh. You need a reality check. You are dreaming. It is time to get back to the real world. The anxiety of wait can sometimes be offset with small endeavors. I prefer to have some simple diversions when time seems to stand still."

"A watched pot never boils?"

"Precisely, now for me, I kind of like to travel. An exotic beach with a good currency exchange rate is a good thing to find. I prefer a small sailboat or a jet ski, with a well seasoned man to pull up anchor for me." Cheryl just about dropped her brush. "I could wear a mini grass skirt with strands of glitter and learn to hula. My assistants could fetch me food and drink. What about you, Cheryl?"

"I am going to live on a tropical island in a cheap, bug free, five dollar a night room. I will do my sculpting there. The plaster and molds will be sent back to the mainland. I can wear just my glitter thong and run the beach with handsome young men in loin cloths. Fetch, will be my assistant." The girls were howling.

"If you keep me laughing like this, you will have to finish the statue by yourself."

Once again, the latex bucket was empty. The women lowered the scaffold and opened another bucket.

"You know, Cheryl, you should just take off this weekend. The latex is not going to be dry before Sunday. Go ski. Go have fun. We could plaster Saturday but that will ruin everybody's weekend. We can plaster Monday. Tuesday you can take off with your assistant, Fetch, and go to San Francisco. I hope you get to see a bit of the city. When you get back we can pull the plaster. Call in and I will keep you up to date. We just might pull the molds for you after everything has dried."

"You know, Mary, you are absolutely right. I forgot to tell you that I went to the Loveland art festival last weekend. Goodman was there. I think she is going to bring a project to you. What a neat lady."

"Now I am jealous!" When the prairie people were latexed the women posed for photos. Cheryl took pictures to record the progress.

The bottoms of the clouds were a bright yellow with a touch of orange. Max left the employee bus and walked up Sixth Street. Cheryl slowed beside him to a stop and rolled down her window.

"Hi, Cheryl. Good to see you."

"How did it go with Bob?"

"I start next week."

"Good work, Max."

"Hop in. I will take you home." He opened the back door and sat behind her. "I signed up for the accelerated freefall class this Saturday. I can't wait. It's all I think about."

Max said, "Unbelievable. No cross country skiing this weekend?"

"I would if the commute was not so difficult."

"I have to work this weekend. I won't be able to see your jump."

Cheryl felt a touch of disappointment, but she was looking forward to a great weekend. "I might put in a days work with Hal and Cheryl. AFF is expensive. The first jump is two hundred eighty dollars because you have to pay for the two jumpmasters. You also have to pay for the first jump course and you have to rent a reliable parachute. Jumps two and three are one hundred ninety dollars each. After that it is one seventy for each of the next four jumps. Seven jumps altogether. About thirteen hundred dollars."

Max listened respectfully to Cheryl. "A reliable parachute. I like your choice of words. Let's go to your house and practice, okay?

"You must have read my mind."

"Stop at my house. I will get my parachute."

He reappeared in less than three minutes. He opened the back door and sat his parachute and the Skydiver's Information Manual on the seat.

"The old 1953 twin beech may be ready this weekend."

"Now you are trying to make me jealous. The tube dive last weekend is going to have to hold me for a little while."

"I do not know where I can get all the money for this and my heat bill."

"But you have your priorities in order."

"You bet! Bob Robertson might give me a one week advance. I told him it's for insurance and a down payment on a new car."

"I knew that you were a morally corrupt scammer."

"I'm going to tell my parents the same thing. Karen said the first two jumps are cash. For the rest of the jumps you can use a credit card. They will give me a ninety day payment agreement. She said the DZ isn't cash rich right now. They just overhauled a couple of Lycomings for their 206."

"I know a cheap place that will be open in a week, if you want to move."

Cheryl gave Max a suspicious look. "Tell me quick, Max and don't you lie to me. Is it still available? It would be better if I found another place, but it is ski season. There are no rentals to be found and I do not want an instant roommate. By the way, my parents want you to work for them. I told them about the financial squeeze you are facing. Hal says he won't pay you a dime for the first week because he has to see if you can go the distance. I told him that I would pass the word."

"That would be great. Right now I have too much work to do here."

"They want to look around Leadville and pick up a house if there are any cheap ones left. Mom moves fast on a good thing."

"There is land up for sale at bargain prices down the river valley all the way to Canon City."

Cheryl wheeled in beside the landlady's station wagon. Max carried the videos and groceries. Cheryl carried her tool bag and the parachute rig. They climbed the stairs to her second floor apartment. Max was tempted to poke Cheryl in the fanny. She gave him due warning after turning the key. "You so much as touch anything in here you are dead."

"Duh, do that include you sweetie pie?"

"Down boy!" Cheryl responded, "I ain't your sweetie pie. So keep your fingers out or I'll cut them off along with anything else you might be thinking about in your dirty little mind."

Inside, Max took in the environs. "Wow. You managed to get the place presentable. No clothes on the floor. You must have sent them to the laundry. No potato chip crumbs." The table and easel caught his eye. Cheryl watched Max closely. In front of him on the table was the replica of the miner she had conceived. Out of twenty entrees, she made the cut to the final five.

"Who did you steal this from?"

"Don't you mock me or denigrate my work. I'll have none of it. I will not let you cheapen my resolve or attitude with your lowlife language. You always try to bring everyone down to your shallow standards." She paused. "Max, have you ever been serious?"

"Not as serious as the person who made this statue on your work bench."

"Oh, that. I bought it at a garage sale last month." Cheryl paused. "Max, I have decided to change the way I talk to you. Ten per cent serious with an up front warning, and ninety per cent bullshit with no warning."

"Yeah, that is about right."

Max had been close to greatness a couple of times in his life as far as meeting the right projects and people. There are achievable levels of basic talent and skills that most people can reach with a little work and sacrifice. There are higher levels, but they require a supreme effort. Cheryl was at the level of national acclaim. No one in the art world knew Cheryl Pritchard, but they would soon hear about her work. Determination and resolve were captured on the face of the miner. He exuded enough energy to pound the hand steel one inch into the rock hard wall with a single blow. "This is truly a great sculpture." On the back of the table Max noticed several photos. He asked Cheryl, "May I look at the photos?" She nodded.

Max looked them over. They were unremarkable workers just marking their time. He looked at Cheryl. She was extremely proud at this moment. Her face was not a smile of arrogance. She knew her work was good, and she was giving Max all the rope that he needed to hang himself.

"They were hand steel workers in the 1940's from the look of the photos. Just another day banging the wall. Not a lot of enthusiasm here. But your miner is all fired up and ready to pound a hole in the rock. Maybe he hit a little bit of silver and is going to dig a nugget out for his stomach. How did you make the leap, Cheryl? How did you make the conception?"

Cheryl was satisfied with his answer. "I played a little, what if? What if he was working his own claim and he had just hit some traces of silver in the rock? Max, let's get on with the practice. How long is this going to take?"

Max opened the gear bag and pulled out his rig. "Oh, maybe twenty minutes. This will be the crash course."

"That is a pretty poor choice of words."

"You are quite right. This will be a condensed version of a couple of important things. Now don't laugh at me, okay?" He slipped into his harness and laid on the floor. He arched his back and lifted his arms and legs off the floor. "I kid you not. Practice holding this arch at least ten seconds. Pelvis and belly button forward. Tighten the gluts." Max balanced on his pelvis to a count of twenty. "You have to be able to produce a hard arch when you go through the door. The plane is moving through the air at ninety or one hundred miles and hour, so that is how hard the wind blast will hit you. There is a second reason. After five seconds this hard arch will put you face to earth and it will keep you there. If you do this you can freefall side by side with other skydivers. On every skydive, you have to work on matching fall rates and staying even with the other jumpers in your group."

He demonstrated the following movements while arched on his pelvis. "Pull your hands closer to the shoulders, if you need to fall a bit faster. Move them out, and you will fall a little bit slower. If your knees are bent and your hands are out in front of you, then you will slide backwards away from everyone. If you need to move forward, point your legs and toes straight and pull your hands in to your shoulders."

Max arched again. His elbows remained in the same place but he pointed his forearms to the floor. His fingers touched the floor. "This is a hand track. Believe it or not, it will scoot you forward. I would drop the hands a little lower, but the floor is in the way. There are several ways to turn or spin. Leg turns are fun." He bent his left knee so his foot was straight up in the air. "This will turn you to the right. Easy, huh? Most people throw an elbow. He threw his right elbow to his side. You can also throw your hand to your back pocket and the inertia from the sweep of your arm, if you do it fast enough, will spin you like a top. That one is called a salute turn."

He stood up. "You can practice the arch while you are standing up. Try it on one foot. Always count out at least ten seconds, and then wave off, deploy, and check your canopy for damage."

"If you break your arch when you jump out the door, the wind will flip you and spin you. When you reach fifty miles an hour or more in freefall, the wind will flip you, and spin you violently, if you break your arch. You must practice the arch. Eventually, it will become automatic to you. Your canopy emergency procedures have to be automatic responses. You do not have time in the air to try to remember what you read or practiced. It is all in the information manual. You have to memorize it and you must provide the correct response. It will save your life. If you don't know the correct response, you might have a short skydiving career. Your instructors will test you on everything. So, practice with this gear. Visualize all of the canopy malfunctions, so that you can deal with them. I am going to leave this parachute with you so that you will have one for practice. You should also learn how to pack the parachute. When you get a chance, open it up. Spread it out and do a four line check and S fold the canopy. Now if you can spare ten more minutes I will be finished and on my way."

"Okay, no problem"

"When you look for your pilot chute, hold your arch. Don't move your body. Just tip your head until you can see the handle. Pull the pilot chute and throw it far away from you. Do not hang on to it. What is next? Check canopy. You must grab the steering toggles and pull them out of the velcro keepers. Look at the canopy for rips and tears, especially when it is used gear. If the canopy is all balled up and a sniveling mess or if it has big rips in it, then you have to pull the red cut away handle and get rid of it. If you don't, then the tears will get bigger, and you will have no canopy by the time you reach the ground. You may still be going to the earth at eighty or ninety miles an hour, feet first, with a messed up canopy." Max began to fly his imaginary canopy around Cheryl's apartment much to her laughter.

"There are two concepts for you to remember. One is your transition and the second is your laundry list. The laundry list is all of the planned maneuvers on your skydive. The transition is everything associated with leaving the plane and reaching a stable face to earth position. You have to pick out your heading and do your circle of awareness. I am going to use your furniture to demonstrate." Max stood on her seven foot long naugahyde sofa. "This is a beauty, truly a collector's item. It must have really set you back."

"Twenty five dollars and a yelling contest at a yard sale."

"Okay. Here I am in the door, which happens to be a passenger side cargo door. I am terrified and I am kneeling. The left knee is on the floor of the plane, and the right foot is on the edge of the door. I am going to push off with the right leg to go out the door. First, I have to locate the spot of ground that the plane is flying over. To find the position of the plane over the ground, you look to the propeller of the plane, and then you look past the end of the wing, to the horizon. You can use the wing tip if the plane is level. From that point, drop your head straight to the ground, and you will see the location of your plane over the ground. Now you can direct the pilot to your exit point.

Max gave her a warm smile. "Now we need to talk about two concepts that will separate you from the rest of the crowd. These two concepts will reduce your fear and keep you on a healthy path to improve your performance and advance you to the next level. When you look at the end of the wing tip, two words will come to your mind. They are transition and laundry list. They will remind you of all the things you are supposed to do and those things will get your brain in gear. The uncertainty and doubt will still be there, but not to the great degree that it was on your tandem jump."

Max smiled again. "Once again, look at the wing tip, and tell yourself that you are going to transition through the door, to a stable face to earth hard arch. As you go out the door, you can actually review your laundry list. It will keep your mind full, and it will keep you thinking about the maneuvers that you have to do. Everyone has there own technique to induce this level of consciousness. The wing tip is a little bit late to induce the mental exercise, but it works."

Cheryl was smiling at Max. He continued. "So when you put it all together to practice, it goes like this. Head outside the door. Look to the airplane nose, up to the end of the wing, and drop your head a full ninety degrees, straight down to the ground. Give the correction to your exit point to the pilot. Corrections are expressed in degrees of the three hundred sixty degree circle. Think transition and laundry list. Begin your count. Rock back on 'Set.' Roll forward and push off through the door on 'Go.'" Max moved forward. He stepped of the couch and hit his arch while standing. "When you go through the door you want a hard arch. Keep your hands in close to your shoulders and your heels up on your fanny. Head back." At five thousand he laid down on the floor. He counted to ten and then gave the wave off signal and pulled his imaginary chute.

"Now, the chute will stand you up, and then you want to check your canopy. One more thing. You have to rehearse these movements with the thought sequence. If you just memorize the movements, you will not be able to produce the motions when it is time to perform them. You have to understand this condition. You will think that you know what to do, but the actions, in the correct sequence, will not happen. It has to be automatic."

"Okay, Max. I've got it. That will give me plenty to work on. Thank you for taking the time."

"My pleasure. I am going to walk back. You have a great skydive and don't forget to smile." They said their goodbyes and Max stepped down the stairs for home. He knew his time had not been wasted.

CHAPTER FIFTEEN

Cheryl turned off the interstate and drove for the parking lot at Fort Collins airport. She parked the car and stared straight ahead. Twelve thousand foot Long's Peak stood in the distant snow capped mountain range against a brilliant blue morning sky. She carried Max's gear bag to the loft. Karen was sorting through student videos in the tiny classroom. "You know, Cheryl. I am going to skip these videos. You can watch them later. Let's get some quality one on one training this morning."

"That sounds good to me."

"Has Max been working with you at all?"

"We practiced together Thursday during lunch. We have been concentrating on the no contact door dive. He told me that you would have a different approach for the first three jumps. He told me that I would be a floater outside the aircraft on exit."

"Yes, we are going to be floaters on exit. Did you talk about that?"

"He explained the concept and we walked through it. He told me you have to be in the plane or the mock up to understand the footwork."

"You know ground practice will accelerate your learning and improve your performance, especially at the beginning. So that is what we are going to do today. Let's begin over at the layout of the airport on the table in the corner. This is how the airport will look when you are under canopy." At the layout they talked about spotting and the obvious ground reference points around the airport. They talked about canopy approach around the airport and how to set up for the textbook student landing pattern. They talked about the dynamics of the canopy, how to steer it, how to slow down, how to brake, and how to land. They discussed airplane emergencies and canopy emergencies.

"Let's take a short break and then we will meet up in the hangar at the hanging harness for your torture session."

Karen strapped Cheryl into the hanging harness to practice the canopy emergencies and the cut away. Cheryl went in to the arch and count. She was suspended about a foot over a big foam cushion. Karen held laminated posters depicting tangled suspension lines, line twists, bag lock, blue sky, rapidly deteriorating canopies and a good canopy. The motion exercise helped to connect the eye and mind to interpret the problem and provide the correct solution. It released the student from the harness system when the red cutaway handle was pulled. Cheryl landed safely on the foam cushion several times before the exercise was over. The red cutaway handle was in her right hand and the reserve handle was in her left.

"What do you think of that action, Cheryl?"

"I think the harness is great training. You actually feel the resistance when you pull the handles. You actually feel the sensation of falling when you cut the canopy away. It is good mental preparation. You realize that your gear works for you before you go out the door. It gives you some mental comfort. You realize that, yes, the gear does work. And you realize that, yes, I have a reserve parachute in case something goes wrong. You know, that kind of helps me inflate my comfort factor." They shared laughter.

"You are right on all observations. It greatly increases the likelihood that the student will initiate the correct steps to get a canopy open without hesitation."

"It does make you stop and think about what is going on. And it does require you to actually perform the cut away instead of just dreaming about it. It is a great teaching aid."

After the hanging harness, they moved to a small platform two feet off the ground, where they practiced the parachute landing fall. Cheryl performed the correct techniques for getting her feet on the ground, along with the recommended body roll.

Karen was pleased with Cheryl's progress and knowledge. She had the ability to produce the correct responses without having to think about them. She was serious. She was going to be the next new woman at Skies West. Instead of videos, Karen continued the hands on training to give Cheryl all of the special attention she could handle. Just before lunch, they donned their parachutes and moved to the mock up. It was an actual Cessna 206 fuselage that had given up the ghost years ago. The cargo door was on the passenger side.

"Cheryl, pay attention to the hand hold bar that stretches across the top of the door."

"Is this our plane? What happened to the wings and the engine?"

"Okay funny girl, climb aboard. This mock up will give you an idea of what it is like to shuffle around in a small plane, while everyone is trying to get to the door as fast as they can." They practiced the actual motions of moving around to get to the door and get the door open. They practiced moving around to get outside the door. Cheryl found out that moving in a crouch, with a parachute on her back, required a little bit of thought and extra effort.

Karen reminded Cheryl of the things she experienced in her tandem jump. "If all of your muscles are tight and immovable, then you must consciously force yourself to relax. Keep breathing. Wiggle your fingers and your toes. Mentally focus on all of the goals of your jump." They rehearsed the arch and the transition.

"Your heart will be pounding in your throat. It will sound like it is right next to your ear drum. It is because you have just done something really stupid. You have just jumped out of a good airplane. It is against every instinct in your mind and body. You will have to force yourself to go out the door and take the floater position. Once you are in free fall, don't fight it. Just let it happen. Take in all of the sights and sounds, so you become accustomed to the sensations of freefall, and your body position. Keep running that laundry list of maneuvers and objectives through your head. Execute them when it is time. Believe it or not, if your mind is occupied, then your fear and anxiety will subside."

"Cheryl, your first three accelerated freefall jumps are going to be from the floater position. You watched a couple of floaters on your observer ride, remember?"

"They moved fast and they were all business."

"That's right. This maneuver is not as easy as it looks. I will walk through it first. Afterwards it will be your turn to practice. There are three or four things to do here all at once to make it work. You have to have a little bit of momentum to get your body out the door into the wind blast." Karen talked as she walked through the drill. "Place your left hand above the door on the inside to keep from falling out. Reach outside and up for the bar with your right hand. It's there. You can't see it from inside. You have to find it with your hand. You need a tight grip here or the wind blast will blow you off the plane. Try to visualize a good choke hold on Max with your right hand. Next, you have to duck your head through the door and spin at the same time that you pull your body outside and up. Your left hand has to grip the bar as soon as possible for balance and to help hold your body to the plane. Once you have both hands on the bar, you can get your feet where you want them and be comfortable for about half a second. Next, the count will be given. On 'Set' pull yourself to the door and lift your right knee. On 'Go' kick your right leg back behind you. Spin on your left foot, and arch into the wind blast. Point your belly button to the propeller. Here is what it looks like." Karen demonstrated again.

"Got that Cheryl? Okay, it is your turn."

Cheryl found the bar and slowly pulled herself out side. She teetered a little bit. She had to shuffle her feet a little bit. She almost fell off, but finally she got both hands on the bar. "This is not easy. You kind of have to catch yourself, as you are falling outside, backwards."

"That's right. Your right arm has to be ready to hold your weight until you get your left hand on the bar to help hold all of your weight. It takes some practice. It is an acrobatic move. Use a good pull with your right arm to help you spin. Kick your right knee forward, but not too hard. That will give you a little momentum to help you spin. You have to get your left hand on the bar as soon as possible so you don't slip off. So think about it for a minute. Take your time and do a couple of more. Once you get the hang of it, a little forward body momentum with that right leg, as you spin and pull, will help. Keep it slow and smooth. Find the rhythm and then you can speed it up."

Cheryl did three more.

"Good enough for now. You understand the technique, so you can practice later on. Now, here is the scenario on the exit for the three of us. Steve will be front float. I am going to be Steve for a couple of exits. You follow him out the door. Ready?"

"Okay."

"Here we go." Karen took the front float position. Cheryl followed her out and took the middle float position. Karen held the bar and grabbed Cheryl's harness with her left hand. "Here we go with the count in unison. Give a slight head nod on 'Ready.' On 'Set,' pull yourself to the door, and lift your right knee. You will kick it back behind you and spin when you turn to the wind blast. Now, kick out and spin on 'Go!'" They stepped down from the mock up. "Face into the wind blast with your hard arch. Present your Elvis Pelvis to the wind blast. Remember, ninety miles an hour is a small tornado. That's right, Cheryl. Good arch. You may see a brief flash of airplane."

"Karen, this floater position is going to have my heart pounding. Let's practice that a couple of more times all the way through."

"That's the spirit, Cheryl. What happens on this exit is that Steve and I leave just an instant before you do. His move into the wind literally peels us off the side of the plane as a group. You got that?"

"Yes. Make every effort to go as a group, and I should not be surprised when I feel some tugs on my harness."

"Absolutely correct. It can be smooth as silk if we leave together. And remember, the anxiety level is very high on jump run. But once you start thinking about getting to your float position, you will have so much on your mind that you will forget that you are at ten thousand feet in the air without a ladder. Once you have your A license and become an intermediate jumper you will be looking forward to all of the fun you will have on your skydives. Now remember, remember, remember, no matter how scared you are, release your grip on 'Go.' If you do not, then Steve will literally pull you free, and it will hurt! Before we take a break here, let's go over the spotting one more time." They practiced spotting. One last time, they practiced the exit and they picked a heading once the transition was complete. Karen commended Cheryl on her performance. She was more than ready. She had advanced. She was confident, alert, and knowledgeable.

"What do you think, Cheryl? Are you ready?"

"I am really anxious to get this over."

"All you need now is a couple of jumps to put everything together. Let's break for lunch and we will meet back here with Steve at twelve."

Cheryl watched her instructors approach. Steve was wearing a gray T shirt and black bermuda shorts. He was tall, tan, and muscular. His hair was short and black. His brown eyes were wide apart. He had a square jaw and he was easy on the eyes. Hopefully, he was as knowledgeable as he was good looking, though looks can be misleading. She hoped for the best.

"Cheryl, Karen tells me that you are ready for your first jump."

"That's right, Steve. I am ready. Throw me out of the plane and let's get it over with. The suspense is killing me."

"Alright, we are almost there. We are going to hit the high points very quickly one more time. This will take less than twenty minutes. Are you ready?"

"I'm waiting on you."

"That's the spirit, Cheryl. The first three jumps are basically the same, and there is a reason. They give you time to gain confidence with the parachute gear and the airplane. They give you time to become comfortable with your transition to a stable face to earth arch. They give you time to work on your skydiving ability, and to match fall rates with your instructors. Your knowledge, and your ability, and your mental awareness will continue to grow, and it will enable you to overcome the fears of the unknown that we all feel in our first three jumps. These jumps are important. You pay big money here for three minutes of air time. Take it very serious. This is the foundation for your growth and your student progression all the way to your A license. We expect your skills and your flying ability to improve with every skydive. That is our goal."

Cheryl looked Steve straight in the eye and deadpanned, "Okay! Good pep talk Steve. Can we go now?"

Karen belly laughed. "Can it, Karen. What we are looking for on jumps one, two, and three is a good, stable, face to earth body position. We will be watching for mental awareness. We need to see you relax and be in control."

Cheryl interrupted again. "My bladder is going to relax pretty soon if we do not get going."

Karen laughed again. "Steve, I think Max is behind this."

"Okay everybody. One more interruption and this class is over. There are six objectives on this jump. After we exit the airplane and make the transition you must pick out your heading. Pick an object on the ground that you can easily refer to throughout your skydive. It will let you know if you are falling straight to the ground, or if you are spinning in the air. If you are spinning, then your arms or legs are too stiff. You will be checking your circle of awareness, your COA, after every maneuver. You have to perform three practice deployments of your pilot chute. In the remaining time, relax and enjoy the rest of the free fall. Work on your arm and leg positions and your arch. Wave off is at five thousand five hundred feet above ground level. Do you know what backsliding is?"

"If you are head and shoulders up, you will slide backwards away from everyone. If you are head and shoulders down, you will slide forward into everyone."

Karen gave Steve a steely look. "I told you."

"Okay, let's check the hand signals." End of thumb and end of fingers touching is the circle of awareness. Open and close the circle of awareness three times means you are potato chipping, so kick your feet together and relax. A victory sign formed with the first two fingers means you are backsliding. Extend your legs six inches and leave them there. A victory sign with the fingers curled means that you are moving forward. Retract your legs slightly or bend your knees slightly. The fist means practice deployment, and when I point the index finger, it means throw your pilot chute. Let's suit up and meet at the mock up. We are going to practice the exit until we get it right."

Cheryl wore a clean white jumpsuit from the gear rental. Steve and Karen wore tailored, light yellow jumpsuits. They rehearsed three exits. The first one was slow. The second was better. The third one was good.

"Alright, Cheryl, for these first three jumps you can practice your emergency procedures on the ground. Do not think about them when you are in the plane. We want you relaxed and ready to run out the door. By all means it is okay to run your laundry list through your head. Let's do one more dirt dive from the mock up with all of the maneuvers. Pay attention."

"Relax. Keep breathing. You will hear the engine fade away. You may hear Karen shout at me. Rub your fingers together and wiggle your toes. Remember, you win by the hard arch on exit. Head back, belly button and pelvis forward. Elbows to your sides so you don't flip or roll. You want to snap into it. You will feel off balance because your feet are not on the ground. Let it go. You must trust your arch. You have experienced the sensory overload, but it will still be there for a couple of more jumps. Leave your brain on, and remember everything. The strange tingling sensation will be the adrenaline. Do not fight any of this. Accept it like you are the world's greatest sinner on your way to confession. Just let it happen. Just like your first good orgasm."

"Steve! I warn you!"

"The thing to feel is your arch. Hit the arch and hold it as you buffet through the air stream, and as you begin to transition face to earth. Your body will loose the forward momentum from the airplane and gravity will take over. At count five thousand you will rotate face to earth. On seven thousand you will really pick up speed. The air seems to give you support and you can relax your muscle tension just a tiny bit. Change your count to thousand seven, relax eight, relax nine. If you are too rigid and tense at this point, then you will potato chip and bounce around. What would you do if you are bouncing?"

"Kick my feet together and rub my fingers together."

"What is your first objective?"

"Stable body position within ten seconds."

"And pick out your . . ."

"Heading and do the circle of awareness check."

"Good. When you finish your COAs click your heels and rub your fingers together to remind you to relax. Next you have three practice deployments. Your count should be 'Arch, reach, and touch.' Make eye contact with the handle." Cheryl did so. "Hold that arch. Do not move a muscle. Move your chin slightly to your collar bone and look for the handle out of the corner of your eye. There is a tendency to make an exaggerated head movement and bend at the waist. If you break your arch what will happen?"

"I will tumble to the earth and splatter like a water melon."

"Yes, you will. Before you can snap your finger you will be tumbling non stop until you regain your arch. What is next?"

"The second circle of awareness check."

"Good. If we have altitude, and you are not bouncing, Karen and I will release our shoulder grips on your sleeve piping. Stay relaxed like you fell face first onto a water bed. We will remind you of deployment at six thousand. Do your wave off then.

No pressure, Cheryl. If you mess it up you have to give me ten kisses."

"Damn it Steve!" Karen feigned anger. "You promised me you wouldn't say that." She winked at Cheryl and said, "Just like a guy! Right Cheryl? Huh? A big sex machine!"

Cheryl laughed and did her wave off. "Next, after I throw the pilot chute, is check canopy."

"There is no wind today. You are on a large canopy so there should be no problem. Increase the distance of your landing pattern, or use your breaks more to lose altitude. Just this one time, Karen and I will set up in a textbook landing approach. You can follow us to the landing area, but it is up to you to do your landing. Your canopy will be moving at twenty miles an hour. There will be ground crew with a bull horn to assist you. If you do not slow down, then you will have to PLF. It is feet and knees together, and elbows at your sides. Hot! Eye on horizon. One leg. Tension or resistance in your legs as you strike the ground. Once your feet touch, do a slight twist so that the side of your knee, thigh, and fanny hit next as you complete your roll. If you are completely taken by surprise, you can use the expedient landing that Karen used last weekend. Feet, knees, hands and face.

"Awwww. You big galoot."

"I saw that one. She burned in big time."

"At one thousand feet above the ground, face into the wind and do two flares to get you warmed up for the landing. What are you going to do before you set up for your textbook landing approach?"

"Check the wind socks to make certain the wind has not changed."

"Okay, Cheryl, show me the hand signals, and then we will take a short break for the bathroom and some water."

Cheryl gave a sideways piece sign with two straight fingers. "Legs straight because I am back sliding." She went palm up with the peace sign and curled the two fingers. "Bend the knees a little bit because I am moving forward." She touched thumb and fingers to form a circle. "Circle of awareness and altitude check." She made a fist. "Practice pull."

"Good. Stay fired up. The plane will be here soon. Let's break for ten minutes."

Cheryl took her rig off. She sat in the grass packing area beside the hanger. Light fluffy clouds passed lazily overhead about six thousand feet above the ground. In the distance above the mountains they seemed to be pressed together into a solid white ribbon on the horizon. She thought of Max working I lift. She wondered if he was thinking about her skydive. He was going to pick up a ski guest pass for her. The winds were calm. No dark clouds in the distant sky. She shuddered. A small tremor of fear ran through her body. It was the third one today. She was scared, but she was anxious to go through the door on her own. She knew she would be safe.

Cheryl reached into her carry all bag for her water bottle. She would be on her own and there would be two incredible jumpers with her every second of the jump. She could pass out and they would get her chute open.

They could do a canopy stack and get her to the landing area. Cheryl could swear Max was thinking of her at this very second, wishing her well. Her feelings were heightened. What a great feeling that someone cares for you or is cheering you on. A smile came over her face. Thank you, Max. I am going to love you or hate you for this. What would he say to me? "Have fun, Cheryl. Enjoy the ride. Don't forget to smile." She hoped that her jump would be good. She was ready to do the laundry list.

The 206 Cessna pulled up twenty yards away.

"Cheryl, let's go. Somewhere around eight or nine thousand feet, run your laundry list."

"When are we going to start moving for the door?"

"I plan to have helmet and goggles on at ninety five hundred and the pilot will give the signal at jump run. Just like rehersal, Karen is going to spot this one. Follow me out the door. Get to your float position as fast as you can. When we shake your harness, that is the signal to start your count. The wind will be cold and brutal. Got your gloves?"

"Yes."

"Anything on your mind?"

"A good jump. I hope to make your job easy. I ain't skeert, but I got the hee bee gee bees."

"This is your first jump. We do not expect you to look for a spot or look down for that matter. When you go out the door to float, think transition and laundry list. You are a winner, Cheryl. The pilot is waiting." The little plane used less than one fourth of the runway. It was just the pilot and the three of them. On jump run Karen and Steve rolled up the fabric door together. Puffs of breath were clearly visible. Cheryl felt her chest tighten and her stomach did flip flops, but it was all gone in the same instant as she focused on the motions she had rehearsed. She relaxed. She knew when she saw the edge of the wing that she would transition from the plane in a beautiful hard arch, without any hesitation.

Goose bumps covered her body. She forced herself mentally to go through with the jump. No performance anxiety here. Above the incredible noise of the engine ten feet away, and the ninety mile an hour rush of air, the two jumpmasters focused on Cheryl like elephants balanced on a hat pin. Karen quickly sized the DZ with her calibrated eye ball and gave the correction, "Twenty right." A couple of seconds later she yelled, **"Straight."**

Cheryl looked at the end of the wing. It was still there. She was thinking now. The fear passed away as her mind became conscious and focused to perform.

Steve watched Cheryl the entire time. "Ok, Cheryl. Get ready."

Karen yelled, **"Cut!** Go get 'em Cheryl!"

Steve spun through the door to front float. Cheryl and Karen shadowed him in less than a second. She felt the instructors grab her harness. She made quick eye contact with both and they shook her harness. She tipped her head back on **"Ready!"** All three pulled to the plane on "**Set!**" They kicked out to the wind on **"Go!"** Cheryl was head back and hips forward. Her arch was solid and smooth. Karen and Steve were right beside her like bees on honey. There were a few light bumps and tugs on her harness as the instructors worked for a good exit. Her heart was pounding. Her body tingled all over. It seemed forever. She was suspended in blue sky and she felt off balance. The airplane engine dopplered away. Cheryl was running the laundry list through her head. Heading, COA, three practice pulls. COA, body position stable face to earth. Wave off and throw the pilot chute. On five thousand the group rotated. The blue sky disappeared up past her forehead and the ground came up to her eyes from her chest. Wow! Talk about visual stimulation! On seven thousand their freefall picked up sixty miles an hour in the next three seconds. The acceleration was incredible. **Yahoo!** She felt the increase as a rush of air against her torso, arms, and legs. Relax eight, relax nine. She picked a heading and performed her circle of awareness.

She was bouncing around a little. The wind tried to peel off her jumpsuit. She was potato chipping and straining to find the right muscle tension for her arms and legs. She finally gave up and kicked her heels together. She relaxed and melted into the oncoming rush of wind pelvis first. Relax and enjoy. She performed another COA. She looked at the sky, the heading, the jumpmasters and her altimeter. Steve's fist appeared. The hand signal for three practice pulls. She performed her move smoothly and slowly three times. Look, reach, and touch. She barely moved her head. Steve's thumb touched his joined fingers three times. Cheryl kicked her heels together and rubbed her fingers.

Karen and Steve kept their grips on Cheryl's leg straps. They released the shoulder grips and Cheryl beamed satisfaction. Her arch became comfortable in the rush of wind. The jumpmasters nodded and released the leg strap grips. Cheryl was lively and aware. She spread her arms away from her body to slow down and she brought them back to her shoulders to speed up. They were able to match fall rates. She grinned at the funny winkled faces of her jumpmasters. Smiles all around. They went through six grand at one hundred twenty miles an hour.

Steve gripped her leg strap again and he pointed his index finger. Cheryl waved off. She moved her left hand to her helmet. At the same time her right hand went to her hip. She moved her chin to the right shoulder. All other muscles in her body remained perfectly still. She watched her hand make contact with the pilot chute handle. She pulled her pilot chute out and threw it away from her. She did it faster than any hired gunslinger in a spaghetti western. It felt good to get the pilot chute out. Maybe she would make it through the jump. She felt tugs on her harness as the parachute inflation system reacted to do its job. The risers grabbed her shoulders and yanked her up to a standing position. It was a jolt that left a bit of saliva on her goggles. Her chin went to her chest and the altimeter on her chest strap right in front of her eyes read 4900 feet.

Wow! That kind of stretched her out. It opened. She was safe. She was scared to look up, but she knew it was a requirement. She felt out of balance because her feet were not on the ground. All of her muscles tightened. She shivered. Her eyes followed her hands up the back risers for her steering toggles. From there, her eyes went to the canopy. She shouted, "Thank you Jesus!" It is always good to pay your respects any time you have been saved. She released the toggles for steering and braking. She put the canopy in full brakes. She looked up and inventoried her canopy for any damage. She watched the canopy as she turned to the right and back to the left. No tears or tangles. Her slider was not quite to the risers. She pulled her toggles to her chest three times and the slider dropped down to the top of the risers.

Here she sat. Four thousand feet above the earth in a parachute harness. She eyed the far horizon. She looked up at her canopy. As her eyes looked up her shoulders and spine moved backward while her feet moved out in front of her. Her brain cued her that she was falling over backward. Her muscles twitched again. The leftover fear caused her muscles to involuntarily tighten up. She checked her canopy again as she pushed the toggles past her waist. The canopy stopped, but her momentum swung her forward. Yikes! She felt as if she was standing in mid air. The muscles in her back between her shoulder blades seized. She was frozen with fear. She felt like she had fallen forward out of the swing seat. She visually checked the metal snaps on her leg straps to make certain they were secure. At that instant, she realized that parachute systems are remarkably safe and well constructed.

Karen stayed to the side and above Cheryl to watch her complete the canopy checks. Cheryl buried a toggle and spiraled her canopy. The spin accelerated and threw her to the side, out from underneath the canopy. Woah! She stopped and gazed at the mountain horizon to soak in some magnificence. This is crazy! Here I am sitting in a harness with a parachute overhead three thousand five hundred feet in the air. What in the hell am I doing? It was then that she saw Karen cut underneath her in a beautiful, fast, sweeping turn. Wow!

"Stay away from me, you witch!" They chased each other back to the drop zone doing stalls, slow turns, and lots of spirals. The trio checked the wind sock at one thousand feet, and Steve led the way on the textbook landing approach. Karen was two hundred yards behind Steve and Cheryl was one hundred yards behind Karen. Cheryl could hear their words in her mind. "We will lead you back to the landing area, but the landing is up to you."

Mike Unruh was ground crew for the jump. He held a battery powered bull horn. As Cheryl turned on to the final approach to land, she recalled that this is one of the obvious places for injury. She could understand why. She felt drained and overjoyed, but she had to pull herself together for one more minute of forced concentration. Stay with it. Don't let up now. She checked the sky around her for more canopies. It is a safety check and a habit to be performed every time she would enter a landing area. She was pretty certain that no one else was around. Concentrate! She was moving across the ground much faster than she could run.

"Feet together!" Mike's voice reached her ears. She kicked her heels together to remind her to relax and be ready to hit and roll. She remembered the instructions. Look out to the front where you are going to land. Hot! Eyes in front to the horizon. Both legs together as one big spring. Legs with tension for recoil, but knees not locked up stiff.

"Half breaks!" Cheryl pulled her toggles to her armpits. Her canopy began to slow to half speed and she was closer to the ground, almost touching. Look in front, look in front!

"Flare!" Cheryl pushed her toggles past her waist. The canopy stopped. Her body momentum continued forward just like she was stepping out of a moving swing when she was a little girl at the playground. She felt a wave of warmth wash over her. She was on the ground. She pulled one toggle past her waist and spun to collapse the parachute so the wind could not pull her over backward.

They all cheered for her. "Yahoo, yahoo! Hooah, hooah! Way to go Cheryl!" Steve and Karen closed in on her to read the excitement in her face.

"How was it, Cheryl?"

"Your lips are quivering!"

"Cheryl how do you feel?"

"I feel like I could pick up a car."

They dropped the canopies on the packing mat outside the loft. Steve signed off on jump one in Cheryl's logbook. He wrote, mental awareness good. Arch good. Smooth exit and transition. Good heading. Performed all maneuvers. Some buffeting. Good pilot chute and canopy check. 30 meters from target. 1500 feet of no contact. Cheryl was elated. She was proud to see the good words. It boosted her ego and her self esteem.

"Alright Cheryl, share some of the feelings that you have about your first jump with us. Give us your observations."

"Mental awareness. The laundry list. I looked at the edge of the wing and my mind was totally blank. I was numb with fear. My muscles twitched. I knew there was something that I was supposed to remember. Transition was the first word in my mind. It is unbelievable. I thought about the laundry list and the fear went away. I am actually thinking about the job at hand. Nothing is automatic yet, but I am learning that I can deal with the fear and anxiety. My mind is receptive to this. My body is still a little slow. On the observer ride I was scared spitless. When you released shoulder grips I had a better position to the wind. Is it possible to think of two laundry lists at the same time?"

"Good question. It is possible when everything is comfortable and automatic. Today you accepted the threats and you dealt with them. You forced yourself to go out the door. You remembered your laundry list. You are learning how to perform a calculated risk in the midst of fear and uncertainty . . ."

Karen interrupted, "And you are doing great! Now, let's get over to Bev's and celebrate. We want the beer and the pizza you owe us."

"I just have too much right now. I promise I will make it next time. I know that I am supposed to buy the beer. You all want me to get you drunk as skunks. I can't do it this weekend. I have to get back while the weather is holding. I will do it next time, I promise." Cheryl stowed her carry all bag and other things in her car. In Denver she stopped at a grocery store and bought the usual sandwich material. Then she pointed the Swinger up I 70 and headed for home. She wanted to get to Leadville before nightfall. She encountered a late afternoon spring snow storm at Idaho Springs. The big fluffy flakes of snow were melting as fast as they hit the warm highway. She might make it to Leadville before there was a serious accumulation of snow on the ground.

Dusk had fallen at Georgetown. Cheryl made it through the Eisenhower tunnel and down to the six thousand foot Summit County valley floor. Several snowplows were on the highway traveling both directions. She coasted down the west side of the Continental Divide past Silverthorne to Frisco. The snowfall was plentiful and it reduced the visibility. The thick cloud cover turned the light of day into the dark of night. Night time had closed in on the mountains. She was rolling into Ten Mile Canyon when she noticed something unusual. There was hardly any traffic from Vail. As Cheryl drove through Ten Mile Canyon, a state patrol car passed by her with the red lights swirling. This was not a good sign. She cleared Ten Mile Canyon, and she watched for the turnoff to Leadville. Vail pass must be closed. As she drove out of the last turn she saw the flashing lights of the state trooper parked broadside in the middle of the interstate just in front of the Copper Mountain and Leadville turnoff. Cheryl took the off ramp uphill and she crossed the interstate on the overpass road. Two pick up trucks were leaving the A lift parking lot at Copper Mountain. She could barely see the expert runs. The A and B lift ran twenty five hundred feet up the steep side of the mountain. Priceless. Man, oh man, talk about skiing. Few resorts in the world equaled what Copper Mountain could dish out.

She was now in another narrow canyon at about six thousand feet in elevation. She began the climb to the ten thousand foot Fremont Pass. Cheryl was on a narrow two lane road with no guard rail. The road was crowned and dangerous to drive whenever ice and snow were added to the equation. A gulch and river provided an emergency stop for run away cars that went over the shoulder of the road. The highway rose up to Fremont pass in a gentle, lazy, zigzag climb. She had a fifty minute drive to Leadville under the current conditions. Eighteen miles to the Climax mine and pass. Cheryl maintained forty five miles an hour. She wondered how soon the frantic tourists and commuters would be on her bumper. Five minutes later a pair of headlights on high beam glared into her rearview mirror from the last turn two hundred yards back. She let the first insane people pass her as the road was fairly straight. She put her foot lightly on the break pedal. She looked in her side view mirror for red tail light reflection on the road surface. There was a little flicker now and then. The road surface was still rough. She knew that as the temperature dropped, the moisture from the river would turn to glare ice on the highway. She forced herself to maintain the forty five mile per hour speed limit. Anything could happen.

A line of cars bumper to bumper were soon on her tail. They were all set up for their chain reaction. The road was fairly straight and two cars passed her. The idiot behind her could not see the curve coming up in front. He would never make it around the curve. She laughed at the thought. It would be great fun to watch him slide off into the gulch. What if he spun around in a circle and back into her uphill lane? Who would be laughing then? Cheryl flashed her brake lights at him. She watched him closely and when he pulled over in the other lane to pass, she did the same thing. He laid on his horn loud and long. He hit his brakes and slid on the icy road just slightly. Cheryl could tell because the headlights danced left to right in her mirror. A real lunatic. He dropped back, so that he would have more room to build speed, and pass her. Cheryl was not about to let this idiot endanger her life. She stepped on the gas and negotiated the curve. She recognized the up coming straight away as the glare ice stretch. She was just completing the curve at forty five miles an hour and she knew the sheet ice was forming. She thought she saw a flicker of red tail lights through the falling snow about two hundred yards up the road. Someone must be in front of her. She could see no headlight, but once they are covered with snow and ice, they barely illuminate. Now there was nothing. She blinked her eyes thinking she could be getting tired. Maybe she had squeezed her eyes too tight when she yawned.

The impatient driver behind her going to try again! She kept her foot on the gas, and with her left foot, she put a feather touch on the break pedal. It brought up her red tail lights. It caught him by surprise, and he hit his brakes too hard for the ice on the road. He was definitely an amateur. His headlights dipped and went into the side to side shimmy dance of the glare ice highway. He managed to stay on the road. Cheryl noticed that the car behind him had slowed to increase their safety distance. At least there was someone back there who had an ounce of sense.

Something was up ahead in front of her. She began to slow and pulled onto the centerline just as the guy was moving up to pass her for the third time. She saw a very dim light at the snow bank on the right side. This was no dream. A flash light? Some one in distress? Hikers? People stranded on the road? For an instant, it was a bright light again! What the . . . ? There it was again, brighter this time. Cheryl hit her horn loud and long. She had to stop. She lightly tapped her brakes to warn the cars behind her. The light ahead outlined an object on the shoulder. It looked like a boulder. Stop. Stop! It could be an avalanche and equipment attempting to clear the road. The light grew from the snow bank out two feet and it was brilliant. She held her ground on the centerline. It was the safest place to be right now. She carefully gripped the wheel like she was choking a rattle snake in each hand. Her tailgater braked and swerved back and forth and back and forth. Cheryl hoped that he pissed his pants. His horn blared again. The lunatic must be all of eighteen years of age.

Holy Shit! A car is broadside on the road! Her high beams faintly outlined the car. Cheryl applied break pressure slowly and evenly until the tires slipped. A car was in the ditch! The back bumper was sticking out into the uphill lane. One of the idiots had passed her earlier had slid headfirst into the ditch and buried the headlights into the snow bank. They were trying to push the black Chevrolet out of the drift and back on to the road. If they had left the doors open the interior lights might have provided an early warning of impending disaster. They were oblivious to the fact that the cars they had passed were right behind them. The car backed a couple of feet out of the snow bank and the bright light appeared. Then, it disappeared as the Chevy rolled back into the snow bank. She laid on her horn again and left her hand on it. What if they pushed it out of the ditch? Four feet off the left shoulder was a steep cliff. There was no guard rail. Oh! My God! They expected her to stop! She flashed the lights on and off, on and off, and on and off. Would the bozos get the message that she was going to pass them, or hit their lousy car? The driver fled the driver's seat. The interior light flashed on. *Now they figure out a warning system and it was by accident!*

She had to stay on the crown of the road even if she hit the Chevy. Screw them. She was going straight for their back bumper. She was at twenty miles and hour. She pumped her brakes a little deeper but to no avail. She left her foot on the brake pedal. The two suspects fled. Cheryl let up off the horn to prepare for impact. She realized she would have to go off the road to squeak by the Chevy. She steered into the downhill lane and her rear bumper began to slide slowly to the riverside edge of the road. She was ready for impact. Her brakes were buried. The wheels were not turning. The car was sliding forward on the glare ice. Lordy! She was slightly panicked. She felt her rib cage tighten.

The Swinger continued to slide forward on the mirrored surface of the glare ice at ten miles an hour. The left rear tire was almost off the highway. She might clear the Chevy. She was watching it all in slow motion. She could see the two offenders. They wore dark rain coats, down to mid calf. How gallant! How cool! Nice color selection, Cheryl thought bitterly. They stared at her as the Swinger slid past the rear bumper. She was sliding sideways now. The offenders would probably yell at her if she hit their beater. She lifted her right hand and flipped them the finger. One broke to run for cover when he figured out the other cars would not be able to stop.

Her speedometer read 0 miles an hour. Big as life, she was still sliding forward at an angle. She would touch the gas pedal as soon as she passed the Chevy bumper. Just a touch to try to move back to the centerline. She wished she could drive forward and pin the clowns into the snow bank so they would suffocate. Her back tires went off the road. She lightly touched gas pedal. Her tires spun. She pushed the pedal a little more. Gravel spit out from under her tires and the Swinger launched forward to the centerline at five miles an hour. She made herself release the death grip she had on the steering wheel. Some hasty corrections were needed to stay on the centerline. Just like sliding around the Food Town parking lot.

Unbelievable. She had no time to be scared. She had just slid sideways around an obstacle on a glare ice road. Her speed continued to build to ten miles an hour. She allowed her self a glance in the rear view mirror. She could see headlights pointing all different directions. She even saw red tail lights of cars off the road. Truly, it was the demolition derby finale. Cheryl was breathing regularly now. She was easy on the gas pedal. She was still on glare ice.

She had been able to detach herself from the danger at hand. She had made it because she had used her mind and stayed with the fiasco to find a solution. There was absolutely no logic to it. There was only reaction and anticipation. She refused to freeze or be hypnotized by fright. You just can't give up until you are past the danger and safe.

Geese, the highways were more dangerous that skydiving. She secretly hoped that some of the drivers would beat up the problem children. She could have lost her life back there if she had not deciphered the headlights as fast as she did. Now her anger raged. She just could not get over it. She needed to let it go and concentrate on the pass.

Twenty minutes later, she crested Fremont pass on the snow packed highway. She thought of all the miners who died of silicosis after working in the mines for three years. She thought of all the blind donkeys. Boy. The animal rights activists could have had a hey day with the blind donkeys. Seven pm and it was pitch black. The low clouds cut off the tops of the mountains. The big snow storm had set in. The fog was down to street level.

As she neared the north side of Leadville, an ambulance raced by in the other lane. Someone had been hurt in the glare ice incident. The ambulances from Copper and Frisco were probably at the scene by now. Copper had plenty of tow trucks. A few more twists and turns. A tow truck sped by in the other lane. The high mountain valley began to open and she drove on to Leadville. She was glad to be back. She was grateful to be alive. She wanted to share the skydive with Max. She wanted to get the plaster on her miner. She felt terrific.

Maybe she should avoid Max and see if he would come looking for her. Nah! That was left over shit from the last relation. No games here with Max. They were friends now. Best buddies. What should she say to him? Sorry I am late honey. All the teenagers wanted me to give them a ride in the Swinger. Then they wanted to park and neck for awhile. A light was on in the dining room. She parked beside the Meteor. Cheryl looked in the living room bay window. The floor was finished. She pounded on the door. Through the light mesh curtain she watched him fly down the stairs. She never felt so confident and good with someone before. How should she make her entrance?

Cheryl wondered if he was strong enough to lift her up. No time like now to find out. He opened the door and stepped back. Cheryl took two quick steps and jumped into him. She threw her arms around his neck and her legs around his waist. No problem here. She stared into his eyes and grinned at him.

"Oh, honey, you are alive! You didn't biff it. You look to be in perfect health. Did you give any kisses to some really ugly men today? I want one." Cheryl gave it no thought. She was breathing deep. She locked her lips to his and laid a hot one on him. Max turned in a slow circle while they kissed. He felt some rapidly building energy from the sudden physical encounter.

"Mmmmm."

"I passed my first jump with flying colors!"

"I knew you would. You are so competent and capable. You are so rough and domineering with your boyfriends. That's why I like you."

"Steve wrote glowing praise in my log book. No one ever wrote glowing praise about me."

"I was thinking about you today while I was bumping chairs. I figured your jump was after lunch around one or one thirty." Max leaned against the wall and continued to savor the contact and the warmth. He gazed at the fire in her eyes. What a lovely moment.

"I left the ground about one. I left the plane at twenty after. Karen said she was going to jumpmaster for me come hell or high water. They are going to try to keep me around." She waited for a response. "She promised she would get all of the guys lined up and that I would not have a dateless weekend for the next two years."

"Gosh, you don't have to tell me everything."

Cheryl licked his glasses. They both laughed. She slid to the floor. She squeezed him and crushed his face to her chest. She tried to break his nose and mess up his glasses.

"Can I stay right here for awhile? My neck really hurts. Could you do that again?"

"Maybe next month." Cheryl released him.

"Maybe next month." He mimicked her.

"I want to go to the Dollar and celebrate. I need to brush up on my pool game. They all went to Bev's pizza bar afterwards to shoot pizza and drink pool."

"Let's go. I want to check out the women's rest room. All the nurses were talking about it last weekend."

"I'm driving." They were out the door in two heartbeats. Max locked the door.

"Wow, the snow is pouring down. We are in the cloud."

Cheryl drove to the Dollar. Max dug into her carry all bag and found her logbook. "Wow, where did all of the tourists come from?"

"Vail pass is closed. It was a hell of a commute home. I will have to tell you about it."

The Dollar was still open. It would stay open until one am tonight once all the tourists found a motel and the bars. The nice lady with light brown hair was working in the saloon.

Max asked her, "What is one of those tasty drinks for women? Kind of a chocolate . . ."

"Your talkin' about a kahlua and cream, a brown cow. It has a great chocolaty taste."

"One of those and Early Times and seven. Make it a double in a large glass." Max gave her a ten. "Keep the change."

They went to the Leprechaun room which was a large open area rented for parties and special occasions. They sat the drinks on a table beside the pool table, and Max slipped into the girl's restroom. There on the wall for ten feet to the stalls was space filled with posters of half naked male models in various stages of disrobing. Some artistic interpretations using magic markers had been added to the denim that covered the genital areas. The eyes of every face had been scratched out. A large eye had been added to one forehead and Max laughed when he saw it. Cheryl had the table racked and waiting. She was anxious to see his facial expression. Her grin matched his!

"Isn't that hilarious?"

"Why are the eyes scratched out?"

"Lyin' eyes. Lyin' eyes, Max!"

"That's right, baby, that's right. Did you draw any of the extensions on those posters? There is some pretty big equipment on that wall." He gave her the enquiring evil eye. "You better practice your break. Any shots you want to shoot again, by all means, do so."

Cheryl sipped the poisonous brown cow. Her head cocked sideways and she made a small sip again. "Mmmm. This tastes good."

"Two should be plenty."

Cheryl stared at Max defiantly. "I have never had a big brother to protect me, so I will determine the number of drinks that I have tonight. Got that, old man?" His smile disappeared into a slight twist. Cheryl laughed at him. "It will be my decision. I have made my own for quite some time now." She broke the rack. One ball dropped in the corner pocket. Max opened the log book and read the entries.

"I really nailed the pilot chute on my first jump. Did I tell you that? I got fifteen hundred feet of no contact freefall."

"Fifteen hundred feet. You must be part eagle. You really had a great first jump. Good for you."

"Karen told me it would be a good idea if I got two jumps on the same day. It gives your level of confidence a boost. She says that all of your nerves are shot from the first jump and the second jump is calm and not so nerve wracking." Cheryl smiled and nodded her head to the corner pocket. One of the solids went in. Max was not surprised. His eye still had sympathy pains. He swore silently to himself. Sure you clown. You think you know all about this girl? You pile of cheap putty! Right now you are so blinded and infatuated you are like a little kid with a parent at the cotton candy stand. You make me sick.

"Karen told me to practice twice as much. She said some people think they can do it again because they did okay on the first jump. They do not practice at all and they mess up the second jump. They break their arch and they tell her that they don't know what went wrong. So, she writes in the log book that they did not practice and that they broke their arch. They get pissed and some of them do not come back. She will not jump master them after that."

"You better practice every week, no matter where you are. Please learn to pack your own chute. It has an extraordinary effect on calming the nerves. Never rush the pack job. You better be able to pack your own chute by your fourth or fifth jump. I am serious. Please do not graduate and then start asking people to pack your chute for you. That will drive your friends away and it could get you hurt. You never know if someone else is in a hurry. If they do a sloppy job, you just might have a canopy malfunction that will really leave you hanging. You are the one who gets the cutaway and the reserve ride. Then you have to pay for the reserve repack by a rigger. You haven't sold my rig yet have you?"

"Are you a little paranoid?"

"You know strong vindictive women turn me on. I love strong women. But, then again, I love it when you pout and sneer."

"Was your mother a strong woman?"

"No, she mostly looked at me and cried. She was an only child. Let's skip it for now. I want to enjoy the evening." This one bears watching. Man, oh man, can she set a trap. "Are you out to get my credit cards? That is what you're after, right? Is that all you want?"

Cheryl nodded. "Pretty close. Sometimes you seem devised."

"You mean devious. You are just trying to find something wrong with me, so you can kick me to the curb after you have used and abused me."

"There is plenty wrong with you. Sometimes I feel you are just not being genuine with me. You just pop off with the first thing that comes to your mind instead of giving me an honest, complete answer. My life and livelihood depend on honest answers."

"And as soon as you prove that I was intentionally dishonest, let me guess, off come the nuggets?" They laughed.

"You are fun to talk with, especially in such deep, meaningful conversation."

She sank an angled combination. Max knees grew weak. "I like the way you positioned your body when you were going to sink that ball. You have so much style and control. You make Tiger Woods look like he is stumbling around the golf course."

"Styling and profiling."

"That's right, baby."

"I nailed my plot chute so fast they couldn't believe it. It hit Steve's shoulder."

"Super. You do not want that thing around your arm or wrist. It will ruin your jump." They looked longingly at one another.

Cheryl confessed. "Max. This has all been so much fun. It is almost as if it is not actually happening to me."

"It is all a big dream, you know. You spend your whole life trying to make it happen. Some work at it more than others."

"Oh, Professor! I do know one thing for certain. You do make me laugh, and I love you for it."

"It was a dreary family. I started in childhood. I was the only one that could make my brothers and sisters laugh. Mom and Dad made them cry. I learned a couple of things from it. When you entertain people some are really selfish and expect you to do it all the time. Like you owe them something. I just hope you appreciate it. Hey, take it easy on that cow! You have to pace yourself." Max had the next shot. The cue ball careened off the rail and nicked the eight ball at an odd angle. It rolled into the side pocket. "Forfeit! Well, that is a relief. This game stresses me out."

"You need to practice more. I don't mean to change the subject, but do you think we could car pool to work?"

"You are asking me?"

"Right now, Max, and don't dilly dally. I do not like wishy washy men."

"You aren't going to wait for me to beg you?"

"I want an answer right now and I want to see your face. And, Max . . ."

"Yes?"

"Don't try to lie to me. I can read a lie."

"Thank you, Jesus!"

"I did say that when my canopy opened today." Cheryl laughed. "Lord! Talk about hanging around and watching the earth! Mass, let's get another drink." As he walked to the bar to put in the order, it occurred to him that he should ask her to move into 304. Why not? That was all he had thought about all week. Why wait? He returned with the drinks. Cheryl was on another practice game.

"Move in to Mac's house with me, Cheryl." It hit her like a freight train. "You pick out your area and put a crime scene tape around it. I will stay away and not bother you. There is an upstairs bedroom and a down stairs bedroom. There is only one bath. I won't bother you. You will have no rent to pay." Cheryl wanted to leap one hundred feet into the air.

"I really like you, Cheryl. Move in with me. Let's be roommates for awhile. You can always keep looking for your own place."

"Max! You are asking me?"

"You are too young to be deaf. You just want to hear me say it again. But I think that I would rather beg you to move in."

"Don't make a scene."

"I can move everything out of your apartment and you will be out before the end of the month. You can give your mean old landlady at least a week's notice. Let me have a key to your apartment and I can move all of your things Tuesday afternoon."

"Okay, okay. Enough, enough. Let's not ruin the evening." She still wanted to run some tests on him so it was a good idea not to start things rolling too soon. "But I will clue you in. I know one of the nurses might take a chance with you. They say your breath is a little rough, but you are a good catch." Cheryl snickered. "Look, Max, Everything is decent right now. Let's just leave it that way. Don't give me the rush job." Max was considerate. A girl could drop all defenses and her social arsenal of acquired protective measures and he would not take advantage. A girl could just relax and not worry because he would always ask her first, for anything. She would always be included and she could always have her own choice. "Let me think it over. I've had several better offers. Young men have actually promised to pay me to live with them. I can give you an answer in a week or two." His face registered shock and dismay. Then, after the message sank in, he laughed freely.

"Oh, that is a good one. You are really funny."

"It is you. Your bullshit is so contagious. That is why everybody likes you."

"I agree. I am almost irresistible in that department. Let's toast to 304." They toasted to sharing the house at 304 West Seventh.

"Let's figure it out Wednesday. We are carpooling, right?"

"I am going to drive the Meteor if I can get all of the virgins out of it."

"Five am, my place."

"Let's pack the parachute some night this week. If we don't, then you should take it to the DZ and have someone help you. It takes only fifteen minutes."

"You just keep pushing and nagging, don't you?"

"Hey! That's my line."

"I don't know yet. I might."

They called it a night.

CHAPTER SIXTEEN

Cheryl went to the classroom. There was no trace of a hard rock miner. There was no trace of a rugged or determined individual. He looked as if he had been standing in pigeon park for thirty years. For a sinister moment Cheryl decided that he might pass for "The Mummy." She also saw a snowman. The latex was dry as cactus in the desert. She was ecstatic. There was new hope and energy. She looked where his eyes should be and pointed a hard straight finger at him. "I am going to get you plastered today! Ha!"

Cheryl went to her locker for her tools. She was on the clock by eight. She was psyched up and ready for work. She had half a dozen sculptures to chase. Nash and Casey were waiting for her out on the foundry floor. Casey was an eight foot statue of some dude with a handle bar moustache and sideburns in a baseball uniform leaning on a baseball bat. Strike three! Cheryl did not like the concept at all. She had three ideas in her head that would be more desirable to the fans and the players at the ball parks. She said to herself. What a waste of metal. There was ceramic in the shoe laces and the pants. A moderate amount of air bubbles were scattered in the hair. The weld lines needed extra attention. Some statues put you in a good mood and kept you there. Working on them was a joy. Some statues were just bad ideas. You almost had to force yourself to work on them. She would certainly be glad when she finished working on this freeloader. Her mind wandered just for a second. She had to force herself to go out the door of the airplane. She did it. But was it really fun?

Nash Mendoza was leaning over Casey. The statue lay on a floor dolly face up. "Wha ta hey Cheryl." Nash stood. His bandanna was soaked and some perspiration from his forehead ran into his eyes.

"I was just wondering if the dremel in your hand was actually making contact with the man here."

"You will have to stand a little closer to me senorita."

"Hah! It is a trap."

"Hey, let me work on this guy."

"Nash, just going through the motions and faking work is more difficult than actually doing the work."

"I have the appearance of earning a paycheck, but right now I just can not concentrate and I do not want to score the metal."

"Migraine?"

"Ha!"

"Okay, Nash. You take the feet, legs and crotch area cause you know more about weenies than I do. I will work on the chest and head."

"All of a sudden I just started over heating."

"It is the onset of the flu, you big swine. Grab some aspirin from the break room. Molly should have some headache tablets."

"You are right senorita. How will I ever repay your kindness?"

She carefully pulled the player over to the welding area. A hole the size of a nickel needed to be filled in where the belt loop met the billow of the jersey. Some one or something broke a corner of the wax mold. It was still good enough for Marty to weld it to the other sections. He knew the imperfection could be mended by a good chaser. She found a piece of bronze in the scrap barrel and she plugged the hole. She had just set the welder's helmet back on the portable cart when Marty appeared. He had been almost an hour late this morning and Cheryl wanted to share her good mood with him.

"Big management meeting this morning Marty?"

His face had a dour look. "Why, good morning, Miss Pritchard. My, you are here so early for a change! Will this continue?"

"Ha! Good one. Maybe. Raise my pay another two hundred dollars. Gas has gone up, and it is not exactly a hop, skip, and a jump, for me to get to work."

"Write that request up for me, and leave it on my desk."

"The big mahogany one or the beat up metal table in the corner?" Marty had no office or desk. They dropped the conversation. It would continue later. He needed to get started physically and mentally. He returned to welding the kids, dog, and hose. Cheryl never wasted time guessing what worries he had besides the day's work. Marty checked on everyone. He did not want to be blamed for something that was left unfinished. He knew the capabilities of everyone and he knew the priorities of the projects at hand and the new projects starting up. He was proud of the creations the artists and the foundry produced for public display.

All Friday and throughout the weekend, the foundry had been blessed with Wes Culpepper. He sported a maroon beret. He wore a long sleeve khaki shirt and pants and a sleeveless artist jacket. Scalpel in hand, he slashed away on the bronco. By Monday morning he had put some serious sculpting all of the way around the horse and rider. Finishing touches were the order for Monday. He took of early, in the middle of the morning.

Midway through the morning, Marty strolled over to Cheryl and casually announced, "My wife has been nagging for us to visit her folks in California. She is not speaking to me." Her deadline passed through her mind.

Cheryl posed a question. "Did she lock her legs on you, Marty?"

Marty appeared momentarily startled. "She is ready to start the vacation this Wednesday."

"You mean she wants you to take her to California or else!" Cheryl couldn't keep a straight face. "Marty, I do not want to tell you how to run your life, but if I were you, I would establish the fact to your wife that you are the head of the house, and that you wear the thong in the family."

Marty laughed. He appreciated the humor. "Oh, sometimes you are such a vile woman."

"Thank you Marty. That is the nicest thing you have said to me in the last six months."

Lord. It was obvious that Marty was going to be gone for at least a week. Cheryl's head was swirling. "What are we going to do, Nash?"

"I guess it is going to get pretty busy around here. But do not worry, Cheryl. Everything will be fine. No need to jump to any contusions." Nash was right. She gradually settled down. They would survive without Marty. Production would continue. Someone else would do the welding. Soon she and Nash were chasing away on the miner. There was a need for her to conserve some energy for tonight. She moved off the foundry floor and down the hall to the break room for lunch. She searched the refrigerator for her plastic bag. Items had a way of rearranging themselves in the refrigerator during the day. Cheryl secured the plastic bag with her sprouts, provolone, and avocado. Today there was a small slice of turkey. Karen had insisted that she get some meat protein in her body to fight fatigue. After lunch, she looked in on the buckin' bronco for Mary. It stood all alone. Wes was no where to be seen.

Mary cut the overhead light off on the bronco to save a few dollars. "What do you say, Cheryl? Help me break down this scaffold and we can start work on your miner and the prairie people."

"When are you going to shim this buckaroo?"

"It will be soon. Gonna need some help on that. Let's get working on your miner. I'm just sitting back there feeling guilty about not helping you. I have no touch or finesse today."

"Shall we go find some plaster?"

"You bet. There is no sense in wasting time and we are still waiting for the new shims to be delivered." Nash heard the commotion and decided to lend a hand. They set the scaffold around the miner.

"Let's get to the shell room." Cheryl and Mary pulled two forty pound bags of plaster to the mixer. They filled half of the mix bowl with plaster powder and added water. They set a three by two by one foot metal pan on a floor dolly. They mixed up two bowls of plaster and the big pan was full. They pulled the dolly to the miner room and they were ready for business.

"Mary how long is it going to take for this to dry? Three days?"

"It is a big statue. Four days to be on the safe side."

"Okay, Mary. You are right. Not a problem."

"Cheryl, I need help with the bronco. I don't think we are going to make the deadline."

"You want it when?"

"That's right, baby, that's right. I have to get shims on it tomorrow. I will grab Nash, Cindy and Johnny. They are working good together. I am thinking latex on Wednesday."

"Okay, Mary I will be on your team. I owe you. I will keep your spirits up. So you are going to ride the bronco again, huh? Do you want to borrow my spurs?"

"Ha, ha, ha! Oh! That is good!"

"You were way overdue. We have not laughed since Thursday."

"Done deal. The shims are supposed to be here today. Bob got the sheet metal shop to make a thousand of them."

"We will get it done. Have no worries. So what is Marty dragging his feet for? He needs to get going."

"I don't know. He has been so vague. I told him to give us the dates and go. His wife is arranging all kinds of outings with the relatives."

"Mary, he was really funny this morning. He was hemming and hawing and all whimsical, like he really did not want to go and leave everybody hanging. So I asked him if he had finished packing his bags!"

"Ha! I'm going to tell him to leave now and that he gets seven days. By the time he gets back, there will be sections of bronze piled out the door."

"Good for you. Wear the bloomers in the family."

"Some days nobody wants to wear the bloomers."

"That is a problem if you have some responsibilities."

"We just got another project in. It is a jazz trio."

"I heard it was a quintet. Super! Who is the artist?"

"It was a referral. Someone I never heard of before. It's for the city of Saint Louis. It will make things crowded, but we like it that way and we certainly have the room. Bob called a couple of chasers from the Boulder Longmont foundry over the weekend and he found two that would be able to come up to help out part time. We don't want to dump every thing on you and Nash."

"Mighty kind of you Mary. Ordinarily It would not be a problem, but I have the miner hanging over my head. It might be good to get the names of a couple of welders while you are fishing around down there."

"Exactly. Not to worry. Let's get this plaster ready." They put on their disposable latex gloves. Mary had the bread pans to hold the plaster. Cheryl was on one scaffold and Mary was on the other. "Hear we are looking at this old go to hell hat again. It will not be too much longer before it is time for the patina, huh Cheryl?" They attacked the miner head and hat together. The latex surface was not slippery. It had a sticky feel to it. The plaster mix stuck to the coat of latex.

"It stays in place without slipping."

"I guess you understand the gravity of the situation. If the plaster is too thin or watery it will slide off. It has to be a thick consistency and just right." They worked together. Their hands were on each side of the head and down the neck to the shoulders. A hand full at a time had to be carefully placed against the hardened latex. The surface shape of the clay could be disfigured if the contact was too rough. The plaster would be applied evenly in each of the thirty two sections outlined by the metal shims.

"On these big statues, it is best to have two or three people working together. It keeps the flow going until the statue is finally covered. Less chance of deformity. One person might get tired, or might try to hurry, and the statue could end up with a pug nose. It sure is a good thing you made that big metal frame to hold all the weight on this guy." All of a sudden Mary started laughing. She stopped as if it was wrong or improper to laugh and covered her mouth. Cheryl gave her a strange look. Mary had a few spots of plaster on her work shirt from the mixing. She looked at Cheryl's quizzical face and burst out laughing again.

Cheryl inquired, "Are you going to keep me in suspense?"

"I remember one falling over!" Mary started hiccupping. Cheryl thought it was great to be able to share some laughs with the boss. "You should have seen it! This woman was bound and determined to get her project done and no one would help her. So she decided, come hell or high water, that she would do it herself. Aaaah, ha, ha, ha! She was so up tight! She was too slow and the plaster was drying in the bucket. She was mad. She lost her attention and balance, and fell on to the statue from a scaffold. The statue was pretty well smashed up. It kind of broke halfway into two pieces. Everybody ran outside of the building to laugh. She was pretty devastated. One of her boyfriends helped her up and they got the statue kind of back together. I think she had three boyfriends. They patched it back. It worked out okay. Then she went on vacation. She told us to call her when the rubber and plaster dried. Then she came in to work on the waxes."

"Speaking of waxes, Molly just about volunteered."

"I knew she would. There hasn't been any construction work this winter with the so called recession and all that we are in. Molly is a terrific person and a sweetheart. She would do it without the money just to help you. She thinks you are a young, blossoming artist, and by the way, I think so too."

"Good. Loan me some money."

An hour later they were past the arms. The big arms had proven difficult and time consuming. Cheryl watched Mary scoop the last bit of plaster out of the big metal pan. Finally, the pan was empty. A quick break was in order to stave off the hunger pains. They returned the dolly to the shell room. Cheryl returned with the sandwiches and her DVD player. She watched Mary mix up more plaster. The pan was filled and they were right back to the miner.

"Mary, why should I listen to a commercial radio when I can pick and choose my own music? Life is too short. Besides I am too worldly and soffissicated to listen to the nerds on commercial radio."

"Have you heard the guy in Breckinridge on the radio? The talk show host Biff America. He is funny! They are trying to get his program into Vail's station."

"Ha! Yes. It is good laughing with Biff. It has been a long time. Cheryl paused, "You know, some of these relatively unknown artists get their melodies copied or stolen."

"Oh yes. They do the music 'copy cat' thing."

"Scourges of the art world. Is there pride in stealing?"

"Nobody really cares unless you are the one stolen from. Then it is time to sue."

"But don't you want the whole world to sing your song?"

Bob stuck his head in the classroom. "I want the world to sing my song. I am out of gas."

Mary replied, "Mark could take us home."

Cheryl fished out the keys to the Swinger. "Here Bob! Ride to town in luxury!"

"Bless you child. I was going to ask you if I could."

"I wouldn't deny anyone the chance to drive my Swinger. It is a classic. Tell your friends that you have become a collector and watch out for the young girls." Bob disappeared as fast as he had appeared.

Mary continued. "That is one of the sad things about art. We have these people on the fringe with money. They wait for someone else to come up with an idea and then they jump in with look a likes or sound a likes. What are you going to do?"

"Just keep jumping in?"

"Ha, ha, ha! And ride the tide."

"They figure any angle to make a buck."

"In music and books, the publisher or agent make a few additions or changes, and then they claim part of the copyright or royalties because of the additions they made."

"Harden your heart and soul. Don't get mad just keep making music."

They got down past the knees, and once again the scaffold was moved out to the hallway.

"It looks like this shift is coming to an end. The prairie people will have to wait until tomorrow. After that I will have to hop right back up on that bronco!"

"Yee haw. Ride 'em cowgirl! Were you in Little Britches?"

"I was in 4H. I had a couple of county fair entries when I was a girl."

"I wanted to enter my little brother in the pig contests."

"Cheryl, I sure could use your help with the plaster tomorrow."

"Sure Mary. It will give me a break from Casey."

"He's a brute. He sure got some plaster in the metal. I have a team ready to go on the bronco. I am going to shoot for the shims and the latex on the same day. Cheryl, can you put in an extra hour of work every day for the next two weeks?"

"I can help."

"The work is piling up. Marty is going on vacation."

"I can put in extra hours during the week. I was hoping to put in any extra time on the miner, but right now there is nothing to do. I guess I gave you an automatic answer with out thinking."

"We will all help you on the miner."

A faint mist of deception clouded in Cheryl's mind. In the past, the rebellious Cheryl would just stubbornly blurt out the truth. Never leave the lie unanswered. The old habit prevailed. "Oh, sure! Just like everyone is helping you with the bronco!"

They stared at each other in awkward shock and disbelief. Then they both laughed. Mary covered her mouth and pointed at Cheryl. "Lordy!" She held her stomach and laughed. "My, what a bitter critter you are! Have you been keeping that one buried for awhile?"

"Well, I'm glad that's over. Nothing like the truth."

"You know you are certainly right."

When they finally finished the lower legs and boots, and the rubble of the mine floor, it was six thirty.

"Darn, Cheryl. This is a big statue!"

"I think the bronco is bigger."

"Well, yes it is. There is more there. Are we bushed? Ready to call it a night?"

"I sure am!"

"Then tomorrow we will meet at the prairie people. See you an hour early?"

"I will be here."

CHAPTER SEVENTEEN

They were right back at it Tuesday morning. The scaffold was set to go beside the prairie people. Mary and Cheryl were in the shell room mixing up the plaster. The prairie people were suited up in a layer of plaster before the day was over. Mary knew how she wanted to section the bronco. She explained it to her team and they all went to work on the horse and rider early that morning. It was nothing short of a celebration. She had worked on the sculpture for more than a month by herself and she was grateful to have help. The crew surrounded the horse and rider after lunch and the latex was carefully applied. By the end of the day the distinguishing features of horse and rider were no longer visible. The bronco now resembled a melting marsh mellow.

That night, Cheryl put in her second night in a row of uninterrupted eight hour sleep. There was a small dose of heaven in an extra hour of sleep. In the morning, she shut off her alarm clock on the makeshift, wood box table. She moved across the frozen floor in her long flannel nightgown to freshen up in the bathroom. She looked out her window at the new layer of snow and the lights of a few early morning risers. Her thoughts returned to the new phase of her project. Soon the sections would move from the wax room into the ceramic shell room. Hopefully, her shells would make it straight to the metal pour before the others. She wished she could move time forward and be done with it. Since that was not possible she promised herself that she would enjoy everything one day at a time.

She had a few minutes to spare while she waited for her ride. She recalled her first day at the DZ and wondered if she would ever jump out of a big plane with nine other jumpers. She eased into an arch and counted silently to ten and check canopy. She performed two cutaways.

The headlights of the Meteor signaled her ride. She was out the door and down the steps ready for the new day.

"Good morning, Cheryl. How was breakfast?"

"Just a fast left over sandwich." Cheryl eyed his big blue coffee mug. She shook her head from side to side. "You getting a hit off your gallon of coffee this morning?"

"One weakness of mine. I only have two."

"I won't ask." Cheryl enjoyed the ride. She had some time to appreciate the scenery and let her mind relax. "You seem pretty calm for your first day. Is that house project letting you sleep?"

"Yeah. I'm getting enough sleep. The body is tired from the amount of work at ten thousand feet."

"Well, you will get some variety today and the Vail valley floor is six thousand feet. You can work for an extended period of time."

"Oh, my. You are so good with trivia."

"I hope you have a good time." They entered the foundry from the side parking lot. It was a short distance to the Single Jacker. Cheryl was thrilled with the progress she made in the past week. She wanted Max to see the shocking difference.

"Oh, my! What happened? The last time I saw him he was green and ugly."

Cheryl shushed him. "Ssshh! He is sensitive about his appearance."

"He looks much better now."

"He does look a little stiff today, don't you think?"

"Was he in an accident?"

"He looks great in a plaster cast don't you think?"

"I think it looks like a flock of pigeons have made him a strafing target."

"Ha! How dare you! We need to leave the doors open in case he wants to go for a walk."

"It looks like he needs a catheter and an IV."

"You have been around the nurses too long." Cheryl led the way to the break room where she and Max would clock in an hour early. They moved next door to the wax room to see what all of the commotion was about. The early workers were rearranging the wax room. More metal storage shelves were moved in. Two more tables were added to double the size of Molly's work station.

Mark stuck his head in the door. "Bob is out front with four more shelves. Let's move them into the lobby area."

Molly greeted Cheryl and Max. "Hi, Cheryl. Help me move these two shelves to the window. There will be plenty of room for your molds now. This place will be swamped in a couple of days with three sculptures. Bob has designated the injection mold room as the new storage area. He said to keep the molds well covered. Blankets and bubble wrap on the ground and plastic bags for the molds. He is bringing in four more metal shelves this afternoon for the injection mold room."

"Molly, meet Max."

"Hi, Max. You know where the room is. Would you move the molds on these three shelves down there for me?"

"Sure will, Molly. Nice to meet you."

Molly shook her head. "It seems like all of a sudden everyone in the states wants to have their statues poured here."

Cheryl quipped, "We do good work."

"A lot of it is the economy. Costs and salaries keep going up. The marginal foundries are losing money."

"It is beginning to look like a library in here."

Cheryl and Molly moved a metal shelf from the hallway into the wax room and placed it three feet in front of the row on the back wall. "It is going to get crowded in here. It is a good thing though. There will be a total of eight wax pots and I will have two new assistants."

The flow of workers in and out of the wax room continued. Molly gave Cheryl a warm contagious smile. She hooted at Cheryl. "I saw your man this morning. Don't know what you did to him but he is looking much better!"

Taken back at first Cheryl quickly recovered with a chuckle. "And he is all mine, Molly. He sure is handsome ain't he? I ain't sharing him with no one else." Cheryl fluttered her eyebrows for effect.

"He certainly is! I would never let another woman within fifty feet of him. I would keep him all to myself. A handsome cuss he is!"

"I guess I could rent him out now and then by the hour if I get short on food or cosmetics."

"I think he looks like the Mummy!" Molly laughed.

"He looks more like the Pillsbury doughboy with bad mix ingredients."

Molly wore one of her usual mountain dresses with white lace around the collar and wrist cuffs. Today the solid color was purple with a thousand little flowers on it. "Molly, will you let me work on the waxes here early in the morning?"

"You mean morning and night don't you?" She grinned mischievously

"Teach me how to wax and sprue, Molly."

"No! Get out of here!" Cheryl laughed. "You know I will. When are the molds arriving?"

"Maybe by the weekend or Monday."

"It just never gets anything but busier around here. How many molds do you have?"

"Thirty two. Do you have much to do?"

"There is always something to do. I am swamped. I can come in an hour early. Carl and the gang mostly eat cereal for breakfast. I have to be home in the evenings for dinner or they abuse me. After dinner, I could sneak over one or two nights a week, after they are safely glued to homework or the television. That would be for two and a half hours. That would make you late getting home."

"I imagine that I will be sleeping here most of the time."

"We are just going to have to be open about it and do it regardless of the time or day, I have that feeling. By the way how about eight dollars an hour? I was going to ask eight and a half or nine, but I know you will share your fortune with me. You can keep the fame."

"I can do that, Molly."

"In advance."

"Awww, I will not have money until payday."

"I heard a rumor about a jazz quartet."

"Yes, so did I."

"It is going to be a big one. Trumpet, bass, trombone and a piano."

Cheryl questioned, "Plus the players? Oh, boy!"

"Plus a female singer. They are talking about a few extra part time workers for a month."

"That works down in the flatlands."

"I know what you mean. Most of us are broke and starving which makes it pretty impossible for us to afford a good running car." Molly added, "Someone told me to ask you if your car is for sale. They saw you driving a different car. What is that all about? Did you find yourself a sugar daddy?"

"I wish. Cheryl avoided the subject. I trade cars on the weekend if I have to drive to Denver. I am worried that my car won't make it."

"Are you going anywhere else with him?"

"Aren't you the persistent one? I am single again, as you know. Right now, I think I will try to enjoy things as they are. I need this free space and time for the rest of the summer."

"When we work on the waxes you can define 'things as they are' because I think that you are lying."

"Me? I never!"

"Are going to wait until fall to get married?"

"Molly! I am married to the miner right now. I have to wait until the patina is dried before I can even begin to think about another adventure."

"Adventure you call it, eh?"

"Well sometimes it is like being in a haunted house and sometimes it is like looking in dumpsters."

"I like working with you Cheryl. I don't get to talk the women's talk very much. Well, we will BS some more, later. Adios."

Bob and Max were in the shell room. Mr. Robertson had the slurry tub swirling with liquid ceramic. He explained the shell room operations in greater detail to Max. "Max, it is time to dip some waxes!" Bob dipped the first coat on several new waxes. "Leave the motor off for the first three coats. The sprues are much too fragile." He observed Max as he dipped. Bob gave him some suggestions that would enhance his performance. Bob pointed out to him the shells and rows of priority. He instructed Max to find him when the slurry was low. They planned to spend the afternoon on the mold machine.

After lunch they walked to the wax injection mold room. Bob turned on the master switch for the machine system, and then he flipped on the switch for the wax melt container. He thoroughly explained to Max the operation of the injection mold machine. Max wrote the sequence of valves to open and close in his pocket notebook.

"There is some patience required here. You have to wait two full minutes for the wax to cool. Then you can break the mold open." Max opened the mold carefully without damaging the wax impression.

"Now you must allow a full minute before you remove the wax impression. If you remove it any sooner, it will bend as you pry it off the mold. But, if you wait long enough, it will pop up when you touch it." Bob touched the bottom edge of the wax with his pocket knife. The wax popped free. "Isn't that amazing? Got it Max?"

"I understand, Mr. Robertson." Only flat waxes. No curved ones. I will not hurry or become impatient."

"Good. When the room is filled up, call me." Bob checked the melting container again. "Go ahead and empty this container and shut the machine down. That will give you time to get another coat of slurry on the small shells."

"Aye, aye, Mr. Robertson."

"There is a beat up radio on the table if you care to listen to some music." Bob turned and left for the foundry floor. Max recalled the Tenth Mountain reunion and Charlie's conversation. Max was grateful for Charlie's kindness. I am truly fortunate to be here.

Thursday Cheryl was back out on the floor as a dedicated employee to work on the shepherd girl. The girl was a small preteen who stood with a baby lamb beside her. She chewed on the edge of her head cloth and stared numbly ahead. Cheryl thought the statue was a little dreary, but the kids and babies are so cute. Marty was all smiles this morning and functioning smoothly. Cheryl guessed he was leaving soon, so she hit him swift and low.

"Are you going to fly or drive, Marty?"

Marty laughed. "We leave in the morning. We are driving."

She felt her stomach hit rock bottom. She spoke unexcitedly. "How conventional." Driving meant Marty could return anytime he wanted. A plane would assure his return. "Just remember, the car gets smaller with three kids in it. There is nowhere to throw them when your ears are bleeding."

Marty beamed. "You are so kind and thoughtful. You don't often find people in the world who are really concerned about one another anymore."

"Well, drive carefully. You don't want to drive off any curvy mountain road on your way. That's child abuse!"

"Oh, how would you know anything about kids?"

"It might be good to write down all the things that need to be done here and leave it with your parents. That way you will be able to concentrate on the eggs you are going to steal from the little kids." Marty seemed to jolt a little bit. Was he feeling guilty?

"My brother has met some people in California. They may order some sculpture."

"Yours?"

"You have no mercy."

"Do you feel guilty?"

"Of course. I hope I can enjoy my vacation."

"Woah! But do you care?"

"Of course."

"When you get back do I get two weeks off?" He flinched again.

"A little jumpy are we?"

"We really don't have a vacation policy. We let people have time off without pay." Marty sneered, "But if you were willing to visit the Dead Sea and do some cliff diving, I would put in a good word for you to Mom and Dad."

Cheryl beamed. "Good one! Marty you're a big guy. Kindness overflowing. You must have gone to church last Sunday." She knew his wife made him go every Sunday when he could be getting some valuable ski or golf time.

Marty registered no facial expression but the miniscule smile. "You are on a roll this morning. Please do not stop until you are in the landfill."

"And don't forget your map and camera."

"Now I know you are being insincere. You're killing me. I'll remember them both. Matter of fact, I should take some pictures of you and Nash working. I can put them on my dashboard and wonder if you are getting everything done while I am driving."

Cheryl headed for the rest room across the hall from the wax room. On a whim she opened the door to the shell room and walked over to Max at the slurry tank.

"How are you doing?"

"All the big shells have one coat and the little shells will get their second coat later this afternoon. I am just about ready to head to the injection mold room with Bob."

"I am concentrating on my work as usual. When I am not working I am visualizing skydiving all the time. It helps me through slow time. I even get little hits of adrenaline. It is all I am thinking about."

Max snorted. "See how selfish and withdrawn you are? It is not advisable to think about skydiving when you are working with equipment. You might reach for your cut away handle and accidentally grind your mammary off. You might stab yourself in the butt with the dremel when you reach for your pilot chute. I got more advice."

"What is it?"

"Work now. Play later."

"It sure keeps a girl powered up. Want to wrestle?"

"If you promise not to throw anything at me."

Cheryl beamed. "Ha! You mean like a big ice ball?"

"I knew it! See, you cheated. You threw an ice ball!"

"No rules! I'll get back to you."

"It certainly is nice to know someone at the new job. And a skydiving buddy to boot. Thanks Cheryl. This is a great place to work."

Cheryl entered the women's rest room. After she finished her business, she practiced her arch. She visualized standing in the door and looking down ten thousand feet to the ground. The sound of the engines filled her head. The wind slapped her face. She remembered the feel of the control wheel of the DC 3. Heady stuff. She hit a hard arch to five thousand and check canopy. She walked out to the foundry floor calm and collected. She was all business now. She picked up her dremel and started chasing the cute facial features of the shepherd girl.

An hour before the end of the day, she walked to the mold room to join Max.

She was happy to see that he made it through another afternoon of work. "Bob has the slurry ready. It is time to dip the small shells again. Are you ready?"

"Sure. I just ran out of wax. I have to clean this beast so it will be ready to go in the morning, and then I will be right there. I should be about fifteen minutes."

"I can help you dip the small shells if you would like me to join you."

"Yes."

"After that we need to move more molds before we go, so we will work a little bit late tonight."

"Sure thing. Cheryl, would you let me know if these leaf patterns produce a good result on the metal pour?"

"They are lousy. I heard Bob say that he was going to fire you."

"Thanks."

"Molly sprues them and they go to the shell room. No matter who makes them there are some tiny air bubbles to chase. They talked about shipping the waxes to Japan to let them finish the job. I think they agreed that there would be too much damage. So get after it, boy."

Before she left work, Cheryl went to the miner room. In her sleep the night before she dreamed that the metal framework gave out and the statue collapsed. She wanted to see how things were holding up. She entered the room and inspected the big snowman. Everything looked good. Nothing had fallen apart. She briefly admired her work. The statue would move into the next phase. She hoped to get the miner into the wax room before the prairie people and the bronco. When the miner was dry she would go back to work on it. She stared at the base, the rubble of the mine floor. She would pull those sections off first. She could relax and do her job as an employee this week. It was her turn to help Mary and the foundry. Chase metal. Pitch in and contribute to the other sculptures that need work. Show up early and work in the wax room and help wherever help was needed.

Just before the end of the day, a white three quarter ton van backed up to the front entrance. Mary was quickly located. The driver opened the twin rear doors and seven layers of stout foam padding greeted her. One hundred molds of the jazz quartet were carefully moved to the open shelves in the wax room. Molly directed the efforts of all the available employees.

"We will be doing this again. The van will be back tomorrow with another hundred molds."

Friday morning the van returned with another eighty molds and the previous night's effort was repeated. Cheryl and Nash finished the Mudville Nine man. Marty took off in the afternoon for California. Before the end of the foundry day, Cheryl stopped in the injection mold room to check on her new friend.

"How many squares did that machine make for you today, boy?" She gave him a warm smile from the doorway.

"I have been here all day and I am close to two hundred. I may see some more tonight while I am trying to sleep. I will probably count squares instead of sheep. Have you made any decision on moving over to 304? There is plenty of room for two people to coexist."

She pulled her foundry key ring from her jeans pocket. She slipped off the extra house key and walked over to Max. “Max, I have mixed feelings about the whole thing, and basically, it is because I do not know you very well. Hopefully, you will not be inclined to steal any of my valuable jewelry. I have also heard rumors of your unsavory character.”

“Ha! Aren’t you the funny one? Good luck on your AFF class. I know you will have really good people to take care of you. You will still have to force yourself to go out the door. I bet you are excited.”

“I am. I am anxious, but I don’t know if my stomach will let me go through with it.”

“The fun and the thrill will eventually override the fears and uncertainty. Have fun, and don’t forget to smile”

Cheryl gave him the spare key. “Don’t you dare sell any of my things.”

“You are in a great mood. Please stay that way. It makes everything easier.”

“Don’t hurt your back moving my gold bars. See you Saturday or Sunday.”

CHAPTER EIGHTEEN

Karen and Cheryl sat in lawn chairs in the packing area. The atmosphere was calm and relaxed. They reviewed emergency procedures and the exam on Cheryl's reading assignment. Steve picked up a lawn chair and joined them as the time for the second jump neared.

"All right, Cheryl it is a beautiful day. Are you ready to skydive?"

"You know, it is all I have been thinking about all week long. I had plenty of practice this week. I hope to make your job mundane and routine. I probably won't need you at all."

"Just like last week, Cheryl, what we are looking for in these first three jumps is body position, stable face to earth freefall, mental awareness and the ability to relax. There are two new maneuvers on this jump. You get to fly forward and you get to turn. You get to test your wings, and move around in the air. When you change body positions, you will be able to sense the movement and experience the results."

"When you do the circle of awareness check we want you to add 'arch, legs, and relax' to your thinking. We are trying to increase your focus on your body position."

"Your fears and anxiety will still be with you for awhile. You will find out that your anxiety and fear will subside, as you increase your knowledge and your ability. You will gradually get used to dealing with these emotional issues."

"Alright, here are the objectives for jump number two. Your first objective is stable free fall, heading, and COA. Karen and I will release our hold on your shoulders. Your second objective is to do two practice deployments. The third objective is another COA. As you know, you do a circle of awareness after every maneuver. Be sure to add arch, legs, and relax. Your fourth objective is to move forward for three seconds. We will do this two times. Your fifth objective is a ninety degree turn with us.

Karen and I will release our grips and let you turn back to your original heading by yourself. Wave off is fifty five hundred feet and deploy by forty five hundred. Alright?"

"I am with you Steve."

"Okay, Cheryl, let's see your arch. Good. If you are rigid and fight the airflow or wind resistance, like you are doing pushups, then you will bounce up and down. Remember relax eight, relax nine, relax ten thousand on your count. Now, how do you move forward?"

"Straighten my legs and point my toes, and I pull my hands closer to my shoulders."

"Good. You will probably drag us. On this leg maneuver, hold your legs straight for three seconds. If we do this two times how much altitude are you going to lose?"

"Three seconds and then relax, will be less than one thousand feet. Probably around eight hundred. So call it sixteen hundred to two thousand."

"Good. Show us the arm positions for a turn and tell us which one you are going to use."

"In the stable arch, if I throw an elbow and my head to one side, that is enough inertia to turn and that is what I plan to do. I do want to try the salute turn and the leg turn sometime."

"Okay, Cheryl. We will do that leg turn. Plan for it on jump five. One more thing, when you throw the pilot chute, stay symmetrical so you don't spin or slide. Get that left hand close to your helmet as the right hand goes for your pilot chute. Just like you did last week. Then you go right back to your arch and hold it until your parachute opens. You want to be nice and stable so that canopy will peel out of your container for a good, clean opening."

Steve increased his volume a little bit. "Do not take this second jump for granted. You are going to have to work just as hard as you did on the first one, maybe more. Just like last week, Cheryl, do not let up! We need the same amount of enthusiasm and commitment. So be fired up, and ready for that exit. You got that Cheryl?"

"I got it Steve. I will be there."

"Let's meet at the mock up in a couple of minutes in full gear."

At the mock up, Steve explained that there would be a tandem going with them. "There will be a tandem jump with us on this load. Cheryl, you and Karen will be in the back of the cabin. I will be by the pilot. The tandem will be in the middle. They get out first and we get out second on the same jump run. Cheryl, that means that you have to make an extra effort in movement here. You have to be right behind them and when they exit, you have to get to the middle of the door and be prepared to float. The spot has already been picked. We give them five full seconds of separation and then we take the float positions. Do not get caught flat footed. It will happen fast."

"I got you Steve."

They rehearsed the exit and the entire skydive two times.

"Okay, folks. We are comfortable with this one. The plane is due to arrive soon, so let's take ten for water and the restroom."

They waited patiently as the 206 taxied in. Cheryl took her assigned seat and she watched the tandem slide into the middle area. It triggered her memory of her tandem jump. She stole a glance at the tandem. She detected a look of determination accompanied by a set of raw nerves on the tandem passenger. Cheryl wondered what it would be like to be an instructor or tandem master. Her thoughts drifted to her observer ride and her level of excitement and anxiety increased. Her body temperature and pulse rate increased. Enough! She forced herself to relax. Just another jump. She relaxed and looked at the beautiful mountain scenery on the ride to altitude. She watched her instructors and recalled her laundry list.

On jump run Steve and Karen opened the door. The wind blast filled the plane with a foreboding of stupidity and fear. Cheryl felt her chest tighten. Her anxiety level flared a warning. Her stomach felt as if a large hand squeezed it into a small ball and threw it down into the bottomless pit of sinking feelings. Fear had come back to find her. In the back of her mind she heard a deep, growling voice. "You should know better than this, Cheryl Pritchard! What are you doing here?" She tried to force herself to be calm. This was not supposed to happen. She knew what the tandem rider was experiencing. Cheryl told herself that she was supposed to be above that level of fear and consternation.

The tandem pair scooted for the edge of the door and positioned themselves for the effort of the team exit. It would be fast. Cheryl needed to move now. To get away from the pending sensory overload, she took an offensive posture. She looked at the ceiling and ran transition and laundry list through her mind. It worked. She watched the tandem launch from the door, and she arrived a second later in the center, feet positioned, and left hand at the top of the door to steady her. Steve counted three thousand, float thousand. Three hands reached for the float bar. Cheryl spun through the door and pulled herself to the plane as if she were Steve's shadow. Karen appeared from nowhere and the instructors tugged on her harness. Their glands were pumping and they were tight to the plane on "Set." Three legs kicked out and three hands released the hand bar. On "Go" the group peeled off into the wind blast. The exit was flawless.

They held their arch patiently through the transition. Cheryl ran her laundry list and was on heading and COA, legs, relax, at thousand seven. The instructors released shoulder grips. They were thrilled by the fast acceleration. Their hearts were pounding and they let the glandular secretions fill their bodies and brains at relax eight, relax nine. Cheryl's early eye contact encouraged Steve to give her the fist signal to practice deployment. She finished two maneuvers with ease and the instructors moved in to side dock on Cheryl.

They shook her harness as a signal to move forward. She gave a vigorous snap to straighten her legs and she pulled her hands in. She felt herself move forward. She felt resistance as her instructors held on and moved with her. She moved for three seconds and finished with a COA. The maneuver was repeated with ease. There were smiles all around.

The wind pulled at her suit and pushed on her goggles. It whistled around her helmet as she COA, legs, relaxed. Steve and Karen nodded to one another and shook her harness for the cue to turn to the right. Cheryl threw her elbow and head to the right and almost ran into Steve. She saw the earth turn ninety degrees, and she felt the grips release. She turned on her own, to the left, and they flew no contact for the rest of the dive.

Their lips and faces were comical as they shouted cheers over the rushing wind to one another. Steve moved for the leg strap grip on Cheryl. He pointed his index finger in her field of vision, the signal for her to wave off and deploy. Five minutes later they were back at the landing area, safe and sound. They reviewed the jump there. Steve allowed Karen the chance to do the critique.

"Wow, Cheryl! You wild woman! You stepped up the pace on us on that jump. You were way ahead of us. You captured your heading and COA on seven thousand. You must have been hungry for that jump, girl, you were just chomping at the bit. Steve and I are impressed. You want to tell me what inspired all of this?"

"I got a late start in the plane. I over compensated to catch up. Mentally, I was in fast forward, and I just decided to stay there."

"Well, what happened?"

"I was not ready for the wind blast. When the wind blast came through the door, I was scared again! Big as ever! It pushed my pause button. I knew I hesitated so I cued on the ceiling and ran transition and laundry through my mind. I snapped back into the play mode and went to the door so fast I thought I was gonna fall out right behind the tandem. I don't know how I got my composure back, but I was in a hurry to get to that floater position."

"You were ready to get out and get some one twenty. Am I right?" They shared smiles and laughter. Steve spoke up. We will talk about the fear later. What other observations, Karen?"

"Cheryl, I'm telling you. You were hungry to perform. I noticed it on your very first jump that you were ahead in anticipation and anxious to perform your maneuvers. You were right back at it on this one. I am not going to pick any knits here. You did buffet now and then. It seemed to me to be random. I was not able to link it to anything specific. Do you have any ideas?"

"I felt it and I swear it was muscle spasms. I mean my muscles just cramped after a maneuver. I think it is associated with the fear. I try hard, but I am not one hundred percent confident in my ability. I just can not totally relax yet."

"I follow you. It is not absence of thought. It is the frozen with fear syndrome. A little bit of it is still around and nagging at you, like your little brother when he shows his ugly face once in awhile. They looked at Steve and laughed.

"I agree all the way around. Cheryl, you keep up the intensity and the practice. That's what is pushing you ahead here. Let's go ahead and plan jump three right now. Karen, lead the discussion."

"Cheryl jump three objectives include the continuation of the practice deployments. Other than that it is wide open for us to pick and choose the maneuvers and plan our own objectives. I think our group could handle one hundred eighty degree turns. Steve what do you think?"

"I will agree. It would be nice to have forward movement, but let's keep it simple. Plan for four one eighties. Cheryl, I know you stepped up the pace on that last jump. On number three, let's go back to the slow lazy pace, and relax and enjoy this easy skydive. No pressure. Sometimes when the pace is picked up a mistake or two is made. Let's turn the pace down just a tad. The pace picks up in level four and level five. We will talk about that later. We want you to participate with the spot. That will give you something extra to do."

Karen asked, "Cheryl, are you up for two jumps today?"

"I am good with the idea of four or more one eighties, but these jumps drain me."

Steve jumped in. "Two in a row is a confidence builder. You have the first intense exposure over with now. The second one is not as nerve wracking."

"I believe you. I don't think I have any nerves left right now. They are all frazzled away. I am willing to give it a try. It is not as cold at altitude today, as it was last week, so let's go get some more one twenty!" They shared more laughter.

Karen added, "The exertion after the jump is from falling through the sky at one hundred twenty miles an hour. You have to push two miles of air out of your way with your arms and legs, and your stomach."

Suzy Dishroon, CJ Shanaberger, and Liz were manifested on the same load as Cheryl's AFF jump. Cheryl savored the recognition and the camaraderie. The six of them were all dressed up and conversing in a relaxed easy manner when the 206 taxied over to them. Cheryl was genuinely relaxed and calm on the ride to altitude. She was mentally prepared to deal with the rush of new wind and anxiety. She vowed to ignore it. She had some new positive thoughts for the skydive. She was going to get some one twenty and a wild canopy ride with her new friends.

She was outside for the float. She risked a quick peek back inside to see the three ladies plastered together. They stared right back through the door at her with big goofy grins. They were going to monitor and critique her exit. Cheryl choked out one sympathetic laugh. Stay with the jump! She made quick eye contact with her instructors who were waiting patiently for her to stop the shenanigans and get back to business. The shake was given. The count began. The release and transition was instantaneous. If Cheryl could have looked back to the door, she would have seen three smiling faces following her transition.

After the jump they assembled in the loft at manifest and the gear rental area. Cheryl wrote a check for the day's activities and turned in her gear. Steve made his notations in her log book. Transition and awareness good. Two 180's. Good exit. Consistent improvement. Shows dedication and growth. Cleared for Level four. He signed her off for jumps two and three. No one seemed to be in a hurry to go anywhere. "Good work. Cheryl, you are cleared to level four. Would you like to share any thoughts or observations, good or bad, with us on your jumps today?"

Karen jumped in with a big grin and bright eyes. "Come on Cheryl. Tell us what is bugging you and don't sugar coat it."

"Boy! I've got some things to tell you! Jump number two. Here I am in the plane. All of this is supposed to get easier, right? Well, my mind and body are still spastic. Let me tell you about my anxiety level. I know you can skydive and live. I have watched people do it. I already have one jump. So this jump number two should be no big deal, right? Here I am at altitude and I hear or imagine this big ominous voice, 'You don't belong here!'" Everyone laughed. "My subconscious brain is telling me, warning me. It said, 'I can't believe you are stupid enough to do this again!'" Again, everyone shared the laughter. "I just about froze up again. The negative thoughts were still there. My stomach flip flopped. It tied itself in a knot, and it squeezed some really sour juice out to let me know that it did not like what was going on."

She stopped for breath and Karen interrupted, "This is the reason jump two is so tough on people who come back unprepared. They have the mind set, 'I did this last time. It was easy. I am cool and good.' They do not practice. They have forgotten half of the emergency procedures. They fake their way through the drills before the second jump and pretend to be up to snuff and ready to go. So when they get to the door they are overwhelmed even more than they were the first time. Most all of them break their arch on deployment if they don't do it before then. We have to wrestle with them or chase them down and get their chute open. You know, it is human nature to let up or take the short cut."

Steve interrupted, "There is a point here, a fine line. This is all about sensory overload. If you get to the point where you are frozen, and have no positive thought process or sequence to save yourself, then things just get worse in your mind. You freeze mentally and your muscles seize up. The negative thoughts just keep piling up, and it is all over but the crying. To a small extent, the student will unravel a little bit mentally. They lose their nerve. Fear overtakes them. That is what happens. Like a youngster who witnesses a terrible accident or fight. That event can disturb them and stay with them for awhile."

Karen jumped in again. "What we do in this training is present to you the instruction, which also happens to be the positive train of thought that you pick up. Once it is ingrained in your mind, you begin to monitor the situation yourself, a little bit at a time, as you advance and get a couple of jumps. What saved you on your observer ride?"

"The activity of the next group of jumpers who lined up for exit. That pulled out all of the negative thoughts that were going through my mind. On the jumps today, I still had to force myself to go out the door. My body was hesitant. I had to tell my brain to shut up, that I was going to do this thing again. I still feel my heart pounding, but it is down in the chest area, and not up in my throat between my ears."

"I would like to thank both of you right now. There are some other reasons that capable people do not return."

"Who have you been talking to? You are supposed to avoid the experienced jumpers. You know that."

"Max told me all about it. Students do not come back if they were exposed to a bunch of braggers, smart asses, and show offs who think they are cool because they are experienced skydivers. New students want to be with instructors and people who are genuinely interested in saving their lives, not a bunch of clowns and bozos."

"Well said, Cheryl. Steve and I accept that comment as high praise. It is too bad that some individuals are counter productive to student retention. Jobs and society are the same way. Tell us about your last jump today."

Suzy and Liz stepped into the circle.

"You know what? My nerves were so shot from the first one, it was like I didn't have the energy to respond to fear. I was just numb to it, or maybe my brain was too overworked to care. I ignored it. There was something else at had. I am beginning to get some positive reinforcement from my brain. My brain is signaling some positive feedback. It says, 'You did that right. Okay, so far so good. Remember to get ready for the wind blast when the door opens.' My brain is beginning to calm down and monitor my movements and thoughts. It tells me I am okay."

Suzy threw in, "Kind of the way Houston monitors the astronauts?" They shared some more laughter. "That is what mental awareness is all about. You are actively anticipating and performing the moves."

Cheryl finished. "A new positive influence has entered the picture. It is the enjoyment and the feedback from the thrill, that incredible rush to one hundred and twenty miles and hour, and the incredible canopy ride. It takes a couple of jumps to understand the gear and build the confidence level. It takes awhile to get over the mixed signals you get, because you think that you are off balance in the arch and under canopy. But I am getting used to those things now."

Karen questioned with a big smile. "What about that Cheryl? What about that difference between your first observer ride and your third jump? It is all pretty overwhelming, isn't it? Just think about it. A month ago you had an observer ride and a tandem jump. That is about twice as much exposure or air time as most first jumpers get. And now, here you are at the end of your third jump. You did some dancing in the air. You moved forward and you made some turns. Next time you will spot, fly no contact and do turns and flips."

"It is just unbelievable. I never knew if I would make it to this point or not."

Liz interrupted, "And don't forget. You only have three minutes of air time and twelve minutes of canopy ride. And how much training do you put in? I bet you put in two to three hours every week here and at home, with the ground training and reading the manual. I betcha."

"Now my mind is having another reason to do these jumps. I have gone from total fear to, yes it works to, oh my gosh, let's do it again. Let's go get some one twenty and a canopy ride!" The group shared laughter.

Steve interjected. "Let me give you one of a few perspectives and then I have to get going. There are two sides to this coin of skydiving. Basically this is a life and death situation versus a calculated risk. There are two absolute perspectives here. Life and death at the first meeting. We can't save ourselves. We are frozen with fear. We are totally incapacitated. But, our training and exposure allows us to bring the calculated risk viewpoint to the situation. We understand the system and we understand why it works. The acceptance factor of all of this has to do with exposure, and how many times you have jumped, and how much you have enjoyed it."

"There is one more aspect that is undeniable." Suzy continued, "And that is the determination of the individual. You still have to force yourself through the first five to ten jumps. There is no comfort zone or reward system."

Karen offered, "Liz is going to work with you on ground drills next time. She is looking forward to the day you graduate so she will have a new jump buddy because no one likes to jump with her, right Liz?"

"I'll get you for that one. Cheryl, it is really important to build a new skill into your repertoire of talent and knowledge at this point. We want you to learn how to pack your own rig. No one here likes a new jumper who does not know how to pack their own rig. We are going to let you take some equipment home to practice with during the week." Suzy turned and picked up a light blue gear bag. She brought it back into the circle and placed it at Cheryl's feet.

"Why don't you take a minute and check it out for us. See if the fit is any good."

Cheryl knelt and opened the bag she pulled out a near new blue and white Vector. She rose and stepped into it all in one smooth movement. She bent to snap the leg straps and straightened as she laced the chest strap. She tightened the leg straps and arched. "Wow! Nice rig. Good fit. I like it."

"That is a good thing. Cheryl, we shopped around for two weeks and we found this rig just for you. It is a sweetheart deal. If you want to keep it, there is a low down payment with easy financing." Liz did not bother to tell her about the card in the bottom of the gear bag.

A smile spread across Cheryl's face. "How does this happen?"

"A skydiver over at Herson's drop zone is getting married. He is selling his rig for a ring and the ceremony. He claims that he does not like the fit or the colors. It sounds good, but the truth is his wife will shoot him if he makes another jump. That's the way it goes."

They all laughed and congratulated Cheryl. The group broke apart. Liz and Cheryl walked down the steps and out of the loft. Cheryl turned and thanked Liz again for the equipment.

"Cheryl, there is a card for you in the bottom of the bag. We all signed it. Just one thing, lock your gear in the trunk of your car. Wherever you go anytime you are going to be separated from your gear, make certain that you lock it up. Even around the DZ. We get the usual lookie loos around here moving in and out of this place. It is too easy for someone to pick up gear up and carry it away. Congratulations, Cheryl, you are on your way. Keep up the good work. If you continue to practice and do your ground drills then everything will grow from here. It will only get better. Have fun at the pizza parlor, and don't forget to smile."

Cheryl arranged to buy four pitchers of beer for the skydivers. She ordered two sodas and moved to the less crowded end of the bar to join Sherry.

"So you and Max are an item?"

"Max and I are good friends right now. We have known each other for a couple of weeks."

Sherry searched Cheryl's face. "So you want to find out what Max is like? You are looking for dirt on him aren't you?" Sherry's abruptness caught her off guard. "Not to worry Cheryl. I know the answer. We are always looking and searching for answers that will save us time and keep us from going through unnecessary motions or painful relationships, aren't we? Cheryl, I am going to be blunt and run some things past you to get this conversation going and save us some time. Max has a good support group. Most jumpers are single and Max is not afraid to stay single. He is good with girls. If you get close to him you will run into his wall. His wall is Gloria. He lives off her memory. He feeds off that memory like some people live off of hate or channel stress. I really think he lives every day as if she is still in town living with him. I mean honestly, he can be so happy all the time."

"Are you still in love with him."

"Good grief! Max and I split up because of Leadville. No one is too blame. It is the world's fault. People want to live in the frickin' mountains. It is the biggest wet dream in Colorado. I wouldn't stay in a one thousand square foot rough hewn log cabin in Leadville. Would you? If I had a signed pre nuptial agreement that I would get one million dollars I might live with someone like Brad Pit for a year or two."

"You are funny and very direct."

"People around here don't hide their emotions. We are an open group with nothing to hide. This group shares its experiences. We still get some selfish, greedy types once in awhile. Max is a good guy Cheryl. He is fun and he makes life easy. Go for it. Get him to commit. He is a giver. He is an open person. He won't drag you around with him everywhere he goes or make demands on you all of the time. He is not a control freak, but he expects trust and mutual respect. We were going good and strong. We were free to go and do as we pleased. There was no fooling around. We were always thinking of each other. We began to move down the road to our future together. It was a great direction. That's the stuff I dream about."

Sherry paused to sip her soda and check the crowd. "He went for the mountains. I'm a transplant from out of state. It was hard for me to get settled and hang on. Some people call it getting established. I call it painful sacrifice. I don't want to go anywhere else. No small mountain town for me. I am a worker. Put anything in front of me. A word processor, typewriter, assembly line, it doesn't matter. I'd pump gas or turn a wrench if I knew how to work on machinery. I like people and towns but I do not care for the metro areas."

Cheryl leveled her eyes and smiled. "So what can you tell me about his ex fiancée?"

"Well, I never knew her personally, but I can tell you all of the bits and pieces that had been floating around. It will be up to you to decide what is fiction and what is fact. All of this is twelve years ago and it is second hand information. They bought a small house and lived together in Glenwood Springs. He was a clerk at the local electric co op working towards assistant accountant. She worked for the phone company. They were engaged. There was some money in the family. An uncle called one day and offered him an obscene salary to work in the family business. His brother had been there seven years and was hoarding his second half million. He put his first half in real estate in Malaysia. One year the Malaysian economy collapsed and his brother had a minor stroke. He lost everything."

"Another real estate market blow out. So Max went to Indiana? Why didn't Gloria go with him?"

I'm certain they talked about it. So, off he goes. He gave her the house. She was furious. She told him to burn in hell. He tried to convince her that he was only going to stay for two or three years. She told him to make the choice between money, or their marriage."

"Money sucks?"

"Her family had it. She told him that 'If it wasn't his money it would haunt him and bite him in the ass.'"

"What happened in Indiana?"

"The relative was in the motions of selling the business. He tricked Max. It was kind of a family trap. They wanted Gloria and Max to live down the block so mom and dad could watch the non existent grand children. He was back in Denver in three months."

"Three months?"

"Gloria was gone."

"Why didn't Gloria go to Indiana to meet his parents?"

"Ha, ha, ha, ah, ha, ha! I forgot to tell you! His parents visited Glenwood Springs twice."

"And?"

"No one invited them the second time. They just showed up to take over."

"What?"

"His parents had nothing better to do except to visit Max and tell him how much better off he and Gloria would be if they moved back to Indiana. They could have a Noble Roman's Pizza or a Dairy Queen franchise. That was their plan. She told them she did not need any help from a bunch of lame assed, back woods hicks. She called the police and reported them as trespassers. She filed a restraining order against them."

"That is just unbelievable."

"You are not going to believe the rest of this." Sherry continued. "His parents stayed in a motel room. The next day they show up with a realtor to sell the house! They said that Max had a history of indecision and did not know what was best for him."

"No way."

"Gloria filed first thing in the morning. Gloria called Mrs. Mason 'a lying, manipulating, two faced bitch' in front of everyone."

"Ha!"

"So goes the story. Look, Cheryl, I am out of time for now. I am going to tell you one more thing about Max and then I'm gonna forget this ever happened. Max never resisted his parent's will or their plans. He never stood up to them. All of their lives they always thought that they had perfect harmony with their oldest son. They destroyed his two older sisters. I think Gloria could sense that they were destroyers and not cultivators.

If you are trying to find out if Max is mentally disturbed or messed up I will be the first one to tell you he is."

They shared a laugh. "Well I guess that answers all my questions."

"What you are going to have to do is destroy his memory of Gloria, or beat that memory somehow. Maybe you can convince him of the harm it does to others because he has neglected your thoughts, your feelings, and your emotions."

"Damn, Sherry! That is good! You need an advice column!"

"His logic is going to fail. He is getting older and he thinks that the river of women will always be there. They will not. That will be his break point. Is he under your skin yet?"

"We are friends. It is platonic. No intimacy. He is under my skin with all this new skydiving stuff."

"Has he bought you a brown cow yet?"

"Oh no!" Cheryl gasped. "He is plying me with alcohol to reduce my frigidity!"

"Well, I guess that might be a standard MO for all men."

They laughed again and stood up to leave. "He is a good man. Stay with him. Get the ring. You have got to kill the image or refill the space in his brain that the girl occupies. You just have to figure out if it really matters to you or not. If he doesn't, then who does? No problem."

"Who does? That is a good one, Sherry. Thank you. It's always nice to meet someone with a sense of humor. You sure filled my ears. What a bunch of bullshit." They laughed. "I think you are bitter and that you just want to knock Max down to make yourself feel better."

"Longmont, Lyons, Loveland are all right for me, but not Leadville. It's the same as living at the North Pole and you better have everything paid for cause there is little work in the mountains. We lived here on the front range for a year and a half. I said no to the mountains because relations ships are meant to grow close and be consummated. I just saw too much potential for it to go the other way."

A pause. Nothing was said. A troubled look appeared on Cheryl's face.

"I still have a soft spot for Max and the brown cows, but mentally he is gone. Go get him Cheryl. Keep in touch."

CHAPTER NINETEEN

Cheryl decided to head for Leadville. It was the last weekend to move out of her apartment. She hoped that Max moved her worldly possessions. It would be great to be out of the rent bill and the heat bill. The second reason was her miner. She was focused on her miner with the intensity of a herd of stampeding buffalo. If the plaster was dry then she could work tomorrow. She could pull some mold sections and get them ready for the wax room. She headed up the winding interstate past the Mother Cabrini Shrine on Lookout Mountain. The mountain peaks cut the sunsets and last hour of daylight. There were enough clouds that she saw a short sunset of fire yellow, and a little bit of orange with a few touches of red.

A light snow began to fall as she rolled into the Food Town parking lot. She suddenly remembered that Tuesday she would be on her way to the mining convention. She made a U turn in the lot and drove over to Starvin' Marvin's for gas.

"Ssssup Buddy? The place is deserted. Where is everybody?"

"Oh, the guys are tired of tires and mechanicin'. They left this afternoon to go to Turquoise Lake for some ice fishing. Where have you been?" He eyed the gear bag in the back seat. "What's in that big bag?"

"You don't want to know. A couple of glocks and some extra ammo. I have been thinking about shooting up your station and looting your cash register. Buddy, the way you can check out the backseat of a car, while talkin' to the driver, could have made you the best policeman in Leadville. Do you know that?"

"Been down at your folks hanging drywall?"

"Gotta make ends meet. Working drywall in Denver on the weekends for some extra money to pay the heat bill."

"Ain't it the truth? More and more folks are putting in the pellet burners. Then once the pellet burners are hooked up, the utilities will probably buy out the pellet companies and run the pellet price up."

"You are right about that. Thanks Buddy." She handed him a twenty.

"All right, Miss Cheryl. I will get you twenty dollars worth and you can be on your way."

She rolled out of Marvin's and drove four blocks to Eleventh. All was quiet as she passed Nash Mendoza's home. Uphill two more blocks to 510. She noticed that her trampoline was no longer in her front yard. Max had picked it up. She climbed the stairs to her apartment. Cheryl turned the key and opened the door. Her apartment was empty. Everything was gone except the easel. My, the man had been busy. She spotted the miner replica on the floor hidden behind the easel. Three drawers to her dresser were on the floor where the bed used to be. She decided to move her art supplies and equipment in the drawers. She would need a few cardboard boxes to pack up what was left and the apartment would be empty. She was out of East Eleventh. No rent to pay. No utility bill to pay. A new parachute! Damn! She would have an extra eight hundred a month to keep for savings. It would keep her in avocados. Life was good. Today it was a little bit rearranged, but it was rearranged in a good way.

She headed for 304 West Seventh a one hundred and twenty year old mining home. The cost back then was three hundred dollars. Guggenheim had the house built for his daughter. The house was originally twenty five feet wide by twenty feet in length. It may not seem like much, but at the time, it surely beat a canvass tent in the winter. Another twenty feet in length was added in the fifties. Cheryl had searched Leadville for pictures of Guggenheim. Tabor's wife, Baby Doe, was all over the town but there were no pictures of Guggenheim's daughter. Maybe she was a dog. Maybe she was a potential kidnap victim. Not even a picture in the mining museum. The IRS was probably looking for her for inheritance taxes.

She drove down Poplar Street through the snow fall, and around the corners past the fire station. Harrison was lit up looking like a Christmas card. Just picture perfect. A soft glow from the street lights reflected off the snow in pools of light orange. Cheryl eased her car off Harrison and on to Eighth. At the three hundred block she turned left on Spruce.

A drop off existed at the entrance to the alley, where the side street ended, and the edge of the hill began. The neighborhood kids were sledding down the thirty foot hill and on out to the Seventh Street sidewalk. She turned into a snow filled alley and pulled into the carport. She grabbed her gear bag and passed through the iron gate. She carefully negotiated the half inch of fresh snow on the recently shoveled path to the side porch. Plastic bags and cardboard boxes filled with trash, lined the fence by the snow covered path to the side porch. The rubbish would be hauled to the dump when a truck could be borrowed from MacDonald. That would probably happen whenever Max found ten dollars for gas. A fifty foot snake to clean clogged sewer lines rested next to the door. Not a good sign. She opened the door and set her gear bag down next to a wood table by the kitchen door. She gave the table a quizzical look. Ah, ha! It was her table! She looked through the window. No one was in the kitchen. Cheryl tried the door. Warm air hit her face and a fragrance from the kitchen wafted under her nose. Where was Max? Ordinarily, he would have been out to help her. She returned to the car one more time to lock up and retrieve his gear bag.

She quietly entered the kitchen to sneak up on him. She spied her pots, pans and dishes on the sink counter. A light scent of lemon clorox mixed with the heavy smell of hamburger chili. Damn, the hombre had hamburger and kidney bean chili cooking in the crock pot. I bet he could do the French Onion soup with my favorite cheese. What a guy. It wouldn't be long before she would rip his clothes off and nail him. Goodness! Miss Manners! Where did that thought come from? Is it the effect of the house? She knew it was. She turned the croc pot off. She hung the keys on the peg by the door. A knotty pine counter, with overhead glass door cabinets, ran the length of the back wall. A lazy Susan and hidden trash collector were built into the counter in the corner. She heard a noise in the bathroom. Max entered the kitchen all smiles.

"I must be dreaming. There is a beautiful lady walking around in the house. Would you like some chili?" Max picked a bowl and spoon from the counter and began to fill his bowl. "There is OJ and sandwich material in the refrigerator. Help yourself. Pardon me, but it is time for me to eat. I need a break." He poured a glass of water and moved to the yellow metal table in the dining room. Max eased himself into one of the chairs. Cheryl helped herself to a glass of orange juice and sat across from him.

"You are taking a break when there is so much left to do?"

"Hhhmph!" He wanted to laugh. He gave her a small smile. "I guess now is a good time for a situation report on the sewer line."

Cheryl inquired. "And the problem is?"

"Oh, the main drain line is slow right now. The tub and bathroom sink back up pretty fast. Then it backs up to the utility sink and the kitchen sink. The line was clogged."

"The house line to the city line?"

"Yes ma'am. Something is clogging the sewer line. Don't use too much water to shower or you will be standing in half a foot of soapy water."

"Okay, who says I want to take a shower?"

"I can smell your sweat stained garments from here you fox. They are heavily stained with fear sweat, and I think you might have dumped your drawers. I bet you went to Bev's Pizza Parlor today. Did you win any pool games?"

"We can talk about that later."

"The large power snake at the rental center was loaned out. This skinny one did not have enough ummph to knock the clog out. I'll rent the heavy coil one some night this week and put the finishing touch on it. I thought that it might have been ice. But that did not really make sense because the sewer line temperature should be above freezing. Later it occurred to me that it could be grease from the kitchen stove dumped down the line for the last forty years. So I filled up the tub with hot water. Then I ran the snake while the hot water washed the line. It worked. It opened up about twenty five per cent. Just outside the house there is a ninety or forty five degree turn to the alley line. There is some kind of obstruction at that point. Cast iron pipe leaves the crawl space." A nuisance look clouded his face. "In any case either the house settled or the alley settled from years of traffic. It may be that the joined pipe no longer matches up out side the house." He looked at her beautiful face and grace. "I just set the commode back when you showed up. There is water in a drywall mud bucket to flush the toilet for now."

Cheryl stood. "You got a plan and you are working on it. Good for you, Mr. Fixit!" She chucked him on the shoulder.

"It will be my summer pick and dig project."

Cheryl concealed her excitement and curiosity. She said blandly, "Hey, Max. I need a place to put my rig. Mind if I look around?"

His face lit up like a little boy at Christmas time. "You got a parachute? You lie!"

"It is out on the porch. I will bring it in. I just want to look around right now, okay?"

"Feel free to take the better home and garden tour. I am going to have a little more chili. Thanks for turning off the crock pot, by the way."

"Do I get a brochure with a comment section?"

"I am afraid I am fresh out. This is an emergency shelter. What you see is what you get. I can't be buying or adding any extra things."

Cheryl stuck her head in Mac's old office room. It was now a bedroom and an office. The floor had genuine white vinyl squares designed to look like imported marble. MacDonald's heavy hide a bed had been moved in from the living room. It was fully open. Cheryl identified her queen sized mattress on the fold out bed. In the center of the mattress was a pile of bedding and clothes that she did not recognize.

A fresh coat of paint covered a long closet area from the door to the outside wall. An over head shelf in the closet was about five feet off the ground. A stout clothing bar ran parallel half a foot below. A mixture of clothing and stowed items were in the closet on the left half. Cheryl recognized a few of her own things. Momentary storage she thought. It reminded her of how sudden the move had been. In the right half of the closet was a makeshift office. Her cinder blocks and a two drawer file cabinet were holding up a wood door that served as a desk top. On top of the table was a computer, a printer and a photocopier. A fax machine and a telephone were under the table. Oh, boy! Another new learning experience. She eyed the photocopier and the computer.

"Where did you get this plastic stuff?"

"I leased it so you could go to secretary school and get a decent job."

"Are you going to collect workman's comp while I support you?"

"Ha, ha, ha! Please, let me finish dinner in peace and quiet."

"Hey!" Cheryl said accusingly, "Where did you get these cinder blocks?"

She stuck her head into the dining room and said in her best small voice with a slight twinge of whine, "Honey, can I pick out the contact paper for the desk top?"

Max laughed. "Yew shuwer can, baby."

"I have seen this kind of thing before. New contact paper is the only way to go."

"Gawd! I'm in heaven! Yew got impeccable taste baby!"

The room had a nine foot ceiling. It felt spacious. There was a rickety chest of drawers she recognized as hers. Three of the drawers were back at her apartment. She opened the top drawer and saw his clothes. This was going to be his room. I bet I know what is in the upstairs. Cheryl left the bedroom with a smile and asked Max, "Is this my room, honey?"

"There is another one upstairs. Pick the one you want."

"What did you do with the thousand dollars under my television set?"

"It paid the bill for my eye surgery." Max rose from the chair. He quietly refilled his bowl in the kitchen and returned to the table.

Cheryl had never been upstairs, although MacDonald had teasingly invited her. She walked into the utility room and eyed the handy sink. There were washer and dryer hookups and enough space for both. Two sliding track doors concealed the empty storage space under the stairway. This would be a good place to store her paintings and tools of the trade.

She peeked in the bathroom on the right. A small sink was in the corner. The bath tub was to the left. The commode was in between. A five gallon bucket filled with water sat beside it. State of the art plumbing! She returned to the utility room and she climbed the stairs to the second floor opening under the peak of the roof. The roof of the house over the kitchen had been raised. The result was a large upstairs room with a low slanted ceiling.

Cheryl stepped into the bedroom. The entire length of the east wall was windowed for passive solar. Six windows lined the wall. They were one and a half by three feet in size. Every other one had a lock on the top and two hinges on the bottom. What an incredible view. She could see all over the small mountain town. Snow covered rooftops were everywhere she looked.

She was pleased that she would be able to see the Silver King's Loop and the head frames. The mountains usually blocked the sunrise colors ninety per cent of the time, but Cheryl was always anxious to see the view anytime day or night. The colored neon lights of the retail shops and the familiar orange glow of the downtown street lights reflected off the snow. After seven blocks the lights began to thin out. A few lights were on in the houses on the mountainside. The lights of a group of snowmobiles were going over Mosquito pass into Fairplay. There was a small one by three foot vertical window to the front. It allowed a view south down the valley.

The four poster bed looked inviting. A low, double drawer dresser rested against the footboard of the bed. Cheryl knew she would put her miniature oil lamp and notebook there. All the comforts of home. A familiar sleeping bag and two bundled sheets with the corners tied up like a big hobo bag were in the center of the mattress. She tugged at one of them and she could see that her clothes were inside. Obviously, Max has given her the upstairs bedroom. A long closet under the apex of the roof was three feet deep and divided into three sections. Maybe she could set her chest of drawers in one of them.

She realized that Max had made this incredible gesture of kindness to her. This was a really good set up. The view of course was everything. What a stroke of luck. Cheryl was moved. She could deal with this. No rent and a chauffer to drive her to work. The house was one of those places where you felt as if you were sleeping in a tree or a low hanging cloud. You could see your entire neighborhood first thing in the morning. This was like being a bird living in a nest at the top of a tall tree. She liked this dream. Maybe she would be part of it. Time will tell. She could always continue to look for an apartment if things got out of hand. She turned to go back downstairs. A small closet was on the left. On the stairway there was a small door that opened to a storage area among the roof trusses.

Cheryl took her time going down the stairs to get use to the steps and the small amount of overhead room. She had to tip her head slightly to the side to avoid the sloping ceiling. The place smelled great. The entire house had been thoroughly cleaned. She would be sure to tell him the place is a pig sty.

"I don't think this is going to work out. Do you really expect me to live in this run down hovel?" Max recoiled. "The upstairs bedroom is way too small." Was he dreaming? Did she just say she didn't like it? Cheryl continued. "I want my bed in the living room in front of the bay window!"

"Arrrrr! This pig sty is not good enough for her. She wants to be head wench and chief pirate!" He laughed. "You got me, Cheryl. Good one. I almost put mine there."

"And I want you to sleep outside. You can't be in the house when I am here."

He laughed again. "I would settle for the front closet with a swinging dog door." Max looked up from the empty bowl of chili. He rose from the chair. "Let's check out the front room together. I worked for the last two days and nights trying to arrange this place to trap you and then I realized that it is the house and the view that springs the trap. I am sorry for the bathroom. It will be fine by the end of the week." They walked through the open square arch into the living room together. A 1970's Montgomery

Ward wood stove was to the immediate right. The legs of the wood stove were on flat slabs of rock.

"This area around the stove is all fire proof." Behind it was a wall of Z brick with four different colors. It had the used brick look. "There is a metal screen that covers the front of the stove if the doors are open. It will keep the hot cinders from popping out on to the carpet. If you look close there are a couple of burn marks on the rug." There was a stack of wood in the corner beside the stove along with a large can of lighter fluid and a box of big wood kitchen matches.

The front door was at the left corner along with a five by ten foot open area and a coat closet. The off white acoustical squares that made up the ceiling showed signs of cigar and cigarette smoke. The light green wall paper was holding up well. The light green short loop rug on the living and dining floor sported a worn path from the front door to the kitchen.

They stopped in front of the huge bay window and stared out at the magnificent scenery. What a view! Simply gorgeous. Snow capped peaks on both sides of the valley reflected the light of the full moon. A small beige two seat sofa was in front of the window. A large rectangular storage box filled the space beneath. It served as a bench and a coffee table.

"I thought this was a nice spot for a love seat."

"Turn the lights out. I want to see the stars."

He flipped the light switch. Here they sat for the first of many times to come. They stared at the heavens and mountains, something more vast and imminent than they. "Please be seated, your highness." Cheryl sat on the love seat. "May I sit with you?"

"Oh, by all means. Please sit next to me."

"It is a great honor for me." He sat next to her. Their eyes adjusted to the stars.

Cheryl decided to see if she could startle him. "Want to start a fire?"

Max turned to look at her. His body temperature was up. His breathing increased though he fought to keep it in check. He was not shaking yet, but he soon would be. He voluntarily made his lips quiver and his legs twitch. "You, you, you mean in the wuh, wuh, wood stove?" His eyes darted about. They were unable to focus. "I was hoping you would say that. Th, th, the wuh, wuh, wood is outside."

"You are very attractive when you are nervous."

"Thank you."

"Let me phrase it this way so I do not scare you. How is the fireplace working?"

"Heck fire! Fire it up. Don't wait for my approval. As far as I know, women have been burning down log cabins as long as men have."

"Are you kidding? You are going to let me make the fire? Max, I do not want to make your head explode with my next question, but isn't that one of those traditional male chores?"

"I am not going to do everything for you. That would spoil you. Sooner or later in life you are going to have to learn how to take care of yourself. I believe in sharing work. I'm one of the new millennium men. I even cheat and use lighter fluid. It gets the draft going right away and it keeps the room from filling up with smoke. By the way, I need something under my feet. A foot stool perhaps."

"You are so masculine and you have so much charisma when you give orders. Get it yourself, honey." Cheryl was all smiles. Finally! The first thing she wanted to do when she walked into the room was to start a fire and sit in front of the bay window in the dark. They moved to the fireplace. In a few swift movements she had tinder in the stove and three logs on top. She applied a generous coat of lighter fluid. She was ready to light the fire.

"You might want to stand back a bit before you throw that match."

Cheryl stepped back. She struck the match and tossed it in. The woodstove erupted in flame. It startled her.

"Ha, ha, ha! Happy now?"

"That is a lot of fun with the lighter fluid. Does it have the same effect with clothing?"

"Whose clothes? What are you talkin' about? Stop! You're scaring me!"

"Fires have that satisfying feeling of warmth and security." Cheryl stared at her naugahyde couch disguised with two white sheets. "Hey! Where did you get that couch? Is that a monster to move or what?"

"I was going to cut it up and use it for fire wood." They returned to the love seat and continued to stare at the beauty outside the window. The contrast was overwhelming. Inside was warmth and comfort. Outside was the harsh reality of winter at ten thousand feet. They could see the flames of the fire dancing in the reflection of the window. Max was beginning to fall asleep. He secretly hoped they would be sitting here and reminiscing about this move ten years from now. They could make it. So far they were getting along as friends united against the harsh economic recession in a small mountain town. Hang on. Don't rock the boat. Try to chalk up a year.

Cheryl broke the silence. "The alcove in the dining room would be a good place for a sewing machine. Would that be alright with you, Max?"

"Sewing machine? Sure! Is it in Arvada?"

"No it is at my Grandmother's house. My grandma said I could have her sewing machine. She lives in Carbondale. It would fit perfectly right thar," Cheryl said in her best grating voice. It sent chills and goose bumps to his torso and arms.

"Sure thing. That would be terrific."

"Max, I have a few more things in the apartment. I am going to try to clear everything out tonight."

"Would you like some help?"

"It won't take long."

"There are two extra keys by the door."

"Okay, Max. Thanks. I am going to pick up some extra cardboard boxes at the liquor store. Do you want a couple? I might stop at the Movie Store and pick up a couple of DVD's."

"See you later. I am going to eat another bowl of chili and clean up some more."

Cheryl found five sturdy boxes at the liquor store. They would be stout enough to hold her heavy books and her sculptures. She drove back to 510 East Eleventh Street. She had to be careful of the new wet snow on the steps, no slipping allowed. The apartment had served her needs for a brief transition. Now it was ready for someone else. Her nagging financial problem suddenly disappeared. She collected her books, her paints and brushes, her paintings, her kitchen gear and the few remaining clothes. She stowed them in the drawers and the cardboard boxes. She moved it all down to the Swinger. She loaded the trunk and back seat. The legs of the easel stuck out of the back window. The car was packed. Maybe Max would be up for a snowball fight when she got back. The moisture in the snow was just right for packing.

This was going to be fine. The move seemed sudden. It just fell into place. A pretty decent offer. Nothing was forced. Cheryl left a note in the landlady's mailbox to keep her deposit to pay the electric bill. She coasted past Nash Mendoza's house in the quiet of the early evening. She rolled down Harrison on the new snow past Sayer Mckee pharmacy and retail store. At the end of the block she turned the corner at Sixth Street and parked by the Movie Store. She jumped inside and shopped the comedy section. She picked up Naked Gun, The Adams Family, and Happy Gilmore.

She returned to the house, one of the little jewels in the crown of the hill. Three small ones were on the east half of the block and four big ones were on the west. She opened the door to the kitchen. The knotty pine wainscot was sparkling. The stove and the refrigerator were pulled out and cleaned. The doors were still open. She closed them. A few pots and pans were tucked neatly away in the cupboards. The crock pot was clean and the remaining chili was tupperwared in the refrigerator.

"Hey, you old fart! Do you want to toss a couple of snowballs? The snow is perfect for packing." There was no response from Max. She teased him a little bit more. "Just for your little attitude I am going to tell my parents to come up and visit."

"I do not want any city folk tramping around here, nosing in my b'ness and tellin' me what a dump I live in."

"By the way, what happened to the trampoline?"

"It had a bad memory on it so I sold it. I got seventy dollars for that piece of hospital furniture."

"That is seventy times that I will hit your right eye."

"It is wrapped up and stored in the half basement. Max tilted his head. He had an inquisitive look on his face. "Honey, you have changed. Your attitude and the way you are bossing me around, it ain't right. Dang! I thought you would be a good roommate."

Cheryl set out some air fresheners. She put two strong ones in his room. She stashed her art supplies and easel under the stairs. The bathroom needed a dresser or closet. She stacked two cardboard boxes next to the tub for make shift shelves. That would do for now. When she returned to her bedroom one hobo sheet was in the middle of the floor. A heavy duty yellow extension cord ran to the electric blanket control dial parked on top of the double drawer dresser. The dial was set on four. Max had made up her bed while she was running around. What a guy! She checked the bedding. There were two flannel sheets that sparked big flashes of static electricity, and two blankets. One of them was a brown electric blanket. The idea appealed to Cheryl. She lifted the sheet and slid her hand underneath. Wow, an instant hot tub! The bed was warm. She turned off the temperature control box. Oh, man! What comfort. What luxury. Probably better than a hot tub. You can sleep in a hot bed and not drown. If you can be indoors at ten thousand feet during winter with a wood stove and an electric blanket you can bask in luxury.

Next to the blanket control on the dresser was a large three ring binder used for family photos. She would put her DZ photos in it. She placed her new cloth covered logbook and the skydive information manual next to it. She put the oil lamp on the dresser and set her notebook next to it. She arranged her clothes in the closets. She stored her artwork and materials under the stairs. An hour later they settled on the couch in the living room to watch a movie.

"Cheryl, what movie would you like to watch?"

"The Adam's Family. Have you ever seen that?"

"Great comedy. Probably a true story. I will be right back."

He went to the kitchen and returned with two plates, two knives, a square of provolone cheese and one of cheddar, a box of wheat thins, and a box of regular salted crackers.

He sat them down under the TV table. Max made a second trip to the kitchen and returned with two large plastic drinking cups, a gallon of sangria, a bottle of Seven Up, and a pitcher of water. He sat them under the TV table. He went into his bedroom and brought out two pillows and a sleeping bag. He dropped the pillows against the couch and left the sleeping bag on the love seat. He returned to the couch and sat on the floor. He put a pillow against the couch and leaned back against it.

"I will pick up some big pillows from the Rose." He opened the bottle of sangria and poured a bit in his cup. He then added the Seven Up to it to make a wine spritzer.

"What kind of wine is that?"

"Carlo Rossi. You can't beat it. We started that winery in Italy three hundred years ago and I have been rich ever since. It has the best taste for provolone and crackers."

"Would you make one for me?"

"You better get your own."

"Okay. I see how this is going to be. What is the sleeping bag for?"

"If you interrupt my movie, I am going to stuff you in it and zip it up."

"I'd like to see you try. Do you think you can take me?"

"You better be careful. It might happen."

They relaxed and laughed with the movie. They enjoyed the evening, the snacks, and the light conversation. The evening was over when the movie ended.

Cheryl turned out the bedroom light. Before she crawled into the warm bed, she went to the small corner window and looked out over the town and down the valley. She went to her knees for a good view through the glass that separated her from the cold. Her thoughts shifted to a higher spiritual level. She prayed to her God. "Heavenly Father, I have been living in the mountains for two years now. I have been working in a craft that I like. Now, I have the luck of my own project. Will it carry me to other opportunities and keep me alive and working in this craft that I have chosen? My father and mother have the ability to provide a job and wages to me for a living. What an incredible safety net. How fortunate I am. My partner is a comedian with a good heart and a strong work ethic. What is going to become of this situation? There is really no worry at the present. We will see what unfolds. Thank you, Father. All things are possible through Your Son our Lord and Saviour, Jesus Christ. Amen. Cheryl absorbed the view for another minute before she turned to slip under the covers.

Before Max went to bed he looked out the bay window. All the lights were out in the house. He felt that it had been worth it to leave the big metro area. As things turned out, he found a low priced home in a place he dearly loved. He slipped out on the porch so he could glimpse a few stars. What was he going to do now? If he and Cheryl stayed together how would he provide? They would have dry wall work galore with her family. He could rent the houses in Leadville. That seemed to be the only direction available to him at this time. He was where he wanted to be right now, yet the means of support were not readily apparent. Would God provide? God always provides. There had always been something for Max. It would be up to Max to fulfill his needs. Now, with Cheryl present, he could no longer take off on a whim. She would not put up with a random life. He thanked God for the blessings that were given to him. He was thankful that he had the determination and ability to make this new effort a reality.

He prayed. "Dear God, thank you for all of the blessings you have given us. For many years I have lived my life with only memories of love. Now there is someone that I would accept into my life. I need wisdom and guidance in order to provide for Cheryl Pritchard and keep her happy. If you have any ideas, please pass them on to me. I ask this in the name of Jesus Christ, Your Son our Saviour. Amen."

After eight hours of sleep, Cheryl woke to her new environment with a smile on her face. Where was she? Oh, yes! Donald MacDonald's house. She liked everything about her new room. She stretched. The she did the usual isometrics. The flannel sheets sparked around her. Who played this trick on me?

On her back, she pressed her elbows into the mattress. She lifted her feet off the mattress twenty times. She did some crunches. She pressed her heels into the mattress ten times to lift her fanny off the bed. She needed to get a foam mat. The floor was a little more supportive. The mattress was for recuperation and rest. She rolled to her side and arched big time. Look, reach, pull thousand. Check canopy. The water was softly flowing through the hot water heat pipes.

She practiced a door dive out of the bed without hitting her head on the low ceiling. Cheryl put her feet into her thick wooly socks. She pulled off her faded yellow nightgown. Then she remembered the shades were not drawn last night. She could be seen. Oh well, the neighbors would have to suffer. No one lived next door anyway. She figured that she could close the first three window blinds, and no one in the green house on Eighth Street could see in. Cheryl liked the shades open at night so she could view the great outdoors.

She coasted to the open closet by the stairs. It held her foundry clothes, long johns, jeans, and sweaters. She pulled out a pair of jeans and stepped into them. She pulled on a plain white thermal top and covered it with a navy blue sweatshirt. The middle closet held her out and about clothing. Her paintings were stored in the last one.

She walked down the stairs slowly to get rhythm and co ordination flowing. She stomped her feet loudly on the last five steps and jumped to the floor. She ducked into the bath to brush her teeth and braided her hair to one plait in back.

"Did you fall and break your neck, sweetheart? You got the whole herd up and running." Max was using the microwave to prepare his lavish breakfast of coffee and oatmeal spiked with brown sugar and instant hot chocolate. It was his favorite by price and speed. Sometimes he nuked sausages. He moved his oatmeal and coffee mug to the bay window.

Cheryl joined him on the couch. "This is great. I love the view."

"I'm not quite used to seeing the whole valley in the morning. Do you think we could get spoiled?"

"One can always hope. What is on your agenda for the day?"

"Anything and everything. I could work at 407. If you go skiing, I would like to go with you. Are you plotting or planning anything special today?"

"I want to give myself a full day off. I would like to move the work table into the dinning room."

"We have to take the legs off one end to get it through the door. What else?"

"The noise in the pipes. I can help you drain the air out of them."

"There is a trap door in the kitchen pantry closet that goes to the crawl space to get to the heat system." He admitted to her that he did not know an awful lot about the baseboard heat and the Stewart Warner boiler. "Mac left some good notes when they installed it, so I know which pipes go upstairs which ones go to the kitchen and the front rooms, bath and so forth. I just need one more trip underneath to find the drain valve. It should be on the hot water line right close to the boiler. Come to think of it there are probably two. One for each zone right by the boiler."

"I leave Tuesday for San Francisco. I planned to take it easy this weekend and do nothing. I thought I would be moving all day today, but it is all done. Thank you."

"You are most welcome."

"It would be great to have another day at Ski Cooper."

"I certainly agree with you. I could ski a couple of hours and still put some time in on 407."

"I have a tentative plan to go to work two hours early Monday and stay all night. I am going to pull the molds and get them to Molly. She is going to rush them through the wax room. I need you to rush them through the shell room as fast as you can. If it does not get done, then I will be two weeks behind when I get back and there will be two or three projects in front of the miner. I would miss the deadline by a mile."

"Is it burning a hole in your head?"

"You know, the more I think about it, if anything comes up out of the blue, and the molds do not get to Molly before I leave . . ." Cheryl paused for a moment.

"It is burning a hole in your head."

"If I don't do it today and something comes up Monday, then I am screwed."

"Cheryl, did you just ask me to give you some preferential treatment?" He tried to keep his face straight.

"That's right, bucko! You have to work with me and for me on this project."

"Why don't we take care of it today before your brain is engulfed in flame? The roads and weather are good right now. We could sneak over and back easily. What would it take, four or five hours? I will drive for you."

"I can tell that you really care for me. You know, the more I think about it, the more I need to pull those molds today."

"If you pack the food, I will start the car."

"We have a nice place to come back to this afternoon. Will the house still be here?"

"Yes it will, and so will the movies."

"Let's go. You talked me into it."

CHAPTER TWENTY

Cheryl examined the base. "Okay, Max. Mary and I tried to keep the plaster off the top of the shims. You can see a few places on the base where the plaster covers them." He nodded his head vigorously. "When you find a spot where the plaster covers the shims, you take this miniature drywall saw and saw the plaster away. You may have to saw the plaster away two times in small layers. Do this very carefully, without bumping the shims. Once you are down to the latex, you cut open the latex on the shims with a utility knife. Got that Max?"

"Aye, aye skipper."

"We will take a couple of molds off the base for practice. Then we will start up top on the hat." Cheryl spoke the words she had been eager to say since her miner had been covered with the plaster. "Alright, Max, watch me get the first one. Watch closely now." Cheryl selected a section where the shims were covered with plaster. Max watched her go through the plaster with the small dry wall hand saw. Once the latex was exposed, she used the utility knife to cut the latex open along the shims.

"Now, pulling the mold is tricky. The first one is the most difficult. You don't want to tear the rubber." Cheryl used four flat screw drivers on the plaster section. It released, but the latex held to the clay surface. They examined the plaster. "It is as dry as a pile of sun bleached bones in the desert. We put a thick coat of latex on the statue. The thin ones tend to tear easily. Now, to remove this latex, just take your time." Cheryl rolled the latex back, and then she gently pulled it away from the clay. Finally, the section of latex separated from the clay surface. "Sometimes small amounts of clay will stick to the latex. Don't worry about that right now." She carefully placed the latex impression into the section of plaster.

"Okay, you do the next section. Take your time. Don't mess it up." Max was able to get the plaster mold off without any problem. He rolled the latex back and peeled it off slowly. "Nice touch, Max. Let's move up top." They set their tools on the scaffold. Cheryl was up on one side of the hat and Max was on the other. "You want an easy touch on the bill of the hat. Be careful. This is a delicate situation." Once they removed the molds from the hat, they began to work in earnest. An hour later they moved the molds out to the hall, and they lowered the height of the scaffolds. In another half hour they set the scaffolding out in the hall. It was time for a break.

"Let's find some carts and get theses molds to the wax room. We can clean the latex and eat lunch at the same time." They rounded up two small table carts and piled the molds on the top and bottom shelves. In the wax room, Cheryl showed him how to remove the clay from the latex with a cloth and acetone. A small wood cuticle stick was used in grooves where the clay was caked in to the detail.

"Excuse me for a minute. I will be right back." She took a short break to go to the office. Cheryl phoned Molly. "Happy Sunday, Molly. I am in the wax room cleaning off the miner latex. Half of them are ready for you."

"That's great, Cheryl. I have been thinking about you. I will be over in about thirty minutes. We can get your waxes started today and be ahead of the prairie people. I'm glad you called. I'm glad you came in today, that was a good idea. See you soon."

Cheryl and Max pushed the carts back to the miner room to pull the rest of the molds. The plaster and latex sections released without a problem. She inspected each one of them. They loaded the carts again and pushed them back to the wax room to clean the latex. There were six molds on the large work bench. Molly and the help were doing two at a time. It was going to be a group effort today. It would reduce the extra hours they would have to put forth during the week.

"Molly, do you want any help from us?"

"Nah, Cheryl. You can catch up with me when you come back from the coast. Our team is going to put in four or five hours. Have you finished packing for your convention? I'll bet it is waiting for you back at the house. Am I right?"

"Molly, you are so right, and we will see you tomorrow." Cheryl and Max took the hint and returned to Leadville.

They removed the legs on her work table and wrestled it outside in order to get a better angle through the kitchen door. They bounced around until the table was set in the dining room along the wall and adjacent to the alcove.

"Max this is really a good setup here."

"Looks like you have plenty of room to hold material and slide it to the sewing machine."

"Let's go look at your noisy pipes. Cheryl opened the kitchen closet and pantry door. Aha! A trap door! Cheryl raised the floor door. "It looks kind of homey down there with the utility light. Is this Mongo's new home? It could be a viable alternative for you."

"You are way to kind. Yes. It is a good secure feeling to have a back up space available for me. You are pretty scary at times but I pretend not to notice. By the way, I like the braid in back. It makes your ears look smaller than they actually are." Max gathered two empty buckets. He collected the tools he needed. A pair of large and medium channel locks, a pipe wrench, a screw driver, utility light, and WD 40 were placed in the bucket. He dropped an extension cord into the half basement and he carried a broom to knock the cobwebs away.

"How about a pair of heavy gloves?"

"That is really a good idea with the hot water lines. You never know when one might leak or a fixture might break."

"Just trying to keep you straight."

He dropped through the trap door and Cheryl handed the buckets down to him.

"Okay, plug the extension in." The light went on and Max moved to the boiler to sweep the cobwebs away. He looked at the two zone tags and traced the lines back to the boiler. "Got it." One faucet was rusted shut. He applied WD 40. The two drain faucets and shut offs were in good working condition. "Okay, turn the thermostat up and get the pump going." He barely opened the drain faucet and he placed the bucket underneath. Water dribbled out along with the occasional whisper of air as it escaped from the line. "Hey, Cheryl?"

"Yeah."

"The instructions on the pump say 'Lubricate with sewing machine oil.' Do you have any?"

"Sure do." She passed the small can down to him. "Don't drink it, Mongo, it will upset your dinner."

"Oh, ha, ha, ha. It's a good thing good thing you pushed me. The pump was out of oil. It is all stout equipment. Nothing cheap here." Max added oil to the reservoir. "Runnin' smooth."

After thirty minutes, the lines were free of air.

"Here you go Cheryl. I have a bucket of hot for you."

She reached down for it. "Dump it in the commode?"

"Unless you want to gargle a little bit first."

"Oh, ha, ha, ha."

They cleaned up and worked on business cards for her convention trip. She decided to use "Sculpture by Cheryl" as her logo. She added her Arvada address and phone number to the card. The sixty five pound paper Max had available would do for now. She used a picture of her replica and made up some tasteful flyers. Now she was set to hand out cards and flyers at the convention. She disappeared to her bedroom to put together the coal miner outfit she would wear. She packed her replica, the cards and flyers, and her other clothes and necessities. When she finished there were three cardboard boxes by the kitchen door. Marilyn would have her suitcases ready in Arvada.

Max was up for the twenty minute drill Monday morning. He turned the thermostat up and punched the button for the micro wave. Before he finished his teeth the coffee and oatmeal were ready to eat. He set Cheryl's plastic food bag on the counter. He carried two of her boxes out to the Swinger and fired it up. Coffee wafted up the stairs.

Cheryl went into the bathroom and slammed the door.

Max taunted, "Not awake yet sugar cakes."

"Don't you sugar cake me."

"No worry, lassie. I'll keep my distance. Did you sleep on a wrinkle last night Princess?"

"Maybe I did. It would not be any of your business anyway."

Oh my gosh, a roommate, and a female at that. I must be out of my mind. She is kind of cute though. "Are we playing roommates from hell this morning?"

"If you want it to be roommate from Hell day, I can give you that. You ain't seen nothing yet, mister. Say, Max, there are three boxes by the door. Would you take them out to the car for me?"

"I don't see any boxes."

"My thirty eight is in one of them."

"Oh! I see them! Right away, dearest. Your smallest command is my greatest desire. My, oh my, this sure is some mighty glamorous luggage you have here, Miss Cheryl. You sure you want to take a chance that the baggage system will lose it for you?"

Cheryl emerged from the bathroom and gave him a serious smack on his fanny.

"Thank you. Does everything meet your expectations?" Are you enjoying the relaxed lifestyle at 304?"

"I am very happy. I got to admit the sleep was fantastic. I think this is going to continue to be a good routine."

"Mongo happy too, Princess." They exchanged a quick thank you kiss. "Ready to go?" Max picked up the third box. Cheryl followed behind and locked the doors.

Cheryl stopped in the wax room to talk with Molly. Six pots were going and six molds were on the table. The wax was flying and Molly was giving directions to Cindy and Johnny. Her face lit up. "We will work overtime on the prairie people and the bronco all week. Don't you worry, Cheryl. I will do your waxes right along with them. We got two coats on your molds yesterday. It was Cindy's idea. All of your waxes will be in the shell room by the end of the week. The spruing will take time, but we will get it done. Cindy and Johnny are going to be here all week with me, so I have plenty of help. You go have a good time in San Francisco! And please, send us a post card."

Bob and Mary kept busy with their new routine in the front office. Mary had several greeting cards in front of her. She penned, "Please make an immediate payment and follow it up with a phone call, and your project will have our undivided attention. We would be delighted to hear from you." Bob put a similar message on the answering machine. More materials were ordered to increase inventory for the four projects that would consume the foundry for the next month. Two shipments of materials arrived this week. The mining museum wired a fifty percent up front payment to the foundry checking account, and Wes Culpepper's check cleared.

Before Cheryl left for Arvada she stopped to see Max in the shell room. "Max, I should be back to Denver by Friday. I've got a key to 304. How about you?"

"Yes. I have mine. You have a great time, Miss Cheryl."

"Max, work on 407 and stay out of trouble. Don't do anything else. Wait for me and be a good boy, okay? I should be in Leadville Saturday."

"You must have been an older sister. You are kind of controlling and bossy sometimes. I love you Cheryl. See you next weekend."

CHAPTER TWENTY ONE

Marilyn picked Cheryl up at the airport when she returned from the San Francisco trip. When they arrived home, Cheryl thought they were at the wrong house. A metallic burgundy pick up truck with a gold stripe from nose to tail, was parked in the driveway.

"Cheryl, your beautiful new truck is waiting for you to take it for a drive. The salesman called Wednesday and agreed to your terms."

"Yea! A reliable vehicle. I want to pick up a washer and dryer over at Salvation Army. I have been thinking about it all week. Go with me, Mom. I will need help to load them up!"

"Sure, let's get all of your things inside the house first."

That night Cheryl shared a relaxed evening and pictures of her convention adventure with her parents. Hal and Marilyn came up with the idea to follow her to Leadville in the morning. They wanted to visit and look for low priced homes. Saturday morning they were up early and out of the house with a plan to explore Leadville. They devoured eggs and pancakes at the Pancake House in Idaho Springs. They rolled into Leadville at nine. Cheryl drove to 304 from the opposite end of the alley so her parents could see the larger homes on the block and the view. The view was appealing, but the three feet of snow in the alley had a negative effect. Max was dragging sewer cleaning coils to MacDonald's truck on the car port. He was astonished as the Pritchard's pulled up. He eyed Cheryl's metallic burgundy pick up with a pang of jealousy.

"Lord, have mercy! What a beautiful truck Cheryl."

"They took an even trade for my Swinger. Mom put one hundred and fifty miles on it. Hal gave me six quarts of synthetic oil. If you change engine oil every three thousand miles, you can get three hundred thousand miles out of the engine with no problems. You look a little grungy this morning. Any luck with the drain?"

"It's working. It's new again!" Max and Hal unloaded the washer and dryer while the Pritchard's parked on Spruce Street. They walked around to the front of the house and began the home tour on the front patio.

Marilyn cut the first grating remark. "Max, this certainly is one incredible view, but look at this pitiful front yard. All you got here is this steep avalanche chute down to the street. It looks like you have to ride a saucer sled down to your mailbox. How do you get your mail?"

"Slowly. You have to wait until summer to pick up the mail."

Hal loved the patio. "Right here. Put the grill right here. This is a beautiful spot for a barbecue grill right here. You have a great spot to relax."

Max believed in courtesy and offered, "Y'all come up this summer and I can fry us up some locusts to eat out here. Them are a delicacy in the eastern hemisphere. It is a good source of protein, and you are soffissicated if you have grass hopper legs sticking out of your teeth. I should have a bunch of patio furniture out here by summer time." They climbed the front steps to the door.

"Come on inside where the view is warm."

They stood in front of the bay window and admired the view. Hal recognized the wood stove. "An old Montgomery Ward catalogue wood burner. I bet it cuts your utility bill by seventy five percent." They moved towards the kitchen

Marilyn stopped in the dining room. She was staring at the alcove space.

"There is a little bit of a slope on the floor here, but I think the old treadle sewing machine would fit perfect here. Cheryl, your Grand Ma in El Jebel has a family heirloom."

"Yeah?"

"It would be perfect right here! I'll call her and tell her that you will be over to pick it up."

They checked out the office bedroom. Cheryl told Marilyn, "I'm learning word processor and computer. Maybe I can get your drywall books on the computer. Max has an accounting program and payroll program."

"Nah! We pay by cash. No sense in keeping written records around."

They moved on into the kitchen. "Well, Cheryl, you ain't gonna have any fun in the kitchen. There is no sink sprayer. You have no water fights to look forward to."

Max knew that insult was for him. "Oh, no! They are ganging up on me."

They entered the utility room. Max stepped into the bathroom to place the commode over the sewer drain.

Hal stuck his head in the door. "Mercy! I see nothing has changed with you. You smell like shit. Does this contraption automatically retrieve your food for you?"

"I just a had a fresh shower this morning and a powder. If anyone needs the bathroom, go ahead. It is okay."

Cheryl commented, "My, sugar! No wonder MacDonald calls you Dip Shit!"

Hal eyed the blue coffee mug. "Good thing we caught this alky before he primed his pump."

Max admitted that he added a little whiskey to his coffee. "Alcohol reduces the bad odor from the sewer." They all laughed.

Marilyn chided, "Cheryl, you have to move out. You can't stay with Mr. Blood Vessels."

Max related his drain encounter. "I spent this morning cleaning the sewer line. It is a good thing you were not here. There must have been forty years of kitchen grease from cooked meals. I snaked the line two times with the big coil. I filled up the bath tub and the sinks with hot water. I opened the drain plugs and left the snake running as the hot water drained through. The line is open fifty percent now. Everything is fine.

"Thanks for that update. We are quite impressed."

"Actually the plumber's friend will take care of anything now. Have I ever shown you our family crest? It is a shield with a garbage can in the center. Centered on the can is a pair of crossed plumber's friends. It really is quite the crest."

Hal commented, "That seems to be fitting."

Marilyn and Hal surveyed Cheryl's bedroom. "Nice place Cheryl. You sleep up here by yourself. Don't you let that old flea bitten bag of bones sneak into your room."

When the tour was over, Max begged the Pritchard's for some help. "With three trucks I could move all the trash outside, and the trash at 407 to the landfill in one move. I could really use your help"

The Pritchard's agreed to help him.

"We feel sorry for you so we will help you move your trash. But it is going to cost you. You have to buy lunch."

"No problem. I got it covered. I will buy at Wild Bill's Hamburger Shop."

The Pritchard's pitch in and filled up the back end of MacDonald's pick up with all of the trash bags along the fence and they drove to 407.

Hal and Marilyn liked the old house at 407. It had potential. Cheryl gave her parents a tour while Max hauled out old worn out rolls of linoleum, rugs, trash bags, and cardboard boxes full of plaster to the trucks.

Hal commented, "My Mom used to tack the linoleum to the floor. When she got tired of it, all she had to do was roll it up and give it to someone. If you have cats and dogs that urinate all over the floor and each other, linoleum is the only way to go." Hal and Max loaded the old cast iron tub into the Power Wagon.

Marilyn spoke up for the group. "Your feng shui is pathetic. You should gut this place and make it an artist studio. Well, let's get moving because we do not have all day up here."

Wild Bill's was the next stop. Cheryl beckoned Max. "Wait outside and save a table for us. Your bio odors are a little strong. We will bring you a cheeseburger and fries." He handed her a twenty. They ate their sandwiches outside the Shop and took in the view of Mount Massive and Elbert. They drank the sodas and milk shakes on the way to the landfill.

The landfill opened at eleven and closed at two. What a glorious day for Max. He paid the entrance fee and slowly drove the gauntlet of prizes that could be reclaimed. Leadville was remodeling a few houses at a time. New fixtures from stores in Grand Junction or Denver were put in the homes and the old fixtures were left at the landfill. After a clorox bath and some new paint on the recycled items, no one would know the difference. There were kitchen tables, kitchen wall cabinets, and floor cabinets. There were bathtubs, commodes, double sinks, bathroom sinks and cabinets, vanity mirrors, beds, coffee tables, end tables, and drawers of all sizes. Max saw two floor length mirrors in the furniture pile. They could use a couple of mirrors at both places. He rolled for the edge of the landfill and backed up to it. The Pritchard's were laughing as they backed up along side him at a safe distance.

"Cheryl, my Gawd! Did you see that grown up man salivating like a dog over those used items? He ain't never gonna have nothing more than trash in his life! You ought to get rid of him now before things get complicated. Try the slow poison routine."

Cheryl yelled at him. "We saw your eyeballs pop out back there!"

"Ah gots to get that bath tub. That there is a modern convenience. I need to get me a high standard of living in 407."

"The pink one?"

Max finished flinging the trash into the landfill and looked over the spoils. He felt like a little kid at Christmas time. He quickly loaded two metal bathtubs, light blue, and bright white. The blue one was open on the right side and would fit against the bathroom wall at 407 just below the window that viewed Mount Massive. There were five kitchen floor cabinets and five overhead cabinets loaded into the power wagon. He set two double sinks and three bathroom sinks inside the floor cabinets. Cheryl picked up a folding cardboard table. Max looked around and noticed the representative was watching him.

"Did I do something wrong?"

"Well, it's starting to look like you are taking away more than you brought in. It is alright. We are glad someone has a use for it. Just about everyone who visits has had a chance to pick out anything they need. Are you going to sell those items?"

"No, sir! A remodel on East Fifth. The one across from Duran's."

"Good man. I know the miner who used to live there. Take care."

Cheryl was keeping a close eye on her new friend. It took a fat bank account to remodel a house. When Max was finished the color scheme would be light and bright. His craftsmanship could not be beat. He had probably just picked up five thousand dollars worth of items. They bid the operator goodbye and on the way out Max eyeballed the large pile of scrap wood. The wood could be used to cover the worn out steps on the porch at 304. There were some massive four by twelve inch wood beams. They would be handy to fashion some steps on the small slope beside the house. The steps down to the mailbox needed repair. The wood could be used to build a small deck for the front door of 407. He would be back to pick up the wood.

The trucks were emptied at 407.

"Thanks you both. You are welcome anytime."

Hal shook Max's hand. "We will be back up to visit. See you next time. You should gut this dump and turn it into an art studio."

Max bid farewell to Cheryl and her parents and moved the materials into the house. The Pritchard's drove all over town. They considered the possibility of buying a house in Leadville and doing drywall on the never ending expanse of the interstate corridor in the mountains. At the end of the day they had to decide against it. Denver was paid for. All of their referrals from fifteen years of diligent effort were there. The foot hills had plenty of work for them. There was always a small subdivision opening up somewhere. A small cabin in the mountains would be nice to have for getaways, but they did not need one. They would visit Max. Cheryl bid goodbye to her parents and returned to 304. She called Molly to see what was cooking at the foundry.

"Cheryl, put some gas in your car and chase some local men. All of your molds are in the shell room. It is great that you feel guilty, but why don't you think of it this way. You live all the way in Leadville. I live fifteen minutes away you live fifty minutes away. Why not let me and the people who live within a half hour do the wax. You do the chasing and the welding. Take a day off and go ski. Have some fun! Bring my check for my hard work on Monday. See ya." Cheryl prepared the living room for a romantic evening of sodas, munchies, and DVD. Max returned with a mirror, a landfill bathroom sink, and cabinet, and a bottle of Mr. Bubble. He had to get the bathroom decent for Cheryl.

Cheryl's alarm rang in her head. She stretched under the covers and tightened and released various groups of muscles. Six times she pressed the heels of her feet into the mattress and lifted her fanny in the air. She gradually increased the pressure until the muscles on the back of her legs were about to cramp up. She tightened her neck muscles and worked her way into a hard arch. She wasn't too groggy today. She slept with a knit hat to ward of the cold. No stuffy sinuses this morning. She pressed her elbows into the mattress and touched her shoulder blades together. She kicked the covers off and did twenty leg raises. She lifted her feet into the air and held them to a slow count of thirty. No mid riff bulge for Pritchard. She rolled over on her side, hit an arch, and tightened all muscles in her back. She turned her head just slightly and rolled her eyes down to the side of her hip, to the imaginary pilot chute. She grabbed her pilot chute and threw it out. She felt good mentally and physically. Outside the snow covered peaks and the Silver King Loop were still there. Wispy clouds streaked the sky. My, gosh! What a way to wake up in the morning! No sirens. No interstate traffic noise. No garbage trucks banging the dumpsters at five in the morning. She heard the water softly moving through the water lines. That settled it. No need to get up for five minutes until the house was warm. She knew Max had the furnace and coffee going. She would deal with him later. Maybe she would playfully test his abuse level today. Was it not the way of the world? Was it not great fun to have some unsuspecting soul to playfully antagonize?

Most men would have been at her bedside by now to accost her and seek favors in the early morning. Not Max. He was playing indifference up to this point, and that was just plain considerate. What an easy guy to be with. Live and let live. What a beautiful sleep. She used ear plugs at night. They helped her sleep. She made a mental note to pick up some more at Sayer McKee. She listened for sounds of life. She heard three soft dings of the microwave. She looked through the window for a full view of the Loop. She heard the bathroom door close softly and the faint sound of a shaver and a tooth brush. She yelled out, "Better use some Janitor in a Drum! Mongo's breath like old elephant." The bathroom door creaked lightly. In his thermal underwear and moon boots, he shuffled to the stairs.

"Oh, my gosh!" With a mouthful of tooth paste he managed, "The Queen is awake! God, save the Queen! The world awaits your presence this fine blustery morning your Majesty. All wait for your approval. Are you ready to begin another work week Princess?" Max retreated to the new bathroom sink. His items were in the cabinet now. He planned to add a few shelves and wall hooks to hold towels and bathrobes and other tems. Progress is wonderful, especially with no price tag.

"Hey, Mongo! Hang a couple of deodorizers under your armpits, would you?"

Max yelled "Cut away! Your chute is tangled. Cut away! Please hurry your Majesty! The fresh smell of your goat and camel are waiting for you, along with the brisk morning air."

Where was the plane? She was ready for a low hop and pop on the morning sunrise load. After that she would have a hot breakfast to get the system pumped up with all of those hot greasy sausages and bacons. Max promised her a sunrise load when she got off student status and a couple of night jumps. Her feet went into a pair of fluffy slippers. Cheryl hit her fourth hard arch. She stood on her left foot and held it until the muscles in her back and hips were cramped. She hit her imaginary pilot chute and threw it out as fast as she could. She ran through her emergency procedures three times. She thought she felt a sympathetic squirt of adrenaline. A tingle and a chill ran up and down her spine as she imagined an emergency malfunction. Could she stop all thought and focus on her cut away handle and get her reserve open in an instant? Could she do it if she was spinning or flailing about in the sky? Would she pull the handles? When in doubt whip it out! She checked her canopy and practiced some turns and a landing in her bedroom.

She picked up her photo scrap book. The first nine pages were filled. She wondered how soon it would be before the book was full, and where the pictures would be taken. She looked at the pictures of the drop zone and the jumpers she had met. They were going to be friends for a long time.

Cheryl and Max both needed a day off. They enjoyed a relaxed day together. They dinned at the Burro. They visited their favorite hangouts and met some of their friends. In the evening they watched comedy DVDs. They practiced turns and flips for Cheryl's next skydive weekend. They turned in early, as they planned to be at work two hours early everyday.

CHAPTER TWENTY TWO

Max executed the roll and lunge before the second muffled ring of the alarm clock. He would practice a couple at night before he went to sleep. He pulled out his ear plugs. Five in the morning. In his moon boots with a green sleeping bag around him, he crossed the floor. He shuffled to the bay window and looked out on the serenity. Every fourth street light cast an orange glow. There were a few signs of activity. One car rolled through the downtown intersection at Sixth and Harrison. All is well. At the south end of Harrison, where the street curved west, he saw headlights of a car coming in to town. The back kitchen window light was on at MacDonald's new place, just down the hill in front of him. He was grateful for his house and its location. He returned to the dining room and turned the thermostat up to seventy five. He quietly entered the kitchen. He picked up his bowl of oatmeal and slipped it in the microwave. He flipped on the switch of the coffee pot. He slipped silently into the bathroom to brush his teeth. He returned to the kitchen to claim his morning breakfast and a cup of coffee.

Cheryl dressed for the day in jeans and a sweat shirt. She threw an extra set of foundry clothes in her carry all bag along with two fresh bandanas. They would go into her locker at work just in case she stayed overnight. She raced down the stairs to the bathroom. In five minutes she was in the refrigerator. She reached for her plastic bag stuffed with the morning meal. A bread roll and a knife went into the bag along with a cluster of green grapes, enough for two people. Her new truck was running so Max must be dressed. She heard him at the porch door and then the kitchen door opened. She flashed a warm smile at him. He returned it and added a nod of the head. "It's a beautiful day today."

"They all are. Feel the flow. It will remain so. Is my coach ready, Mongo?" Cheryl stowed her carry all bag behind the seat. They hopped in and quietly left for work. It was time for her to relax for the drive. At the foundry she would release herself into the day's routine with boundless energy because she worked for the pleasure and the beauty. Cheryl loved the beauty. It was captivating. It was powerful and hypnotic. It was a luxury to work on beautiful sculptures of art and help to move them through the process towards completion. They sat in the comfort of her new truck and Max drove to Minturn.

"I need to visit my Grandma. She has a family heirloom just waiting for me in El Jebel. You may have heard Marilyn say that yesterday." He was munching a grape.

"Marilyn who?" He did the mental calculation. One hour and a half to I 70. Forty five minutes to Vail. One hour to Glenwood. Half an hour down to Carbondale. "It is about three and a half hours over to Mount Sopris."

"You don't say."

"We could camp out. We could visit the hot springs pool."

"You know, that is really a good idea. We could leave from the foundry after work and make Carbondale by eight."

"That's why you keep me around, Princess. Just the slightest nod of your approval keeps me all tuned up. I have a tent and a queen size air mattress."

"Max, let's do it. We can pack everything Thursday night and Friday we will celebrate this week with a camping trip."

"Your greatest wish is my smallest desire. Here we are your Majesty. Two hours early at the Robertson Foundry."

Cheryl made a quick early morning tour. The metal was in several piles on the foundry floor. There seemed to be a shortage of copper, mica, and silica as well as slurry mix and plaster. Max began his routine in the shell room. Cheryl moved to the wax room. Mark must have turned on the melting pots. The hard chunks of wax were just beginning to transition to thick liquid. Molly walked in a minute later.

"Cheryl, I certainly appreciate your extra help this morning."

"I owe you Molly. I will try to help as much as I can."

"I can use you early every day this week."

"I will be here to help you."

"We will get it done Cheryl. We will get it all, the prairie people, the jazz quartet, the bronco, and your miner. There is nothing that I can not do! It may take a couple of extra weeks, but who the heck cares? And then we will do even more statues! Do you realize that while you were gone the molds were pulled off the bronco and the prairie people? Let's start with the prairie people."

"Yes, I know. It is going to be a race to the finish line. I brought pictures of the convention. They are in my locker."

"Excellent! I am anxious to see them. Man, oh man. Bob got these extra work tables in here just in time. There is enough room for four people to wax the molds. Let's set out eight." Molly set up two more pots. Cheryl moved eight molds out to the table.

"Did you work this weekend?"

"Saturday morning our family went for an early jeep ride around the Horseshoe Lake area. We cooked out. Everyone wanted to get out of the house for awhile. The weather was really nice. We would have camped, but I worked Sunday, and the kids have their final exams coming up in a couple of weeks. They needed study time. It was dry enough to camp at the lower elevations. Cheryl, are you here? Are you deep in thought, or are you sleeping? Where did you go?"

"Max and I are planning to camp this weekend. I can't wait! I am wondering how it will go."

"You don't know him very well, do you?"

"What if he attacks me Molly?"

"Gosh, Cheryl. That might be a good thing, but he probably would have done it before now, don't you think?"

"You might be right about that. I do have a few options available to me. I could tell him that I have aids. That usually defuses the excitement level."

"Well, now, that is an original idea, how romantic."

"Then again, I just might crush his head with my powerful mandibles, and drag his husk into my tent, and lay my eggs all over him."

"I can see his feet squirming and kicking now."

"What if he starts talking to another girl in his sleep?"

"That would be a clear sign that you should look for a new apartment."

"So, Molly, tell me about your view here behind the windows. Do you just sit in here on your throne and view your kingdom?"

"Ha! That's for sure! I know everything. I know when the materials are low and when they get ordered. I know when Bob and Mary are arguing. I know when someone walks in with a go to hell attitude. I know it all!

And I get paid twenty five cents an hour less than you do. Bob sticks his head in here in the morning on the foggy days, and I rattle off the first thing on the list and the second and the third. He thinks about it and nods his head and takes off. It does not seem like much, but when you throw in the burden of a payroll and the money for materials, then the juggling problems emerge. Bob and Mary do a good job with the operation here. Hey, Cheryl, there is a rumor out that you found a new apartment."

"Yes, I moved in with Max. There is plenty of room. It's a great place with a nice view."

"Johnny and Cindy found a vacancy in Minturn. Do you have a platonic relationship with him? Enquiring minds want to know."

"You mean everyone in the foundry rumor mill? I don't know yet, Molly."

"Okay, Cheryl. I won't press you. If anything happens I hope it goes good for you. My husband is so good to me. He makes my life wonderful. I think Max might be the same type of person. That guy can move some shells. He dips twice a day. The racks are not full now but they will be by the end of this week. They will be full for a month. We will find out if he can keep up the pace or not. He is consistent and a conscientious worker and he hasn't made any mistakes. Haven't you noticed by now, or is love blind? See the stack of two hundred leaf squares? They are for you and Nash to chase next week. Bob has Max make at least one hundred every afternoon. It takes about five hours. You and Nash will have a steady stream to chase next week."

"Okay, Molly. I will take your word for it. You scored a point for Max. You are the woman to be the boss. Those leaf patterns are a pain. The small air bubbles hide in the tight twists. They are hard to chase."

"Let's get after these waxes."

"How are they going to get four projects through the foundry at the same time, Molly?"

"You know, they are going to need a herd of welders around here. The jazz quartet has one hundred seventy six pieces. That will be over three hundred sprues. You will be chasing that party for three weeks. Do you have a headache yet?"

Cheryl laughed. "Oh, Molly, you are so right."

Johnny and Cindy entered the wax room to begin their regular shift and Cheryl moved out to the foundry floor. Every day of the week was a repetition of Monday. Cheryl arrived early every day to help Molly wax the molds. Her regular hours were filled with her work on the foundry projects. She applied herself as a talented, dedicated, and loyal employee. The regular topic of conversation among the employees this week was where they were going for their first camping trip. The push was on to get the bronco to the metal pour area. The foundry operation began to expand from overtime for all employees into a second shift. The sand blasters were busy. Metal pours were a daily and nightly occurrence. The foundry was alive and working non stop on a skeleton crew.

CHAPTER TWENTY THREE

Friday after work they took off like rabid dogs for a mini vacation with no pressure or work. No money was thrown away at the drop zone. They had no cares and no worries. The camping gear was prepared Thursday evening and loaded in the truck Friday morning. Cheryl enjoyed her new truck. It was a beauty and a pleasure to drive. She raced through Minturn to the interstate and on to Eagle. They zipped past beautiful homes and chalets owned by people from all over the world. New construction had pared the mountain sides in a terraced effect. The top of the ridges were pushed into the gullies until a new plateau was formed. Then, a narrow road would be cut up to the next level where the same procedure would take place again, on the new level. All of this just to get a few more half million dollar home subdivisions within five or ten miles of Vail, Beaver Creek, or Eagle Vail. There were big names behind the big money. The available area was now five or six times the size of the original valley floor.

As Cheryl drove along, it occurred to her that they would be camping out and sleeping in a confined space. In a short amount of time, some awkward moments would arrive. This was just like their first venture to the DZ. There were a bunch of ifs, but her parent's house had been available as a refuge. Was anything going to happen tonight? If anything went wrong she could always sleep in the truck, or take off for that matter. Was it time? Did she want to go through with this? He was holding up pretty well so far. It is a little early in the relationship. A thirty five year old man with glasses. But he is such fun! She decided it would not hurt anything. It just might be time to find out if they were going to fall in love. Maybe he is in love with me. Maybe he is hiding it. She decided to find out. If things really got out of hand, she could always sneak into the truck and take off. She could use the charge card at the local hotel.

The beautiful Eagle Valley opened up to them. The big raindrops of the usual late afternoon shower began to thump on the windshield, the cab roof, and the hood. Dusk began, and the bottoms of the heavy gray clouds were brushed with red and orange. Cheryl wound her way through the Glenwood Canyon past No Name and into Glenwood Springs. She did the reverse loop to get under the freeway and head south to Mount Sopris and Carbondale. She had kidnapped Max and she was going to visit her grandma and get her sewing machine.

She turned into the Sopris entrance. They rolled along on a gravel road in the dark, to a dirt jeep trail. She shifted the transmission to four wheel low and continued up the trail for an eighth of a mile to an open field where she turned off the trail and parked the truck.

"How does this look?"

"Fantastic. It looks like we are the only two people around. Let's find a couple of dry spots for the tent."

The air was chilly. Cheryl put on her full length rain coat and Max wore a jacket and a knit hat. The ground squished beneath their feet as they unloaded the truck. Several dry spots were located and the gear was unloaded.

"This is great, Cheryl. There is some slope to the area which will help us keep dry if the weather moves in. A penny for your thoughts."

"Hey, that is my line."

"Your Majesty." Max spoke calmly. "The tent will not go up by itself. It is one of those sacred male rituals to set up the tent. Would you care to be in charge this evening?" A sly smile and a smirk crossed both of their faces.

"That is so typical of you. You have given me another little dare. Not to worry, Mongo. Stand aside! I know that it is impossible for you to put the tent together. Your mind is much too feeble." Cheryl looked at the innocent tent in the nylon bag.

"That's right. That's right."

"I might warn you that I smell a rat. I am certain there is a trick to it and you want to laugh at my fumbling efforts." Cheryl opened the draw string and dumped the contents on the ground.

"Would you rather watch me snowboard?"

"This is elementary and straightforward." She grabbed two corners of the tent. She shook it up in the air and guided it to the ground. There were three brass hooks on each corner. They would snap to the poles and the rain fly would cover it all. Cheryl eyeballed the twenty one aluminum poles on the ground. It was obvious that the poles would fit together. Get on with it. She quickly put together four sections with four poles in each section. She had five poles left, the rain fly, and two metal cylinders about the size of her hand. The cylinders were identical. One side had two holes close together the other side had two holes a little farther apart. It was obvious that the cylinders held two sections of poles together at each end of the tent.

"Obviously these hold the tent poles together somehow. I have done all of the work for you. Why don't you finish the rest? I just want to relax and enjoy the evening.

"We tied, Cheryl. We both made it to the same point. It was awhile before I could figure out the cylinders." Max rotated the cylinder and turned it left to right.

"I see how it lines up now." Cheryl got the two sections of poles attached to the cylinder on her end of the tent.

"Now, three poles connect the two cylinders over the tent . . ."

"And then the rain sheet goes over. Too easy Max."

"The last two poles push the rain fly out a foot in front and back."

They threw the rain fly over the tent.

"This is a nice tent, Max. Your front porch is a little small, but I am not complaining. Lets get the gear inside, and then, if you have no objections, I would like to check for stars between the clouds, and run a couple of thoughts past you."

They threw the sleeping bags, cooler, and a very small camp stove for backpacking inside the tent. A couple of pillows followed. This was going to be a good time. They had a dry setting, and an adequate shelter that appeared to be water proof.

Max kept the large air mattress outside.

He quickly volunteered to blow up the mattress. "I have more hot air than you."

They were in a primitive setting in a huge forest on the side of a mountain. They leaned up against the truck. Cheryl's eyes were sparkling. It may turn into a romantic evening. She could feel herself heating up. Max sensed the fires might be raging.

Keep your mouth shut and you could have a wild night in the tent Mongo. He felt his testicles twitch and his manhood stir. Better relax fast there trooper. Don't get ahead of the campaign. The reflection of starlight on his glasses made it look as if he had big frog eyes.

Cheryl thought of Karen and her comments at the DZ. She could not help the laugh that slipped out. "Ha!"

"That funny, huh? You laugh at my castle and my offerings?"

"Just laughing at something that Karen said."

"Cheryl, you picked a good spot. I like it here. This is terrific place and the mountains make me look good."

"This is wonderful. How far are we from El Jebel?"

"I guess about six miles."

"Max, I guess I have not really expressed my feelings to you on a couple of things. I wish to do so now."

Max exhaled air into the mattress in a calm controlled rhythm. "Really? Have you have been hiding deep thoughts and feelings from me, Princess?"

"You have really gone out of your way to provide a place for me to live. You rescued me from the rent and all the utility expense."

"Hey. That is the way it is in these mountains. Everyone has to help one another just to get by. Everyone has roommates and car pooling. No easy feat to be independent, especially with this stinking economy."

"Thank you for helping me. The move has been a wonderful escape from my old dilemma."

"Yes, yes. Go on. Am I to be rewarded?"

"Now I am to the point where I really do not know what else I can possibly use you for."

"Ha! Oh, that hurt. You cut me. Good one."

"We have been friends for only a short time but I want to take our situation to the next level. I am comfortable and I know you care about me without having said so."

Max began to huff on the mattress. He would be dizzy and pass out in another thirty seconds if he did not take a break. He covered the quarter sized hole with his hand so the air would not leak out. "I guess I should thank you. You have been a really decent roommate." His mind shifted to hyper drive, but he needed to slow down. He had to have some innocent charming answers. Keep it clean. She gets to decide to make the moves.

"Do you have any feelings for me beyond the friendship stage? Because I think . . ."

Max interrupted. "I know what it is, Cheryl. You and I have become friends. We are sharing the rent burden. We enjoy the Pac Woman game at the bowling alley. We respect one another and we have feelings for one another. But there is a subtle and maybe a subliminal force at work between us. We both share that force and it is pulling us together. It is similar to skiing and camping in the great outdoors. We are immersed together in these wonderful things. Your statue and the work you do. You have created a phenomenal work of art that will go on public display. It is a visible product of your talent and creativity. It is powerful and captivating. There are two more things that draw us together. One is 304. The view is powerful and captivating. Actually, it is overwhelming for me. We both love the great outdoors. The last attraction of course is skydiving and the open cargo door of the airplane at ten thousand feet. It is powerful and captivating. It is haunting because of its unknown, hypnotic force. The thought of jumping through the door is completely unnatural. These events have contributed to our interests in each other. They play part in the equation of why we are attracted to one another."

"Oh, my, how eloquent. You should lecture at the university. What else, Professor Max? Do you have anything to tell me on this romantic evening?

The clouds became a blanket, and random raindrops began to fall. Bright lightning lit the clouds, and a huge roll of thunder washed down the mountainside.

"Max, it looks like the weather is moving in. We better get the gear in the tent."

Once inside they left their wet boots by the front door. The down pour was cold. The big drops burst loudly on the tightly drawn rain flap. It sounded as if they were inside a popcorn bag in a microwave oven. Max sealed the mattress air hole with the plug and screwed the plastic cap over it. He turned on the nine volt flash light and put it on the cooler.

Thanks to the rain, the whole environment had changed. They were together in a primal crib. Stay cool. This could be explosive. The mattress filled all but two feet along the side of the tent. The cooler with the food and drink went into the corner. They moved in a crouch or on their hands and knees. Cheryl dug into her back pack to check a couple of things. The interlude gave her time to recall her chat with Sherry. He plays unaffected and uninterested and indifferent. His thoughts are otherwise. "He is waiting for you to come forward. He is waiting for your approval. When that happens, nail him." Wow. Sherry maybe right on the button. "Don't let him get away into the non commitment role. You got to nail him if you want him." Sherry was right. Cheryl could feel her juices flowing and her body temperature warmed up a notch.

"Now what were you saying?"

Cheryl watched Max as he recovered from the ten minutes it took to blow up the air mattress. She knew he was week and vulnerable. "I am grateful for what you have done. Thanks for the tent and the mattress. Are you going to sleep in the truck tonight?" The question caught him off guard. That was when she attacked him. She put both hands against his chest and shoved him backward onto the air mattress. He saw it coming, but he did nothing to stop her. He was looking into her eyes to see what she was thinking. She had a small, vexing smile on her face. It grew when she heard him exhale as he hit the air mattress.

"Huaahhh. And here is the bell for round one."

She took satisfaction in the push. She had not shoved a man since she pushed her little brother around. A primal, animalistic sneer crossed her lips. "You are mine!" Cheryl knelt in front of him as he rose to a sitting position.

"Honey, you look absolutely devoid of morals."

"It is your lucky day, Max. Count your blessings."

His wood grew a little bigger. Good she was playing. Max stammered, "I like women who are not afraid to initiate sex."

She leaned forward and responded to his stupidity. "I guess I don't mind helping you a little bit. She helped him take his jacket off, then she gripped his shirt behind his shoulders and pulled it to her. It ripped off over his head."

"I think you just tore my expensive Second Hand Rose T shirt. Is this your idea of foreplay?"

"Oh. Do you want to do something about it? Relax, Max. We can burn it tomorrow. Later, if you feel like you want to scream, be my guest."

"What, honey? No foreplay? You know some men like foreplay. I'm not like other men, Cheryl. I like foreplay." His skin goose bumped in the cool air.

Cheryl had never really verbalized during love making. She decided to play along with him. It was awkward at first. She began to converse as if nothing was going on. Say anything. Let out the first thing that comes to your mind. Do not hide the thoughts, dirty or otherwise. It was fun to see the astonished look on the partner's face. Let the other person come up with the comeback line. Max was good at that. He could handle it. He was not offended. He would not harm her. She slowly moved into him and he fell back on to the mattress. Conversation began to flow more easily for her. Cheryl whispered to Max. "Shut up sweetheart. Tonight you are going to get it my way." Cheryl set all of her weight on top of Max. They were both pleased with the contact and the warmth.

"Wait! I need to brush my teeth."

She looked him straight in the eye and said, "That's it. Cooperate, baby, so I don't have to rough you up." Max emitted a slight chuckle. "You laughin' about sumthin'?"

"No, no. I'm scared, honey. I have never seen you act this way. Your composure has changed. You are no longer sweet and demure. You are mean. Don't stress me out. I won't be able to perform."

"Is that really what you want right now, Max? Sweet and demure? I know that you are ready to do the wild monkey thing!"

"I am extended and I am ready for you." Max thought he was going to loose his load before he got his pants off, especially if she helped him. Cheryl was on fire. She was hot and panting with an urgent need to be satisfied. He bumped his pelvis up into her hips two times. "Did that hurt, baby? It felt good for me." They stared at each other. "We have come full circle in a very short time. We might be an item and graduate to new levels right here and now. Are we doing good?"

"Yes, Max. Okay for now." Cheryl was grinding into him. "It could get better if I duct tape your mouth. Where did you put the duct tape?"

"Hey! That is my line! I hid the duct tape from you. You have been acting strange. I had a bad premonition on the drive over." He gave her the low IQ look and made his lips quiver. She laughed.

"Come on, Max. Make it good for me. I really need some dynamite sex."

"Okay, as long as you are not greedy and controlling."

"Hey! That's my line. Max, to tell you the plain truth I was getting worried. I decided to get you hot and all worked up tonight. Otherwise, we would never make it to this level. We would never have sex. I thought that you would ask me to have sex with you way before now. Well, Max, you never told me you wanted to do it. You have not told me that you are crazy about me. Why have you not told me that you want to marry me and make wild passionate love to me?" They were grinding and arching into one another.

"Oh, yeah. Here we go. I guess that was really inconsiderate of me. The man has to ask because it is customary and politically correct. Am I am supposed to send you an engraved invitation? Is that one of the requirements? Dear Ms. Cheryl Pritchard, your presence is requested for a night of sex and debauchery. Please RSVP. Now, tonight, you are going to mercy fuck me, and then I will owe you for the rest of my life. I will be at your beck and call if I ever want to get laid. Cheryl, I promise on my word of honor that I wanted to get intimate with you the third or fourth time I saw you. Think about it from my point of view. I never told you I wanted to hose you because then you would have called me a sleazy hood."

"Great. Got any more excuses, Max? I was just off of a bummer. I needed a break. I was not ready to jump back on a roller coaster. I did not want to be on the rebound. I could not take the chance to become involved with some sleazy hood."

"See! I told you! You were afraid that you might ruin your reputation."

"I had to be cautious because I heard some rumors about your mental abilities. That required some first hand assessment on my part."

"Flattery will not help you at this point, Cheryl. You have said too many hateful things about me. Be careful. This talk is making me extended. I should tell you that I am extended. This conversation has aroused me."

"Don't denigrate the moment, Max. You spineless coward. Shut up and take it like a man." Cheryl let her hormones rule her actions and words. The fire was roaring uncontrollably. "I knew you would have an excuse. Well, here is mine. After we had thirty of forty conversations, I decided that it would be a risk to become genetically involved with you."

"Good one. I wanted to do it plenty of times. Just an ordinary animal response. No emotional calculating, or scheming, or thinking involved. I did not think it would be right. So I waited for you to decide and to let me know."

"You mean dirty, impure, animal lust? What a terrible reason to have sex. Casual sex cannot be tolerated early in a relationship, Max, but commitment sex is alright."

"Is that where we are? Commitment sex? I was just worried that it wouldn't be the right time as far as what is socially acceptable in our relationship. Now it's true that we are friends, but at what point did we get past friends? I'm thinking we are still friends and that's all. Now you want to go to this new level. I'm confused." They talked softly to one another as they ran their hands over each other's bumps, lumps, and hot spots. The fires were beyond smoldering. The small tent warmed up nicely.

"We might find out in the next hour. Then again you may never find out if you do not shut up and take your clothes off. That's right, Max. Be a good little boy and take your clothes off!"

"Wait a minute!"

"Shut up, Max! I have decided that I am going to get intimate with you. It is time for me to check out your extension. I need some dick. Is that okay? Can you handle it? Or do I have to leave you here and drive around to find someone who can?"

"Honey, that is up to you."

"Don't call my bluff! I'm warning you!" Cheryl rose up on her knees. She unbuttoned and pushed down her jeans. She stood and took them off. She left her rain coat on for warmth. She wore no underwear. "Let's get started, Max."

"Honey, it is raining loud and there is no one around for miles. You aren't going to hurt me are you?"

"I am just going to bump you a few times, Max. That is all it is going to take for this first one. I might rape you the second time. It won't be demeaning, I promise you. It won't bruise your ego. You don't have one, remember?"

"Rape is a felony!"

"Well, I will apologize later. Right now I am going to have some fun." She was down it front of him on her knees unbuttoning his pants. She ran her palm over the denim that covered his wood and squeezed his sausage. "Ready, Max? Arch your back and lift your butt off the mattress so I can take your stinking jeans off." She pulled them down slowly along with his mutant ninja turtle underwear. "I hope you have more to attack me with than a turtle." The hormones were raging on both sides. She watched his penis flop over to one side then it began to roll back to the center like a fighter getting up after being knocked down. And it kept growing, and growing and growing.

"Whooeee! Damn, that is a big old dick, Max. Nice to see you rise to the occasion."

"A present for you, Princess. Let's put the turtle in the dark castle. That is, if you want to go through with this."

She reached out, grabbed it, and pumped it up and down. She pulled the stretch limits and it began to stiffen up. She shook it from side to side and said, "This is gonna be more fun than I thought. Nice work, Max. This will only take a second." She moved her knees on each side of his waist. She moved on top of him for position and entry. She held his manhood and moved her hips in a circle to position his extension.

"Oh, that's a wet one. Wet and wild."

"Are these the wrinkles you have been talking about, Max? All your dirty little jokes? I am going to ride you like a dime store pony."

"Like Mary's big gray bucking bronco? I guess this means we aren't going to have any foreplay."

"Shut up, Max. You had your chance. Time's up. You have just been running your mouth and protesting." She moved up imperceptibly and then lowered her self. He moved his hips imperceptibly at the same time, and they got the turtle through the castle gate. She grimaced a little. "It's ok. Sometimes I don't mind a little discomfort. I'm gonna ride you like that goofy bucking bronco at the foundry."

"That's right, baby! Giddy yup! Vent Baby! Get it all out! Get rid of all that pent up frustration. Pound me brains out."

"That won't take long, Max." Cheryl slid slowly down the throbbing member to the base. She began to stroke them both with a series of hot, wild humps. His head was bouncing up and down on the mattress. "Take your glasses off! You are spoiling my vision."

The down pour continued to batter the tent fly. "Don't stop now. It is perfect, dear. There is no one around to hear us. So are you going to own me after this? Am I going to be your little slut puppy? Am I going to be bound and beholden?"

"Max, I just thanked you for all you have done for me. Things are good now. My life has changed for the better. Thank you. Now shut up."

"Wait a minute! What do you mean 'for the better?'"

"I swear. This is going to be your only chance."

"See! You are going to manipulate me from this point on. You are going to claim this as your starting point."

"I swear, if you don't shut up now, I will get my thirty eight. I will have a hard time hitting such a small target, but I will shoot your brains out."

Max feigned deep thought. It made good sense. "Nights like this are perfect nights for murder."

"I'm thinking about it. There is no one around here for five miles in any direction. I would be able to get away with it."

"How utterly romantic. Over the top. That is why I am madly in love with you, Cheryl." Max pulled the sleeping bag over his head for levity. "Now there won't be so much pressure, baby. I am just an object for your hidden pent up desires."

"Oh! Yeah!" She said between thrusts, "That really is much better. Leave your face covered, Max. It works for me. It does take a little bit of the tension off. I am just about ready to gush like a geyser!" She released and shuddered a few times. Cheryl resumed hitting him again. Hard and fast. She loved Max passionately. She bumped him hard. She pushed hard into him and ground down against his pubic arch. He pulled the sleeping bag off his head. She watched his face contort with a little bit of discomfort. "How is that, Max? Do you like that? It turns me on when I see you wince a little bit."

His eyes were crossed and turned up in his sockets. "It's good for me. Don't stop. I am going to try to go the distance. Are you fantasizing that I am Brad Pit?" Their eyes burned holes in each other. They continued to enjoy the pleasure of the slow strokes, the stopping, the alternating, the slowing and picking up speed. Max felt himself move to the edge of release. "Don't move. Please. Stop, just for a little while."

"Are you going to give me directions now, and tell me what I am doing wrong?" He let the urge go. He took a moment to think of something totally different than what the current situation was. The release stalled. He started to deflate a little. "You didn't come did you?" He shook his head no. "Good."

Cheryl was gorgeous to Max. "Honey, scoot back towards my knees, just a little."

She knew what he was doing. This was just getting better and better. "Okay, but first I want to take it all a couple of times." She rose up slightly and then relaxed and sat down on him. She took two more, long, deliciously slow descents. Then she bumped him hard and fast. He could see fire burning in her eyes. They felt the fire burning in their bodies. Cheryl leaned forward. Her breasts held his eyes. He caressed them lovingly. He reached inside her raincoat and gently pushed them to her rib cage. She moved back toward his knees enough that she was stroking them both, slowly back and forth, for a good length and maximum stimulation. Cheryl did not think she could ever get this hot. She moved forward again for more contact. She rose up, and arched her back. She sat down again and ground into him.

Max watched as her face began to contort. "Don't fight it, baby. Just let it happen." He sensed the vibration like a rabbit detects an earthquake. Her thrusts became sporadic. "I feel it coming, baby! Here comes the earthquake." Max pulled the sleeping bag over his head a second time. Thunder, overhead, rolled again down the mountainside.

Cheryl felt the overwhelming turbulence build. She shuddered and clamped up on him. "Aaah!" She hit Max with a couple more short fast thrusts. She let go and shuddered again. She got off one more though not as heavy. Two light convulsions shook her body. Aftershocks. She emitted a fairly loud, "Ohhhh." Max ran his hands over her breasts. He moved them lightly all over her nakedness to tickle her. She kicked her legs back along side of his and fell forward on top of him. She was finished! Then she laughed. "You should have seen your head bouncing up and down. It was funny."

"I'm glad you liked it."

The temperature level in the non porous tent was up thirty degrees. Cheryl was all tingly and sweaty. Max pulled a towel out of his backpack to tidy up with. "Ladies first."

"My, what a gentleman." He quickly zipped the two sleeping bags together.

She felt him snuggle to her back and drape his arm across her stomach. His hand cupped her breast. The night wind lapped at the tent and the rain splattered on the surface. They were glad to be away from the foundry and happy to have some intimate time together. They had finally found one another. They were complete. They were resplendent. They fell sound asleep oblivious to the storm and the cold. They slept all night through the downpour.

CHAPTER TWENTY FOUR

Early next morning, Cheryl unzipped the bedroll and crawled toward the front of the tent. She unzipped the entrance door and appraised the situation. "The sky is clear and blue like your eyes." She dressed quickly. "Hey, boy! Can you pick up this poor excuse of a campsite for me?"

"Got an itch?"

"Yes, but not for an old coot."

"Is there a fire sale?"

"Since you are tired and no fun, I am heating up for some four wheeling. No hurry on the tent here, Quasimodo, or whatever your name is."

"No need to dis me is there?"

"Hey, that's my line, boy! You did pretty good last night, Max. You kind of surprised me. Right now, I have an itch to test drive the truck. I will be back in a little while."

Cheryl was anxious to go four wheeling. She had waited long enough for a test ride. Her grandfather used to drive on the narrowest roads on a mountain side that he could find. The sheer drop offs scared his daughter Marilyn and his granddaughter Cheryl. It stood to reason. She was going to go four wheeling up the mountain at least to the next open area if conditions allowed.

The shift was still in 4 wheel low. Cheryl rolled away from the tent for a little safety distance. She cranked the wheel and did a three sixty. On the tight turn the mud arched beautifully through the air for ten feet. She laughed hysterically. She knocked out three donuts close to the tent. She observed that the tent was covered with mud but still standing. She yelled out the window. "Wake up, Max you are missing all of the fun." Max heard the monster truck move to the other side where the despicable event resumed its course until the tent was covered with mud. Satisfied, she took off uphill on a narrow rutted jeep trail, through a grove of aspen trees. The morning sunlight filtered through. She laughed happily into the morning.

Max did not question this sudden impulse whatsoever. He felt a little anger flare when the mud hit the side of the tent the first time. His tent was supposed to stay clean. Those were his rules of camping. After the fifth deluge of mud and water he decided that he had to laugh. The metal poles were still supportive of the situation. The tent would dry out. He waited for her to leave before he opened the cap on the air mattress. He began to pick up their things and stow them in the gear bags. He looked outside the tent. There were puddles here and there. He located one high and dry spot to place the gear. He put the mattress down first. Everything else was placed neatly on top. He wanted to keep his shoes dry so he hurried back and forth in the cold water in his bare feet. He folded up the muddy tent and waited patiently for his new camping partner to return.

She raced down the road out of the forest towards Max. He purposely wore his long sad face and stared at his cold feet. She missed him wide to the right and peppered him with a few splotches of mud. She slowed and circled to him. Her pickup was covered with light brown mud.

The driver window opened and she asked him, "Why the long face, snookums?"

"Must you always desecrate and disrespect my manly world? I bet your little brother ran away from home because of you. And my name is not snookums!"

She laughed at him. "Hey, Mongo! Toss your duds in back and let's find some breakfast." She picked up her camera. She stepped out to record the event. This would be a good addition to her scrap book. They left the campsite and rolled five miles down the road. At the El Jebel Trailer Park they found Grandma's trailer. Grandma saw the truck. She asked how it got covered with mud. Cheryl admitted she spent most of the morning trying to run over Max. They laughed. Grandma told Cheryl to use the shower and freshen up while she whipped up some breakfast for everyone. Cheryl declined. Grandma started a small fire in her wood stove and the ambiance was welcomed by all.

"I just thought the thing to offer is a fire, some of my hot coffee, and some dry socks and underwear. Course I wear the big old cotton kind. I don't wear the skimpy frilly lacey stuff like you youngins wear. I don't let my underwear hang out when I am out in public either. Grandma was on a roll. "How about some left over turkey sandwiches from last year?

I'm just teasing you youngins." Grandma Julie Pritchard heated turkey sandwiches in the micro wave while she scrambled up a big batch of eggs. Max helped himself to a cup of coffee. They talked about Cheryl's new skis, her art work, and how much they enjoyed living in the mountains.

Grandma was an accomplished skier in her day and an outdoors woman. "Yep, I tolt yer Granddad just to move on back to that big city and make his money. Anytime he felt he needed to see me, he could drive back up into the mountains and visit me for a spell. You got to be thankful for the time you have in the great outdoors the way people were supposed to live. If the old man takes off on you, why it's just tough shit. You don't have to go with 'em. It's hard to find a good one these days. Wally Dallenbach lives just up the hill. He likes my coffee and he stops over in the morning sometimes. Every once in a while he would tend to my garden now and then."

Max questioned, "Which garden?"

He received an open mouth stare from Grandma Julie, and then she let out a hoot.

"Ain't he a kick Grandma?"

Grandma cast a suspicious glance in his direction. "It looks to me like this one here needs a lot of cleaning up." Granny gave Max the evil eye, and then a cold hard stare. Max jerked his head away from her gaze to avoid direct eye contact. "You know sometimes they pretend like they are listening to you. But they really don't have a care for nuttin' but theyselves."

"Well, what do you do then Grandma?"

"Well, honey, you can't hold back. You just got to double up your fist and put a good one right into they's eye. You have to let them know they better pay attention and do as you say."

Cheryl looked at Max with a full grin. "That is some pretty sound advice. I will remember that." Max wanted to throw his hands up in the air.

"Hey, Grandma, why don't we go cruise the town a little just you and me. We can pick up some groceries and wash the truck."

"Maybe Wally is eating breakfast at the Sopris Grill this morning. If not we can drive to his place and kick his door down." Cheryl and Grandma left for the main drag. Max remained in the overstuffed chair for some shut eye.

Cheryl finished up at the car wash and Grandma Julie admired the brand new metallic burgundy truck. "Where'd you get all that mud? Are you runnin' from the law?" They stopped at the Sopris Grill and bought two sweet rolls and tea. Wally was not there. Grandma Julie opened her purse. She penned a check and handed it to Cheryl. She looked at the check. It was written out for a seven hundred dollar down payment on one of her Single Jacker replicas.

"Ooohweeeee, Grandma! You sure about this?"

"No po' folk in the Pritchard lineage. All us Pritchard's come from good stock. Yer Maw and I decided to pitch in and buy one. I want some new meaningful decoration in my house." As they left the Grill, Grandma told the cashier, "When you see that Dallenbach fella, you let him know that I have been lookin' for him and that I am gonna find him. He can't hide from me." They returned to the house to wake up Max.

"Cheryl, this old sewing machine is a family heirloom. I have decided that it should be yours now. Your mother used it quite a bit to keep you clothed when you were little."

"Grandma Julie, I remember. I used to watch her. Mom would let me push the cloth, but I had to be very careful and follow the pins."

"I got some material for you. It is almost the same color as that purty truck outside. Use it to your liking."

Cheryl and Max moved the sewing machine to the back of the truck and placed it against the cab. They covered the machine with the tent fly and secured both against the cab with two flat straps.

"Now, baby girl, you remember to send your Grandma Julie some pictures of your work and hurry up and git that miner made for me. Take care, Cheryl. Come back and see me."

They made their good byes and Cheryl drove to the hot springs in Glenwood.

They basked in the one hundred degree temperature of the hot pool for ten minutes. They moved to the large pool to play Marco Polo and hide from one another in the mist that rose from the warm water. She rode on his shoulders, her head above the mist. They embraced and kissed in the mist until it became obvious that Max was aroused and it was time to quit.

Max whispered, "Last night in our intimacy I discovered that we are very compatible. Thank you for that experience. You really know how to show a guy a good time. I think you like me and I would really like to make love again. We should go home and experiment some more."

"Hey, back off. I had a physical urge that got out of hand, nothing more than that. You just happened to be there. It will never happen again in a million years. Consider yourself lucky."

"I am not certain that you enjoyed my performance. It took so long and you kept moaning all of the time. I may need some practice and some extra coaching."

"Is there something wrong with a long time?"

"Maybe we should have a code word or something. It is not good to leave that kind of stress unattended. I don't want to let you down. How about, 'Is it time for tea?'"

They return to Leadville. Cheryl placed two folding chairs on the patio and ran a power cord from the living room out to the chairs. Max unloaded the truck and he helped her move the sewing machine to the alcove in the dining room. It was a comfortable fit with room for material and odds and ends. Cheryl handed him an electric hot plate, an aluminum pan, and a box of tea bags. She filled a water jug. She picked up a plastic bag and filed it with half a loaf of bread, provolone cheese, alfalfa sprouts, avocado, peanut butter, two knives, and strawberry jelly. The items were placed in a cardboard box and they ventured out to the patio. They ate their sandwiches, sipped hot tea, and did nothing but gaze at the scenery for an hour.

"What are you thinking, Max?"

"I really had fun camping."

Cheryl rose from her chair. She clamped down on his ear like a mother with an errant child.

"Owwww! Owww! Hey! Let go! That is not funny!" Max rose from his chair.

"Let's go watch a movie, Mongo. I need a back rub. Eventually, you will learn to follow me naturally without having your ear held all the time."

They collected everything the cardboard box could hold and returned to the living room. Cheryl stretched out on the floor on her stomach in front of the TV.

"Happy Gilmore, please."

Max readied the DVD and joined Cheryl on the floor to pamper her with a soothing massage.

"That is great, Max. Keep up the good work. I will let you know when I am tired."

"Cheryl, I really enjoyed the intimacy we shared last night. Would it be okay with you if I moved some of my things upstairs?"

"Move your what?" She laughed and rolled onto her back to gaze into his eyes.

"Well, I mean we slept together last night. Didn't we?"

"Yes, and I did enjoy it."

"I interpret it as being a step forward for both of us to a life of more pleasure, stress reduction, and relaxation. I don't think we should lose our momentum or quit. We need to stay current on our physical lovemaking so we can improve and move to a higher level. You know, just like skydiving. You told me there were some things that I was doing wrong, and the only way I can improve is with practice, and more of your instruction."

"I have a lot of things on my mind right now. Let me think about it this week." She put her hand behind his neck and pulled his head down for a kiss. "Now, if you don't mind, let's go back to the movie and the massage."

At the end of the movie, they made their way to their separate rooms. In the middle of the night, she tiptoed into his room and slipped under the covers next to him.

"Don't get excited. I just want some company, some creature comfort. I have not slept close to anyone for a couple of months."

"Last time I slept close to anybody it was my brother and sisters. We fought over the dolls and stuffed animals."

"Thank you for that sumptuous bed. I feel kind of guilty hogging it all to myself."

"If I start to snore, just hit me and tell me to stop. I will go back to sleep. Feel free to use a pair of my ear plugs if want to try them out. There are a couple of clean ones in the top dresser drawer."

"Thank you for camping with me. I never camped out like that before."

"Oh, sure. That was something, wasn't it? What a down pour. I need to tell you my side of the story though. The altitude sickness took over my actions and behavior. My screams were from the dementia and not from any passion or intimacy. I was near hysteria and I was delirious. It was an accident, just a sterile animal act. I really meant to kill you because I knew no one would hear your screams. Rainy nights are good nights for murder."

Cheryl poked him in the ribs and stuck a finger in his ear. She snuggled close to the brute. "Gosh, Max. Even with my mattress you can still feel the fold out bars."

"It's nothing. You have to adjust your body to the bump to be comfy. It truly is much better than the alternative."

Cheryl looked offended. "What is that?"

"The crawl space me lady. The day you moved in you told me that I could live underneath the house."

"My dear Lord! Come on. We are going upstairs but don't you try anything funny." They retired to her comfortable king mattress. "I don't want to be hurt, Max. I don't want to plunge blindly into another relation until I am certain."

"It has all happened so fast. Never this fast for me, but you have no worries, dear. I will buy you a seeing eye dog and a sonar walking cane. I have been really worried. I thought you might expect me to become attached to you."

She gave him another poke in the ribs. "That one was free."

"Anytime you want to visit your grandmother again, just say the word." They drifted to sleep in the warm heat of their bodies. Cheryl placed her head close to his chest and listened to the beat of his heart.

CHAPTER TWENTY FIVE

Sunday morning Cheryl quietly negotiated the sparks and left the bed in her flannel night gown. She picked up her notebook and the manual and negotiated the stairs. She flipped the coffee switch for Max as she went through the kitchen. She stopped in front of the fireplace and fired up two logs. She sat down on the sofa in front of the bay window with her books to soak up the beauty of the morning. She admired the majesty of the great outdoors. Snow was still on the peaks, but the heavy blankets in the green forest below had diminished. There was snow in the avalanche chutes and a few shaded areas the sun could not reach. She wondered what would happen between her and Max now that they had crossed the threshold of intimacy. She knew that they were taking a step into the future together one day at a time. She knew for certain that there would be many more camping trips this summer and that they would enjoy intimacy again. She was grateful from the reprieve of rent and utility bills and she was happy that she did not have to work at the foundry today. She thought of Marilyn and Hal. She figured they were already hanging sheetrock this morning. She felt guilty not being there to help them. Cheryl opened her notebook to her spreadsheet and turned her thoughts to the completion of her miner. How would the week unfold, and what were her objectives and priorities?

She needed to get tabs on her shells. Her waxes had made it into the shell room and some of them were out to the wax melt furnace. Cheryl realized that the task at hand was to get her ceramic shells to the metal pouring area. That would be her priority. To do this she would have to make certain that every shell made it through the wax melt furnace. She had to locate them and keep track of each one of them. Gosh, how do you do that when there are a couple of hundred ceramic shells between the shell room and the pouring area? She decided to mark them with a piece of tape on the sprue hook or she could mark the shell with a magic marker. She had one in her sewing basket. She turned to the next clean page and wrote "Wax melt furnace week." Beneath that she wrote, "Locate shells in the shell room. Move all shells through the wax melt furnace and assemble them at the pouring area." She thought strongly about that for a moment. There were what, four projects going through the shell room and the wax melt furnace? All of the projects were in a race to the metal pour. She would move her shells through the wax melt furnace in the morning, at lunch time and again in the evening before she went home. She might be able to do fifteen shells a day. She could sleep in this week. Oh, heavenly bliss!

Surely there were some snags waiting for her. What would they be? Oh, yes! The hand steel. She needed to make her own. She would have a backup, and no last minute worries. Where is the marble base and when will it be delivered? She heard Max enter the small bathroom to use the toilet and shave. He stopped at the coffee pot to pour coffee in his blue mug. Max made his way quietly into the living room to sneak up on Cheryl. She knew he was behind her and she turned as he neared just in time to receive a light kiss on her head. He put his coffee mug and the skydive manual on the lid of the storage box in front of the bay window. He sat down beside her on the sofa. He thought he might tickle her feet this morning for getting his tent all muddy. Maybe he would tickle them until she was hysterical.

"Where do you want me to set up the tent, baby? How about here in the living room where we could be close to the DVD? You know something? I would even agree to the dining room so you would be close to the sewing machine and the computer. It would really be good for you to learn how to use the computer and type fast. Then you would have another job skill. It is good to have as many skills as possible these days." Cheryl turned to him and kissed him lightly on the cheek. This was the man she had recently had glorious orgasmic contact with. "That reminds me, Max, I am going to make a jumpsuit from the cloth that Grandma Julie gave me. I need to get your measurements because I am going to make a straight jacket for you."

"What do you have on your agenda?"

"I know you will be glad to hear this. We can sleep in late this week. It is going to be wax melt week at work. I have to get the shells through the wax melt furnace. What do you want to do today?"

"I am going to put in a day over on East Fifth Street. How about you?"

"I have several choices. I could work on the computer today. I would like to learn more about the word processor. I could start on a pattern for my jumpsuit. I need to practice dirt dives for jumps four and five and I could help you over on East Fifth. What do you think?"

"Wow, I can use help today. You could put me ahead of the curve. I have to locate a path for water and drain lines to the second floor bath from the downstairs kitchen. I have to cut two holes in the dining room to get the gas line to the new furnace under the stairs. I need to drop the electric wire from the attic down to the second and first floors. Your help would be greatly appreciated. These things would take days for me to do by myself. It will take us more than an hour, but less than two."

In half an hour, they were standing in the kitchen of 407. They were in the corner close to the wall furnace. "It would be nice to be right in the corner, but the second floor joists probably have some support under them along this outside wall. If the drill does not make it through, then move out a foot from the wall and tap the ceiling. If that spot is no good, then come out another foot and tap again. Okay?"

"Just cut a hole in the floor."

"I wish I could. I might end up cutting two or three holes in the floor to find a decent opening. The distances between the second floor joists are not uniform. It is creative architecture." He raced up stairs. In the bathroom he had a skill saw, a saws all, and a 3/8 inch thick drill bit that was twelve inches in length. Cheryl used a broom handle to tap the spot on the ceiling. He drilled through the bathroom floor above the tapping sound. The drill bit was in far enough to pass through the floor board. It was still spitting out wood shavings. He knew he hit an obstacle, maybe a cross support. "Move out one foot." Max pulled back a foot and experienced another obstacle. The third time the drill went through to the kitchen. He quickly opened up a square foot of flooring with the skill saw. The opening was right between the joists with no cross supports or obstructions.

Cheryl ran upstairs to look over his shoulder. "This will work. You can even move it out another foot and you would be right under the bathroom sink counter."

"How did you know the bathroom sink counter is going there?"

"There is no other place for it if the tub and commode go on the window wall."

"You are so right. It will work." He drilled four more holes through the ceiling to mark the small rectangular opening to the kitchen. "Now for the gas lines."

They returned to the first floor. He pointed out two spots in the dining room where he needed holes in the floor, one on each side of the room. He entered the crawl space under the house through the trap door by the kitchen window. Cheryl drilled the first hole. She hit a floor joist. She moved the drill three inches and drilled through. She let the drill bit fall deep under the house past the floor joists. "Can you see the bit?"

"I see it. Drill one more a foot towards the living room and a foot towards the far wall." The bit went through again. Max would be able to splice into the existing line. They did they same for the second hole. He went to the dining room and marked the openings with the magic marker. Next he filled a coffee can full of small rocks. They went to the second floor and he climber the ladder into the attic. He dropped the first rock inside the area between the studs and the outside wall and the inside wall of the back bedroom.

"Got it right here. It is half way up the wall. It is probably a two by four cross support for the wall studs."

"Mark it, please."

"It is a good thing you said please."

"Okay, go across the room to the wall behind you."

And so it went for the entire upstairs. "That's all for now, Cheryl. I have to cut some holes with the skill saw and then I have to drill through the floor to the stud space in the first floor walls. There will be some heavy sawdust in the air on the second floor for at least an hour. After that I would still like to mark the paths to the first floor, if you will help me.

"Listen, Max, let me stay for another hour or two. I can cut sheet rock to cover the lathe board where you have pulled the old cracked plaster off the walls. I can do all of those and I can slap a layer of drywall mud on it for the first cover. The holes will be dry in a couple of days for you. I can do some painting. I mean it is the least I can do to return all of the kindness that you have shown me for the past three weeks. So let me help."

"I have to keep my eyes off you or I will get nothing done."

"Do you love me Max?"

"No! He reached for her. "You will have to wait and find out." He gave her a strong quick hug, a quick kiss on the lips and a smack on her fanny. "Okay, Cheryl, you are on. Knock yourself out. There are some dust masks in the dining room." With a skill saw he cut open the eleven marks Cheryl had made to catch the wire. He drilled a hole for the wire to pass through the cross supports to continue the journey to the floor. At the floor level he cut holes for the electrical boxes. Beneath these holes, he drilled through the floor to the first floor stud space, to drop wire to the first floor.

He made the measurements for the total length of the water lines, the drain lines and the black gas pipe that he would need to buy at Ken's Lumber. He wrote them down in his pocket notebook. On the second page he listed all of the fittings he would need, the tees, elbows, couplings and the shut off valves. The dust finally settled. They resumed marking the wire drop to the first floor. Cheryl marked the sound of the rock where it landed on a cross support or the floor level.

Max returned to the attic and cut eleven fifteen foot lengths of romax number twelve and ran them down to the openings on the second floor. Cheryl cut drywall to fit the spots where the old plaster was removed. She screwed the drywall to the lathe board. The dry wall was not quite as thick as the original plaster. She opened a five gallon bucket of drywall mud. She made fast work of spreading the mud to fill the cracks. It would take a second coat to get one smooth wall surface.

Max left for Ken's Lumber to buy the P trap and the tee fitting for the commode drain pipe. Ken had the fitting he wanted. It was in the inventory of parts for the toilet expansion in the mining museum. The fitting had an extra two inch opening that would accept the tub and sink drain line. Max dared Ken to sell him two tee fittings. He gave Ken an extra ten dollars. He returned to 407 where Cheryl was waiting for him.

"I want to work on my jumpsuit and the word processor this afternoon. What time do you want me to pick you up?"

"Whenever you are ready to beat me in a Pac Woman game."

Max returned to the upstairs bathroom. The first floor commode drain and vent pipe ran up through the upstairs bathroom. He secured it to the wall with metal tape in two places. He changed the wood wheel on his skill saw with one that would cut metal. The metal dust was flying as he cut the metal pipe at floor level. He lifted the pipe two feet with the help of a two by four and his floor jack. He strapped the pipe to the wall again. This may have broken the roof seal on the pipe, but he could easily repair the break. Job satisfaction and the hope of a functional rental property filled his mind and heart.

He moved his tools to the down stairs bath and repeated the effort there on the vent pipe. He made his cut three inches above the floor to allow room for the tee to slip on the end of the pipe. He raised the pipe with the two by four and the floor jack. He coated both ends of the pipe with plumbing cement, slipped the tee in place, and lowered the pipe into the top of the tee. Too easy. He beamed with pride. He moved his tools back to the second floor bathroom. Once again he cut the pipe three inches above the floor. He repeated the cementing and the fitting of the tee.

The top of the P trap would come to rest at the new level seven inches above both floors. He did have to open the original floor enough to accommodate the curve of the P trap. The big question was solved. With scrap wood from the landfill, Max would build supports for the new floor. Upstairs, the clothes washer, the sink, and the tub would drain into the commode drain and vent pipe. Downstairs, the kitchen sink, the bathroom sink and shower, would drain into the commode line. The drain lines would be easy to install.

They played like kids at the blowing alley. They sharpened their pool skills and Cheryl won two out of four on the Pac Woman machine. She pressed Max for the tie breaker. He asked her to save the tie breaker for another day. They picked up fresh DVD's. Max disagreed with every selection Cheryl made. It was annoying at first, but Cheryl caught on to his game. She added her own chiding of his bad taste in the shop for everyone to listen to.

"You have no taste. You have no class. I can't believe that I go out with you."

The evening was upon them. Max cleaned up the living room and put three logs into the wood stove.

Cheryl went to her room to meditate. She meditated on the sayings of power that were in a tiny book her mother had given her. They were proverbs of a sort, modern day thought and wishes. She remembered all the good things and the fun things that had been part of her life. This helped to diminish some small traumas and disappointments from her past. Cheryl knew in her heart and mind that the best way to forget any trauma from her past would be to step out again into the future. What was her future? The future would be her new plans and dreams of what she wanted for tomorrow and the rest of her life. It would unfold only one day at a time. It would not unfold unless she worked toward it every day. No matter how small her steps were, they would be toward her dreams. The statue, the drywall, her art work, and her journey with Max. It all began one step and one day at a time.

She read her notes from the morning. She had five weeks left to finish her miner. She would have all of her thirty two sections at the metal pouring area by the end of the week. That would be her goal. When the bronze metal was poured in the shells, she would once again work two hours early in the morning and two hours in the evening. She looked at the replica next to her logbook and the skydive manual. Where would she start? How would it go? Weld the base? No problem. Weld the chest together and then the arms. No problem. The boots and the legs to the hips might be a little tricky to get everything lined up. She had doubts that her shells would be poured all at once. They would arrive a few at a time. Oh, well. Even if everything was poured on the same day, she could only work on a few sections at a time. She was getting ahead of herself now. She would go through the week with loyalty and dignity. The miner would be finished when the patina dried and not before. That was the reality of the situation. She told herself over and over that the deadline was not really an important concern.

Max snuck up the stairs on his hands and feet. He flattened to the stairway and stuck his eyes above the floor level. His thoughts were a silent prayer. God, look at this beautiful lady. All disciplined and plotting the upcoming events of the week. I love her. God, I love this woman. Please be with her and keep her from harm.

"How is it going, baby? What has your notebook told you tonight?"

"I need to put out poison for undesirable vermin."

"Any good news, Princess?"

"Yes, there is some good news. We have regular hours this week. We can sleep in."

"You know if you stare at the lamp much longer, your brain is going to burst into flame."

"Oh? What else do you have for me, Max?"

"I just want to warn you. I have set out some poison in the living room in front of the TV. Some pillows, a pitcher of water, white zinfandel, provolone cheese, and crackers. I am trying to snare a large red haired rodent that has been running through the house."

"I'll be down to investigate. My neck and back are a little sore. I might need a massage for an hour or so."

CHAPTER TWENTY SIX

Cheryl was awake just before the six thirty alarm went off. She was spooned with the recent object of her desire and affection. They were wonderfully warm under a pile of blankets. Sleeping alone has a few advantages, but there is fun to be had with Max in the morning. The alarm clock would ring any minute. Cheryl decided to mess with Max just a wee bit. She backed away from him. She drew her knees up to her chest and pushed her feet against his back. He began to slide towards the edge of the bed. He faked a couple of snores and took the covers with him ever closer to the edge. Cheryl remained warm in her flannel nightgown. The alarm clock began to ring.

"What have I done wrong now?"

"Would you get the alarm clock, please? It is time for you to rise. Mongo, start the fire or I will dot the other eye! Bring me my bowl of swill! Fetch the chariot!"

"Is there something important about today, m' love?"

"That was not called for you incompetent lackey! You insolent servant! I have worked my ass off to get the miner to this point. I make your sandwiches that you eat for lunch without gratitude or even a thank you. I deserve to bask in luxury."

"You sleep with me do you not?"

"Go, Mongo. Go now!"

"That's right, m' lady. Piss on the peasants."

They entered the foundry through the front doors. The air was almost cold. She followed Max to the shell room. He secured the entrance door open for ventilation. Cheryl looked across the roomful of shells. She was eager to get her shells through the wax melt furnace.

"The miner shells are on the back of the second rack. The prairie people are in the middle and the bronco is up front. That is how I separate three or four projects." He opened the back door and positioned two fans to circulate air past the hanging shells.

Cheryl counted thirteen. She pulled her black magic marker and drew two dime size circles on the inside of the sprue cup. They walked out to the wax melt furnace. Close to forty shells were lined up for the furnace. She noticed a horizontal black line two inches long on the side of the bronco sprue cups. The others were the prairie people with a vertical line. They located eight miner shells. She pulled her magic marker again and marked her shells. They arranged five of them under the hood of the wax melt furnace. She dialed the furnace for heat and fired it up. They moved to the other side of the furnace where the finished shells were stacked. Cheryl located eleven more. They were the ones she had run through last Friday. She marked them with two circles. She was gathering pieces of her project. Her miner used to be a large clay sculpture. Now her shells blended in with all of the other hundreds of shells in the foundry. "Thanks Max. Put them on the table carts and get them to the metal pour area. And don't crack them! Catch you later."

Bob left a note in the slurry mix bowl for Max to add four buckets of water. Someone put some overtime in the shell room this weekend. Max was adding the water as Cheryl returned.

She inspected her shells again. "How many more coats Max?"

"The first ten need two more coats minimum. They should be done by Tuesday evening. The last three need three more coats. They should be ready for wax melt on Wednesday. The slurry materials are available. It will happen."

Cheryl eyeballed her shells again. She had them all accounted for. Excellent. The rest of the miner would be through the shell room and the wax melt furnace by Wednesday. "Boy, you know it would really help me out if you paid a little extra attention to these here shells with the two dots on the sprue cups. I just might throw you a couple of chicken wings for lunch, boy."

Max delivered a face full of twisted smirk across the shell room and nodded his head profusely. "I meant to thank you for helping me remove my wrinkles. Do you want me to set the tent up outside during break time? Maybe we could do some four wheeling after work on the way home?"

"You know after six months of cohabitation in Colorado we are considered legally married. You might want to increase your insurance policy. I will need some extra cash after your husk is empty."

Max stepped on the slurry pedal. The blade began to stir the mix. "I'm sorry. I can't hear you. Any other instructions for me?" He gave her the goofy grin.

"Oh, yes. You will get them later."

Cheryl moved to the foundry floor. Her spirits were buoyed. The process was under control. She would keep her shells moving through the stages. Her spiritual state was fulfilled. She was alive with love and harmony from the weekend camping activities. Her Granddad used to say, "Just hold what you got and keep 'er steady." The girl on a swing and Casey were almost finished and ready for patina. She put the touch ups on both. Her two foundry priorities for the week were the shepherd girl and the newspaper boy. She made progress removing the ceramic from the head shawl on the shepherd girl. An actual bath towel had been used for a shawl to cover the girl's head. The latex and the wax picked up the fine detail but the hot metal pour washed the tiny ceramic spikes smooth in a couple of spots and particles of ceramic scattered in the surface of the metal. Cheryl would eventually clean them off the bronze surface.

She spied Marty in back wheeling the welder over to the pile of bronco shells. She was in a good mood as she usually was when she tried to tease Marty. "Hey, handsome, how was the vacation, are you glad to be back?" Cheryl liked to pretend that she was the boss with Marty. It worked if she did not push it too far. It was somewhat amusing for him.

"Hey, Marty! Good of you to return. Are you planning to rescue us from our impending deadlines? I just need to make sure you know the jazz quartet is being pushed through the wax room. It is five figures plus the piano. That should give you something to do. One hundred seventy six sections. Do you remember the prairie people? The metal pieces are piled over in the center section."

"Hey, there, thank you Cheryl. Mary got me up to speed yesterday."

"Gosh, Marty, you been back in town since Friday? You had lots of phone calls. Some people have stopped here looking for you, bill collectors I think. Ha, ha, ha! I hate to tell you this but the bronco is due in about two weeks. That won't stress you out will it? I guess if you can weld about eight sections every day you can get most of it knocked out, but the prairie statue is due in a couple of weeks. You may be working evenings and weekends to get it all done."

"We have two welding machines now. I will have one rod in each hand and I will finish it all by myself. If you want to help me I will have some girl scout cookies for you when you pick up your pay check."

Mary and Bob walked though the front door to the office. They pulled the dialing for dollars file folder out of the desk drawer and arranged their work on the desktop. They discussed the important aspects of the foundry work for the week. Mary gave Bob a run down. "The girl on a swing and Casey will get patina this week. The flatbed trailer is supposed to be at the truck dock Thursday to move them both. We can load them up and they will be on the way. The news paper boy and the peasant girl should be ready for patina before Friday. We have four partial payments in, the prairie people, the gate mosaic from Japan, Casey, the girl on the swing, and a final payment from Frank Wier for his stainless steel cranes. The first partial payment for the jazz quartet is supposed to hit Wednesday, and the final bronco payment should be here next week. We need to stock up on materials for wax, ceramic, welding, patina, and metals mix. I will order three times what we normally ask for. This week we have materials coming in tomorrow or, well, all week. How about you, lover boy?"

"I have the pouring crew help out with the wax melt furnace. I split them into two shifts so we will be open around the clock, just the same as last week. Everything went smooth. This week beginning Wednesday or Thursday, we will pour metal around the clock until all four statues are complete. How about them apples?"

"Wow, I bet you that will be three weeks of metal pour. The welder will be delivered today. The metal sections for the prairie people are going to be stacked in the center partition and the sections for the bronco will be stacked on the other side."

At the end of the day Cheryl picked up eight shells at the wax melt furnace and moved them over to the metal pour area. There were now nineteen empty shells at the metal pour area. She was irritated that her shells were last in the line order.

Thursday morning, she put the finishing touches on the shepherd girl and the newspaper boy and went to work in earnest on the kids, the dog, and the water hose.

Cheryl thoroughly enjoyed her job. In between fits and bouts of concentration she occasionally took a small break. Instead of heading for the break room, she would think of skydiving. In two more days she would jump again. She visualized the maneuvers for her new jump. She would fake a stretch, but actually she would ease in to a hard arch and silently count ten seconds. If she did not think of skydiving then she would recall the ecstasy of her last camping trip. She had never been so worked up with a man. Max certainly knew how to keep his companion hot and wet. Cheryl suspected he had very strong feelings for her. He sometimes seemed unmoved, but she knew otherwise. They were best friends and they were now sharing an intimate relationship. Love was in the air. Cheryl took a small break to check in with Molly.

"What is the scuttle today, Molly?"

"I heard that the girl on the swing will ship Thursday. Nice job on her face, Cheryl."

"I just thought of you and I made her beautiful. Man, oh, man. Have we got some projects going on or what?"

"It is a good thing the wax room got a make over. The larger work table and the new shelves made it possible for this big push. Cindy and Johnny have really given extra effort. They have great personalities and attitudes. When they are not helping me they are rotating on the sand blaster and the wax melt furnace with the pouring crew. Cindy bought four old sheets from the second hand store in Minturn. She cut head holes in the center of the sheets and hemmed in the neck hole. Now the sandblasters have some home made smocks to cover their clothes from the dust. I'm telling you, they care about what goes on here and they really help out. We have one hundred forty molds in here and we are putting on two coats a day. The jazz quartet will be next of course. It has a grand total of one hundred and seventy six pieces.

"Molly my miner just up and went to pieces."

"You stand by them and care for them. You put your time and money into them and you do the best you can and what happens?" She raised her voice slightly, "They just up and fly to pieces. It can happen to anyone, Cheryl."

"Talk to you later Molly." Good old Molly. Molly never had a negative day. If she had a feeling that something was amiss or that something needed to be done, then she would resolve the situation. Her motives and thoughts were always for positive outcomes. As Cheryl left the wax room she ran into Mary.

"Cheryl, would you pick up the old man on the bench and the girl on the bench? They need to be worked on by a couple of good chasers. Get Nash to help you."

"Will do, Mary. I was really glad to see the shepherd girl go, so I will help you out on the bench people. I am ready for a change of scenery for a couple of hours."

Mark, Bob, Moose, Nash, Ernie, and Johnny loaded the girl on the swing and Casey at the bat on the flatbed trailer at the truck dock. Casey went lying down and the girl on the swing was vertical. They literally carried both statues on to the trailer by hand. There was a flurry of shoring up on the flatbed trailer. Wood framing with two by fours and sixes were used to support the statues for the road. The statues were wrapped up and protected with cardboard and moving blankets.

Max dipped the bronco and the prairie people all week. Everything was under control. The wax crew continually brought waxes for the jazz musicians to the first rack in the shell room.

The whole complexion of the foundry began to change once the pouring marathon was under way. The lights were on twenty four hours a day.

The metal pour area was set up for non stop production. Large quantities of copper silica and other metals were in close proximity to the furnace. The pour crew began at ten am and was scheduled to pour all weekend. It was one hour for the mixture of metals to melt. It was fifteen minutes to pour into the ladle and fill five or six ceramic shells. The foundry would pour forty shells every twelve hours.

That afternoon Cheryl found Max at the injection mold machine. They stared at each other longingly across the room. The memory and the fires of the camping trip resurfaced. They had a mental and chemical attraction that surpassed ordinary physical desire. They could feel the circuitry in their bodies begin to over heat.

"Max, do you love me?"

"Yes, I do. I am crazy about you. I care for you. You are number one in my life."

"Would you jump of a cliff if I asked you to?"

"I might if you promise to catch me, but first, I think we need to work on our personal relationship. I think we need to work on our relationship from the verbal standpoint. Do you mind if I ask you a personal question? That night in the tent, you were not your usual self. You were, ah, different. You treated me like an object. It all seemed so detached, and impersonal, and cheap from my point of view. I felt like you were using me. Like the way some people use a mop to clean their dirty floors."

"Hey, that is my line. Maybe I did, boy. Maybe you had it commin'. But that is my business and none of yours. Besides, so what if I did? What are you gonna do about it?"

"Do you have multiple personalities?"

"I think I am going to go to Sky's West this weekend."

"That is exactly what I would do. I wish I could go with you. I will be at 407 again."

"I will explain everything to you this evening." She turned and left the room.

In the spirit and flow of their intimate time spent after work, the living room was prepared for the three M's, the movies, the munchies, and the massages. The foundry clothes were washed. Cheryl packed her equipment for the weekend and stowed it next to the kitchen door. They agreed to take two cars in the morning so Cheryl could leave from work. Eventually, they settled on the floor and the furniture to view a comedy DVD. It entertained them for about fifteen minutes before they decided to continue their wrestling matches in a more formal manner.

"Cheryl declared, "I am the Assassin! I am going to use the claw hold on you tonight. You cannot get away from me."

Max countered, "Your claw hold was outlawed last week. I am Dick the Bruiser. I am going to attack your groin area, and you will not be able to walk tomorrow. We will put you in a wheel chair with a safety belt so you can move around at the foundry." They tired of wrestling and returned to the movie. Max paid loving attention to Cheryl with a luxurious thirty minute massage. Afterwards he tortured her with soft light touches over her back and her breasts and between her legs. Cheryl was on fire. Max could feel her heat on his hands. He slowly peeled away her wet jeans and her blue plaid flannel shirt.

"I have been waiting since four o'clock this after noon to get your clothes off." He removed his own as he continued to run his fingers lightly all over her back. His fingers lingered between her legs. "I think we need to work on a transition from a back rub and clothing removal to wild monkey love."

Cheryl rolled over and gazed into his blue eyes. "Max, you are so cute when you try to be funny. I am ready for you Max. Give me what you gave me in the tent. Don't be stingy. Give me multiple orgasms. I need you. I want you to love me tenderly and I want you to love me forever. You do love me, don't you Max?"

"Yes. I do love you Cheryl. I am going to show you how much I love you right now and every day after this moment." Max moved over her. He kissed her lips and teased her with slow strokes. Later he rolled to his back and let her mount him to take what she needed.

"Give me enough to get me through the weekend."

"Your greatest desire is my ultimate wish."

That night Max induced the greatest fire ever in her lower abdomen and breasts.

An hour later she told him. "Let me rest. I haven't an ounce of energy." They turned out the lights and went upstairs to share a night of sleep. Cheryl listened to his heart beat as she drifted off to sleep.

That peaceful night, deadline dreams began to appear. Cheryl could monitor her shells and their movement, but there was no visible reassurance. With no visible signs of her miner a little bit of doubt worked into her subconscious during her sleep. The restlessness began to turn into movement. There was only a small amount at first. The last three nights in a row Max was awake at one am. He was freezing. The nearest blanket and sleeping bag was a foot away from him. Cheryl was warm and toasty comfortable in a huge pile of blankets. It happened to them both in the tug of war nights of restless sleep. He made a mental note to pick up three more blankets from the Second Hand Rose along with four or five pillows for the living room floor.

Friday morning at the foundry, Max followed Cheryl straight to the pouring area. She was wide awake now and eager to find metal in her shells. Six of her shells had been moved. They looked in the finished pile. One by one they found six poured sections of the base. She would be certain to thank Mark and Moose. "Max, we will be here Sunday to weld this base together."

"I love it when you give me orders. Maybe you will have some more for me tomorrow night."

Cheryl was back out on the floor as a hired employee to perform the task at hand and to do it with style and flair as she always did. She was even and steady today. She prepared the backup hand steel that Nash brought in for her. She latexed the steel and left it in the wax room. The plaster would be taken care of next week.

The push was on to get the bronco out the door as soon as possible. Both welders were in the bronco area. The Robertson's were rotating on the welding duties. Before the end of the day, Cheryl stopped to see Max in the leaf room. They argued briefly.

"Max, leave your car here and go with me to the DZ. We can rent a room nearby."

"Cheryl, it kills me not to go with you, but I have to work on 407. You will have fun tomorrow at the DZ. If you do really well on your jumps, then I will have a big surprise and a special treat for you when you get home, remember that. It is going to have to hold you, Princess. I think you might be a little bit spoiled with all of the preferential treatment you have received lately. I may have to spank you in the wrestling ring when you get home. I am planning to pick up some extra pillows for the wrestling stadium and three more blankets for your medical stretcher. You are going to need them."

"Thanks Max. I'll remember that. I think you have some serious personality flaws and disorders. I am going to put you in traction and a rehabilitation program when I return."

"Bring it on, baby. You think you can take me?"

"You are on. I will prove it to you. We will settle the dispute once and for all tomorrow night in the stadium."

"Have fun this weekend and don't forget to smile."

They embraced in the parking lot after work. "You will be home before you know it. Stay away from Bev's or drink soda if you go. Only one alcoholic drink. Stay away from the townie teenagers. If you get home late, I will know. You will get a brutal spanking from me."

Saturday morning Max treated himself to a sausage burrito for breakfast at The Golden Burro. The day was clear and beautiful. He knew that Cheryl would have no problem at the DZ. He stopped at Charlotte's and picked up three blankets and two big floor pillows for the wrestling arena. He assured Charlotte that Cheryl was fine and still working on her project in good health. He moved on to 407 for another weekend of the work he loved to do. He had been at it for nine months now. This was his second remodel. He fished the rest of the electrical line down to the first floor. He installed the electrical boxes for the light switches, the receptacles, and the ceiling lights. One fine day he would make it to the discount light store for the ceiling lights.

At one o'clock, Max thought of Cheryl. He went outside with a cup of coffee to the small deck. The winds were surprisingly calm. He felt a real or imagined link with her. He knew they would think of one another today, but probably not at the same time. He focused his thoughts to the drop zone and her jumps. He sent her a message of safety. He meditated. He was worried about her overconfidence and the other things that could go wrong, but he knew she was safe at Sky's West, especially with the instructors she worked with. Max cleared his mind and prayed to God. He expressed his thanks for all that was good in the world and he asked for Cheryl's safety.

He returned to the house and he started in the upstairs bath. He used the wood from the land fill to build supports for the floor. Upstairs, the new level would come out three feet from the wall. There was enough room for the tub and the commode. There was plenty of room for the washer and the dryer in the corner between the sink and the door. He installed the drain lines for the clothes washer, the sink, and the tub, to the commode drain pipe. He included access fittings on the drain lines. Next, he installed the water lines for the washer, the sink, the tub, and the commode. He included shut off valves, and drain faucets for the water lines. He was a believer in the convenience they would provide over the life of the system.

Downstairs, in the kitchen corner, he cut through the wall into the bathroom. The drain line from the kitchen sink would join the bathroom sink, and the shower. They would empty into the commode drain line. He installed supports to raise the floor level seven inches, just like he did in the upstairs bath. The drain lines could be run without tearing up the floor or working under the house. The P trap for the shower could be installed with no problem. Max planned to have a large shower downstairs because of the small amount of available space. The corner sink from 304 would leave room for a tall narrow section of shelves for towels and accessories.

He installed the water and drain lines. He moved the landfill bathtub, sink cabinet, and commode to the upstairs bath. He would install them after the new floor was down. He lined up the floor cabinets in the kitchen. He shimmed them until they were level. He braced them to keep them sturdy and then he attached them permanently to the wall and the floor. The counter top would be next. He knocked off at five thirty and headed for home to be ready for Cheryl's return and an early evening to bed.

CHAPTER TWENTY SEVEN

Cheryl was glad to be away from the work routine and ready for some excitement and fun. No one dished it out quite like the Sky's West Drop Zone. She was in good spirit today. She wanted to see her new friends and release some energy. She got together in the morning with Liz to pack her new parachute.

"There are three phases of folding up your canopy Cheryl. If you think of it that way it is easy to remember." She laid the container down pack tray up and stretched out the canopy and suspension lines. "Alright, grab the tabs at the top of the canopy and lay all seven cells down on top of each other, like an accordion on its side. "Now pick up the two outside lines on the nose where the open cells are, and the two brake lines on the tail. Walk them down to the risers. Notice that there are no suspension lines running through or around those four lines. The four lines must be clear all the way to the risers."

"Let me show you what the tangled suspension lines look like." Liz picked up the container and flipped it through the front and rear riser on the right side. She stretched the lines out and laid the container down. Both women could see the tangle of the suspension lines.

"Cheryl, I know you can see the tangle, but try that four line check again."

Cheryl picked up the four lines at the bottom of the canopy and walked down to the risers. She made it half way to the container when her hands encountered the twists and the overlap in the suspension lines.

"Is there any doubt in your mind?"

"No. It is really obvious. No doubt about it. So this can happen if you roll through your suspension lines on landing?"

"That's right. It will also happen if you just dump your parachute in your gear bag at the end of the day. When you pull your parachute out of the gear bag the suspension lines will get tangled up."

"So that is why everyone makes the effort to daisy chain the lines right after a jump while they still have the rig on."

"Absolutely correct. It is also the reason that you pack your own chute. Do not get in a hurry to manifest for your second or third jump. You need to be packed first or at least have plenty of time to do so. If you packed this mess it might open with lines over the canopy. There is an amazing amount of stress on these suspension lines once the chute is open. If you have a line over your canopy, it will cut through the material. Now, to untangle that mess, take the outside line on the nose, and follow it down to the snag." Cheryl followed the line to the snag. "Now pull that line towards you."

Cheryl pulled the container towards her. "I can see the path of this line to the riser. So I pull the container through that opening?"

"Right. You figured it out. Keep your eye on the container and pull the container through the tangle."

"That is pretty slick."

"It's not difficult at all. It just takes some extra time and it will save you an ambulance ride."

They shared a laugh.

"Now for the second phase, you have to S fold the canopy. The A line group is at the nose, where the cells open. The D group is back there on the tail. Leave the A group right where it is. Grab the top of the canopy above the B group and pull all of the canopy material over until the B group lines up on top of the A group, then set it down. Cheryl knelt at the top of the canopy. She picked up a handful of the canopy above the B line group. She pulled the material across to the nose of the canopy and repeated the motion for the C and D group.

"Now there is a little variation with the tail, the D line group." Liz demonstrated how to arrange the left side of the tail and the right side of the tail on top of the folded canopy.

Cheryl watched attentively and memorized the procedure.

"See how the four suspension lines on the left side converge to one line that is the brake line?"

"Yes. It ends up tied to the top of the left toggle that you use to brake and steer. The same for the right side."

"Correct. Have you done this before?"

"I have been paying attention. When I get the chance to watch someone pack their chute, I take the time to watch."

"Then move on down and stow the brake lines."

Cheryl moved to the risers and set each line and toggle in the "keeper" on the back of the risers.

"Do you have riser turns on this jump?"

"Yes, I do. On the first jump."

"Hang on a second." Liz fished out her role of duct tape and wrapped a small amount around each toggle. "Just a reminder. Be sure to work your canopy requirements into your dirt dives. Do you feel good about this pack job, Cheryl?"

"So far I do."

"Are you going to use this parachute on your next jump?"

"That is kind of a scary thought isn't it?"

"Yes it is. I certainly remember mine. The funny thing is that you may think about it when you get in the plane or on the ride to altitude. But you won't think about again until after the jump is over."

"Would that be because you are too busy thinking about all of the other things on your jump?"

"I think it you are beginning to catch on, Cheryl. Okay, follow me through this third phase, where we close everything up. The end of the pilot chute ribbon goes through a hole in the top of the canopy bag and it is tied to the top of the canopy. You have to pull the ribbon all the way through the opening in the top of the canopy bag, until the bag is at the top of the canopy. No knots or twists are allowed on the ribbon." Cheryl pulled all of the pilot chute ribbon through the top of the canopy bag. "Next, you place the top part of this pile of parachute into the canopy bag. Now, believe it or not, there is room for the rest of the canopy in here."

Cheryl knelt down across from Liz with the canopy and the bag between them. Cheryl folded the canopy into the bag carefully so the suspension line integrity remained undisturbed. When the entire canopy was tucked into the bag, Liz spoke up.

"There is one more thing to do. Bring the slider up here, would you please?"

"You have to do about twenty deep knee bends to get this rig packed."

"Yes, you do. It will help keep our legs in shape." Cheryl returned the slider from the risers to Liz. Liz folded it into the bottom of the canopy bag. "The slider slows the opening of the canopy. If you do not have a slider the opening will be fast and uncomfortable."

"Why do I have the feeling that was an understatement? If you are going a hundred miles an hour and you have a sudden stop, something is going to break. Am I right?"

"Absolutely. You have to know your gear and how it functions to have confidence in the process." Liz helped Cheryl close the bag and fold the suspension line groups back and forth from side to side on the canopy bag. Cheryl wrapped a rubber band around each line fold to prevent tangles and to maintain line deployment integrity. The suspension lines were neat and orderly back and forth on the bottom of the canopy bag.

"Whoever figured out how to put this big canopy into this tiny little bag had a twisted mind."

"Ha! That's for sure!"

Liz had Cheryl flip the bag into the container pack tray lines down. Her strong hands and fingers threaded the pull up cord through the locking loop on the bottom flap. She ran the pull up cord through each grommet on the other three flaps. She strained to get the loop pulled through the grommets. With her free hand, she fumbled for the pin on the pilot chute ribbon. She slid the pin through the locking loop and removed the pull up cord.

"That is not easy."

"Good job. Usually you can find someone to close the container for you. It is kind of a custom to get one of the boy toys to do it. Karen whistles for them."

Cheryl deftly stowed the pilot chute and placed her rig in her gear bag. "Thank you Liz. I will let you know how the opening goes."

Together they made a relaxed tour on the hanging harness and the PLF stand. Afterward, Cheryl looked for Karen.

The sun was shining and the winds were calm. They sat on lawn chairs under the red and white stripe canvass sun screen in the grassy packing area next to the loft. Both were enjoying the relaxed moment and the day. Karen quizzed Cheryl about her reading assignment in the Skydiver's Information Manual and reviewed canopy emergencies.

"Why do you throw your pilot chute?"

"If you hold on to your pilot chute, the ribbon can wrap around your arm and wrist. The pilot chute will not pull the locking pin to open your container and deploy your canopy because it has wrapped around your arm. When you let go of the pilot chute it will be right there on your arm. There was a death in California last month. It was in Parachutist magazine."

"What if your pilot chute slips into the burble on your back?"

"I roll on my side and let the air stream pull everything off my back. It will take your pilot chute and your gear off your back like a kite on a windy day. I can make eye contact with the gear at the same time for inventory purposes." Karen laughed. "If the gear is tangled then I cut away and deploy the reserve."

"Describe one more type of total malfunction."

"Bag lock is a form of a total. The pilot chute pulled the pin and the container opened, the suspension lines are out, but for some reason the canopy is still folded up and stuck in the in the canopy bag."

"What is the corrective action that you take?"

"Go to the hard arch, head back, and pull the cutaway handle and the reserve handle."

"What is a partial malfunction?"

"A partial is when the canopy comes out, but it does not fully inflate. The material may be caught in the suspension lines. It will look like a mess. It might be all rolled up in a big ball of garbage. Usually, it is due to a bad pack job. The chance that you are falling vertically at eighty miles an hour or more is pretty good."

"What corrective action do you take?"

"Get that hard arch and pull the cutaway handle and the reserve handle."

"What is a horseshoe malfunction?"

"A horseshoe malfunction is when any part of the canopy, or the pilot chute ribbon, or the suspension lines wrap around you. The canopy might be all rolled up or it might be open."

"What corrective action do you take?"

"I think I would take a big breath and pass some gas in my jumpsuit." They shared laughter. "You have to clear the material away from your body. If the material is snagged on you, it will still be right behind you and attached to you after you pull the cut away handle. So, if you deploy the reserve parachute, it will open up in the mess of the main canopy. You will have two canopies tangled together and a really painful landing."

"After you deploy your pilot chute you have a loop of suspension lines snake around your side to your stomach. What do you do?"

"Push those lines back behind you and you might want to roll a little bit to the other side so the wind will blast everything off your back."

"You were somersaulting through the air when your canopy opened and you have a few suspension lines around your arm or leg. You have a good canopy. What corrective action do you take?"

"If it is just a couple of suspension lines, then you pull your knife and cut them. If there are a bunch of them, just cut everything at the risers and get your reserve open."

"Alright, Cheryl, stand up and cut a couple of lines. Play act it. One thousand, two thousand, hurry girl, three thousand, four thousand, five thousand."

Cheryl stood and drew an imaginary knife. She went through the motions of cutting the imaginary suspension lines.

"So, Cheryl, tell me what is the point of the drills? Why do you practice them?"

"Basically, if you have a canopy emergency, you have to deal with it correctly. You have to be able to perform the correct action and you have very little time to do that. If you allow yourself to be distracted, you might have a hard landing. Distraction is the danger. The motions take two seconds and eye contact and recognition will take at least another two seconds. I am still moving at one hundred miles an hour and I have lost one thousand feet of altitude."

"How much altitude is required for a reserve canopy to inflate?"

"After you have pulled the reserve handle, the fast ones are rumored to open in five hundred feet. So, if it takes five seconds to recognize a canopy malfunction, and pull the handles, that will eat up one thousand five hundred feet of altitude."

"Five seconds goes faster than you think it will. Practice under canopy. The reach to your knife should be the same as the reach to your pilot chute, automatic, but twice as fast. The cutting must be just as fast, one hand to hold the material and one on the knife. If you have one arm tangled up then one hand may take longer to get the knife out. That is something that you should really think about. You have the correct understanding here. Let's talk about riser turns just briefly. You will have to do them on jump four or five."

"Alright, I am listening."

"Imagine that you track away from a formation and someone's canopy opens right beside you. You have twenty feet of separation, but you are flying right into the other jumper. How would you dodge the canopy? Would you take the time to release the toggles from the keepers and steer away?"

"Let me guess. The riser turn is faster."

"The riser turns are a safety feature. If someone is in front of you on opening you can dodge them quickly by pulling down on a front riser. Your turns with the riser are just an instant away. This allows you to make a quick dodge. Reaching for your keepers to release the brakes will take longer and might result in a mid air collision."

"Don't look now, but here comes trouble."

Steve ambled up with a lawn chair in his hand. "Mind if I join you ladies?"

"That all depends. Did you bring lunch for us today?"

"One of these days, I just might do that. Right now, it is just another gorgeous day, and I am trying to find out what you women are up to."

"Karen has me all fired up for level four and five today. She has been pushing me this morning."

"But it is a good push from ten thousand feet. Steve, now is a good time. We are ready. Is it okay if we sit right here?"

"Yes we can sit here and talk about jump four for awhile. Cheryl, remember to include the mind set of COA, legs, relax after every maneuver. Alright, here we go. There are five objectives for jump four. You have your usual transition and heading. After that you have five maneuvers to make. One ninety degree turn, two one hundred eighty degree turns, and two three hundred sixty degree turns. Five seconds a maneuver is one thousand feet and five maneuvers would convert to five thousand feet. We exit at ten thousand five hundred. You must be under canopy by four thousand feet so there may not be any extra freefall time. Are you with me?"

"Gotcha Steve. I will try to do each turn in less than five seconds. If I do each turn in four seconds, then we will have an extra five seconds of freefall."

"Cheryl, describe how to make a three hundred sixty degree turn."

"From the stable free fall position you have to snap your right elbow hard to your waist. You snap your head that direction as well. The left hand snaps to the top of your helmet. A fast, hard snap will have the pinwheel effect where you spin on your belly button just like a toy top. I hear it is possible to make a three sixty in three seconds. If you do not put in a good snap, then your turn will be slow. Your body will drift or slide sideways around in a circle. It may take five seconds or more to complete the turn. I plan to use a salute turn. I will throw my right hand hard and fast to my right hip."

"Good. Let's go to the hanger and dirt dive this jump with the floor dollies."

They moved to the concrete hangar floor and laid on the floor dollies. Cheryl was in the middle with Steve on her right and Karen on her left.

"Alright, Cheryl initially we need to what . . . ?"

"Initially we all three have to get heading and circle of awareness."

"Right. I want you to count the seconds for each maneuver as well as your circle of awareness. Now back up to the open door and take it from there. Talk your way through the jump."

"Spot and give corrections. Ready. Set. Go! This is a no contact jump after the exit. As much as possible we have to match fall rates. Okay, we made the transition, I have a ground heading, and we are at ninety five hundred feet. I look to you for a signal. You nodded your head and I do the first ninety to you."

"Good, Cheryl. These first three turns do not take much time. Don't worry about your COA until you are on the three sixties. We will have some time left over. Okay, turn right to me and that is your first ninety. Now, turn left to Karen and that is your first one eighty. Turn back to me again and that is your second one eighty. What should you do right now?"

"My second COA. I am with you. Do both the five second count per thousand feet and the COA on the three sixties."

"Good. That will work for us. We might be at eight thousand feet. You will have plenty of time. So do not feel pressured. Okay Cheryl, take the first one to the right."

Cheryl spun her dolly around past Karen's smiling face and back to Steve. "Hey that takes a little muscle on these floor dollies. We're not going to take them with us are we?" Karen and Steve laughed at the question.

"All the way back to me and make eye contact. Look for a cut off signal because we may be out of altitude. Okay, we have altitude. Next one to the left, and all the way around. Okay, we made it. We are at five thousand above ground level. Go ahead. Wave off and deploy."

They sat on the floor for awhile.

"Cheryl, there are a couple of what ifs to watch for on this jump. If your turns are slow, there is the possibility that you will slide around. If that happens Karen and I might have to push you a little so that you do not bump into us. Your heading is really important on this jump. To get credit for this dive it must be a three sixty. A two seventy, or a four twenty turn will disqualify you. I feel positive about the three of us. I think we are going to be all right on these turns. We match fall rates easily. We have some positive no contact time. All of the good, hard work you have done adds up, and I think this jump will be smooth." Karen readily agreed. "Alright, let's do this two more times and Karen and I might include one or two hand checks in the ground drill. After that we are out to the mock up."

Cheryl opened her gear bag and pulled out her new jumpsuit and parachute. The thought that she and Liz packed it earlier crossed her mind. She did not dwell on the thought. She knew it would open. She met Karen and Steve at the mock up.

Steve congratulated her on the new gear. "You look great Cheryl. You made a good move to pick up that sweetheart deal. I thought I detected a little nervous twitch there for a second. Did anyone help you pack that snivel?"

"I am not going to let you jinx me. Liz and I really checked everything out down to the stitching. I'm good to go with it. I have every confidence in her ability and I am comfortable with the gear." She boasted, "Besides, I have a reserve. Man, oh man. I did get a good deal."

Karen assured her, "Yes you did. You have a really good system there. You were wise to make the move."

Steve opened things up to the jump at hand. "We are manifested with a tandem just like last week. Our first jump is scheduled for close to eleven and the second one is scheduled for one this afternoon. Cheryl do you have some canopy maneuvers to perform on this jump?"

"That's right. I am going to do one turn with each riser. Karen suggested I do them with while the brakes were on and again after the brakes are off."

Karen reminded her, "Put those turns on your laundry list and in the ground drill as well. Cheryl you have the spot today. Do you want to let me be the pilot for a minute, and tell me what is going on with your group of jumpers?"

"Right. We need a south to north jump run one quarter mile east of the runway. We have two groups. A tandem will be first and the AFF student will be second. Both groups will get out on the same jump run with a five second interval between the two groups."

"Alright, that will work. What is next?"

"You and Steve get the door and I will take care of the spot and the corrections to the pilot. And I would like to do a door dive on this jump."

"Cheryl, tell me about your door dive."

"Well I have practiced for three weeks now. I have to get my heels up on my fanny to reduce my leg exposure to the wind blast."

"If it is all right with you, I would like to have a grip on your left leg strap. It won't slow you down. Steve, what do you think and where do you plan to be on this exit?"

"The leg strap is a good idea for all of us. I am going to rear float so I have a bird's eye view of you ladies as you exit. Agreed, Karen? Okay let's walk through this exit and the dive two times. We have a plane rolling up in about twenty minutes."

The fourth jump came off without a hitch. Cheryl's turns were complete and on heading. She watched the green earth and the clouds below turn beneath her. After her canopy opened, she saw the duct tape Liz wrapped on the toggles. Cheryl performed four riser turns. She released the brakes and did four more.

They packed their parachutes for the next jump together. Steve was interrupted with a phone call. They were pressed for time so he decided to speed things up. "Karen? Do you want to take over here? Go ahead and run through the objectives on jump five. Skip the mock up if you need to. We are short on time." Steve headed for the loft.

Karen and Cheryl continued to pack. "Okay, Cheryl. As you know, there is a Z Out on this jump. The purpose of the Z Out is to prove to you that the hard arch position works any time, and all the time. Tell me about your Z Out."

"I kneel on one knee in the door, and I hold on to my ankle with both hands. I roll out the door and I hold the ankle for five seconds. Then, I go to a hard arch and transition face to earth."

"Good." Let me highlight the objectives for jump five. You did such a good job with the pilot and the spot the last time that you get to do it again. Your second objective will be the Z Out. You are going to leave the plane holding your ankle with both hands. The wind blast is going to bounce you around on the exit, so grip that ankle like you are choking Max. After five seconds of the Z Out, you hit your hard arch. That is your third objective. It will prove to you that the hard arch will return you face to earth if you are tumbling. It is a confidence builder. Circle of awareness, legs, relax. Your fourth objective will be to perform a complete and stable front loop or front flip as we call it. Your fifth objective will be to perform a complete and stable back flip. Check your altitude between each maneuver. Wave off is five thousand and be open by four thousand. This is going to be a feel good jump. No stress here. There is extra time on this jump. Probably fifteen seconds. What extra maneuvers would you like to do?"

"I have been thinking about that. Two back flips and two leg turns is what I would like to do."

"Let me caution you here. It is easy to forget about altitude when you are having fun. The back flips will go fast. If you are above six thousand you will have time to knock out two leg turns. If you are at six thousand you only get one because you have to . . ."

"Wave off at five thousand feet."

"Alright. Let's get a quick bite to eat and meet Steve at the mock up in ten minutes."

The plane ripped through the air at ninety miles an hour straight north, on the east side of the runway. From two miles in the air the two mile runway appeared to be about six inches long. Cheryl stuck her head out the door on jump run. The wind blasted her face and shook her goggles. She located the plane position above the ground and hollered the corrections over the engine noise to the pilot.

"Cut!" Cheryl was on her left knee with the toes of her right foot at the edge of the door. She held on to the leg cuff of her jumpsuit with both hands. She gave the count and she rolled out the door into the wind. The blast pounded her and flipped her over. It partially knocked the wind out of her. It was all she could do to hold on. She spun and flipped out of control until the count of four thousand and she let go of her ankle. For a split second she was upside down on her back. All she could see was blue sky. As fast as you can snap a finger, she flipped face to earth. She rocked head up and down in a big time, teeter totter, potato chip. She finally relaxed into the column of air that her body was pushing out of the way. Her life guards were right beside her and in the next few seconds they enjoyed the acceleration to one hundred twenty miles an hour. Karen gave the signal for the front loop. Cheryl lifted her head slightly and then snapped her head and shoulders to her feet. She drew her knees in to her stomach. She felt the wind blast tear at her parachute and try to pull it from her body. Her momentum carried her through a complete flip, and she returned to a stable arch. Karen gave her the nod for the back flip.

The back loop was fast. She pressed her hands down flat against the wind. She snapped her head back and brought her knees up to her stomach. Her momentum carried her through, and she returned to the arch. She made her COA legs, relax. Her altimeter read 8000. They had fifteen seconds of free fall left. Karen gave her two fingers for two more back loops and she knocked out two for herself to match fall rates with Cheryl. They were at seven thousand and she gave Cheryl two fingers. Cheryl made a right leg turn and a left leg turn. Karen closed and grabbed Cheryl's leg strap as Cheryl checked her altimeter.

She shouted, "Good work Cheryl!" Karen gave her the deployment signal. Cheryl waved off and threw her pilot chute. The risers snapped her shoulders straight up in the air. Her chin dipped to her chest. Who packed that hard opening? She checked her canopy and buried her right toggle past her hip and spiraled the canopy four times. She repeated to the left. She raced Karen and Steve back to the landing area.

On her way back to Leadville, Cheryl thought about her relationship with Max.

She was having a great time and so was he. They loved to do chores and errands for each other like going to the store or the laundry or just cleaning around the house. Max washed dishes for her. Things were under control. Cheryl wanted to give things a little push to move Max to the commitment stage. She would approach him tonight and openly discuss how close they had grown together. Then she would suggest that he make a lifelong commitment to her. She turned right on to Spruce Street. She drove past the Meteor into the alley and parked in the carport. She grabbed her gear bag and locked her truck.

Ever since the camping trip everything had cranked up a notch. It was simply the best sex encounter that she had ever experienced. It lingered in most of her thoughts. Could it happen again? Would she remember it forever? She wanted Max to commit to her because she wanted to commit to him. She would have to come right out and speak her mind. No beating around the bush. She needed to be up front and tell him in direct words that he should dedicate his life to her. Max might not be the best catch in the world, but she had seen more than her fair share of bad catches in the sea of humanity.

Her hormones were raging on their own when she finally saw him that evening. She had to work to keep herself in check. They might have another encounter this evening. Hopefully, it would be enough to get her through the next couple of days.

Max was waiting for her. He knew that Cheryl would put a few hours in at the foundry tomorrow. Tonight it would be early to bed. The living room was set for a luxurious evening of movies, munchies, and massage, the three M's. Max had the new pillows on the floor.

She approached the object of her affection and kissed him lightly on the cheek. "Max, I want to ask you a favor. My hormones have flared up. I just had some real excitement today, and now, I would like to add a little nightcap to that. Do you think you could help me with my problem? You might have to put out a fire."

"I have fire proof mittens."

Cheryl took time to listen to Molly's message. "Cheryl, you have six pieces of metal. It is the base. You might have a couple of more shells poured tomorrow." Cheryl thought for just a second and then she hollered at Max. "Max, we work tomorrow."

"Yes, my love."

"Let's plan to turn in early and get to work early."

"I am all for that. Let's get started with the three M's right now." The lights went out and the movie went on.

"Do you know what I want to do, Max? I want to repeat our Thursday night love making session."

"I do too. You were not paying attention to me or anything I said."

"Aren't you the funny man? And I want to talk about commitment first, Max, so be strong for me."

"Commitment as in forever? I understand that you might be looking for a license to steal my hard earned monthly paycheck."

"You may look at it that way if you like. I choose to look at it from the standpoint of a marriage and a fifty fifty partnership. You need to answer the questions that I am going to ask you. Would you be willing to make a commitment to me and dedicate your life to me? Would you be loyal to me?"

Max gave her a warm smile. "Let me think about that. Can I get back to you next week? I have a lot of projects and things on my mind."

"Do you love me, Max?"

"No!"

"I want to hear you say it!"

"It! Yes, Cheryl, I love you. Things have changed haven't they? From buddies to sweethearts to lovers. The next thing you know, we just might tie the knot."

"Really? Do you have any idea when that might be?"

"No, I don't."

"You know the next level is engagement. First I have to see if I like the ring you get for me."

"Oh, but of course. How silly of me. How do you know I will propose to you?"

"Because I have decided to shoot you if you don't."

"You are serious?"

"Trust me, Max."

"You have been hanging around Karen too much."

For the second time in three nights, Max provided a relaxing massage. He was in heaven and he liked to please. He slowly worked Cheryl to a heightened level of warmth and desire. He teased her and slowly peeled her clothes off.

Cheryl panted, "Oh, Max, I am hotter than the forest fire in 'Always.'"

"Are we going shopping? I have a firm commitment for you right now. Here comes the slurry bomber with the fire retardant."

"Max, take your glasses off."

Max rolled over and Cheryl mounted him. She took her time and quenched her desires in her own manner.

When they finished, He went to the kitchen for more cheese and crackers and a new bottle of wine.

"Max, your stamina is so amazing! How do you do it? Do I really turn you on that much? Is that what it is?"

"That is why my name is Dick, the Bruiser!" For about thirty minutes I thought you were Paris Hilton. I think I blacked out after that."

"Okay Dick, it is time for the regional title bout. When I get my strangle hold on you, I am going to keep it tight, even if you try to tap out."

Max backed the truck out of the carport and rolled slowly out of the alley. They drove over the pass to the foundry under a beautiful blue sky amidst the beauty of the mountains on a narrow winding two lane mountain road.

"Is it a little foggy out this morning, Princess?"

"It was a restless night."

"I know. We are taking turns waking up in the middle of the night."

"It is those darn old dreadful deadline dreams again. The extra blankets make it a little bit easier."

Max decided to joke with her. "Honey, you can be proactive with your dreams. You can actively participate in them and have an effect on the outcome. Dreams are subconscious thoughts of unresolved conflicts and problems that you have. During the day, you ignore them or deny their existence. At night your brain gets even with you for all of those unresolved problems. Your brain dumps your fears and misgivings in your lap and lets them run wild! There is something you can do about it. You have to enter your dream and put your foot down."

"I think I am going to put my foot down on your head."

"Before you go to sleep, you have to stage a plot to defeat your foes whether they are people you have to deal with, or dead lines, or goals, or fears of homelessness. You have to have your strategy in place before you sleep. And then, when it is frustration dream time, it all comes in to play. You may not come out victorious on the first attempt, but at least you will find out that, yes, you can interact and have an influence on the outcome. You can even become assertive and demanding in your dreams and push people around. You have to turn the tables on them."

"You are so good with trivia, Professor Max. I am really beginning to have scary dreams."

"Maybe I can help. I will schedule an appointment to examine you and analyze your dreams."

"Then let's do the appointment now. I feel conversational. I had this dream a couple of nights ago. I wore a dress like the 'Black Velvet' girl with a big string of pearls. Everyone in town was at the museum for the opening ceremony and the unveiling of the statue. I was so excited. I was going to be world renown. There were a few speeches, and then the sheet was taken off. So there is my Raggedy Ann doll, only in giant size!"

Max laughed. "Oh, my goodness."

"Shut up."

"It is from your childhood. The Raggedy Ann doll means that you wish you were not there in the first place. You wish that you were safe at home. There is security in running back to childhood. You could get away with little mistakes and not get into too much trouble, except for a scolding. It also symbolizes how you have left the little world and entered the big unforgiving world of adults where mistakes can be monumental and cost you your job. Did you feel like a little girl at the time?" Cheryl chuckled. "What did you say to the crowd?"

"Well, I got all flustered and I was really mad, so I said, 'Ok, who ripped her eye off?' At least that is what I am going to say next time."

"That is a good one, honey."

"Last night I had a different version of the dream. This time the statue was there, but the head and arms were missing. I was wearing the bib overalls and the coal dust make up."

"Well, just the headless miner, it represents the lack of materials to do the job and the foundry bottleneck. You know, the things that would keep you from making your deadline."

Max told her about the dream that he used to have when he was ten years old. "It is called the 'Rolling down the hill backward' dream. The whole family was in the car. We were going somewhere together. Dad was driving. The car was going up hill. The hill got steeper and steeper. The wheels began to spin and the car could no longer go forward. The car began to slide slowly backward. The whole family sat immobile like statues. No one could do or say anything. Everyone but me was frozen and looking straight ahead. As children, we were not allowed to speak when Dad was driving. I jumped around in the seats and tried all of the doors and windows. I was locked in and I could not get out. I looked out the back window, and I saw a big semi truck charging up the hill, ready to plow into the back end of the car."

"Is that why you ran away from home?"

"That and one hundred other reasons. It was an indication to me at an early age that everyone has to look out for number one. And don't look to others for help, even if it is your brother, your sister, or your parents."

The foundry was operating around the clock since the non stop pouring operations began last week. Cheryl's six poured shells for the base were right beside the sandblaster. Max stared at the sandblaster. It was a work table with a big rectangular plastic cover on top. The blasting was done inside the plastic box. The cover kept the residue inside the box so the operator did not have to stand in a cloud of sand. Cheryl picked up the rubber mallet at the sandblaster.

"Okay, Mongo. This is elementary and it can be mildly amusing. Pay attention and you will learn how to sandblast. There is an outside chance that it might be too difficult for you."

Max nodded his head several times in the roll of the dolt, and said enthusiastically, "Uh huh, uh huh, uh huh."

"I pretend that the metal is the high school volleyball coach who used to have all the blonde girls on the first string." She pounded the shell with the hammer. "He was emotionally attached to them. I pretend that I am punching his nose with this rubber mallet. I had to play on the second string. I never got to play in any of the games, and I was better than all of those other bitches." The ceramic cracked and popped off to the floor. "When this pile of ceramic builds up on the floor, you can eat it for lunch."

"That's right, baby. Vent all of those nasty old memories."

When all the ceramic was off, she placed her hands and arms into the thick protective rubber sleeves connected to the plastic box. She picked up the handle of the spray gun inside the box.

"Okay, Mongo. Put the metal inside." Max picked up the section of metal. It weighed about thirty pounds. He opened the door and placed it in the sandblaster. Cheryl gripped the section in her left hand and pointed the spray gun with the other. She stepped on the electrical floor switch, and she pulled the trigger on the gun. High pressure air and sand gently washed the metal surface free of ceramic reside.

"Nothing to it. Do you think you can handle this?" Max nodded his head vigorously. "You get the next one and I will tell you what you are doing wrong."

"Like last night?" He blasted the metal free of ceramic while Cheryl gathered six large clamps by the welder next to the prairie people in the center partition. She visited her locker long enough to pull the base pattern she made just before the latex work. She moved the metal sections to the welder after they were blasted. Cheryl had the sections lined up and ready to go. Together they used the clamps and aligned the metal sections according to the pattern. The fit was good. She tacked the sections quickly. Two of them had to be broken and realigned for a better fit. Within an hour, Cheryl had all of the pieces of the base tacked together in one fine, smooth surface with no gaps or flaws. They took a short brake and scoured the metal pouring area. Molly was right. Seven sections of the head and hat had been poured.

"Max, get these seven to the sandblaster. You know the drill. Give me back the clean metal. Find the dolly or carry them. Blast theses babies. Don't pound the metal too hard."

"You mean pound it gently, the way I pound the princess?"

"When you finish, put them by the base."

Max obediently complied. He loaded the shells on the cart and moved them to the blaster. He knocked off the ceramic while Cheryl put some solid welds on the base sections. He finished blasting the head and hat. He loaded the metal on the cart and rolled them over to her. She clamped two sections of the hatless head together while Max held them even to the shoulder sections. Cheryl lightly tacked them together. Next he held the sections of the hat bill to the miner's head. Cheryl tacked light and fast. After the bills were neatly secured Max picked up the crown of the hat. To their surprise the fit was tight and right on.

"Not bad. The alignment is near perfect. There will be some tough chasing on the weld around the bill."

"I have all of theses white spots in my eyes. I can not see anything. I think I am blind."

"You are supposed to close your eyes when I tack, you idiot." Cheryl would need to match the head section on top of the chest and back to check for alignment before she welded the two sections together. A couple of good welds to the head and hat were necessary so the head could be lifted without the small tacks breaking open.

Cheryl was satisfied with their Sunday morning venture to the foundry and the welding that she was able to do. They stopped for groceries on the way home and a couple of comedy DVD's. In her bedroom, she studied her information manual. She reflected on her two new jumps and ran some of the emergency procedures through her head. Jumps six and seven remained. She read her log book with pride and looked at the photos in her album. She let the skydiving go and opened her notebook. Her mind shifted to the foundry situation and the completion of her miner. How would it come about?

The pours to her shells would continue to be sporadic. The bronco and the prairie people had the priority. Cheryl had expected all of her shells to be poured by now, but even if they were, she would only be able to weld the sections together a few at a time. Why get angry? It was the human condition to have an excuse or something to be angry about. She needed to stay happy and have good dreams at night, instead of the dreary, deadline dreams of failure.

How could she deal with this dilemma to make things work out in her favor? She would make everything work out. That was what she wanted. She would settle for nothing less. She had the base and the head and hat tacked together. Once it was welded she could move it to the big work bench. That left two sections. One was the lower torso, the hips and legs. The other was the upper torso, the chest and the arms. She could tack a torso together and leave it on the dolly. Cheryl would be free to wheel it back and forth to the welder without interrupting the Robertson's or whoever was using the welder. When one torso was finished it would go on the floor and the next one would go on the dolly. This would be a workable solution. The sections would be more than two hundred pounds apiece. She penned the thoughts into her notebook.

She read the small book of positive sayings that her mother had given her back in high school. She meditated and stared at the small flame on her oil lamp. Max worked his way up the stairs on his hands and knees as he liked to do. He poked his head over the last step.

"How are you Princess? What are you up to now? Are you happy with the work at the foundry today? I really came up to see if you have any kisses for me." Cheryl held out her arms and Max moved to her on the bed. She gave Max a generous assortment of pecks on the cheek and nose.

"I could make the deadline, but all I can do is focus on doing a good job with what is at hand and go one day at a time. I am anxious to get that miner back on his feet. I miss him. We have to be at the foundry two hours early every morning so I can use the welder. The shells will be poured this week, but I have no idea what nights the shells will be poured."

"I am all for you and I love you, Cheryl. Would you like to put this out of your mind for a while and let me entertain you? This could be the last relaxed atmosphere that we have for awhile. The living room is set for the three M's. Right now I am trying to figure out how I can lure you downstairs. Would you care to join me in the lap of luxury and watch movies by the fire and the big bay window? If not we could go outside for awhile and you could throw some ice balls at my head. I promise to stand still so you will have a chance to hit me." Cheryl felt Max slip his hand behind her and put it on her fanny.

"Oh, my, how utterly romantic. I will go with you as long as you promise to work on your transition of total commitment and loyalty to me."

They howled at the comedy DVDs.

Afterwards they had scheduled a round of love making. They turned the love seat around. Max sat and removed his jeans. Cheryl moved on top of him and raised her flannel night gown to her waist.

"You got me so hot last night that I thought I was going to melt."

"Enjoy the view and my loyalty to you. Any commitment will require me to find an engagement ring and propose marriage to you."

"Are you ready for that, Max?"

"We could finish our projects and start our engagement."

"Max, that would be wonderful. Let's work on this current engagement right now. We can talk some more, later."

CHAPTER TWENTY EIGHT

Cheryl and Max were at the foundry two hours early everyday. Monday she was disappointed. There was no new metal for her. She knew that her section pours would be sporadic, and she was determined to stay positive about the whole situation. She set her frame of mind to be a competent, dedicated, and happy employee. She would go with the flow of the work on the foundry projects. The big push was on for the prairie people and the bronco. Cheryl shadowed Mary's every move between the two projects all week.

She managed to finish chasing the kids, dog, and hose. She worked on the kids when she needed a break from the bronco or the prairie people. Mary put her quality control eye on the piece and decided that it would get the patina as soon as possible. With the kids and the dog out of the way, Cheryl turned her attention to finish as much solid welding as she could on the base.

Tuesday morning the chest, back, and arms showed up. The metal was clean and waiting for her by the sandblaster. Max helped her move the metal to the welding area. He held the chest and back sections as Cheryl lined them up and tacked them together. It was a good omen. The rest of her shells might be poured this week or next. The thought lifted her spirits and kept her attitude positive.

Cindy and Johnny showed up early.

"Johnny and I think your statue is phenomenal. You are going to get it back together piece by piece, right?"

"That's right, Cindy. It looks like it is going to be piece by piece, but as long as you and Johnny help me, we'll get 'er done!"

"I have really never seen anything like it. We will help you Cheryl. Anytime. You just let us know so you don't have to wait for us."

"Cindy, I can use some help right now."

Johnny and Max held the head and hat over the upper torso so Cheryl could check the alignment. It was off a smidgen, but nothing to fret about. Max and Johnny carried the head and hat to the end of the heavy work bench. The area was seldom used. Cheryl could do some chasing on the head during her free time. It would always be in the same place waiting for her. She would smooth the miner's complexion. There was a touch of ceramic here and there about the moustache and ears. There were a few small air bubble holes in the hair. That would be no problem. She would chase away the few specks of ceramic. She would smooth the section welds away and match surface texture.

He would be handsome when she was finished.

Cheryl was back out on the floor with resolve. She felt fantastic. She would have her two new torso sections to work on this week and next.

A new project, a statue for the Tenth Mountain Division, arrived at the foundry. Goodman handed Mary a check for ten thousand dollars just to get things started. Molly's crew moved the molds to the available shelves in the wax room.

The big push for the next three weeks was on the bronco and the prairie people. The efforts would not stop until the statues were out the door. Each department and employee dealt with the increase in work. Everyone took pride and satisfaction in their efforts. The routines and jobs were the same, only there was much more work to complete. As result every time card had overtime hours, and the employees were grateful.

To save time, the bronco was welded as two separate sections, the cowboy, and the bronco. The work on the bronco was slow. An internal metal support was constructed to support the horse and rider. From the base the support metal ran up through the hooves and front legs, on the inside of the statue, to the back of the saddle. The support was built a little bit at a time, as the bronco was welded together. The fit had to be good for the support structure to hold the weight. Once the bronco was completed the cowboy would be added with the help of the overhead crane.

Mary and Bob put their usual time in the front office to administer to the constantly changing needs of the operation. So far everything was running smooth and they were grateful. Mary planned to patina the girl on the bench and the kids, dog and hose. She ordered a five ton flatbed for the shipment on Thursday. The news paper boy and the shepherd girl were shipped out. Large orders went out for more material for all of the departments.

The foundry received a call from the Rodeo Hall of Fame. Someone at the museum assumed that the statue would be delivered this weekend when actually it was the concrete pedestal that was going to be poured. The statue would arrive two weeks later. Bob handled the call much to his consternation.

"I think signals or communications were mixed up. I believe you are going to pour the concrete platform that will hold the statue. Hey, who am I talking too? I need to talk to a head honcho or the building superintendent. The person I need is the one who will oversee the concrete pour this weekend. Have someone call me back." Bob imparted to Mary, "Gawd! Everybody wants to have the word on what's going on and they may pass the word, but it seems nobody is in charge to get the work done or line it up." The phone rang and Bob picked it up. "Robertson Foundry."

He listened for half a minute. "No. You can tell the statue committee that the statue might be a week late. They should voice their complaints to your payables department and Culpepper. Those are the individuals responsible for the delay. We are not your scapegoat. How about the lift? Did you get the word on the lift? No, we need you to rent one from an equipment rental yard there in the Springs. I do not waste my time calling the Springs rental yards. We are going to need at least a large extension fork lift capable of two thousand pounds, and some fabric lift belts to get the statue off of the trailer. Why don't you ask your statue committee to do it?" Bob laughed into the phone. "That would be funny. What is your job, sir? Building super, good. Are you going to oversee the concrete pour? Yes. We just sent a copy of the pattern to you. You do have it? Good. And you have the anchor with you? It is shaped kind of like a big letter C. It has to be in the concrete and it has to be the exact spot on the pattern. Did you find the diagram and instructions? Good. It will show you the size of the statue base and the size of the two metal flat pieces that will be sticking out above your concrete six inches high and two feet apart. Yes. That is the anchor. Okay. See you in three weeks."

Bob hung up the phone and turned to Mary. "The building super said that the fifty percent up front money was sent to Culpepper way back when."

That night Cheryl aligned the arm sections. Max held them while she tacked them together. "It is ok to leave your eyes open, Max."

"Oh, ha, ha, ha, ha!"

Friday evening over dinner, Max asked Cheryl what her plans were for the weekend.

"You know we will be back to the foundry tomorrow for our second Saturday in a row. If I still lived at 510 East Eleventh, I would stay over night and sleep at the foundry. I would chain you outside the foundry where you could chase the tree squirrels and be comfortable. But for some strange reason, I really enjoy being here at 304. Do you realize that I like to be here in the evenings even if it is only for a short night?"

"Did you want to go to the wrestling stadium tonight? Dick the Bruiser is taking on all challengers. He is going to wrestle blind folded with one arm tied behind his back. Do you think you can take him?"

"You tell Dick that I am going to push my finger in his ear until I poke his brains out. Maybe we should bask in the luxury of the three M's tonight and practice some transitions."

"Just tell me what you need and your greatest desire will be my smallest wish."

It was a marathon weekend for Cheryl. The legs and waist had been aligned and tacked Thursday. A couple of shells had not been poured or they were lost in the pile of finished pours. The boots and the hands. The upper torso was on the floor within striking distance of the welder by the prairie people. The lower torso was on the dolly at the edge of the bronco partition. The first sections of metal for the jazz quartet were left at the sandblaster. Cheryl was off the clock and on her own today. The kids and the dog and the girl on a bench went out the door on a five ton truck Thursday. She found a new rhythm this weekend. She moved from the upper torso to the lower torso and over to the head and then back to the base. If she could not use a welder then she would chase the welds and surface texture on the base, the face, the legs and the chest and back. She had arranged a successful working area in the storm of three ongoing projects. When a section had to be turned over to work on the other side, she would outline her strategy to her co workers, and they would be ready to help her when the time arrived. Today she found them as they clocked in to work the weekend.

"I need your help to check the alignment on the upper and lower torsos."

Nash, Rudy, Johnny, Mark, Max, and Cindy were all there to help. They waited for her by the prairie people. Cheryl wheeled the dolly over. On the count of three, the two hundred pound upper torso was lifted from the floor, and matched to the lower torso at the waist. She made the inspection. The fit and alignment were good. Better safe than sorry.

She outlined her plan to the crew for the rest of the week. "I need to get this statue welded together in the next four days. I am going to need your help. As soon as the boots come through, I am going to weld them to the legs. Alignment is not an issue with the boots and the base.'

Rudy spoke up. "Sure thing, Cheryl. We are all for you. We want to help you, and if you do not ask us, we will be angry. Just call us Team Cheryl, okay? When do you want to do this?"

"It may be Tuesday, it may be Wednesday. I will let you know. It may take as long as twenty minutes. What is going to be the best time for everyone? After work? Lunch time?"

Nash spoke up. "Why don't we get together ten or fifteen minutes before break time or lunch time?" Everyone agreed.

Mark jumped in, "If that does not work we can always get together right at the end of the shift."

Cheryl continued, "A day or two after the lower torso is welded to the base, I will need your help on the upper torso. We will need scaffolding to get the torsos lined up and welded."

"Well, it looks like you are in the right spot for scaffolding," Johnny offered. "We will borrow from the prairie people. Too easy."

"Why don't you use a couple of people to get the base on the dolly before you call all of us together?"

"Good idea, Nash." Cheryl was relieved, once the plan was communicated. It happened. She had a team to help her. They liked to help in any way they could. Such was the nature and disposition of all the employees at the foundry.

Marty was welding on the bronco. Mary was welding on the prairie people. Cheryl pulled her miner in every time either one of them went on break, or ran an errand. She did not have the luxury to work full time on her miner, but she devised a way to finish the welding. She continued to dodge all of the blocks that would stop most people. Marty was amazed at her resolve, her patience, her optimism, and her ability to use the welder for only five or ten minutes at a time. He was amazed at the lengths she endured to get the sections to the welder without delay. Every time he moved away from the welder she wheeled a section over and went to work. She welded during lunch and during breaks. She arrived two hours early in the mornings to weld, and she stayed after work for an hour or more.

Marty teased her. 'It looks like your miner is lying down on the job over there. Does he need a rest? It looks like you worked him to death."

Cheryl countered his remark. "When he recovers from his drinking spell he is going to throw a plastic bag over your cowboy's head and beat him bloody with his hammer." Everything was going to be fine. She would have extra hours this week to get it done. Her energy was flowing. It was her statue, her welding, and her chasing. She was doing it all, and she responded to the test by giving her best efforts. She savored the enjoyment and the satisfaction. Soon her handsome miner would be in a museum on a marble base.

After a full weekend of work, Cheryl made time to sit in front of her oil lamp and meditate. She let anything that had upset her slide away. She was aware of her goals. Still, she meditated on them as if to etch them to the forefront of her consciousness. She had to find the boots and the hands. Moose told her they had been poured. There was one half of a section of arm missing. She realized that she did not have to worry about the boot placement on the base. The boots could fit anywhere in the area and be an inch or two off in any direction. She would simply expand a footprint and no one would know the difference. Only the welds on the base needed chasing. That would save some time. The main focus this week was to communicate with her team. The miner had to go vertical this week. She had to get the torsos welded together on the base. She had only two weeks left, yet she had no regard for the deadline at this point. This miner was not going to be a rush job. She listened for a moment. She heard a squeak on the stairway. Max had become impatient with her absence. His eyes finally cleared the top stair.

"I haven't seen you around. Where have you been? What are you up to now?"

"I have to get the miner vertical this week. It can happen Max."

"Everyone is just amazed at what you have done. You wheeled that dolly back and forth between the two welders like you were playing in an international tennis championship. Everyone is talking about your miner.

The consensus is that it does not matter about the deadline. The museum is getting one whale of a statue. Your team is already working on how to move the miner into the museum. I was not supposed to tell you that. They don't want you to get excited or worry about the installation. It will go smooth. Everyone on your team loves you. Cheryl, could I ask you two quick questions?"

"Oh, I suppose. Don't take too long. I have important work here."

"When are the wheels gonna fall off that dolly, and as you look at me, are my ears level? I think one is lower than the other. It is the one you pulled on after the camping trip. I can see that your teeth are a little crooked too."

Cheryl's wheels stopped turning and she began to warm. "Are you going to sneak up behind me and put your hand on my ass?"

"I might do it right now if you happen to look the other way for a moment. That is the only reason that I am talking to you right now. I am extended and I am hot for you."

"Max we have to get in early Monday and find the hands and the boots."

"We are going to give the miner the boot?"

"Why haven't you found the boots for me Max? What is up with that? Don't you care for me? Do I always have to tell you about everything that needs to be done?"

"I have been helping you, but you have not been paying any attention to me."

"I will talk to you about that in a couple of minutes. It is going to require two stages of effort to get the statue welded together. It is going to be another long week. We are going in an hour and a half early every day."

"It is never a long tiring day when I am with you. I enjoy your company."

"Now, I have a couple of minutes to examine your ear alignment Mongo. Are the three M's ready for me?"

"Yes, your majesty."

"I believe I will require a brown cow this evening for this ear examination."

"Of course, your majesty. What ever animal you have in mind will be no problem."

"Max, I have been having proactive dreams about a wild turtle that I found in the forest. I have invented some new moves to lure him into the castle once I encounter him. I had the Raggedy Ann deadline dream again. This time it is a touch proactive. You will be proud of me."

"Would you like to tell me about it?"

"It is my favorite. This time, I played it cool. One of her eyes was missing so I walked over to the doll and screamed 'All right! Who ripped her eye off?' Then I turned around and yelled, 'Somebody ripped her damned eye out! Who did this? Which one of you ripped her damned eye out?' Everyone was dropping their drinks and walking away."

"I like that one. Retaining control and motivation by fear or tantrum throwing will put the audience back in restraint. You could have ripped the other eye off right in front of everybody and screamed, 'There, you dumb bastards! Now it is balanced!'"

"You got to put them in their place. They all think they are better."

"That's for sure! With all the over weight emotional luggage you have been carrying around you could have crashed and burned a 747 jumbo! You know people in crowds think they can have an effect with their opinions as a large intimidating group. But one on one, they can not hold a candle to you. That is why you give a challenge. No one in the group will stand up or come forward. If you voice strong objection and place blame and fault, then these people, as individuals, will assume their natural chicken positions and break away from the group and run. They are still chickens."

"Okay, Max. Let's go downstairs. I want to see your natural chicken position."

"What is your worst nightmare?"

"That would be at the statue unveiling when the curtain is lifted and there I am, without any clothing, drinking a brown cow."

"Honey, that dream means that you are superior to all of the hacks in the crowd. You are so confident and so superior that you can do anything you want and your body is so perfect that you do not have to wear clothing."

"That is not what you said last week, professor. Last week you told me it meant that I was a failure. Have you fallen out of bed and hit your head on something?"

"I am not sure. I don't remember falling out of bed."

"Don't worry. I like the new Dr. Freud. Come here. I want to see your extension. Show me your firm commitment."

CHAPTER TWENTY NINE

Cheryl was wide awake before Max. She had a big week on the horizon. She had slept, but not enough hours. She eyed the man sleeping beside her. Not a care in the world. No deadline. She decided once again to have a little morning fun. She maneuvered without waking him. She put her feet into his back and began to ease him over to the edge of the bed. "Time to wake up,a sweetheart. Let me help you get to the thermostat, darling. Then you can warm up the house, and prepare my breakfast."

Max coughed and sputtered. He pretended to snore. "I'm having a bad dream now. I'm close to the edge of a cliff. I can't help you. I'm scared."

"Well. Keep breathing Max. Focus on your objectives, if you have any. You will be okay."

Max hit the floor with a thud. He rolled to his back and put his feet and hands in the air. She snickered.

"Ow! Honey! I think I broke my arm."

Cheryl was laughing out loud now. "Too bad it wasn't your turtle."

"My eye hurts!"

"Heh, heh! I think I will start the poison in the coffee today. I can finish up your pitiful houses and sell them."

The first day of the new week Cheryl searched the piles of shells at the sand blaster. Most of the shells were the jazz quartet.

"Here they are Max! You know the drill."

They chimed in unison, "Give me back the clean metal." Max nodded his head vigorously. "Uh huh, uh huh."

He held the boots for her as she tacked them on to the legs. He held the last section of the arm for her. She tacked the hands to the arms, and then they went back to the foundry work. At lunch time she put solid welds on the boots and hands all the way around. She did take a small break after she finished the welding. Everything was coming together. Finally, she began to relax.

The second day of her big week she got the word to her crew to meet before lunch. During the afternoon break, the legs and waist of the miner were lifted into the air and placed on the base. Cheryl quickly tacked the boots to the base to secure the position. She added several long welds for strength to hold the extra added weight. Word quickly spread that the miner was only half the man that he used to be. She did not resent the comments made by several employees. She was smiling. It showed on her face. She was genuinely cheerful. Her miner was beautiful.

Cheryl was back out on the floor with resolve. Her miner would be together by next week. She needed to spend the rest of her free time today and tomorrow to finish the welds on the legs.

It was the day after hump day of the third week of ongoing twenty four hour operations at the foundry. Everything was going smooth. Everyone had hit their stride. The prairie people and the bronco were near completion. Some of the sections of the jazz quartet were moved into the bronco area and welded together. The Tenth Mountain project was being poured. The old man on the bench and the girl on the bench were loaded onto a five ton flat bed truck, and the bench people left the foundry. Cheryl notified her team to meet twenty minutes before afternoon break at the prairie people. They grouped together to formulate their plan of approach. They set up scaffolds on both sides of the miner. Next, the two hundred pound upper torso had to be hefted into the air.

Everyone helped to get the arms and chest vertical and over to the scaffolding. Two people climbed each scaffold. They reached down for the arms and lifted the upper torso. The arms had to be rotated ninety degrees to line up the two torsos. Those that were not on the scaffolds moved onto the base of the miner. They slipped and jockeyed constantly on the base to get the torsos close together. The balancing act to align the torsos together was difficult. On the count of three, a supreme effort was made to do so.

Cheryl tacked at the waist to secure the alignment. The crew had to shield their eyes and hold the statue while the tacks were applied. Next she put a four inch weld on each side of the miner. Once secure, the team relaxed a little with only a few minor muscle twitches here and there, from the coordinated effort to hold the statue perfectly still. For the first time in four weeks, the miner was vertical once again. Instead of a green clay sculpture, this time Cheryl had a bronze miner. The moment registered high for the team members. Cheryl had many exciting moments in her lifetime, yet none of them registered as high as this one. The pride and the emotion was beyond anything she had every felt.

At the end of the shift, she walked to the injection mold room to pass the news to Max. She stood at the doorway.

"Are you slumming around this afternoon?"

She decided to tease him. "You really put a lot of time in on the leaf squares."

"Are they easy to chase? Are they better than the last operator?"

"They are the same as everyone else who has worked back here. Nash and I chase them. They get tiny air bubbles and some zit bumps because of the swirls in the pattern." Cheryl stared at Max until his curiosity spoke up.

"I love to look at you. What are you up to now?"

A warm smile formed on her lips. "Max, the miner is welded together. Everything is winding up and I should be finished in a week. Mary is going to help me with the patina. The patina is scheduled next week after the prairie people and the bronco. The marble base isn't at the museum yet. I am beginning to think that I may as well head for the DZ this weekend. Do you want to go with me?"

"I want to go with you every time."

"How do you manage every afternoon in here?"

"The machine manages everything. All I have to do is inject the right amount of wax and wait for it to cool. The other part of my brain thinks about the priorities on the rentals, the solutions to the electrical and the plumbing systems, and where the money for the materials will come from. Sometimes I review my skills in intuitive calculus. You never know when you might need them. Other times I think of falling down at Ski Cooper and the beautiful girl I met there."

"Really? Did you fall in love with her?"

"Well, I wasn't certain at first. She is really bossy and possessive, but she kind of grew on me like cancer."

"Maybe she had very little when she was growing up. Do you love her, Max?"

"I fall in love with her each and every day."

"Why, Max. That gets me excited. What a nice thing to say. What is her name?"

"Come over here and I will whisper her name in your ear."

Cheryl hesitated. She wanted to take the bait and wrestle with him. "I will check back with you tonight on that."

"Be careful. Dick the Bruiser is scheduled to wrestle in the ring at 304 this evening. It is an open venue. He is taking on all challengers."

"Max, close up. The day is over. Come on, walk the hall with me."

"Be right there. Catch the light for me, would you please?"

Cheryl and Max took a short, leisurely stroll to the prairie people. Max stood with Cheryl in front of her magnificent bronze creation. He thought to himself. "This girl's abilities are just awesome."

"What do you think, Max?"

"Well, it looks like everything is coming to a head here. Any idea how you are going to get it on?"

"Nash and I tried to weld it on the torso. It takes two people to pick up the head and hold it steady. We held the upper torso and there were so many bodies in the way, I could not get in to weld. Then the crew could not keep the sections steady enough. It was so awkward. I really did not have a plan, so we skipped it and welded the two torsos together. That was hard enough. We figured that we would be able to get the head next week somehow. Maybe with the crane."

Max detected an assumption for a hope and a wish to take place next week.

"Come on, Max. Let's get going."

"Hang on a minute. Give me a little time. Max needed time for his own protection. He knew he would have to face this problem next week. No one had a solution for certain. It was the end of the week and the problem was tabled until Monday. He stared at the scaffold next to the prairie people. He eyeballed the height and the distance to the statue. He walked around the base of the miner studying the symmetry and the angles. No. The scaffolds could not be positioned close enough. He was certain.

"Max . . ."

"Okay, okay. Gosh, you certainly are anxious to dash out of here."

Cheryl explained to Max on the way to the car, "I promised my parents that I would put in a full weekend on the dry wall work. They are expecting me. You will have all weekend to work on your house.

Monday morning the crews worked with Bob and Mary on the bronco project. The bronco rider was being assaulted with tethers. The crane sling wormed its way around the back of the cowboy and under his arm pits. The tethers would help place the rider into the correct spot on the saddle. When this was accomplished the crews would move quickly to place the scaffolds near the saddle. The cowboy was carefully lowered onto the bronco using the overhead crane. It was a group effort to get him lined up and held while Marty and Bob got him welded to the saddle.

Nash made a loud comment for all to hear. "Well, that is one way to make it through your eight second ride. Have your ass welded to the saddle."

Max could hear the cheering. He and Molly took a break and walked down the hall to check out the commotion. They had to shield their eyes from Marty's bright arcs. The mood was euphoric among the crews, and Molly and Max were glad that they took time to share in the moment.

Cheryl's day came to a close with no progress at all on the miner. The crane was unavailable for use. The bronco was in the way. The focus was moved to push the jazz quartet and the Tenth Mountain. Cheryl did try to position a scaffold close to the miner. The distance and height was not quite close enough. Her crew assured her that there was plenty of time. They would work on it tomorrow. The crane would be available soon.

That night brought worries and interrupted sleep to Cheryl. It was about three in the morning. Just like clock work. In about two hours they would wake up and get ready for their morning journey. She was perspiring lightly. She had slipped her arm across the middle of his stomach again. Her hand and fingers opened and closed. She was clinging to him. No, she was not. Was she chasing her miner? She was! Her hands were inspecting the welds and she was chasing the welds on her miner. She stared to roll back to the left again. Against his better judgment, Max decided to tease her. Maybe she would talk to him while she was sleeping. "Just about finished?" Cheryl froze. He said it again. "Just about finished?" He rested on his left elbow.

Cheryl answered as plain as the early morning, "Did you hear me?" Max turned to look at Cheryl at the same time she rolled towards him. Her elbow caught him square in his right eye. She nailed him. There was a large white light behind his right eye. Max groaned and he fell back to the mattress. His first reaction was to be up set which was normal.

CHAPTER THIRTY

His eye throbbed with pain. It began an uncontrollable twitch. He had no control over it and Cheryl had no control over her actions. It did prompt him to ask her a couple of simple questions.

"Was it a bad date with a headless miner?" There was not a word. No rustle of sheet, blanket, or sleeping bag. There was only her light breathing. "Are you two hitting it off?" Max let a minute pass. "Who do you like more, the miner or me?" He thought he heard Cheryl mumble "The miner." He asked her, "Would you rather sleep with the miner?"

Cheryl answered, "The miner."

Now he knew she was awake and playfully irritating him. Max was not going to take this personally. "Does your elbow hurt?"

"It feels great!" She rubbed her elbow. It did seem to have a bump on it.

"You rolled over and hit me in the eye."

"I am certain you deserved it. What did you say or do to me?"

"I waited a long time to be certain that you had not done it on purpose. It was just a minute ago. Did the miner make the unveiling without a head?"

"No. You are making fun of me I won't stand for it. It is not funny."

"Nevertheless, we can not let it be a headless unveiling, madam." Max sat up quickly. He grabbed the comforter and pulled it up over both of them. She rolled to him and threw her arm across his stomach.

"Come here, baby," he whispered. She moved her head to his chest. She loved to listen to his heart beat. She knew now, that every one of them was for her. Well, most of them were. One for her, one for the rentals, and one for recreation. She knew that was the order. Cheryl knew it was going to stay that way. It was only a matter of time. A matter of time before what? The ring? The proposal? The marriage? The kids? She kind of liked the way things were right now.

She didn't want to be the center of sick humor at three am. "You can laugh later. I wish you would let me go back to sleep. I feel exhausted."

"Honey, if you go back to sleep, levitate the head of the miner off the ground and place it on his shoulders, would you please? And while you are after it, weld the head on. You are all over the bed at night. It has been four nights in a row."

"I don't recall inviting you up here anyway." Cheryl opened her eyes. "Max. I have to do something. This is ridiculous."

Max whispered softly. "Baby, I am going to get the coffee and the truck. See you in awhile, Princess." He kissed her forehead. Cheryl was physically tired and emotionally upset, but there was a spark of hope this day. She was going to fan the flame with a little drama of her own.

As Max began to leave the bed she startled him. She drew herself upright and yelled, "My, God! What filth has snuck into my chamber to spoon with me in the wee hours? I'll have none of it!"

Max turned his head and said timidly, "No worry, m' lady. Fear me not. 'Tis only your humble manservant, Mongo. I was seeking a little warmth from the colt night's air." Cheryl put her feet into his back and pushed him slowly to the edge of the bed. As Mongo neared the edge, he gripped the sheets that held them together. "There is no need for violence or cruelty now, m' lady."

"Mongo! Your place is next to the coals of the fire, and the pile of wood with the furry little mice! Those are to be your comforts and comrades. Now fetch my chariot and be quick about it!" Max threw the blankets off so his arms wouldn't be caught in the fall. He balanced precariously on the edge of the bed. He flailed his arms and legs.

"We can be civil and work in harmony, m' lady!" Cheryl fully extended her legs and let go of the sheets at the same time. She laughed when she heard the resounding thud as Max bumped the floor. His intestinal gas escaped without a sound. Max turned onto his back leaving two quivering legs and arms in the air for her view and laughter.

She actually laughed with delight. That had not happened in the morning for some time. Max reprimanded her. "I see the misfortune of others brings you laughter." Max felt immensely better.

"And don't forget me luncheon, you miscreant! I'll be having hot tea with me sandwich, Mongo!"

"Yes, m' lady. Your greatest wish is my smallest desire. And your headless he man, m' lady? Will you be having lunch again with the man who has no head about him? You really must do something about him your highness! No work is getting done in the mines."

"Mongo! You silver haired hobo!"

"That's it! Vent me lady! Vent it all out on poor Mongo! I should think the two of you a perfect pair!"

"Mongo, give your self ten lashes! Roll down the stairs and fetch me breakfast."

Max rose on his hands and knees searching out his clothes. He rolled over on his back and pulled his jeans over his feet. The jeans filled up as he extended his feet into the air. He rose and Cheryl pulled the covers around her. She watched him as he looked for a sweater and sweatshirt. He stuck his tongue out at her and gave her the Bronx cheer.

"Oh, ha, ha, hah."

Max removed his earplugs. "Mongo not hear Princess. Mongo wearing ear plugs for good sleep."

"Come over here, darling! Let momma pull those babies out! That reminds me. Pick up a couple for me, would you Mongo? You are starting to snore again. I have to roll you over on your stomach every night. I do not want to use your second hand, wax infested plugs. I want my own."

"Quite demanding this morning. Did your Highness sleep on a pea? Will m' lady be going to her mine today for more drudgery and ridicule? Perhaps today m' lady will find a miner who has a head on his shoulders."

"Mongo ! I will not give you another word! I will call the guard instead! They will make you the headless one." Cheryl rose slightly and rolled back to the windows. She loved the view of the Silver King Loop.

"As you wish, me lady. Your greatest command is my slightest distress."

"Mongo! If you do not leave now I will strike your other eye!"

"So! I knew it! It was an intentional blow. That is battery! And you are always nagging me. That is verbal assault. You think you are so cute and clever. Well, m' lady, do not toy with me." Max leered at her. His mouth was open and his tongue lay out between his lips. His eyes were wide open.

"I'll have no insolence from you this morning nor any other. 'Tis for me to decide. Nothing is for your consideration! Your mind is much too feeble."

"Don't you point your crooked finger at me, you old witch."

Max looked out the windows. The moon light exposed the magnificence of the sky and the Silver King Loop. He started down the stairs. He turned to blow her a kiss. "Here we go again!" Max turned and took the first step. He intentionally bumped his head on the low ceiling. Cheryl howled with laughter.

"It serves you right!"

"We will get the head on your miner today, sweetheart. It is going to happen today, or your name isn't Princess . . ."

"I smell a fart!" Cheryl interrupted. "You farted and did not warn me! I know what that means. That means you have no regard for me!"

Max laughed. "Your timing is perfect, me lady. That's a good one. Princess I Smell a Fart."

"Mongo! Was that a fart, or have ye failed to brush your teeth for another week?"

Cheryl howled with delight. "Now stoke the wood you miserable miscreant. Ready my chariot! That's an order!"

"That's right, me lady. Piss on the poor servants and the lowly peasants." Max slammed the bathroom door.

Cheryl hollered. "That's right! Vent it, baby! You are so confident. It is not your problem. I am not your lady. And 'we' are not in all this bullshit together! I can handle all this bullshit myself. You are hereby banned from the second floor, Maxwell."

"Not surprised. You can not build any more fires in my Montgomery Ward wood burner."

"Tisk, tisk."

Max walked out of the bathroom and turned up the thermostat to eighty from fifty five. He stepped into his moon boots at the kitchen door. He loved his moon boots, a nice warm inch of foam all around his feet. He opened the back door and walked out to the truck. When he walked back into the kitchen, Cheryl put her arms around him and kissed him.

"Good morning, Tramp."

"Good morning, Angel. We will put a head on your miner this morning."

"I'm flipping back and forth. Good, we will get it done. God, we can't do it by ourselves."

"We will be early enough to give it a chance. Something might work out. I am going to pack my bags and move out if we don't get it on today."

"What kind of ultimatum is that, Max? We are too close to quit now, buddy. Good spirits are rising this morning."

On the way to work they conspired. What was the equipment at hand? What was needed to do the job? Use of the crane was out of the question as the bronco was in the way.

"The two aluminum ladders went back to the rental center last week. Molly has a ladder in the wax room." The air was thick with anticipation. The butterflies were in their stomachs. Their heads were swirling with uncertainty as they neared the foundry.

Cheryl suggested, "How about the scaffold? We could set up the scaffold."

"You still have to lift the head up to the top."

"That will work. All we have to do is get a couple of people to help us lift the head up."

"I checked it out last week. The scaffold is at the wrong height and it is too far form the miner's shoulders. If the head only weighed five pounds, it would be no problem. It weighs about eighty pounds and that is the problem."

"Oh, thank you professor. Do you know where you are, Max? Hey! You missed the turn."

"I should have seen it! I should have seen the turn!"

"You are trying to chicken out! Buc buc buc buu waack!"

They were the first workers in the foundry. The miner was waiting for them. He was alone all night on his dolly. They pushed him a short distance to the welding equipment.

"Maybe we can give this poor guy his dignity today." Cheryl mused.

"I agree. Let's get Mortimer's head." They lugged the head over to the miner. They placed the head face down on the floor as if the miner was not allowed to see what was going to happen. Cheryl looked at Max. "I look at you now, and I think of the day I watched you fall down the hill."

"Has anything changed?

"You are not like the others, Max. That is why I love you."

"Well, let me pay you back."

"Would you check the wax room for the ladder?" Cheryl powered on the welder and busied herself at the welding table. She clipped two welding rods in half and stowed the lengths in her plaid blue flannel shirt pocket.

She gathered four lengths of used rod on the welding cart. They would be perfect for the close in work. They were four inches long. She stretched the ground and rod lines to reach behind the miner. Max returned with the ladder. They circled the statue to find the most opportune approach from which to work. The miner's stance was similar to a baseball player in the batter's box. The right leg was back and the left leg was forward and bent at the knee.

"It is going to be better for me to put the first welds at his collar bones. I can reach them without any trouble." She stepped up on the bronze base and easily got her hands on the miner's shoulders to demonstrate. She climbed down and clamped the ground line of the welder to the base of the statue, where it overlapped the edged of the dolly. "I can drape the welding rod line over an arm." She pulled a generous amount of the welding rod line around to the back side of the miner. Holding the rod handle she stepped up on the base. She passed the rod line over the hammer shoulder. The line dropped down the front of the chest. Cheryl climbed down and returned to the front of the miner. Again she climbed up on the base. Counting the dolly she was about three feet in the air. She pulled the line until the rod holder was on the floor. "Hold that for me," she said to the miner.

"What is his name?"

"I'm not telling."

"Festus? Mortimer? Is it Stein?"

"Who?"

Max repeated loudly. "Stein! Frank N. Stein."

"Why do I fall for stupidity?" Cheryl shook her head.

"Are you talking about me or my poor jokes?"

"Both."

Cheryl was positioned as if she was dancing with her huge bronze miner. "I see two, three, actually four tack spots."

"I believe you. Please be ready. Make the welds big, baby."

"Max, you are not going to do what I think you are going to do!"

"I am going to try it one time and I will be very tired, so please, lay a big weld on there for me."

They moved behind the miner to decide where the ladder would go. Cheryl watched him study the wood ladder. It held a light dull brown color that all weathered ladders possess. One half of the wood was missing lengthwise on the second step. The customary metal support bar was intact and slightly bent. *Place your foot in the corner of the second step.* He spread the legs and climbed the steps. He stopped next to the top step. Strength and integrity were present, but would it be enough?

The ladder fit best next to the miner's back and facing the hand steel. Max went up the ladder a second time. He twisted to the right and looked at the hole where the head was going to go. It was even with his waist. Max would have to be at least this far up the ladder, with the head on his right shoulder. He was two steps from the top of the ladder, and one and a half feet to the statue. With a slight twist to the right, he could lean over to the shoulders, and set the head where it was supposed to go. It might be all he could do, just to get the head on one of Mortimer's shoulders. That would be better than nothing. Hopefully, the ladder would not shake or brake. Could he reach the left shoulder with his left hand? He would need it for balance. He tested the move. He leaned over and placed his left hand on the left shoulder of the miner like they were old buddies. There was plenty of space. The ladder moved slightly the opposite direction. *Oh, boy!* How much would it move with the eighty pound head on his shoulder? The head was heavy when he picked it up with Cheryl. It would be heavier just to make it this far. Hopefully, the ladder would not go out from under him when he leaned over to the right.

Cheryl checked the settings on the welder and waited patiently. She had picked two spots to the left and right of the neck in the collar bone area. Then she planned to put a big weld on the chest bone. She would make it a big one, if they got that far. Max looked over the opening in the miners shoulders where the head should be. He looked over to Cheryl.

She looked into his eyes. The moment and suspense was building in both of them. Max thought of the task at hand and the engaging life they were experiencing together. Cheryl was enjoying the fire that was building in her stomach at the moment. She spoke evenly, "Go for it, Max. Try not to kill yourself." Max was not overjoyed. If you fall you fall. Just fall away from everything and not on anything. They were both thinking how wonderful this moment would be when it was over.

"I love you, Cheryl." Max spoke softly to her as if they were in another place doing something else. He watched her fires ignite. She was steeled. It was going to happen. He was going to come through for her. Max again gauged the distance to the spot where the miner's head belonged. Better to be above and lower the head on to the miner. At this point if he lost his grip he could let it go. He might be able to put his left hand on the shoulder if he was lucky. He climbed down and he checked the sequence of his footing. He also noticed that the ladder did not move or wobble as long as he stayed on the middle of each step.

Max thought to himself. The right foot has to go on the first step. Right foot. Right foot. The second step might break, so be off it quickly and on to the next. As Max climbed down he made a guess that the head weighed every bit of eighty pounds. Combined with his weight the total would be about two hundred and seventy pounds. He could not remember if he ever saw a two hundred seventy pound painter on a ladder. Max comforted himself with his final analysis. Oh, who cares? I can't lose. If I fall and hurt myself I will go to the hospital. Cheryl will get some attention, and some one else will put the head on. No problem.

Cheryl was ready. Clamped between her teeth were the four inch rods to work with in the close quarters. One was loaded in the rod clamp. Max picked up the head one foot off the floor. There were no ideal hand holds. The palms of his hands covered the cheeks of the face. The head was balanced, but it tipped forward or backward with the slightest movement. Max sat the head back down on the floor.

Cheryl couldn't believe he was going to do something this stupid. She realized he was calculating his chances and she didn't interrupt. She calmly donned her welding helmet and left the visor up. Her foundry clothes were adequate hot spark protection. They were both silent now. Both were hoping for the best. Cheryl prepared herself mentally to tack. She eyed the spots along the top edge of the collar bones. Hopefully, the tacks would allow her to burn a couple of long welds. Max was awake now, and he was ready for the occasion.

"Let's do it Max!"

Max grinned. "If I drop the head, the molds are in the wax room."

"That's the spirit, you one eyed genius." Cheryl looked around the side of the miner to keep an eye on him.

He moved two steps to the head and dropped to a full squat. His hands cupped the cheeks of the miner's face. Not a great hold to start with. There was a sharp intake of air. He picked the head straight up off the floor chest high. In the following instant, he suddenly dropped to a half squat as the head seemed to stall in mid air. His shoulder came up to meet the head. At the same time, his right foot found a new spot on the floor for balance. The miner's left ear was now on Max's right shoulder. The bill of the hat was resting not too comfortably on his shoulder blade and ribs. It was painful. He refused to acknowledge the pain.

He made an attempt to stand erect. His knees wobbled. He searched for a new center of gravity. The awkward position of the head caused him to bend at the waist and list slightly to the left. A series of small intakes and exhales for fresh oxygen could be heard as he shuffled his feet. He almost went over backwards. He almost dropped the head. There would not be a comfortable position. It was past time to move on. Don't miss the bus. His labored breathing continued. He could not capture a full breath, due to the weight.

There was little time that he could hold the head. He quickly focused on the next and only move. He was to the ladder in two steps and a half shuffle. All the weight was on his left foot. Max moved his right foot onto the first step. It was so fast, Cheryl was not certain that she saw it happen. His left hand shot out to grip the ladder for balance. He attempted to bring up his left foot. Because of the awkward forward lean, his knee would not clear the ladder steps. He returned his left foot to the floor and he pointed his right toe to the outside so much that his heel was off the step. He would have to climb the ladder bowlegged. His knees were bent and pointing outward. Again with incredible speed the left foot found the broken second step. He felt the narrow metal rod through the rubber sole of his boot as the weight bore down. There was no side to side wobble. There was no creak or squeak. It didn't break. The step held the weight.

The right foot shot to the third step and Max quickly brought the left foot up beside the right one. His left hand seemed to be performing independently holding on to the ladder for balance and advancing upward. Both knees pointed out to the side. He tried to straighten them. Oh, mercy! The muscles in his thighs were burning! His head was forced down. Out of the corner of his eyes he could see the miner's shoulders. He knew two more steps were required. He made it.

Cheryl held her expression neutral as she watched Max reach the last step. He was not able to twist toward the miner. He had to turn his feet on the step. He made one foot move at a time until both feet were pointed to the statue. He could see where the head was going to go. Max had only to lean out to the miner and let the head role forward off his shoulder to the hole. He took a millisecond to figure out how much he would have to lean over and at the same time to lower the head. He had to move slowly. Nothing less than absolute balance, would keep the ladder from wobbling out of control, and sending the bronze head to the floor, and Max to the hospital.

His left hand held the top step for balance. From the waist up he slowly rolled forward to the shoulders. He hoped the ladder would not shoot out from under him. Cheryl kept a watchful eye on the leaning process. How does he do it? She took three silent steps back and two to the right. She might be a casualty if he dropped the head now. Max moved slowly as he leaned over to the statue. He used the muscles of his back to lower the head. Suddenly, his neck, shoulder, and back gave out on him. Time and fatigue settled any doubt, whether or not he would make it. All questions were answered. His left hand shot blindly out towards the left shoulder of the miner to keep him from falling on the statue. The lucky grab saved the day. "Thank you, Jesus."

Cheryl saw the hand instantly change from a normal color to all white. Just a little bit of pressure there. She held her breath. At the same time the neck of the miner made slow but solid contact with the shoulders. Max let the statue take the weight of the head. It had been a lucky strike. The placement was only off by an inch or so laterally. His body recoiled when he released the weight, and the ladder wobbled in a tight side to side pattern. He was perpendicular at the waist now. His left leg was off the step and out behind him for balance. He wanted to quit. He really couldn't see anything now. All he could see was the miner's back. The bill of the hat prevented him from moving his head. The ladder had stopped wiggling. He had to hold things in place. He totally ignored the pain and focused on balance. Cheryl was up on the base to the miner in a flash. Max voice came out in small strained spurts a few words at a time with an occasional gasp for air. "Can't see a thing. You call it. Tell me where to move it, by the half or quarter inch."

"Cheryl replied, "It's hanging over in front and it needs to go one half inch to the hand steel." Max had to make just a minor adjustment. With every fiber trembling, every nerve ending frayed and maxed out, he lifted the head section about a quarter of an inch. The head moved to the hand steel and quickly dropped back to the body. She spoke evenly and firmly with a touch of excitement. "Don't move! Right there!" He saw her gloved hand slip over the miner's hammer shoulder for grip and balance. She stood on the base with her feet between the miner's. Cheryl held the rod a half an inch off the surface of the two pieces of metal. She gave a strong nod of her head and the visor of the welding helmet fell over her face.

She was in a world of darkness now. It was familiar to her. With a firm grip she moved the rod towards the metal until a small spark of lightning appeared. The light illuminated the surface of the metal. She could see what was in front of her.

Cheryl put a one inch spot weld where the two sections of metal met on the left collar bone area. She shifted her body to the right and moved her hand, as if it held a wand, over to the right shoulder. She barely grazed the surface for light to locate the spot for her second tack. Max struggled for comfort. He was beyond suffering. He tried to stoop to lighten and rearrange the load. Suddenly the first weld popped. Cheryl hollered, "Max! Don't move!" She replaced the spent rod with one from her mouth and placed a two inch weld on top of the breast bone. She put her last four inch rod into the holder and moved back to the first spot where the first weld broke. She laid a good solid two inch weld on the miner's left collar bone. She stepped off the miner and reached for a half length of rod from her flannel shirt pocket. "Hang on Max! Two more!" She was back on the base. She lined up the weld and she snapped her head forward. The welder's helmet dropped in front of her face.

The welder's helmet with the tiny glass window protected her eyes and face from hot, flying sparks. She brushed the bronze with the tip of the rod, for light, right on the spot where the two sections of metal met on the right shoulder. Through the thick green glass, Cheryl could see the blazing white hot end of the rod meld the two pieces of metal together. A trail of red with a tinge of yellow followed behind. She put two quality welds on each side of the neck. She lifted the helmet. Her eyes saw one big happy white spot floating around in front of her miner. She had a look of amazement and satisfaction on her face. The welds held. The head was on!

Max moved to a standing position to find a little comfort. His hands held the brim for balance and placement. He was more up right now and his legs were twitching involuntarily. He was the victim of a good side to side ladder wiggle. He could finally see the fit and it looked right on except for a smidgen of an overlap along the back. When the welding stopped, Bob and Nash moved forward. Like a wounded duck in flight Max eased his overworked body down the ladder. He had difficulty making contact with every step. He was not in smooth control of his body.

Nash grabbed the ladder and held it. "Easy there, buddy. I got you covered, Max. Good show."

"What ta hey, Nash!"

Cheryl was ready to weld across the back. "Move out of the way Max. Let me get in back. Hurry! Make yourself useful and hold the ladder for me." She heard Max inhale.

Nash beat him to it. "Just say please, Cheryl. You never say please." Nash looked at the red beet complexion on Max's face. "Cheryl, did you feed Max his Wheaties this morning? He sure is macho today. Lucky for you."

She wanted to bear hug Max, but the floor was crowded with workers. "Thanks, Max. I will catch up with you later." She noted his stressed condition. "I need to finish this." She looked deep in his eyes past the strained look on his face. It was done. Cheryl was back in business. She was smiling almost as if nothing had ever happened. She had won!

Max relented, "I can see that I am back to my lowly position as chariot driver."

Nash laughed. "Max, your eye looks a little puffy today. Has the lady been whippin' up on you?"

"I don't know why she gets so angry. I think it is the alcohol."

Max began to walk around with all the mobility of a penguin. He walked around in tiny little circles. He was patiently waiting for his muscles and nerves to stop firing. He let his muscles relax and it was the wrong thing to do. His muscles began to twitch furiously. They were trying to cramp all over his body. Thankfully, the bill of the hat was no longer rubbing the ribs on his back. Max was grateful for the relief. He touched his toes and shook his arms and legs. He looked at the ceiling and tightened the muscles in his neck and arms as he arched.

"Hey, Max. Could you get us a couple of sodas?"

"Hey, Max. Have a soda on me. I put some in the fridge."

Cheryl and Nash were marching on.

"I might be able to pull the head forward a little in front. That may help the edges match up across the back."

"Better not!" Cheryl warned, "You have to pry the edge out. Pry bars will do the trick. Find a couple for me." Nash understood. He went to the nearest tool bench and picked up two flat metal pry bars. Cheryl climbed the ladder with speed and grace. Nash returned and handed her two stout pry bars. She set them on the ladder. She found a likely spot to work on the left shoulder. She slipped one edge between the metal pieces. She pressed against the top section and the metal lined up on the hand steel shoulder.

"Up here, Nash!"

Nash climbed up the base to the pry bar. With one hand he held the miner for balance and the other hand held the pry bar for Cheryl. "Ready for me, senorita? Max is gone now."

"Give me a couple of minutes with the welder first, Nash. Then I will put an arc across your groin for you. You can show it to Silvia when you get home tonight."

The hood snapped down. Nash closed his eyes and looked away from the bright arc. Cheryl put two spot welds along the back. They were up and down the miner and the ladder like squirrels on a tree. They repeated the process on the hammer shoulder. The edges were matched up evenly.

She informed Nash, "It will be easy to chase this weld on the back. Not as much detail as the front."

His moment over, Max limped back to the break room. He was almost there when Molly bolted out of the wax room in a fast shuffle for the foundry floor, camera in hand.

She burst out, "I heard Cheryl got the miner's head on this morning! Just now!" Her medium brown eyes were wide and bright. The short black curly hair on her head framed her warm smile.

"Cheryl got it tacked on real good, Miss Molly." Max returned the smile along with a nod of his head.

"I'm going to go look right now! I gotta see how my work turned out!"

Max felt good. The fun thing about sharing is that everybody gets to be part of something special. Everyone had worked on the miner and they were proud of the wild sculpture in the Robertson foundry. Molly ran down the hall to the foundry floor. Word spread among the workers arriving that morning that the miner was no longer headless. Another transformation had taken place. The old green image was back in a new startling bronze form. Cheryl put one last weld in the middle and then she stepped down from the ladder.

Bob Robertson walked up to her. "Congratulations Cheryl! You are in the big time now!

Cheryl squeezed his hand as hard as she could and added three hard pumps. She answered with enthusiasm, "Thank you, Bob, for putting up with this extra project!" Much to his surprise, Cheryl sniffed and gave him a big hug!

Nash cautioned, "Careful, Cheryl, here comes Mary!"

"I saw that! You messin' with my man?" Mary mocked.

"You wanna fight me for him?"

"Nah, but I might rent him to you some time when you get your big money. He is high maintenance." Bob cast Mary a cold stare. They all laughed.

Nash interjected, "I suppose you won't stop by the house to talk to me and Sylvia anymore!" Nash put his arms out to Cheryl.

She stepped into him. She threw her arms around his neck and gave him a big hug. "Aren't you the funny one Nash?"

"Bob and I walked in at the same time. We were afraid you would have fallen off your miner if we made any move at all!"

"That is a poor excuse, but I would use it too."

Workers were watching Cheryl clean up. Everyone offered their congratulations and commented how good the miner looked.

"I guess no one really looks good when they lose their head," joked Cheryl.

Cheryl put the welding gloves and the helmet on the welding cart. Molly ran right in for a congratulation hug. Cheryl almost lost her balance.

"You did it! You got it done!"

"He's just about done Molly! Ain't he handsome?" Cheryl hiccupped a sob and sniffed.

"Everybody's been talking about your headless miner. We have been waiting for you to put the head on."

"You know how it is, Molly! Just too much going on around here!"

"You can say that again. What pushed you over the edge, you crazy woman?"

"I was out of time! I can't sleep. Big nightmares. I vowed to do it today or take my life."

"I saw Max's puffy eye! There are rumors of violence. Did you have to smack him?"

"He was getting fresh with me you know."

"Those men. They think they know everything."

"In my mental anguish he was making unwanted advances at me. I warned him, Molly, but you know talking never does any good."

"So here you are! No crane! No scaffolds! You flipped, girl!"

"Well, I did. I did, and I got away with it. You know anger and frustration can be a powerful motivator." They shared a laugh.

"Good for you. My, what a bronze! God bless! Cheryl this is the best bronze that has come through here in a long time." Molly spoke loudly to the group. "Now all of you big bad foundry workers stand right around the front of that there miner so Momma Molly can get a picture of all you knuckleheads. Now stand up straight and smile." Molly was greeted with some rude and suggestive comments. Examination of the photo would reveal several tongues sticking out. "What is his name Cheryl?"

"Hector! And I am right proud of him! He is a hard worker." Everyone laughed and Molly's camera recorded the happy event. The group started to disperse, but she was not finished with them.

"Okay!" Molly hollered, "Everybody over to bronco. I'm going to shoot you all with my Canon!" Molly began arranging everyone around the bronco. Smiles and laughter flourished. Jokes about riding the buckin' bronco were exchanged. Mary blushed once. Bob Robertson laughed and turned red. The camaraderie began to surface. Molly did some small group shots of workers and the Robertson's posing for the camera. She clicked the shutter until she had exhausted two large rolls of her 35 mm film.

Yesterday, the cowboy had been welded to the buckin' bronco. The patina would go on the prairie people and the bronco tomorrow.

Moose yelled, "Hey, it's time for a party! Where's the champagne?"

Mark added, "We should have a big break at lunch and celebrate!"

Bob yelled over the commotion, "Hey, wait a minute! There are still plenty of other projects to work on! Why don't we knock off an hour early and have a party? What do you think Mary?"

"Maybe we are overdue. Let's bring lunch in from the Burrito Shop."

Nash, never the shy one yelled, "Let's cater now! Beans for everybody!"

Bob relented. "Okay. We will have lunch catered from The Burrito House. At three thirty we will shut down for liquid refreshments and more pictures of your natural selves." Jeers and cheers greeted the announcement. "Don't tell anyone in town what the goodies are for, and we can make it home safely without police escorts. We will pass the hat now to collect donations for refreshments."

It was over. She wasn't rich yet, but she was famous, well, maybe well known to a few people. Finally, Cheryl might have a good night's sleep. She could come to work refreshed and invigorated. She had watched her parents experience the pressures of deadlines in their drywall business. Now she had physically experienced the havoc first hand. It is different when it happens to you. Nerves. Stress. No sleep. No wonder the boss gets grey hair. Cheryl spied Max returning from the break room with the lunch bags. She walked to him with a big toothy grin.

"I love it when you smile like that."

"Got the sandwiches, Mongo?" Cheryl was beaming with pride from her face to her heart.

Max added, "You are lucky today. Your sandwich is stuffed with fresh alfalfa sprouts."

Cheryl could see the moisture in his eyes. "Want to sneak outside and eat them."

"I need to get in the shell room before someone has to remind me. How about an early escape from work about three thirty or four and a game of pool at the Dollar?"

"You think you can take me?" Cheryl glanced down briefly and returned with a new facial expression. "I would really like to backpack Bear Lake this weekend. I have an incredible urge to denigrate you outdoors again. Is that alright with you?"

"Provided my ears are off limits."

"I will hold my enthusiasm in check."

"We could pack for camping Thursday night . . . Friday after work we could head straight for the lake. Would you like to go to the bowling alley or the Dollar after work today?"

"Yes. Let's do that. Talk to you later."

Max would hold this moment for the rest of his life. All of his emotions were flowing. He returned to the shell room to relive and savor the brief moments that had just passed. He checked the tub and stepped on the foot pedal to mix the slurry. His nerves and muscles miscued. He felt wobbly and sometimes he tightened up for no reason. He would have to be careful with the shells. He would leave the foot pedal off so the blade would not be turning as the shells were dipped into the slurry.

Bob Robertson had dogged him down the hallway. He examined the contents of the slurry tub. He moved to the dry mixer and prepared another batch with great gusto. There was something about him this morning. There was a large smile of satisfaction on his face. "We certainly have a great group of employees. Let me know when you are too low for the small pieces and I will get you stocked up. And you might want to start with the small pieces first for a casual warm up. I noticed that you have a bad case of the DT's. Is it the alcohol, Max?"

Max laughed. "Arrrrrrr! Shiver me timber! 'Tis the rum, sir. I can not hide anything from Mr. Arrrrrrr!"

"Why in the world did you climb that ladder? Were you trying to collect workman's comp?"

"Just groggy this morning, sir. I was trying to clear out the cobwebs."

"Okay, there you go Max."

"Say please, Mr. Arrrrrrr!"

"The beans are on the way. I know you are in need of a little energy."

Max eyed the rows of shells hanging from the bars. His progress in Leadville flashed through his mind. Was it time to tie the knot? He recalled where he left off yesterday. He walked around for a quick check to find the most neglected shells, and then he began to dip one after another. He was in a great mood. There was a smile on his face. He felt the world for Cheryl. He gave her his heart this morning. The relationship was upon them both. It is here. It is now. It is time for a new level. The ache on his ribs emerged for a moment and Max promised himself that he would propose. He should do it today at the bowling alley. No. He should find a good ring first and get everything lined up. He could get half price shopping in the classifieds. How would he find her size? Maybe he should just lay the money down at a store and let her pick it out. No! He would buy used. He could get twice the carat. He would give Cheryl a gift certificate to a jeweler. She could design the ring and the mount for the diamond.

Cheryl was back out on the floor. She was elated. She hadn't felt so complete or so wholesome for a long time. Work left undone will leave you lacking in spirit. It will show and it will manifest itself in unusual behavior. Cheryl was happy and relieved. She might even be nice to Marty today. Man, oh man, imagine that! She tied the blue bandanna over her head to protect her hair from the occasional flying metal sparks. She eyed the bronze miner in the corner. Magnificent! You are looking good!

The miner had life now. He stood tall, defiant to the face of the hard rock wall in front of him. He would pound another hole for the dynamite to be packed into the hard rock. An explosion would follow. Afterward his eyes would search the new surface for the slightest hint or trace of silver. He might even swallow a nugget if he had the chance. She began her work day for the Robertson's. Her work was plenty. Right now she did not care how high it was piled. She was incredibly content. She began to chase the welds and match surface texture on the prairie people.

Bob walked into the office and said to Mary, "I can't believe that is the only ladder we have here."

Mary looked up from her time card routine. "The other two went back to the rental shop two days ago. The contractors have everything rented and leased from the equipment rental shops."

"We should have bought one."

"They could have bought one. I'm sure they talked about it. We have been through this same situation. Remember?"

"How long have we had that ladder Mary?"

"Should we varnish it for a keepsake?"

"After today I think we should. Isn't it amazing what Cheryl has done? She did it all by herself."

"It's important don't you think?"

"Yes. You are right. It is very important, but what they did today was pretty stupid."

"I refused to hash over shoulda, coulda, woulda with you this morning. I ordered the beans. The hat is being passed to take up a collection. Why don't we focus on that? If you keep up your whining, I am going to have to give you a whippin'."

"She kept getting moved back while the rodeo man got poured. All of that was Culpepper's fault."

"It's over, Bob. Forget rationalizing and promise to love me tonight."

Bob tilted his head and said, "Let me think about it."

"If you do not, I will get my thirty eight, and I will shoot you in the ass."

The workers were all seated in the break room. They talked with mouths full of sandwich. They goaded one another about the fast moving pace and the abundance of work. As usual, some of the artwork was subjected to playful comments.

Nash said, "I think he looks worse now. That artist, she must be a man hater to give him a face like she did."

"Culpepper would sit and scratch out a few cuts of clay. Mary did all the work."

They made irreverent fun of the farmers on the prairie statue. "Just like an insurance company. You wait forever for the check. Ernie mentioned he had a marathon coming up in Kansas. Nash mentioned that he and Silvia were going to New Mexico to visit her parents for three days. Molly and Cheryl shared smiles and praise.

Max offered, "I'll be in the hospital next week recovering from my hernia operation and my sore eye."

"Why don't you turn the lady in for beating on you? If you do nothing it will only get worse."

"I ought to. She is possessed. She is hallucinating at night, and she beats on me in the morning."

Max looked at Cheryl's wide smile and bright eyes. He melted inside.

"Cheryl, why are you hitting Max?"

"I'm not talking."

"I think she is oversensitive about the poor quality of her work. Yesterday I told her that the miner looked better headless, and she should leave it that way."

Mr. R walked past the break room. "The tub is filled."

"Okay." Max picked up his sandwich and left for the shell room. Break time was over. He dipped until all two hundred and forty eight shells had a new coat of slurry. He left the floor fans on and moved out to the injection mold room.

Cheryl fell into her Robertson foundry work routine. She hoped to work on Hector, but Marty moved the welder over to the bronco rider. She was a little upset. Then she remembered that Max told her she could not pull his ears if she was mad. She started laughing uncontrollably. She recalled stretching his lobe on the patio. It was all new again. Her life. The fun. The day. The year. What new statue was next?

Around noon time three folding tables were set up. Johnny and Cindy covered them with packing paper. Mark and Moose backed the pick up truck to the dock and brought in the Burrito Shop's delights. Bob carried in a couple of cardboard boxes filed with secret fluids ordered by the employees. There were three cases of beer, and a mysterious box that contained bottles of poisonous fluids. Mark placed a paper sack of four large rolls of film at the end of the table for Molly.

At three thirty Bob announced around the foundry, "Put your tools away and lock your lockers! I am not responsible!"

Slowly, and with certainty the atmosphere looked as if no one would walk away alive. The photos would be left for the coroner and the detectives as evidence.

CHAPTER THIRTY ONE

They drove to north Leadville and turned west toward Mount Massive at the Food Town parking lot. Cheryl stopped at the drive up liquor store. Max ran inside and picked up two bottles of sangria and two liters of 7Up.

"Oh, boy! You are a connoisseur of fine wine. Two bottles, eh?"

"I am a connoisseur of low prices and an extra bottle just in case one breaks."

"What an excuse."

Cheryl drove past two subdivisions out towards the golf course and Edith Sepi's Gift Shop and Restaurant. She chauffeured them slowly around the mountainside on the improved county gravel road. Her foot was off the gas pedal. The new truck rolled forward on its own accord.

"This is the way my grandfather liked to drive across the Terryall road when we would four wheel together, slow and easy. He used to say, 'Let all of your troubles roll away. Enjoy the smooth ride while you can.'"

Max savored the moment. "This will be a perfect way to celebrate! I'm relaxed already. So, how did you find this place?"

"Last year I went with a friend to Bear Lake. There is a rock shelf at timberline that runs parallel to the peaks for a half a mile. I figured there might be one or two more small ponds. We started back home at night. We drifted off the trail. What a beating from the tree branches! I thought I might never go backpacking again. I went back the next weekend to look for another lake and I found this one. I also found a cloud of starving mosquitoes. I used them for meditation."

"Did you hide in the sleeping bag?"

"You guessed!"

"You never think of solutions until something goes wrong."

She turned into a very small parking area that was marked with a split wood fence. They both stepped out of the truck at the same time and moved to the back to don their gear.

Cheryl dropped the tail gate. She stood her pack upright and slipped into the harness. Max copied her move. Together they carried seventy five pounds of gear. They had two gallons of water, a lightweight tent with a rain cover, an air mattress, sliced turkey, carrots, cheese, oatmeal, coffee, the world's smallest oil lamp, the world's smallest butane stove, a flat grill for the fire, veggie sandwich material, two liters of 7Up, and the two bottles of sangria. A green sleeping bag was tied to the top of each pack.

Cheryl walked into the trees. About twenty yards into the trees, she picked up a hint of a foot path on the forest floor.

Max was amazed. "This is wonderful. A secret trail." Forty yards further into the woods, it was obvious that they were on a narrow path. It moved up and out to sparsely populated trees on the mountainside. Three hundred yards in front of Cheryl was a rock field. The field proved to be somewhat of an obstacle course.

"Max, be careful, don't break an ankle. I would have to tie you to a tree and leave you for the bears."

"You are so right. There is no help around us for miles. I would have to die here an unmarried lover. A public disgrace of the worst kind."

They crossed to the far side of the rock field against the warnings and territorial cries of the chipmunks. Cheryl picked up the trail on the other side. The ascent was straight up for a quarter of a mile.

If balance was lost as a prelude to a slip or fall a heavy pack would drag them down. They unbuckled the harness waist belt. That would allow them to quickly slip out of the packs. At the top of the ascent they entered an area of large pine, and they decided to take a break. They leaned their packs against a waist high rock and slipped out of the harness. Cheryl opened a pack pocket and removed a water bottle. She checked Max to see how he was holding up. They held each other close while they shared the water.

"Well, I guess we are about ready to go." Cheryl squeezed the bottle and the stream of water bounced off of Max's glasses. "I owe you one, remember?"

Max gave no reaction, but he did issued a stern warning. "There better not be anymore of that kind of behavior." Max deftly removed his camera from a pack pocket as Cheryl replaced her water bottle.

"Hey, describe your favorite poster in the ladies room in the Silver Dollar!"

"What . . . ?" Her questioned expression turned into a big smile and a belly laugh. She turned to face Max and his finger pressed the shutter button.

"Aha! A good smile against the blue sky back ground."

Cheryl shrieked, "You cad! You can't be trusted!"

"Come on, don't hit me. One more. Lean against the rock. Drop your arm. Brush the hair out of your eyes." He snapped another. "Oh! Killer! Wild forest woman searches for Big Foot. Now you will know what everyone else sees when you wear your disgusted face! I have never in my life snapped a photo of such pure evil and hatred!" Max couldn't stop himself. "Ha, ha, ha, okay, now take your sweater off."

Two tired to fight or argue Cheryl crossed her arms. The light breeze blew a few strands of hair across her forehead. "Alright, you caught me in a good mood. But when I get my breath back you are in big trouble."

Max gave her the Bronx cheer.

Cheryl revealed a childhood fear. "I wanted to have my teeth straightened when I was little. Daddy was always gone overseas and Momma didn't have enough money." Cheryl had one or two barely twisted teeth on her lower jaw.

Max humored her. "Cheryl. You have one beautiful smile. Smiles are remembered. You give people around you a moment of enjoyment in their day. Your lips are sensual. People look at your face, your mouth, and your eyes when you smile. They are not orthodontists looking at your teeth. Forget about the teeth." Max was unrelenting. "And if you have a big toothy smile it means you are a smart ass. Now, let me see the smart ass, and tell me about your favorite male pin up in the ladies room. Tell me why the eyes are scratched out. I forgot."

"Oh, my, Professor Max. You are so good with trivia. Your official name is Dr. Seuss. Is that correct? Haven't you taken enough? Once in a while you have too much fun with me. You taunt me just a bit and it escalates to torment because you never stop."

"So, what are you going to do?"

"I am going to pull your ears."

"That's my girl."

"I'm thinking about growing fangs and biting you."

"Where?" Max feigned fright."

"Oh, aren't we the funny one?"

"It might be okay with me. Tell me! Where are you going to bite me?"

Cheryl belly laughed. "I'm going to rip your jugular out like a vampire. Then I am going watch you die while I drink your blood."

Max captured a clean smile. "Good one. Keep laughing. Let me see the horse teeth. The big teeth. That's it! Bucky Beaver would be insanely jealous. I think Bugs Bunny might fall in love with you."

They donned the packs once again and followed the trail through the trees. As they neared the timberline, the height of the trees diminished until they were as tall as the trees. They walked for a half mile on the granite plateau. Cheryl climbed down a shear rock cliff about twenty feet tall. Beneath the plateau was an open area and there was a small pond just inside the edge of the trees at timberline.

"Wow! What a great spot, Cheryl. Zebulon Pike would be jealous."

"At this point I was wandering around the area. I was just about lost and ready to turn back."

It was the neatest trail Max ever hiked. The walking time was one and a half hours which meant that heavy packs could be carried uphill without too much suffering. It had a little bit of everything. It wound through the large green forest and on up to the small green forest at timberline. The path opened up for incredible views.

"Ah we got lucky. No mosquitoes."

"Only one vampire."

Cheryl delighted in asking him, "Honey, would you blow up the air mattress for me? Do you want to put up the tent?"

Max tried to tease her. "No!"

"Where do you want the fire, baby?"

"I like the fire in our hearts and minds and between our legs."

"You know I just might swing at that there other peeper of yours." She found a good spot with a couple of large rocks to sit on and a ready made campfire. "Over here, Max. Inside the tree line for some shelter from the wind." She picked up her backpack and moved it to the new spot. "We can find the perfect spot later."

"Yes, Miss Manners. This is wonderful. There are plenty of small branches on the ground for the fire. Do you want to light the fire?"

"Let's work on the fire together."

They foraged for pine needles, twigs, and old limbs on the ground. Between the two of them they gathered enough for two days in just a few minutes.

Max pulled out a small butane stove the size of a cup saucer. He pulled the two discs apart. One served as the base against the ground and one served as the pot holder. Inside was a metal cross of stout tubing. The saucers screwed on to opposite ends of the cross tubing. The third end of the tubing held a gas flow control knob. A small feeder pin, to stick into the rubber seal of the butane can, was on the fourth end. A small burner the size of a fifty cent piece, held the pot saucer in place.

She watched Max with great interest. "Wow. Pretty slick."

"Not big enough for a barbeque, but it beats having to carry a full sized grill."

Next Max shoved the broken branches and pine needles into the circle of rocks. He slid the small butane canister onto the metal pin on the cross tubing. With one match he lit the stove burner and turned up the flow control. He pushed the large flame into the twigs and immediately a fire was burning.

"Hey! That is cheating! That is not the great outdoors! There is nothing rugged and individualistic about that. That is blatant suburbanism."

"It is a great way to save matches or light up a fire in the rain. Just keep the butane can away from ignition sources." He placed the metal grill over the small fire. He had three pans that fit inside one another. He filled the large one with water for their coffee and tea and placed it on the grill.

"What's for dinner?"

"Not a gourmet delight. It will be carrots, chicken, and cheese. Just enough to keep us alive."

"I think I will have my turkey, cheese, and avocado. I will work on some new ideas for the menu." She threw a candy bar at him. "I have to stay in practice."

Max set up the tent and returned with tea bags, and instant coffee. He poured hot water into her cup, and filled his coffee mug. "This is the life!"

"Any bears up here?"

"Their food is down below. If you find a gooey pile of berries on the ground make a lot of noise and retrace your steps."

As darkness arrived, Cheryl shared her thoughts on the miner and the events that would unfold next week. Max unrolled the mattress to blow it up. "The marble base will be delivered to the museum this week. Bob will let us use his truck to move the statue. All we have to do is get it to the lobby. Nash will drill the holes in the marble. Danny will braze the pegs to the base. Mary is going to work with me on the patina. That should happen by Wednesday. There is a rumor floating around that the foundry is going to close."

"Is it a serious one?"

"Marty did some scouting on the western slope on his Easter vacation. Rumor has it he found some inexpensive overhead. I am worried, Max. It is going to leave us without work."

Max pondered the thought as he heated the carrots, the chicken slices, and the cheese. "Oh, no, that is just great. Just as everything falls into place, then things start falling apart."

Cheryl bit into her fresh sandwich. She talked to Max as she continued to munch. "That is what I am worried about. Hal and Marilyn have a drywall job in the Chief Hosa subdivision. It is a big contract with some large three hundred thousand dollar homes. They don't like to drive more than thirty minutes to the job. They made an exception this time." Cheryl paused. "They are doing some interesting things like camping at the worksite instead of going home every day. They stocked five gallon water bottles at the site for bathing." She paused again. No response from Max. "That big money just keeps rolling into Colorado. Marilyn told me they might be able to manage two crews if we work for them. They will hire you. They trust you."

Max spooned out his dinner into a plastic bowl and swallowed a spoon full of the warm concoction. "It sounds like they need help right away. How soon do they need the answer?"

Cheryl held his gaze. "Hal and Marilyn will hire you to work for them. I mention it again because I am hoping that you will agree to work for them. They trust us. It would be the summer to do it. How much more time do you need on your rentals?"

"I would guess at least a month working only on the weekends and evenings. I have a little bit of electrical work. The water and drain lines are in. I need to remove the old brick chimney. I have to pass inspections. The plumbing inspector is local, so the inspection would take place quickly. Leadville is without an electrical inspector. The Summit County inspector is doing the work. He stops in Leadville at least every two weeks, depending on the number of inspections. The gas company will want to walk through and check out the new furnace and the water heater. Then, of course, there is the matter of the interior cosmetics, but that is not important."

"Could you do the work on the weekends? I think Hal would let you go Thursday for three day weekends until you get it done. He has been through a few lousy workers. He likes the quality of the work you have done. You could pay the rent out of your salary. It would be better than what you have been making. Would it not?"

"You know, a good two week pay check from Hal would help me get over the next month of expenses. That does make sense, but it will take me forever if I have to do it on the weekends. I would lose a work day just driving up and back. And it is difficult to put in eight hours of physical labor in the mountains because of the altitude. I need to stay here until it is finished. I am not backing out, well, maybe I am."

They finished dinner and Max washed the utensils. He collected garbage in a plastic bag, rolled it up and placed it in the tent.

"Max, I brought you here to this neutral place to ask you some questions that have been nagging me. I need to talk to you about a couple of things. We can converse on equal footing here. Your house would subconsciously give you the upper hand, and you might be prone to dodge some of these questions I have, or blow them off."

"I agree. Go right on ahead, baby. There is no way you can ruin a beautiful night at eleven thousand feet. Are you done yet? Ha, ha, ha!"

"Max, how much do you care for me?"

He stalled for strategy. "Oh, give me a time out. Please? I want to open the sangria." He opened the sangria and made a spritzer for her. He filled his blue coffee mug and added a splash of 7Up for courage. He fished around in his mental attitude and humor archive.

"Well, you know the first forty five days were a real eye opener. I was scared to death. I thought that you might be crazy or schizophrenic."

Cheryl sampled her spritzer. "Ha! Careful, Max. You do not want to be on my shit list."

"It has been what, six or seven weeks? I was infatuated with you when we met at Ski Cooper, and ever since the night we camped out at Mt Sopris, our relationship has moved to a higher level." He tested the sangria. "We found out that night in the rainstorm that we are sexually compatible and that we enjoy sharing the physical aspects of love with each other. So at that point, infatuation went out the door. I am no longer infatuated with you, Cheryl Pritchard. I am in love with you. Words like love, and lust, and commitment, and marriage are in the air now."

"That is good, Max. Can you tell me more?"

"Yes, I can. That rainy night we had it together. There was some serious lust and all of the right chemistry. Now, we have let our relationship continue, and we are trying to determine how much of it is love, and not just lust, or casual sex. We are trying to determine where we are going to go from tonight and how fast is it going to happen."

"Oh, Professor! Please continue."

"Let's keep some perspective on this. We have learned so much about each other in a very short period of time. We are both in that crazy emotional skydiving arena as well. Some people would say that we have bonded. I say that we compliment each other and lift one another physically and spiritually. Cheryl, let me catch up with you here for a minute. What is on your mind? Tell me, and you will get better answers from me."

"Alright. Fair enough." She was ready to approach Max with the questions she formulated last week. It was going to be now or never, just spit it out. All is fair in love. "Max, I need to get some things out of my system, and I need to do it now. My mind is full of a mountain of desire, and I also have just a little bit of doubt."

Max swilled more sangria. "Tell Uncle Max about the little doubts."

"These thoughts have been swirling around in my head all month and I can not get rid of them. All of these thoughts have intensified since we camped at Mount Sopris and I got your clothes off." Max laughed. "I want to talk about them and I want you to give me truthful answers. Don't lie to me, Max. Our paths have converged and now they are running parallel. Love has blossomed and I think marriage is definitely a possibility for us. Now I am worried that we are going to drift apart. There are some things that will move each of us in a different direction. The foundry is closing. I do not want our paths to diverge. Wait Max. Do not say anything. Do not move. Stay right where you are. I want to give you a great big hug." Cheryl stood and walked behind him. He sat up straight. Cheryl put her arms around him and held him to her chest.

"Thank you. That feels great."

Cheryl increased the pressure of her hug. She whispered in his ear. "I am not falling in love with you, Max Mason. I have fallen in love with you. I want to marry you. You have touched my heart and my mind. I am worried that you might get away from me. That would hurt me deeply.

I do not think that I could ever love anyone again. I don't want you to hurt me. Now tell me, without hesitation that I am the only girl in your life, now and forever. Tell me that there is no one else alive or buried in the folds of your imagination that I have to compete with for the rest of our time together. Think about it Max, and then tell me the truth." She loosened her hug and returned to sit on the rock in front of him.

They stared into each others eyes. Max took a small swallow to moisten his throat.

"I always cared for you Cheryl, and I have always valued being with you. I have been by myself far too long, and I know I am in love with you. Tonight things are absolutely serious and on a on a totally new level. Words of love and marriage are out in the open now. Oh gosh. Let me collect myself for a minute.

"Max, let me say it a different way. Commitment. That is what I am looking for. Commitment. I am on a schedule too and if you do not commit, then I will not be here in a couple of months. I am going to move on. I will be down the road. I will not waste time. I will not throw a year down the drain living in sin with you or anyone. I spent my last two years living in sin, and things were pretty bleak for me when the dam broke." Cheryl paused. The silence was deafening. "If you do not ask me to marry you, then I am going to leave you. If the foundry closes down, then I am out of here. I am gone within one month. Inside of three months I will have a bundle of friends in Arvada, and drywall work that I can survive on. I will remember you, but I will not dwell on what happened here in Leadville. My next job is waiting for me in Arvada, Max. It is not the beautiful mountains, but I have safety there. If commitment is too scary for you, and you think you might find someone better, or something else you want to do, then tell me. I can pack up and I can put my efforts towards something positive for me." Total silence. "We are making progress here. This is important to me because I am in love with you. Do you love me? Tell me you love me. I need to hear it everyday. Do you love me?"

Max stood and reached for her hand. She stood and they held one another. Max whispered in her ear. "Yes, Cheryl, I do truly love you. Did you not feel it Tuesday morning?"

"Yes, of course I did. I still feel it with all of my heart. It may seem as if I am asking the same question over and over, but I want to be absolutely certain. I have never asked a man to marry me. Women aren't supposed to do that. See, Max, a woman is never supposed to say those things to a man."

"Who says so?"

"Let me finish."

"It's my turn."

"Be quiet and listen. I'm right for you now or I am not right for you at all. I have been on the love merry go round enough to know that you are a good deal. There is an age difference, but that is my decision. Max, I want a firm commitment."

"Is that like a dedicated woody?"

"I don't want to be with you two years from now and not be married. It is not like we are nineteen or twenty. Do you need more partners to experiment with? I don't. I like the direction we are going and I need marriage. Max, women are different. We have the baby. We can not risk our futures with drifters. I thought you knew that. And guys tend to dump girls for all kinds of stupid little reasons. I want security and I want my future to be with you."

"Cheryl, we should get married."

"I need to hear you elaborate on 'should.'"

Max broke the embrace. "Here. Let me refresh your spritzer. This is getting good. I won't give you as much sangria this time so you don't get upset and fly off the deep end, or rip my jugular open." To stiffen his resolve he added a splash of 7Up to his sangria.

"Just a moment. I am getting ahead of myself. There are still a couple of questions I want you to clarify." She knelt and added some wood to the fire. She poured more water in the pan. "Max, I know about Sherry and she told me all about your old flame, Gloria."

"Oh! Woe is me!"

"Settle down. Sherry told me you have had a few girlfriends in your bachelor years and that you were quite in love with them at one time. She tells me that you live off of their memories, and that you use those memories to help you block out any new affair you might encounter. She claims that you are a confirmed bachelor. So, tell me, Max, are there still two girls in your memory that I have to worry about and compete with?" She looked up from the campfire. "You can live on her memory, but her memory can not touch you like I can. A memory can not cook for you. It can not play with you or snore in your ear. Max, she is gone. I am the girl here with you now. I am your future. I am as good as or better than Gloria, or Sherry, and I realize now that you know it. I am not trying to make you feel guilty. I was just afraid about it, and I had to ask to know for sure. Let's be a team, Max. You and me."

"All of my girl friends were nasty and sleazy, and I loved them dearly. Do you have any more dirt on me?"

"What was the employment thing about in Indiana?"

"You have heard parts of it. I never should have done it. I lost my mind and any rational ability of self examination. It was all about money, relatives, family business, exceptional wages, and a good job. It lasted a little over five weeks. I left abruptly. I belong here in the west."

"No one could believe that you left Sherry. Would you have married Sherry?" "Yes. I would have. It could have been any day. We were both ready for it. She had an open invitation to go with me to Leadville. How did Angie Owens steal your boyfriend?"

"Fair enough. Here is the point. I don't want to keep going down the road and then have the game called because we go different ways. I want completion and commitment."

"God knows I'm overdue for commitment. I have only committed to myself. That is so selfish and greedy. Woe is me."

"Do you still live off of memories of her?"

He thought for a moment. "I did, Cheryl. I recall her vividly just like my first static line jump. Now I have those feelings for you. I live on your memory every single day. Let's kiss to that."

Cheryl stood once more to kiss her love again. "Max, I want you to know that we are making some progress here."

"What a beautiful night. Cheryl, I am so glad you brought me here and not one of your old boyfriends. Look at all of these beautiful stars."

"I want you to know that I care for you. I want you to know how much. I want you to know that this relationship means everything to me. I want it for the rest of my life. I really love you, Max. I just do not know the right way to phrase these questions. I have not thought long enough, but now is the time to ask them."

"Every weekend you go to Sky's West I stay in Leadville and work on the rental. It kills me. I want to be there with you and I want to watch your progress, and your growth, and share the fun. Then again, without me there, you are able to concentrate on your work and mingle and make some new friends. But I have to admit, that all I really wanted, was to watch your lip quiver."

They laughed.

"Karen said that to me after the first jump! Thank God for the Karens and the Mollys."

"Well, I am glad you brought the subject of my memories up. I would hate for you to carry that around inside for a couple of years. One day you might unravel and hack me to pieces."

"Let's move to the big rock and sit together."

"I am so glad that we are here together to share this beautiful night and these beautiful stars."

"Can you imagine from the day at Ski Cooper to today? Did you think it would happen, Max?"

"I left all of the doors open for you."

"So you were trying to trap me!"

"I don't know who trapped who with what, but I certainly am thankful that we are here together. I have a suspicion that it works both ways." Max knelt in front of her and put his hands on her thighs. He took her hands and stared into her simmering eyes. "Cheryl, what are you thinking right now? At this very moment?"

"I want you to marry me."

"I do want to marry you. Just like you said. Let's be a team. I love you and I will marry you because it is what both of us want."

"Seal it, Max. Kiss me!"

"Your greatest command is my smallest desire."

Cheryl laughed and Max leaned forward and gave her a long soft kiss."

"Mmmmmm. Good one, Max, you gave me goose bumps and you made my toes curl up."

"That's so you can't run away."

"Max. I am so happy that you want to marry me. Now, I just need to know where and when."

Oh, God. The ultimatums. "Just a minute." Max took another swallow of sangria. "Okay, okay. Let me shift gears. A couple of places come to mind. Tell me what you think."

"Really?"

"Yes. The drop zone, Arvada, any church in Leadville, or the patio at 304, your courtyard at the castle."

"You know, you might be on to something there. My court yard would be fabulous. Everyone would take pictures of the scenery. No one would take pictures of us."

"We could have the reception at the bowling alley."

"That would be good. So Max, when do we get engaged? I would like to have a little something to flaunt in front of my friends."

"You mean adversaries?"

"Something that is a constant daily reminder that you support me, and care for me."

"Mastercard or Visa? Which one do you want? You can only have one."

Cheryl could not help but chuckle. "Something that also projects hope for the future and that I am spoken for."

"As in the Hope Diamond? The big rock? All custom made and five to ten thousand dollars? Honey, we can look in the classifieds. There are always diamond rings for half price. We could buy a couple of them and have them tastefully arranged in a band that will fit your finger. You could design the band yourself."

"I can deal with that. That might work out fine. I would still like to shop at the jewelry stores. You know, just for grins and giggles. You never know. I might see something that I like."

"Now I have a question for you. The rental houses. They are in my name. Will you sign a pre nuptial agreement?"

"Whhhaaaaat? The rentals? Those old beat up things?" She laughed the threat away. "There goes the romance! How did you ever get my panties off?"

"You weren't wearing any."

"Do you value the rental houses more than me? You would be better off selling them. Ha! See Max, I knew you were a taker."

"I never had anything in my life. Anything I obtained by myself or was given, I had to share with my brother and sisters. If I did not share, then I was punished. They would run and tell mom and dad. You know, they were young liberals. I just handed everything over to them to forgo the verbal reprimands. All I want now is just a few things that belong to me."

"Waaaaaa."

"Okay. I will answer with this question. Would you give up your miner for me or would you let me have half of the proceeds?"

"Oh. I guess I understand."

"It may seem a weak analogy to you, but this is my retirement. This is not a short term thing. This is not just a lark or something to do. The rentals are serious. I purposefully took this path to make a retirement for myself. I got them at a low price, and when the real estate bust ends, they will see some appreciation in value. They will also provide me with five hundred a month for the rest of my life, six thousand a year."

"Hey! I have a solution! You have to sign a pre nuptial agreement that you can not have claim to any of my artwork proceeds or the artwork."

"I will, Cheryl. I would sign in a heart beat. Honey, that is a great analogy."

"Okay Max. When we get home you type them up, one for the rentals and one for the artwork. We can get them notarized at the bank. All I really want is you, Max. I want the claim on you."

They kissed passionately to arousal. She felt his hand cup her breast.

"Max. Let's go to my tent. I can play the Daytona 500 and you can play with the twins."

"Your tent?"

"You just gave it to me remember? We are going to get married and half of what you have will be mine."

Max put his head in his hands. "I am so screwed. I am so screwed." He drew some laughter from Cheryl.

"See how selfish your basic nature is when you are not putting on your facade of the blab and gab? You have double standards, just like the rest of us."

She pulled his yellow underwear till it stretched and tore to pieces. "Shut up Mongo and disappear the turtle. I ain't gonna wait all night for you to figure out what I want right now."

"You are a very vulgar Princess."

"Do you like that in a woman Max, because I am not playing Princess now? You told me you got hot faster when the woman initiated the molesting."

"No, I don't like vulgarity in a lady. But Mongo does." They changed positions many times like squirrels running up and down through the trees. After the gymnastics and the orgasmic release, Cheryl and Max slipped into the sleeping bags and huddled to get warm. They were warm as toast in no time at all with their combined body heat. Contented, they drifted of to sleep.

A wonderful night of warm snuggling passed. They woke up to the morning breeze on the mountain.

"Max, I have a bit of a dull headache. I am going for water."

"Hot please."

"Sure, baby. I will get your diapers changed after that."

"I will be yours forever. Take charge your Highness. I love women who are givers."

Cheryl wormed her way out of the tent with the plastic water jug. She sipped some clear, cold water. She swirled it in her mouth and spit it out. She moved for the butane stove and the small grill at the campfire. She had a twig and pine needle fire going as Max began to deflate the mattress. She added wood and set the grill. She placed the pan on the grill and filled it with water from the plastic milk jug. She could hear the air rush out of the mattress as Max rolled it up. The cups were waiting for her to pick them up. She sat on the stump next to the rock bordered camp fire, and watched two backpacks appear outside the tent. Next was a folded queen size air mattress and a sack full of cheese, bread, avocado and alfalfa sprouts. After that, tea, oatmeal, and instant coffee appeared. Max collapsed the tent and folded it into the bottom half of his backpack. He rolled the sleeping bags and tied them.

Max moved to her and kissed her head. "I love you, Cheryl, and I want to marry you. Will you marry me?" He shook instant tea into her cup and instant coffee into his mug and added hot water to both. "There is no other woman in my life now, or from the past, living in my memory. There never will be anyone but you."

Cheryl sighed. "Oh, Max come here and kiss your love."

"When the backpacks are finished. Wait for me, my love, I shan't be long." Max stuffed the rest of the gear into the packs and carried the plastic sack to her. He went to his knees in front of her. She felt his lips touch hers in the most vibrant medium kiss she ever experienced.

"Oh, Max, I could feel your heart in that one. Good kiss. I think I will put that one in my logbook."

"Keeping track, eh. You might not be able to write fast enough."

"Keep them coming." She let the sack and the knife fall to the ground. Max pleasured her again.

"It certainly does get the blood running in me, Princess. Want to play pass the sausage?"

"You couldn't ruin this moment or this day if you tried to Max."

"How is the head ache?"

"You kissed it away." Cheryl poured the last of the hot water in his blue mug and looked into his dark blue eyes in front of her. She felt good.

It warmed her heart and soul to hear him say, "Thank you Miss Pritchard. What a lovely way to start the morning. With a warm beauty to fill my cup and care for me."

"This warm beauty is going to be your wife."

"Let's toast to our lives."

"Together, Max. Today is the first official day of our journey."

Cheryl made several small sandwiches for future consumption. Max rolled the sleeping bags and tied them to the bottom of the back packs. Cheryl pushed the hot cinders to one side of the fire. She doused the hot coals with the last of the water and covered the pit with a layer of rocks. No embers would be able to escape to the forest floor. Max dumped the rest of the small trash into a plastic bag and stowed it in the top half of his backpack. He closed both packs and tied the bed rolls to the top of the packs. The first day of their future was officially underway. They were moving together on the path of common goal and desire. Cheryl was right. If he ever had another opportunity in ten years it would be too late. He would be forty five by then. Any lass would scorn him unless of course he had a few million tucked away in the bank. Somehow that always warmed a young girl's disposition for five years or so.

"Cheryl, I need love in my life. The opportunity to be with you will never happen again in my lifetime, and I will wind up nothing more than an old coot."

"Well, I have news for you. You are going to be an old coot in ten years. I think I can work with you, Max, but you must prove to me that you have cleared your mind of your past irresponsible adventures and that you have grown tired of them."

"Your dagger is buried deep dear. Do not pull it out or I will surely die."

Cheryl helped Max hoist his backpack. She slipped into hers while he held her pack. They held each other. Max bumped her with his pelvis. "Let's have one kiss for the road, baby. You know I only agreed to all of those things last night because you drove your truck, and it would be a long walk home by my self."

"I will kill you."

"I've lived a full life."

They kissed passionately.

"Lead the way Pocahontas."

The sunlight and the panorama were stunning.

"What are you going to do Max? Any idea yet?"

"I have been thinking about it and I am glad you asked. I am going to move everything into 407 while I finish it up. I will find a renter for 304. Then I will catch up with you and your parents at the Chief Hosa job. I think we should get married shortly after that. Then we can figure out when and where we will be married."

"That will be fun. You have time. Hal and Marilyn will welcome you with open arms. Hal says the State Higheway opened the back road through to Central City. All of the new construction has access to the interstate now so they can zip back to the city for materials. I am going to finish the miner and get him to the museum this week or next. I will leave for Arvada and not look back. A lady has no choice. Security is tantamount to survival for me. Arvada is where my future is for the next six months. By the way, did I mention that I live forty five minutes from a parachute center?"

"Did we talk about love and lust last night?"

"Yes we did. Is there anything you are uncertain of, my darling? Do you need clarification on anything? Is everything on schedule according to your plan? Am I asking too many questions?"

"You are so funny."

"Max, I think that is a wood tick on your ear. Come over here and let me take a look at it." Max shook his head vigorously side to side.

He unloaded the truck and stowed the gear in the kitchen closet. Cheryl listened to the answering machine. There were several messages. Most of it was old news. Mary Robertson left a message for her. "Cheryl, Colorado Springs is covered. You do not have to go." Sandy from the mining museum announced that the marble base would be delivered Wednesday. Cheryl phoned Danny Duran and left a message on his answering machine that the marble base would be at the museum Wednesday, and that the statue would be delivered Friday. The installation could take place anytime after that.

"So what is our next conquest, m' lady?"

"Prepare my bubble bath! And let's have a little cheese, wine, and crackers on the floor by the tub. Get the heat dialed up. After that, I plan to conquer your temple."

"Arrr! Aye, aye skipper!"

After his temple was raided, Cheryl readied her gear bag with her rig, goggles, helmet, gloves, log book, the skydiver manual, camera, and extra clothing. Max loaded her equipment bag and she was down the road for home and the drop zone.

CHAPTER THIRTY TWO

"How is work, Cheryl?"

"Don't mention work. This girl has a big project with lots of production problems and stress from a closing deadline."

"Cheryl, you have to chase the base today. You have to dock on the base formation without knocking Karen and me out of the sky. Your objective is to demonstrate competency in the delta maneuver. You are going to do two of them. You get to spot without assistance. Canopy opening is four thousand feet. Pretty easy, huh? As always we are improving our flying skills every jump. We will fly no contact and work on matching fall rates."

"Let's walk through one. "Believe it or not it is just like walking forward fast or slow. Karen and Steve moved twenty yards away from Cheryl and faced her.

"Okay, Cheryl. We are the base. Run at us." When Cheryl was half way, Steve hollered, "Now walk." When she was five yards away, Steve said, "Okay, now, baby steps."

"Let's talk about what just took place here. We can not create the exact motions on the ground, but these movements give us something to talk about. These ground drills help us remember which maneuver is next and the correct body position for the maneuver. It also helps to set the tempo. Alright Cheryl, explain what happens and what your movements are as you dock on a formation. Karen has trouble docking so please explain it to her." Smirks and smiles were exchanged.

"An example would be a bird landing on a picnic table."

Steve suppressed laughter. Karen chuckled. "Is this example in the information manual?"

"Let me finish. You have to slow down and bleed off your forward speed before you hit the formation. The flare reduces forward speed."

"What happens if you stop three or four feet away?"

"I have to point my toes, and bring my hands in to my shoulders. A good hand track will scoot me to the base. Without moving my shoulders or elbows, I move my hands and forearms down to the ground in a forty five degree angle."

"Great, Cheryl. What if you fly down to us fast and hot?"

"Then I go to the chair position. I will keep moving to you but after a second or two the forward speed is stopped. Then, I have to get face to earth fast, and close on the formation. Hopefully, I can stay slightly above you. It is easy to drop down to you."

"Good point. Once we transition from the plane and are stable, Karen and I are going to do two back flips and back slide away from you. Use the delta position to catch us and dock on us. Show us your delta and explain it to us."

Cheryl stood and spread her feet shoulder width apart. "I am going to ease into it to reduce wobbling. I have to bend at the waist and my hands go down to my hips and out a foot or so from my body for stability. My legs are straight, and my toes are pointed. I am going to set my eyes on you. My head and shoulders will make small corrections. If I need to turn I use the left hand for a left turn. I move it farther away from my side while I pull the right hand close to my side. The hand creates an unsymmetrical drag, and that translates to a slow pivot point."

"Alright. There are a couple of important points here. Karen and I will be stationary. Any movement you see will be your movement and not ours. Do not let that be a surprise to you. On the first one we want you to approach fast. No worries. It is okay to get a little bit aggressive here. If you are smoking in on us, on a collision course, then Karen and I are going to move out of your way. One more idea. Fly right into our shoulders. Bring your shoulders right into ours. Then take your grips. If you have no forward momentum and you reach for us, then you will back slide."

"We are going to try for at least two of these. We will fly a no contact, round formation, and match fall rates. When is deployment?"

"Four thousand feet." Cheryl was fired up. She was excited.

"It is time for a restroom break. Let's break for ten minutes and then meet at the mock up in full gear. We have about twenty minutes. Cheryl liked the mock up. It served as a rehersal and refreshed her memory of the quick shuffling movements of bodies in close quarters. It took the edge off fear and apprehension because she had to think about making a spot, the exit, and the first move on the laundry list. She also prepared herself mentally for the wind blast and the engine noise.

Before a half hour had passed Cheryl and Steve were rolling up the heavy cloth door. They secured the door with a velcro strap at each end. Cheryl checked their location over the airport. Karen moved behind her and Steve moved to the edge of the door close to the rear float position. Winds were west to east and the spot was between the hangar and the runway. Cheryl gave a "ten right" correction. When she yelled "Cut" Steve spun through the door to the rear float position. His right foot was on the door threshold. Cheryl smiled directly into the light blue eyes as Karen made contact on her left side, and gripped her leg strap. The exit was smooth. After the transition, Karen and Steve did two back loops and slid away from her.

Cheryl bent at her waist and moved her arms slowly back. She encountered a slight wobble, but she kept her eyes on the base. Her speed increased and she held her delta as she closed. When she was about twenty feet away she moved her hands in front of her. She sat up in a partial chair position to flare and lose forward speed. She slid past Karen and Steve. She waited too long to flare. She recovered her arch and moved to dock on the base. They were laughing, but they gave her thumbs up.

Karen and Steve flipped and slid away a second time. Cheryl closed the distance. The base grew in size as she neared. She was slightly above the base and she flared to release her forward momentum. She quickly returned belly to earth. She was level to the base and ten feet out. She closed the distance with a hand track and straight legs. Their hands and shoulders almost touched. Steve and Karen broke out smiles. "Way to go Cheryl. Good work." Karen and Steve gave her the COA sign. They flew no contact for five seconds. Steve pointed his index finger and Cheryl waved off and tossed her pilot chute.

They talked about jump seven as they packed.

"To me the turn and track is the most important point on any sky dive. It requires five seconds to complete. When you are down to your last five seconds of freefall you must forget about any other planned maneuvers in your jump. You must wave off from the group, and turn and track. Opening altitude is a safety issue. If you are still working on the completion of a skydive with other jumpers, and you go below the USPA recommended opening altitude, then you have no safety margin if your main canopy malfunctions. You will be notified that you broke a drop zone safety rule, and you will be grounded for one month."

Steve continued. "Okay Cheryl, why track away from other jumpers?"

"A good track will give you a fast horizontal separation from your group and an open space to deploy your canopy."

"Okay, describe the track position."

"You roll your shoulders forward to trap air. Feet close together. Arms out to the side with a slight bend at the waist. Head back. That is the hard part. It makes you like an airplane wing. You trap air around your chest, and that helps keep your body flat in the air. You build up speed and slice forward horizontally. It takes three seconds for the movement to pick up some real speed."

"Good. When you first go into the track position, you will wobble a little bit left and right. You can move your hands farther from your side for stability, and then once you have speed, you can pull them closer to your side to trap and cup the air. We have plenty of time on this jump. Let's work on the ground drill."

"You get to spot without assistance. Deploy at five thousand feet. Canopy opening is four thousand feet, pretty easy. You are going perform one track. We are limited on altitude at this drop zone. So let's plan a couple of maneuvers."

"I would like to do a couple of leg turns and back flips."

"That's the spirit, Cheryl. Karen?"

"Let's stick with the turns. How about a right leg turn and then a left leg turn?"

"That sounds good. We are going to break this dive off at six thousand. Break off and turn and track for five seconds. Wave off and deploy.

"We will exit together and transition to a no contact three way. Make certain that you pick your heading. On signal, wave off, turn, and track on heading. When you finish nine seconds, flare a little to stop your forward momentum. Go back to your arch. Get big and slow down. Karen and I will dock on you and then we will finish the rest of the jump. At six thousand we break off. Turn and track for about five seconds. Get big, and take a second or two to slow down. Wave off and deploy. Alright?"

"Got it, Steve."

"A note of caution here. Do not open in a track. It will injure you. It will give you a severe case of whip lash. When you stay in a track, your speed will increase. Remember, at the end of a track, you want the stable freefall position. Get big to slow your fall rate. If you have to wait two or three seconds, then do so. Slow down. If you open in a track, you will get your bones realigned. You will be uncomfortably stretched from head to toe. You will feel your canopy bag hit the heels of your feet and you could possibly get suspension lines around your legs."

"Okay. I will file that one away for future reference."

The jump run was the same direction as the last. The smooth exit and three way round proved that each jumper was keenly aware of the others. Fall rates were individually adjusted to match the group. Steve gave Cheryl the nod to go ahead. Cheryl turned for her track. She focused on a tiny farm house east of the interstate. After six seconds her goggles began to bounce around on her eyebrows. She must have picked up forty miles an hour.

She flared on eight seconds to slow her forward speed and returned to her arch. She turned one hundred and eighty degrees to the airport. Her altimeter read 8000. Karen and Steve appeared from nowhere. The nod was given and Cheryl did a right leg turn and a left leg turn. They enjoyed the remaining seconds of smooth no contact flying. The wind comically realigned the skin around the bones of their faces. It rushed past their ears with the whistling of fun and it tore at their jumpsuits. Cheryl's goggles were loose from the track and they fluttered around her eyes. Steve and Karen made faces at one another. They broke off at six grand. Cheryl turned and tracked for four seconds. The farm house was larger now, and the barnyard animals appeared to be as big as ants. She waved off and threw her pilot chute. The rustle of her canopy reminded her to brace for the opening shock.

Sunday evening they lay on their stomachs and watched a comedy video. Max pampered her with a medium massage. Between laughter Cheryl shared her thoughts.

"Your promised me a sunrise load."

"How about tomorrow morning?"

Cheryl smiled and stretched to an arch. "That would be excellent. There is just one small problem. As things are going to go this week, tomorrow will be patina week. We have regular hours."

"We can stay up late tonight."

"When are we going to jump together Max Mason?"

"How about into a hot water Mr. Bubble bath."

"Is there enough room for both of us?"

"I thought you would never ask. I bet both of us can fit in the tub."

Max voluntarily began a massage with a lighter more sensual touch which moved along the insides of her thighs and next to her breasts that were squashed to the floor. Cheryl squirmed on occasion.

"My transitions to the delta and the track were really professional and smooth. On the delta, I swooped to Steve and Karen and went past them in a flare position. They were laughing at my attempt." Cheryl continued. You know, it used to be tough just to get out the door. Now, here I am falling to earth at one hundred twenty miles an hour, and all I am thinking about is how to swoop down to dock with Steve and Karen. Isn't that just bizarre?"

"Let me put it in perspective. You can dock on your dream, even in the face of certain death. But to do so, you must have positive thought and focus, and a plan. It is the same thing you are doing with your statue project. You simply have to ignore everything else."

"Oh, Professor." Do you think we should transition to the hot bubble bath?"

"Oh, yes. We should, but we need to transition out of our clothing first."

They removed each article of clothing smoothly and sensually. They kissed frequently with deep rooted feeling of mental and physical passions centered from their love and commitment to each other. Max eventually rolled to his back to let Cheryl go to work on the inducement of pleasure to her body. She took her time as she was in no hurry. After she had released two significant orgasms she rolled off Max.

He headed for the kitchen for more wine, cheese, and crackers. First he stopped in the bathroom to plug the tub drain and ready the hot water for an entertaining Mr. Bubble bath.

CHAPTER THIRTY THREE

The new emphasis and direction for current projects was shifted to the jazz quartet and the Tenth Mountain. Marty was up to his eyeballs with metal sections to weld together. Finishing touches were put on the bronco and the prairie people and most of the employees were back to their regular schedules. Cheryl found time to put the finishing touches on her miner. The final check was received from the mining museum.

Tuesday afternoon Mary and Cheryl were right back on the scaffold. This time they were looking at the miner hat. Mary and Cheryl had the necessary cloths and brushes. The patina materials were close by on two carts. There was white for the candles, and red to add a little color variation to the bronze surface here and there. Mary mixed up a bluish gray color for a cold patina on the hat.

"You are putting it on kind of thick."

"Trust me here, Cheryl. This idea occurred to me a awhile back. I could have told you earlier, but I figured on this present moment at hand. I knew it would eventually arrive. And here we are working together, with smiles on our faces, and sharing this last touch up on your miner." Mary continued. "This is a glare thing. And by the way, Cheryl, I really am proud to share this moment with you. You have been such an asset to this foundry and we all appreciate your loyalty and good work."

"You know something, Mary? This has been the greatest experience in my life."

"Mine too, Cheryl. You know, these big statues on public display indoors get a lot of ceiling light. Usually there is very little light at the floor level. The top of the statue will glare and it will be brighter than the rest of the statue. The top of the statue will reflect the bright ceiling light, just like a light house."

"A light house?"

"No matter where you stand to look at the miner, all of the features of the face and all of the extremities would be diminished because of the bright reflection of ceiling light from the hat!"

"I believe you."

"It will give you an unbalanced visual experience. At the bottom of the statue you have shadow or glare interference and at the top you have brightness. Visitors will have a bad viewing experience and they will not understand why. They will only understand the glare."

"It is a distraction, and the brighter light creates an unbalanced appearance?" "Exactly. Now what we are going to do here is fool the lighting system. This cold patina will be a bluish grey if this mix turns out right. It will darken the hat. It will not really absorb the light, but the important thing is that it will not reflect the ceiling light."

"There will not be a lighthouse. You are brilliant, Mary. Thank you so much."

"The rest of your statue will sparkle, Cheryl. The ceiling light will show the coloration of the patina on the face and the arms and legs. Even the base will sparkle. This statue will really look good! And your boyfriend here, Hector, will look better."

"How did you know?"

"His name?"

"Yes."

"Well, in your frustration to complete this project while things have been difficult for you, a couple of your friends have heard you talking under your breath for the last two weeks. I mean, come on. After all, you heard Bob and me talking privately." Mary gave Cheryl a wide grin. "Didn't you?"

"Well, I don't tell everybody what I hear." Cheryl could only laugh.

"And besides, you want this go to hell hat to stand out don't you? The darkened effect will make it noticeable and different."

That did it. Cheryl had been trying to remain composed, but with Mary's help and knowledge, she could only recall all the growth and experience that she had gained from the Robertson's. Her eyes moistened, but she recovered before a tear could leak down her cheek.

"Incidentally, I am proud to go through this transition with you, Cheryl. You have learned so much and done so well. Bob and I are extremely proud of you."

"I know Marty is jealous."

They laughed.

"Will you ever give my son an even shake?"

They laughed again and a tear rolled down Cheryl's cheek along with a slight sniff. They continue to wipe the chemicals to the surface and rub them in. Afterwards, they took turns working the torch as they moved around the miner.

With great fan fare and ceremony the prairie people and the bronco were loaded up on separate flatbed trailers. The bronco was lifted with the overhead crane high enough to the get a one ton dolly under the base. The statue was rolled over to the loading dock and on to the flat bed trailer. The astonished driver said, "I ain't never hauled anything like this before."

After the dolly was removed, an amazing group effort was under way. Wood supports from two by fours and two by sixes were set against the base and screwed into the trailer floor. A second layer was screwed on top of the first. The support would keep the base from sliding around during transport. The driver placed a moving blanket and some tie down straps across the base, so the horse and rider would not vibrate apart on the road trip. Three wood arch supports were tucked up under the belly of the bronco. One ran from behind the base to behind the front legs on the belly. A second ran from behind the base to the middle of the belly. The third one ran from behind the base up to the back legs. Each wood support was cut to fit the contour of the belly of the horse. Moving pads and blankets were used to cover the supports, so they would not mar the statue or rub against the patina.

The statue of the prairie people was given the same treatment, but it did not require as much extra support as the bronco. A hundred photos were taken for scrap books and the foundry wall of fame. In the excitement of the picture taking, Molly laughed when she heard Bob say to Mary, "Once we get back home tonight, I am going to tie you up like this." Plans were made to load the company truck with the welder, some touch up patina, and the roofing torch for the installation Saturday.

That afternoon the Robertson's held a meeting. They explained to their employees that they had found a building in a small town on the west side of the Colorado Rockies south of Grand Junction. They planned to relocate after the last two projects in Minturn were completed. Bob and Mary visited with each employee and invited them to move to the western slope to work in the new foundry. Everyone had the opportunity to remain an employee, if they could manage to move.

Friday the miner was loaded in back of the Robertson's forest green pick up. Cheryl's crew lashed him down face up on the dunnage and blankets for his ride to the museum. The crew looked over the vehicle. The coils and springs were flattened. They were maxed out.

Mark had an observation about the tires. "Those are definitely May Pop tires. I have experienced them before." Everyone shared a couple of laughs. The conditions would require a slow drive to the museum. Pictures were taken for the record. The miner looked as if he was riding home drunk in the back of the pickup.

The truck was hard to control. Patience and a safe low speed would be required with all the winding curves and switchbacks. Eight hundred pounds of weight would make the truck impossible to control if the position of the statue changed. A hard brake or a sharp swerve would induce the load shift. Max was watching downhill and he verified a car headed uphill, toward the curve in front of him, at a high rate of speed. He put his foot lightly on the brake and left it there. The car cut the centerline all of the way around the curve. Max slowed using the brake lightly. He moved to the very edge of the road to avoid a collision. He pushed the horn loud and long, but the horn was dead. He did hear a loud staccato blast from Cheryl's truck behind him. *Stay way from my miner!* The approaching vehicle swerved away from the center of the road. It missed the front bumper of the Robertson's truck by a few feet.

Max monitored the drop of the front right tire off the edge of the road. It did not dig into the shoulder but bounced back up onto the asphalt. His speed was slow enough for the sharp turn. The rear tire would get the most abuse. Thankfully, it did not blow. No doubt it lost some air.

Everyone in the statue convoy was greatly relieved when they reached the bottom of the pass road. Cheryl and Nash honked their horn as they raced ahead to the phone bank at the laundromat. Cheryl would call Danny.

His father answered. "He is in the garage. I will tell him about thirty minutes."

Nash called his brother who alerted several individuals selected to serve as the installation crew.

The trucks pulled into the small maintenance parking area beside the side door. Max thanked Cheryl and Nash for the horn alert to the careless driver.

"Nash had a premonition that something was going to go wrong, so we started watching downhill for speeders and the usual sloppy drivers."

The installation crew showed up. They unloaded their coolers and placed grocery bags beside them. The grocery bags held your normal everyday working man's lunch. A pile of thick leather gloves appeared next to the bags.

Rob Gage met Mark and Nash at the side door entrance as the installation crew gathered around the miner.

"We can't get the miner through this door. You will have to go through the front entrance." The front entrance was terraced up the hillside. It would require the crew to carry the statue up a flight of forty steps. No one wanted to take the miner up the steps. Rather than launch into a lengthy discussion of the facts, Nash met Rob's excited gaze as straight as an arrow. "Okay, Mr. Gage. We will move the truck around to the front. It will take about ten minutes. We should have the statue at the front door in about twenty minutes. Is it unlocked?"

"I'll pick up the keys and meet you there." Rob returned down the hall to his office. He searched his office desk and sport coat pocket for the keys to the museum doors.

Mark and Nash exchanged smiles. "He may know all about the mines, but he don't know much about double door entrances." Nash and Mark were on the double door entrance in a flash armed with two phillips screw drivers and a five pound sledge hammer. The metal divider in the middle of the double door was removed in a jiffy. The difficult task was in front of them.

They decided to carry the miner horizontal and face up. There was plenty of room for crew members around the shoulders and the head. There was room for only three bodies to lift at the base. Two of the crew made up for the imbalance by holding up the legs. Eight people would have a slippery one hundred pounds to hold. Extra crew members would be close by for assistance.

They reviewed the safety plan. "If you hear any pops or cracks it is a weld. We will have to look at the weld. If we set the statue down, we will only set the base down on the floor. If there is no major damage, then we will march on. If you get a cramp or get tired, then speak up, and one of the extra hands will take your place. Don't wait until you lose your strength. Let someone else take your place. There is no shame here. Only our safety matters. When we encounter a problem, all discussion will be brief, and done at a low volume. Is everyone ready? Okay, let's get 'er done."

The miner was lifted from the truck and carried out over the tailgate. The distance between the hand steel and the hammer was greater than the door. It was obvious to everyone that the arms would fit through if they were on a diagonal from the bottom left corner to the right top corner of the entrance. One quarter of a turn was applied to the statue and a second attempt to breach the entrance to the museum was made. The reach was still a foot too long.

A second short discussion ensued and the statue was slightly angled to the entrance. The hand steel easily slipped through the door at the top corner. The crew shuffled forward and carefully bounced off one another. Now the hammer hand had to clear the entrance. The base would have to be higher and the head and arms would have to go higher as well. Inside, the hand steel touched the ceiling tile. Mark had his eye on the situation and spoke up. "Push the spike through the ceiling tile!" It lifted the white tile, the statue slowly rose another foot and the hammer bumped around the entrance into the corridor. The crew exchanged cheers with one another for their success. They were inside the museum. Clearly the base crew was bearing the brunt of the torture and they called for a break. Moving blankets were placed on the floor and the miner was lowered to rest. Sodas and chips were passed around. The sandwiches and beer would be later. No harm was done to the ceiling.

Rob remained at the front doors for ten minutes. No vehicle had appeared. He checked down the street. Nothing. Inside the building he heard a faint pounding on metal. He quickly retraced his steps to the side door. He arrived just as the statue was midway through the entrance. He was miffed because someone had pulled a fast one on him, but he did not speak of his displeasure. He wondered how they moved the statue inside.

The hard part was over. The installation crew was one hundred feet from the lobby, just one more move down the hall. In the lobby the miner was lowered to the moving blankets placed on the floor. The installation crew took a long break and discussed at length how they would raise and set the miner vertically.

Cheryl moved her carry all bag to the lobby. She had her pattern, the four posts, and the epoxy. Danny Duran parked his welding truck at the front steps to the museum. He uncoiled his one hundred fifty foot long lines up the steps to the lobby.

Cheryl placed the base pattern on the marble. With a magic marker, she dotted the marble four times at the exact locations for the holes to be drilled. She removed the pattern and placed it over the exposed end of the base. She marked the exact location on the four base anchors where Danny would braze the anchor posts. The four base anchors were flat metal bars, one inch thick. They were welded to the base. Cheryl and Danny huddled to discuss the number of posts to be used. They agreed that three posts would be the ideal number of holes to set the statue. Four would increase the likely hood that the posts would not line up with the holes. Danny mentioned that drill bits could not be used to widen a hole in hard marble. Cheryl understood and agreed to his reasoning. Danny assured her that the one inch thick metals anchors were sufficient. They broke from their huddle. He attached his ground wire and returned to his truck to double check his settings.

Ray Mendoza brought his own portable mine wall drill. He removed the drill from the carrying case and selected one bit from the three that he carried in the case. The bits were three feet long. The drill motor was the size of the motor end of a large chain saw. Max and Nash measured the thickness of the base. If Ray drilled the hole all the way through, then the epoxy filler would leak out. They used green duct tape to mark the drill bit with the desired length.

The anticipation grew as Ray drilled the holes. Danny brazed the posts to the anchors.

The installation crew held a brief safety meeting. It was agreed that they would have three verbal checks during the move. A verbal "Okay, go ahead." would be given once the statue was vertical. Anyone losing a grip or strength would speak up "Help me" and move back so that an extra member could take over the position. If for any reason they had to set the statue down, they would holler "Dunnage" and two railroad ties would be placed under the statue base, to protect the three new anchor posts. Cheryl would direct the fine tune movement of the posts to the holes. She stirred the epoxy mix in a plastic water pitcher. The crew holding the base put on their heavy gloves as the edge of eight hundred pounds would injure a hand. Four people actually held the edge of the base. Two others found holds on the front leg. Four extra crew members stayed in a circle behind those lifting the statue.

Wives and girl friends were taking pictures.

It was difficult to get the miner vertical. "Dunnage." The miner was set on the large railroad ties for a break. It was near impossible to pick the miner straight up in the air. Hand holds were scarce. There was not enough room for everyone to get a hand hold and the miner was difficult to balance. The statue moved slowly to the marble base and over it. Cheryl was stirring the epoxy mixture. She wondered how she would get between the legs of the installation crew. She directed the posts over the drill holes. The statue was lowered gently into the holes, in a painstaking match up. "Good. Lift it up. Okay, just scoot six inches toward the stairs, and I can fill up the holes now. Two holes were revealed and she filled them both halfway in less than seven seconds. "Okay. Move back a foot." She moved around the crew to the other side in a flash. "A little more." The third hole appeared and it was filled in the blink of an eye.

Everyone was anxious now. The pain would soon be over. Victory was on the threshold. It was time to slow down and not hurry. The only hazards left were squashed fingers and strained backbones. She lined the posts up once more and said, "Okay, set it down."

The crew lowered the miner to his marble base. He now stood proud and defiant in all of the sunlit glory of the lobby of the mining museum. Cheers and applause filled the lobby. More cameras came out to record the happy moment. Cheryl was ecstatic. In her excitement she congratulated Danny. He chuckled and said, "Wait till you see the bill." He smiled and winked at her. She looked for Max. Max saw their exchange. He smiled and winked at her.

Cindy spoke up, "Remember, Molly wants two pictures from four angles."

Poses were struck for group photos. The mood was festive. Excessive posing soon became the order and beers were opened over Rob's objection.

Cheryl and Max left for the bowling alley to celebrate. They bowled three games for some fresh entertainment and some new laughs. They refreshed the brown cows and moved to the Pac Woman table where Cheryl soundly defeated Max, three games out of four. They returned to 304 with no impending commitments for the weekend. Cheryl made plans to stay home and sew on her jumpsuit, and enjoy a lazy weekend. Max would put in a weekend on 407, and be available for anything Cheryl might decide to do. They enjoyed a relaxed atmosphere of the 3M's. Cheryl conversed in hushed tones to Max as he applied a soothing massage to her body.

"The closure of the foundry will be the first obstacle in life that we will overcome working side by side together. Right Max? See how easy it is? We are going to remain together for the rest of our lives and transition through these trivial trials without any sweat."

Early the next morning, Max had to figure out where he could splice in to the existing gas line system to add a new line to the forced air furnace under the stairs. The kitchen and dining room shared a wall space heater. It attached to the incoming gas line that ran beside the outside wall, all the way to the space heater in the living room. He could add a line at that point.

Inside the house, he disconnected the gas line connection to the wall space heater. He entered the thigh deep crawl space underneath the kitchen floor, through the trap door close to the window. Underneath the house, the 3/4 inch wall heater line ran across the back of the crawl space to a tee fitting on the incoming line. Max disconnected the 3/4 inch line at the tee fitting. Now, through the use of a second tee fitting, he could add new lines. He added a six inch length of black pipe into the tee on the incoming line. He placed a first class shut off valve on the end. He added another six inch pipe to the end of the shut off valve and placed a new tee on the end of it. The middle opening of the new tee pointed directly to the hole in the dining room that Cheryl opened up last weekend. He reconnected the 3/4 inch line to the kitchen wall heater that he had removed earlier.

He was able to pass ten foot lengths of black pipe gas line into the crawl space from outside of the house. The previous owner accessed the crawl space to lift the back half of the house and set it on a new foundation. A nice hole already existed. All Max had to do was breakthrough the accumulated snow and ice. The hole was there for him. He easily passed the pipe to the crawl space.

He fished the new pipe to the two holes that Cheryl helped him with in the dining room. He attached the pipe to the new tee on the wall space heater line. He cut another hole in the floor right beside the furnace, where the new line would come up from the crawl space. He used elbow fittings to connect the lines and he finished up late that afternoon.

Max called it a day and returned home to give Cheryl his love and attention. He had struggled with he urge to leave the remodel effort early in the afternoon, but he managed to work until six. He was in a great mood. There was a smile on his face. His back and shoulder blade felt bruised from the head and the hat, but it had not slowed him down. They would share another week together without deadline fever, or anxiety, or sleepless nights. He parked on Spruce Street and walked to the house. Her truck was not in the car port. He made a hasty sandwich, grabbed a soda, and moved to the beauty of the living room with the big bay window. When he walked through the dining room, he noticed that the sewing machine was gone. That was odd. Max began to get suspicious. He set the sandwich and soda down on the TV table and went up stairs to the bedroom. The oil lamp, her notebook and the instruction manual were not on the on the chest. Her clothes were no longer in the closet. Oh, **no!** His mind reeled as if he had been hit by a bus. She had moved! He looked into the storage area under the stairs. Her art materials and easel were gone. Max turned mentally and physically nauseous at the same time. He had suffered three separations before, but this one was going to hurt. The cold he felt was deep. All of the good times and feelings would disappear and the memory of them would drain him mentally and physically.

Two or three times in his life, Max experienced what he was now feeling. He knew with certainty that this moment and the decision were important, and he had made that decision. Now it was time to act. His future and the rest of his life would be spent with Cheryl Prichard. It would impact and change his life. Their lives. Why get angry? You have to give her everything. What was to be mad about? Nothing. He had to drop everything and move to Arvada. Where would he live in Arvada? With the Pritchard's? That was not the issue at hand. It was time for him to move in the new direction. Get things in order. Why procrastinate? They would find each other in Arvada. Drop everything and move to her side. He could never live alone again.

Max, he told himself, you need to brace up and get a spine. This is all about going through the door. It is all about the relative wind and the transition. If you keep this thought foremost in your tiny little mind, you will make it through this initial phase.

Hold your arch! Have faith! Soon you will be face to earth in the stable freefall with Cheryl. He finally retreated to the sofa to collapse. As he picked up his soda and sandwich on the TV table he noticed a page from her notebook at the side of the TV.

"Max, it was difficult for me to do this. I could not bear to tell you. Please get to Arvada as fast as you can. We can share what began two months ago for the rest of our lives. Love, Cheryl."

He sat in the sofa and opened his mind and heart to the setting in front of him and relaxed. How could he ever leave this view? Did he love the view more than anything else in the world? He would still be able to share it with Cheryl. It was still here. Only a short commute was required. He was so selfish. He looked into the chest storage area underneath the window. Maybe half of the molds were missing.

Accept it, Max. You have known for almost two weeks. Cheryl figured out what she has to do. She is an adult and she has to provide for herself. Arvada is the obvious answer. That is why she harped on you about Arvada and the marriage proposal. With the exception of being on one knee with a ring, Cheryl had proposed. Did he make an offer to provide for her? He did make it clear that he would marry her, but he did not ask Cheryl to stay in Leadville. Would she stay here and live off his meager income? She might, if she was married with a partnership in the rentals. Did he make that suggestion? Did he offer it to her? No. He talked about a pre nup as if it was funny. If he put himself in her place, it would have angered him. Gosh, he was so selfish.

Max found a pen on the TV table and returned to the sofa. He turned the letter over and he began to write down his thoughts. He began to figure out the things he had to do right away. There were only five. Visit or call Lilly at Lake County Realty to find a renter. Type up the prenuptial agreements. Find a wedding band for the engagement. Move everything out of 304 to 407. Pack the car and go. He folded her letter and put it in his billfold. He went to the office room and flipped the light and the computer on. The message light on the answering machine blinked at him. It was a message from Cheryl.

"Max, I have to keep the pay checks coming in. I left the TV and the long couch for you. I hope you do not use them with anyone but me. If you do, and I find out about it, I will shoot you with my 38. I have friends that will be monitoring your activities, so you had better be a good boy. You have your houses to do. Get them done and then come join us in Arvada as soon as you can. We can work together again. We can visit Leadville on the weekends. Who could ask for more, Max? Millions of people would like to be able to have mini vacation to the mountains for just the cost of gasoline. Hey! Stay off the bottle. If you give in, it would be okay to cry in one beer. Max, be a sport and bring the couch and the work bench when you have a chance. Caio baby!"

He pulled up the word processor and typed up the pre nuptial agreements. When he finished, he dialed Lilly's number and left a message that he was looking for a renter for 304 West Seventh. Now two things were out of the way.

He sat in front of the bay window that evening. He realized that his mind was acting as if Cheryl had totally left him. It was the normal human condition. Take the easy way out where you feel sorry for yourself. Let everything slide, until you no longer choose to do anything to resolve the unfortunate situation. He realized that she still loved him and was still with him. She had to cut out on him. It kind of made him mad. It definitely forced his hand, but it was nothing to get hysterical about. He had to calm down. His mind was playing games with him. Max, you and Cheryl are still together. Take a deep breath and dive through the door to Arvada.

Saturday night Max slept alone. He missed the new bubble in his life. The house felt empty. The next morning, he felt as if he awakened to the cruel ending of the most promising dream in his life. He had been happy. He had been genuinely loved. Max intended to keep the dream alive.

He arrived at 407 early the next morning. He told himself that he was happy and content and that he needed to finish his project. He worked on 407 all day with a raging fury. He put down the new flooring in both bathrooms. Upstairs he installed the sink cabinet and the sink, the tub, and the commode. Downstairs he installed the kitchen counter across the top of the floor cabinets. Next he installed the kitchen sink, the bathroom sink, and the frame work for the shower. He installed the faucet fittings for all of the sinks, the tub, and the shower. The only thing left was to hook up the water connections to the faucets on the sinks, the tub, the shower, and the commodes. Once he had the shower faucets hooked up he could close the water line cupboard and install the plastic wall inserts for the shower and the tub. Only the best for his renters.

CHAPTER THIRTY FOUR

Monday morning Max soloed to the foundry. The wind blew the dinosaur off the hood. He muttered, "Damn, now I have no one to guide me." At the same moment a shabby pickup truck barreled around a turn over the centerline towards Max. He swerved immediately to the edge of the road and the wheels on the passenger side dropped over. He was wide awake now.

Mary caught him sneaking in the front door fifteen minutes late.

"Max. Glad you are here. We received some compliments over the weekend from Leadville on the majesty of Cheryl's miner! The museum lobby is magnificent. Cindy brought photos back for Molly and the foundry. We printed them up Saturday. I know how proud you are to be a part of the whole project."

"I sure am Mary. Cheryl might be up from Arvada later today. I don't know for sure."

"Cheryl explained everything to me before you left Friday. She told me that her parents needed her desperately this week. Bob and I prepared in advance and we have some on call hired hands from the front range in here this week. They sleep at our house or here. We need your help. Marty has a couple of projects for you. They need some assistance on the jazz trio. He will give you all the particulars."

Max nodded, "All right. Mary, I would like to join Cheryl and her parents as soon as possible. I can work this week if you need me, but I may take off next week for the front range."

"We figured that. We need you this week Max. I will have more help next week."

"Okay Mary. Talk to you later." He stepped in the wax room to greet Molly and get a lift in spirit from her.

"Hey, Max. What a Friday, huh? We heard you almost ran off the highway! The pictures are on the shelf. My gosh, what a sight that Hector is! Tell Cheryl, job well done. How is your shoulder, by the way?"

"It is about fifty per cent better. I will pass the kind words to Cheryl."

Max was soon involved with work. His thoughts that day lingered on Cheryl's departure. He felt the world for her. The thought of the ring entered his mind again. He had to come up with something. Where would he go? Vail? Frisco? Leadville? Silverthorne? There were plenty of places to shop, but it made no sense to him to go alone. He would not pick anything out. He really wanted to go with Cheryl, together.

Early Monday evening back at the house, Max was on the small patio enjoying the cool evening breeze, and the view of the Collegiate Peak Range. A few snow banks were left on the peaks. He was on his second beer when he recognized the mute distant ring of the phone. He ran up the steps. The recorder picked up and he heard Cheryl's voice.

Max was elated. His heart was pounding. Had he told Cheryl I love you enough? He picked up the phone and said, "You need to know that I tell the moon and the stars every night of my love for you." His short sniff followed.

"That is good, Max."

"I am so glad to hear from you. Thank you for leaving the message and the note. They saved me from going over the edge mentally."

"I was worried that you might become a hacker."

"Cheryl, you dumped me and blew out of here like a whirlwind. I feel like a wood ice cream stick on the side of the highway that some snot nosed kid threw out the window of a speeding car five years ago."

Cheryl laughed. "Max, everything is great here. We are in Arvada tonight to clean up and take a half day off tomorrow while we get the two trucks loaded up with dry wall. The body odor after two days is a little tough, but . . ."

"I could give you sponge baths."

"Yes you could, you big galoot. When would you like to schedule the next sponge bath? Max, visualize a steady pay check and a good one at that. We could commute back and forth to Leadville on the weekends where I can attack you. You could howl into the night. How does that sound to you?"

"Is that a proposal?"

"Yes. Finally! You have picked up on my hints. I was beginning to get worried. I thought you might not propose! Nash drove by your house and said that you were on the patio drinking."

"It really is lonely and cold here without you."

"What are you doing now?"

"Typing up a two prenuptial agreements and looking for a renter."

"How thoughtful! At least you are moving in the right direction. How is your back? You know, I could massage your back if you were down here. Is it going to happen?"

"Yes. I wanted it to be a surprise. Give me a week." They kissed good bye and hung up.

See Max? She has not left you. She loves you. It is the path that you must accept. It is not going to be your way. It is going to be the highway. Time to rejoin society. He pulled the letter from his bill fold. He read the back where he had listed things to do. His phone rang. It must be phone your friend night.

"Max, there are rumors flying all over town that the foundry closed. Are you alright? What is going on?"

"Sue, so nice of you to call. I have been extremely despondent and I have been thinking of calling you, so I could chase you around your living room."

"Terrific. We have been upset with you ever since you abandoned us at the Tenth Mountain Reunion way back when. If you want to get together, leave a message on our answering machine and we will work something out. Okay, Max? We all love you!"

"Thank you, Sue. I will be in touch." Again, he read Cheryl's note. He kissed it and returned it to his wallet.

Like time going backwards, shifted into reverse. He was listless, adrift, nothing of importance, all of those incredibly mind numbing things or mind nothing things. What was life now?

His mind accepted that he was moving to the door. He could feel the open door. It was the right door, and the right thing to do. His life would change. He would become a better person. He was going to make the transition. He felt he would be welcomed in Arvada. He felt joy for it, and hoped that the time would come to pass very soon. He had a skydiving buddy and she was a beautiful female. They shared the same working interests, the same philosophies, the same recreational pursuits. What more could you ask for? Why not work together, and be married?"

In the middle of the week, Max listened to a message from Lilly. "I have a renter for you. Her name is Mary Ross. She has one dog, an Irish setter. She is staying at a house off Highway 285. She does not have a phone. I will give her your number and you two can find out if this is going to work out. Or I could tell her that you will be over this afternoon at two o'clock, if I hear from you. She said that would be a good time."

They met Thursday evening. Mary was from Grosse Pointe, Michigan. Only the finest genetic make up in the USA. No worry about the rent. She won a sexual harassment suit from Public Service of Colorado. Her parents are rich and famous. Max drove her to 304. She took the tour. They quickly agreed to ink a rental contract. She signed and handed Max a check from Public Service Credit Union, for six hundred dollars. She was floored with the view. The rest of the house was a little shabby in contrast to what she was used to. Max knew she was lying through her teeth and that she was lousy at it. He knew she was thirty one and living on a shoestring. She did have a valid motor vehicle license. She was not half the woman that Cheryl was. She claimed to be brilliant and financially responsible, yet she asked Max if he would move her things for her. Max could not believe it. Was he really a dupe or was it a signal, a premonition of the things to come with his rental property? Right now, he did not care. He had other matters on his mind. The rentals were going to be his retirement.

As he tried to fall sleep that night, his mind would not rest. One of the things Cheryl said was burning a hole in his head. "You will slide into your fifties and be a lonely old coot." He thought again about a ring. He remembered that Charlotte had a jewelry counter in front of her living room window. Maybe he would find something symbolic for now. He wanted to pick up one or two pair of coveralls for work. He would check with Charlotte at the Rose tomorrow. Another thought crossed his mind. If he made it to Arvada next week, he would be able to jump with Cheryl. He held that thought and finally drifted off to sleep.

He dreamed of a skydive with five jumpers. A six way round. Five moves were planned. Suddenly everyone was gone. Max was flying through the air. He checked his altimeter and saw the ground come up beneath him, like a pie in the face. He bounced. His bones shattered, the blood splattered, and everything went dark.

He sat bolt upright in bed. The alarm clock read three thirty. He decided to use the bathroom. He stumbled and cursed his way down the stairs. He looked in the mirror at his sad eyes. Where was the smile? The confident outgoing Max? He was still bouncing along the highway after being kicked off the bus. Soon he would come to rest in the ditch, a broken, deserted, homeless man. Stop it Max! You are having a meltdown. A mental meltdown. You are emotionally traumatized and your heart and mind are just too callused to realize just how devastating Cheryl's departure has been to you. What he needed to do was load up his car, get a good nights sleep, and go out in the morning with a hard arch, and a firm commitment to make the new transition. Pack the necessary clothes, gas the car, and oh, yes, the ring.

Friday, Karen gave Max a heads up phone call. "Hi, Max. Is Cheryl there?"

Max thought he heard her snicker. "Why, Karen, so nice of you to call. Cheryl is working in Arvada right now doing some drywall. Do you have the number there?"

"Max, we are one third of the way through the jump season.

Where have you been? We missed you. We thought you were going to be at the DZ this summer just like the good old days. We need somebody to entertain us and keep us in some good laughs."

"I will take that as a comment in the positive sense."

"I looked through my logbook yesterday. I found an entry that I have failed to complete. It is the day you showed up in April. Do you remember that, Four Eyes?" She went on. "I have this rectangle with a couple of dots in it. One of them is me, one of them is you, one of them is Sherry, and one of them is Cheryl." Max stiffened. "Max, Cheryl is coming in this weekend or next for her graduation jump. She is cleared to jump on her own. I wanted to make sure that you knew this."

"Eeeyeah. Karen, I appreciate you thinking of me and keeping me up to date. I hope all is well for you."

"Did you catch that last part, Four Eyes? A couple of the jumpers down here are hot for her. If you ever want to date her again you better show up. There will certainly be a big party at Bev's afterward. You like parties, don't you Max?"

"Of course . . ."

"Max, take a break and get down here to the DZ. You get on your projects and you can't see the light of day. You need to work on your social skills for awhile."

A light went on in his head. Karen. Karen is at the center of Cheryl's sudden departure. She and Cheryl were in cahoots. Karen was behind all of this. He let the thought go.

"Here we are Karen, and you are bold as ever. Would you please show a little respect for those of us who are suffering?

"Max, always the funny man. Listen, you have been gone too long. You do not know what is going on around here. You think you have Cheryl all sewn up?"

"Could you back off just a little? There is no need to come on so strong. It has all been pretty fast here lately."

"Isn't it always?"

"To be truthful with you, I have come to the same conclusion and I am taking steps to get to Arvada, and your precious drop zone."

"Max, just remember, you never really know how much you messed up until the object of your desire is gone. Isn't that right? Am I right Max? Are you listening to me? Don't clam up on me!"

"You are right, of course. How could I be so thick headed? I will be to the drop zone Karen. I will be looking for you. Take care, Karen, and thank you for all of your work with Cheryl." Max hung up the phone.

He called the Pritchard's and left the phone number for 407. He also left the number for Lake County Realty. Lilly would relay messages for them if need be. Once again Max borrowed Donald Mac Donald's truck. Over the weekend he moved everything from 304 into the two story up on East 5th. Max would help move Mary Ross, for free of course. He moved Mary's things into 304, and she moved in Sunday. She set up a funny looking fenced in area next to the house for her dog. Monday, he would be certain to transfer all of the utilities into her name.

He headed for Charlotte's jewelry counter. Charlotte was an attractive lady in her mid fifties. She worked to keep her black flowing hair presentable. They walked to the glass counter in the front room. She stood behind the counter.

"Give me the big, gaudy, cheap looking one."

"You have always been a big joker, haven't you Max? Who is this ring for? Are you buying an engagement ring for Cheryl?"

Just the sound of the question made his breathing and heart rate go up a notch. Unable to think of a stupid, quick quip, he answered with the truth.

"Yes, Charlotte. I am."

"Well, then let's pick out the best one here. I will help you just this one time. It's about time you two got hitched. That was a pretty fast courtship. You two must have hit it off pretty good. Is this your first marriage?"

"This is my sixth."

"I got a washer and dryer back in the garage. I been savin' it for you."

Max did not care if she had said that to her last dozen customers.

"Put my name on it. Say Charlotte, do you have any jumpsuits? Coveralls, work suits, you know for painters, or construction work?"

They found two in a pile of work clothes that fit him. Charlotte had them up stairs in the men's section. "Thank you Charlotte for everything that you do for us. You and Charlie are awesome! I know you keep all of the skiers in decent clothes." Max made out a check to Second Hand Rose, and he included the price of the washer and dryer and a decent tip.

"You might give Cheryl a little bit of time before you start a family. She mentioned she had some ideas for two or three more projects.

"She is back in Arvada right now with the drywall business."

"Well, that was kind of sudden. Everyone in town is waiting to see her statue. The museum isn't open just yet. They say it will be next week." I haven't seen her in a while, so you be sure to tell her I said hello."

"Will do, Charlotte. Max hugged her and kissed her."

Charlotte turned a cheek to him just in time. Charlie walked in. "You messin' with my woman?"

"It's a small town Charlie, you know how it goes."

"There is the Max I know. What are you up to, buddy?"

"Gonna get hitched, Charlie. I reckon you two are the first to know. Don't tell anybody now. It is supposed to be a surprise."

Charlotte laughed. "You know us Max. We won't tell a soul, will we Charlie?"

Half the town would know within the hour.

"Max, just a minute. I have a couple of little jewelry boxes here."

"Could you spare a business card? I want to fold it and fit it in the box."

"Charlie and I think you two will make a good couple. You tell Cheryl to stop by."

"I will tell her."

He typed a two line message to Cheryl. He stated that the ring was symbolic and they would find one together some day. He tore the paper to a manageable size and folded it, so it would fit easily in the ring box. He included the card from Second Hand Rose. He scotch taped the ring box and put it in the manila envelope with the pre nups. He placed the envelope in a plastic bag and hid it inside a dry wall mud bucket that was half full. Hopefully, the envelope would be discovered. His plan was a little bit loose right now. He would try to perfect it. At least he finally had one.

Max loaded up the Meteor. He had all of the important things. His parachute, a weeks worth of clothes, the prenuptial agreements, enough peanut butter and jelly to last a week, bread, oatmeal, a few select tools, and all of his camping gear.

He wondered how offensive this temporary ring would be. Oh, foolishness. It was not like he had six months to get everything figured out and prepare for all of this. It was better to do something than nothing at all. Offending someone sometimes sparked verbal confrontation and fencing. All Max had to do was to ready himself with his usual jokes and his childish reaction. He could redirect the flow and everyone would come out laughing with a workable agreement. Just the thought made him happy.

Get on with the transition. Get the wheels rolling and don't forget the gas.

CHAPTER THIRTY FIVE

He found the directions from Cheryl's message on the answering machine. It included some positive encouragement and the exact directions including street names to the job site at Chief Hosa. He wrote them down and stuck the paper in his wallet, along with some gas money. She left a few suggestions for the air mattress and clothing. The tools and the tent would be optional. He would stop at the grocery store and pick up two five gallon jugs of water, one for washing and one for thirst.

He left a manila folder for Lilly with Cheryl's phone number and how to get in touch with him. He included a letter that he would be gone for three weeks. He would be at the Arvada number every three days or so to check messages. He promised to call her once a week just to check in. Finally he was on his way to meet Cheryl and her parents. Max thanked the Lord.

Under a clear blue sky, he worked his way along the twisting highways that allowed views of the mountains, the river below, and the rail road tracks that ran beside the river. The granite boulders played peek a boo in the pines and spruce. A large curve in the interstate provided a splendid view of the Continental Divide, in the distance, forty miles away. Take the off ramp up to the right. Go on to the winding two lane blacktop service road and through the subdivision entrance. Become lost in the thick red pines. Roll down into a huge green open field bounded by a jutting granite hillside. Nice digs. Go around the hillside into a four square mile opening.

What was once a family farm or horse ranch for over one hundred years had been cut up because of estate tax purposes. These were original homesteads that had been in the family for one hundred and fifty years, four or more generations. The theft of the great estates inside the foothills had been going on for seventy years now.

When he pulled in the drive he found no one at the house. No doubt they were in the big city catching a shower and materials. Max felt great. His nagging conscious had been quelled. He was confident, but he had a small case of the nerves. He was going to greet the folks today, and prove his work ethic and performance to them. He would give it some thought and be ready to go. To pass the time he decided to engage in one of his favorite pastimes and that was setting up his tent. He began to blow up the mattress and he recalled the night at Mount Sopris. Oh my. He was close to heaven once more. He looked forward to the Pritchard's return.

The Pritchard's arrived early the next morning. Max heard their truck and he waited at the end of the driveway, next to the patio behind the house. The Pritchard's saw the tent in the back yard and suspicious eyes were cast in his direction.

Hal was happy to see the help. "Let's get this drywall moved inside." He unlocked the sliding glass patio door and they quickly moved the drywall inside, as the women unloaded the rest of the material. "Glad to see you. We have a big project here." They moved half of the drywall into the living room and the other half went upstairs into a large bedroom.

Max mentioned to Cheryl, in passing, that he brought all of her camping gear. Little time was spent on conversation. Everyone went right to work like pigs running for the trough.

Marilyn stared at him and finally questioned. "So, Max, how long are you here for? Just a day or two?"

"I could be here for the duration."

"Ha! I bet you don't last a day. I got a hundred dollars right here says you will be gone by tomorrow."

"I got you covered. Who is holdin' the money?"

Hal and Max were busy butting the sheets of dry wall together. Cheryl and Hal screwed them to the wall while Max held them in place. Marilyn readied her banjo. The tool held a roll of tape and just enough mud and moisture that the tape could be pulled and lined up to cover the unsightly edges where the drywall met.

Working with Hal and Marilyn required that things be done to a certain level of perfection. Max had always been a quick fixer to save time and money. Now he had to suck it up and strive for perfection on the taping and the mud sculpture. It was upon him to spread the mud over the tape covering the butt joints of the drywall. Max found a wall where the tape work was dry. He smoothed mud over Marilyn's tape work from a day or two ago with an eight inch drywall knife. He made every effort to cover the tape so carefully, that a critic could not discern anything but a smooth wall. He opened a new bucket and added a little water. He used an electric mixer on the concoction to mix the mud to a smooth texture.

Marilyn was an accomplished banjo operator, the fastest west of the Mississippi. She decided to razz Max a little bit.

"Can you speed it up there a little, Max? You are just a slow puppy dog. You are a disgrace to our blue ribbon team."

"As in Pabst?"

"As in excellence."

"I will have you know that I am the m, e, in teamwork."

"Oh Hal! Did you hear that?"

"I feel his pain."

"Well, you got a machine instrument that muds the tape automatically for you."

"You are just a slacker. You are just a natural born, slow worker."

"No, I go for my quality work as opposed to your pathetic, sloppy, fast efforts. And in case you didn't notice, I just opened a new bucket and smoothed out the mud."

"That doesn't count."

They continued to work silently. Max was minding his own business. He knew everyone wanted to talk. He was enjoying the quiet. It would not be long until everyone would be interrupting one another. Be patient.

Marilyn was the first one to break the silence. "Max. You have been awfully quiet over there all by yourself. You have not said a blooming thing."

"You should be grateful."

"What are you thinking?"

"You know, this shore is some purty country. I used to hunt an awful lot of grizzly bear, back in the day with Bill Cody. This country is a lot differnt nowadays. Take this here house fer instance. This house is going to be up for sale within three years because all of these new subdivisions are filling up with people from back east. They bring their big family money out here, and they buy these houses, these damned dream cabins that are way too big to live in, and after they have been here for a year, they begin to figure out that they are really out in the boonies. There is only one convenience store for miles. They have a few neighbors, but the neighbors don't know how big and important the new folk is. They have this false superficial need to be recognized and be known and respected. So what do they do? Do you know what they do Marilyn?"

"No. What do they do?"

"I didn't think so. They go back home to all of the in laws and outlaws, to satisfy some preconceived notion that everyone back there knows who they are, and what big shots they are."

"Oh Hal! Did you hear that?"

"All of a sudden they are in a brand new subdivision development with no convenience store, no gas station, no little church chapel, no anything, and they find out that they can't stand to talk to the wild life for company or companionship. All they have is the TV and the satellite link or cable. Most of them can not handle the loneliness. Eventually, they will sell out and return to the populated areas, or to the family community where they felt part of something, and had friends and someone to talk to.

Hal interrupted, "Could somebody shut that blabber mouth off? Cheryl, do you know how to turn this blabber mouth off?"

"You wanted the extra help."

Max continued on undeterred. "And of course everyone wants to live in the mountains, but it is just too much seclusion for them. They just stay indoors and play bridge or watch TV. They don't do nothin' outdoors. Out doors is only for scenery looking, not participation. They talk their kids to movin' out here, but they ain't no jobs. One day they all pack up and go back east of the Mississippi.

A blob of drywall mud that just barely missed Max's left ear, splattered on the wall in front of him.

"I could have knocked you out. The next one is going to hit the back of your head if you do not shut up." Hal could fling a glob of dry wall mud across the room with incredible accuracy. You could hear it whiz past your ear if he missed the back of your head.

Max could hear movement and shuffling behind him, but he willed himself not to turn around. He was not afraid of anyone.

Marilyn resumed her chatter. "Max, you look so professional in your coveralls that I hardly recognized you."

"Why, thank you Marilyn. That is so kind of you to say so. I have a tape measure and a marking pencil in my pocket, along with a utility knife. I wanted to get the suit embroidered on the back, you know, like the kids do with their jeans these days. Maybe something like, 'Hal and Marilyn's Dry Wall Team.'"

"You mean, Marilyn and Hal's."

"I saw these two tourists yesterday at the Davis Donut shop. They were wearin' cut off jean shorts. One had 'Hot Stuff' embroidered right on her ass. Her sister had 'Fine Ass' embroidered on hers. I wanted to marry both of them right there."

"You could get 'Dumb Ass' embroidered on your suit."

Cheryl and Marilyn opened up a fresh bucket of drywall mud and moved it closer to Max.

"We have been pretty good to you, haven't we Max? I mean cutting you in, a total stranger so to speak." They had moved the mud bucket a little closer to him. Max was facing the wall minding his own business and doing his best to ignore them at the moment.

He could hear movement again and suspected something was at hand. He figured that his luck may have run away. "My life seems more complete to me now. It seems more professional. Here I am with a blue ribbon team. I need to take pride and perfection in my work. Before, it was just remodel and repair, with time and money saving short cuts. This all seems to be faster and smoother when you are part of a team." He needed to say something irritating and annoying, some kind of emotional insult that would trigger rage, and get the juices flowing. It a very calm hollow voice that echoed lightly off the walls he said, "It will be tough for you to keep up with me. I will not make fun of you though." Max continued to blade. His eyes and mind focused on what he was doing.

"Oh, Hal, did you hear what Max said? Isn't he brilliant?

"I can feel his pain."

Marilyn added, "Well, Max, how do you like drywall now?" The women loaded their hands with globs of dry wall mud. Max knew they were right behind him. He knew his time was up. Someone wanted retribution. Apparently, the old score remained uneven in someone's mind.

Cheryl joined in the conversation. "Do you remember the night at our house when you volunteered to do the dishes?"

That was it. Here it comes. Max loaded his knife with mud and moved his foot back a half step to spin around. The time was at hand. He was going to get his beating, and he had no current health insurance for any unforeseen consequence. He let loose a laugh. "You mean the one when I sprayed the black widers with the bug juice?"

The mud flew before Max could spin and engage them. They hit the back of his head and his back. Mud flew past him and splashed on the new drywall. Max could not help but laugh. Should he turn and throw himself into the foray? Or should he give them the lecture. It wasn't fair. The whole thing was not fair. They snuck up on him and attacked him from behind.

"You cheated. That's the kind of people you are. You snuck up behind me. You attacked me from behind. That is the coward's way. Without any warning, you slung your filthy mud at me. You are cowards. Both of you."

They dug into their buckets for another assault.

"Let him have it, Cheryl. Show him that you love him!"

He turned around and caught a line drive from Hal. Even Hal was flinging the mud at him and laughing about it.

"That's alright though. I understand that y'all are anxious to have a lot of fun and everything. If you stop now, I promise that I will not retaliate. I will not try to get even. I know what it is like and how much fun you are having. It sure is hard to stop ain't it?"

Hal pulled his camera out. The intensity of the mud flinging increased along with the verbal disrespect and the laughter. Max looked like a spotted owl. They launched another salvo that hit him in the chest, the fore head, the cheek, and one eye of his glasses. Now he looked like a spotted cow. He dropped his dry wall knife. He stretched out his arms and declared for all to hear. "Hallelujah, I am loved!"

They charged him and he stumbled to the ground to play dead and give up. That was the visual time out when he was a kid, growing up east of the Mississippi, but not with these people. It was the wrong thing to do. The women smeared mud on his coveralls.

Marilyn hollered, "That's right! It looks like the shoe is on the other foot."

Marilyn and Cheryl were laughing and screaming. They smeared the back of his head and neck. They smeared his brand new jumpsuit. They were a well honed machine of destruction. Woe unto him who stood in their way.

"Aw, Max, your brand new jump suit has mud on it! How did that happen? Get another bucket Cheryl!"

"Okay! That's enough now. I will give you one more chance to stop your foolishness before someone gets hurt." He had to back them off. He jumped up and pounced for their bucket of ammunition. The women ran for another. He was wet and ten pounds heavier. Max took on the demeanor of a slow moving mud monster, a giant among sheet rockers.

"Franken Muddy mad!" He loaded both hands with mud and he began to chase the girls with small monster steps. He was clowning more for the camera, while he played Franken Muddy. "I'm Franken Muddy, the drywall professional!"

"Get that embroidered on your ass!" Cheryl found a bucket with the lid pried half way off. She tossed the lid and looked inside. She pulled out a plastic bag with a manila folder and a white cardboard ring box. Cheryl handed the envelope to Marilyn and opened the box. "Holy moly! It's a rock! It's a ring. It's a ring! It's for me! It's for me!"

The mud throwing was temporarily interrupted.

"It's for me! It's for me!" Cheryl screamed. "I love you Max! Let's get married now!" Cheryl smiled and laughed. Moisture was in her eye. She looked at the Second Hand Rose business card. She turned it over. Love was in her heart.

Charlotte had written, "Good luck, Cheryl" on the back.

She hopped up and down. Franken Muddy hopped up and down. "Whoop, whoop, whoop!" Like an insane mud monster he hopped around the stack of dry wall in the living area. Cheryl hugged Marilyn and ran to Max. She bumped flat into him and almost knocked him over. Max took two steps back and they wrapped arms, pressed stomachs and chests, faces, and lips. Hal kept taking a picture now and then.

Marilyn read the note. "Cheryl! It is a cubic zirconia! Here is a note that says he is sorry for the zirconia. I'm telling you, this guy is gonna be apologizing all of his life. You will never get any of the things that he promised you, except for the apology." Max wanted to throttle Marilyn, but he knew she was kidding.

Marilyn read the pre nup agreements. "Hey! This is a pre nuptial agreement on his rental property!"

They read the cover letter.

"In the event of marriage between Cheryl Prichard and Maxwell Mason the title to the following property, is to remain in sole ownership of Maxwell Mason."

Marilyn uttered, "You selfish bastard."

Hal tore the flap off a cardboard box to use as a writing board and he quickly produced a pen as the girls read the pre nups aloud. One has to be able to produce a pen, paper, and a calculator at any moment in the construction business. Hal was tuned and knowledgeable to formalities, yet he had his own character and demeanor when dealing with contractors and customers.

Hal began to laugh. "Who has to change Cheryl? You got him wrapped around your little finger and the po' boy is so confused, he is pissing all over hisself like a puppy? Was that what you said?" Hal cast the order eyes at Cheryl. "You better sign it now." Hal handed Max the art pre nup. He eyed Max. "Don't look at me like that, Mr. Mud Ball. I'm on your side right now, and I sign your paycheck!"

Cheryl did not miss a beat. She grabbed the pen and signed it.

"Ha! There you are Max! Do you know what is going on here, boy? We are married!" She handed him the pen and Max signed her pre nup that he had no rights to her artwork or proceeds.

"I am not going to fall for your cheap ploy! You thought this would scare me away didn't you. Marry me Max! Now!"

Much to her surprise, Max jumped through the door of no return. He fell to his knees and begged Cheryl to marry him.

"Cheryl. Here I am. I am on my knees begging you to marry me in front of your mother and father. Just like I begged you last week. What's the holdup?"

They all start laughed. He looked so ridiculous.

"I bought this ring to be symbolic of the one you will wear. We will find that one together. Marry me Cheryl. Cast aside your selfish ways and your bitter resentment. I want to live with you for the rest of your life."

"Atta boy Max! I knew you would come around. I will marry you."

Hal pressed the button again and caught Cheryl and Max smeared together, kissing in front of her mom and step dad. The greatest step dad in the world.

Marilyn continued her rant, and she was one of the best. "Max, are you trying to pass off a cheap zirconia my daughter? This is dime store shit! You bought this trinket from the Second Hand Rose!"

Max told her off. "That's right! I am a dealer in junk and I am proud of it. Your daughter does not deserve any better."

Marilyn was angered enough to resume the mud fight. "Cheryl this guy is a shyster. I will not let you marry him."

"Ah yup, ah yup, I am a shyster!" Franken Muddy began to skip around the living room.

Cheryl read the brief note. "Dearest Love, this ring is symbolic. Let's be a Team and find one together."

CHAPTER THIRTY SIX

It was Saturday morning, and the end of the breakfast conversation in Arvada. Marilyn graciously declined Cheryl's offer to go to Sky's West for her graduation jump. "No we can't go with you today. We have to go to Home Depot. We promise to watch you next weekend. We will be caught up and maybe even ahead for a change."

It was mid morning when Cheryl and Max pulled into the lot.

"Max, I just can't believe that we are finally going to get to jump together."

"I just can't believe that you are here. After watching you ski at Cooper, I didn't think you had the co ordination to or the determination to make it through AFF."

"Do you have any more stupid little dares for me?"

"The Bruiser wants a rematch with the Crusher for the championship. No holds barred."

"We will have to set up a new ring, maybe out at the job site. Come on, Max. Let's go have some fun."

"Now you're talkin'."

"Hey, Mongo. Be a sport and carry my gear to the loft. I will get us manifested. Okay with you?"

Ever the dullard, he shook his head vigorously up and down. "Your greatest wish . . ."

They chimed in unison, "My smallest desire."

Cheryl went to the loft. She ran into Liz and Karen, and they quickly agreed to a four way. Manifest informed them, "You have about an hour. Load nine. What is your group name?"

"They looked at each other with mischievous grins. Liz offered, "Rusty Zipper?"

The laughs confirmed the name.

Outside the loft, Liz asked Cheryl, "Is Max here today?"

"Yes he is. He is walking over from the parking lot now." They turned to watch him wobble along with two gear bags to the packing area.

"I see you have him carry your gear bag. You have him trained pretty good."

Karen added, "Either that, or he is blind and in love."

"Do you think I should get him one of those sonar canes?" They shared a laugh.

Liz inquired, "What do we want to do for our first jump together? Head dives?"

"I don't know. Ask Cheryl. Let her set the pace. What is it going to be Cheryl?"

"Well, something easy to get started this morning. Back flips and turns are good for me."

Karen nodded with her award winning smile. "You know, just a four way round and three sixties is kind of fun. You have to work a little bit to center point and match fall rates. It is a good one to start with."

"If you alternate right and left three sixties, you will be surprised. It is an easy dive that will put you on your toes.

Max dropped both gear bags in the packing area. "Baby, what do you have in your gear bag? The kitchen sink?"

"That's why I keep you around, boy."

"Let's do the dirt dive now and get it out of the way."

They rehearsed a four way round with alternating right and left three sixties. Cheryl remarked, "I was wondering if I was ever going to get to dirt dive with my boy toy." They shared laughter.

Liz opened up. "Cheryl, we are going to break off at four thousand above ground level. Open by three grand. This will be new for you. You are moving fast and the ground will be close."

Karen smiled. "Don't take the hypnotic express. Don't become overpowered mentally."

Liz agreed. "When you get close, it really opens up. All objects spread apart really fast. It is hypnotic. You can be mesmerized. It will draw you in for a bounce."

"Don't go there. It will give you a strange, distant, stare in your eyes, like the one Max has." They all shared a laugh. "We are glad you are back

Max. We have someone we can vent with. Hey. Let's all do salute turns on this dive."

"I have new rules, ladies. Don't abuse me. You are limited. You only get two jabs a day. It is because of the strain that the Princess puts on me. I might fly off the handle and turn into a hacker."

"You let me know when the burden is too great. I've noticed a few decent males around here to link up with in case of your absence."

"I told you, Max."

"I'm grateful. Let's move on and drill this one more time."

The loud speaker announced, "Tandem 'We are flyin' and 'Rusty Zipper.' Ten minute call."

Karen volunteered. "Let's give the tandem a five count and go out on the same pass. I will go talk to them."

Liz and Karen rolled up the door and moved the pilot to the exit point. The tandem left, and Karen moved for front float, while Liz grabbed the back float. Max held Cheryl's left leg strap with his right hand. Four jumpers left the plane on "Go."

Once through the transition, the wind of fun whistled past their helmets and tore at their jumpsuits. They joined shoulder grips and smiles for the round, four way star. The nod was given and the right turn was made. There was some separation in height and distance, but corrections were quickly made and the group gripped four way star number two.

Max shouted at Cheryl. "Cheryl, will you marry me?"

The nod and laughs were given for first three sixty to the left. For some reason, Cheryl turned to the right. She quickly made the mental recovery, and after some work they had grips on their third star.

She hollered, "I will shoot you in the ass if you don't!"

Liz and Karen were laughing their heads off. The nod was given for another three sixty. All four divers finished and were centered and level relevant to each other.

Karen yelled, "Let's all get married!"

Max was overheating. He moved to Cheryl and gripped her shoulder piping. He pulled them nose to nose and gave her a hot, three second kiss while falling to earth at one hundred and twenty miles an hour.

Liz and Karen completed their fourth three sixty. There was altitude to squeeze in one more three sixty for everyone.

Upon completion the "go away" signs were given. The tracks and separations were made, and the divers listened to the rustling of the canopy material, as it left the canopy bag in the hundred mile an hour wind.

Four canopies snapped open. They inspected their canopy material and grouped up to fly back to the drop zone together.

Liz drew first shout. "I am not jumping with you anymore! I think you two are mental! You need to check in with a shrink before you do anything drastic!"

"Get out of the way Max. You are two slow!"

"Let's go find a Justice of the Peace!"

"When do you want to shop for a ring?"

"How about whenever we leave the hotel?"

"Max. You have your sequence mixed up again!"

"How about this afternoon?"

"Where are we going to stay?

"How about we put the tent up at the KOA camp ground in Loveland? They have a swimming pool. The water is not deep. You don't have to worry about drowning unless I hold you under!"

As Cheryl neared the landing area she noticed an unusual number of people. Must be lookie loos or relatives. She returned her concentration to her landing. She was still on fire from the kiss. Was that Marilyn?

Max stepped out of his gear in a flash and moved in front of Cheryl. "Here let me help you." He unbuckled her chest strap. They stared into each others eyes.

She took her helmet off. "Max, I feel great. I got a jump and you kissed me, and you asked me to marry you, and I agreed. Was I dreaming Max?"

"No, Cheryl I want to marry you right now."

Liz and Karen shouted, "Come on girl! Were waiting on you! What is the hold up?"

They turned around and to Cheryl's surprise a small circle of jumpers had formed.

"Will you walk with me, please?" Max offered Cheryl his left arm. She took it with her right hand.

Hal and Marilyn were in the center standing next to the Minister. Marilyn and Hal walked out and met their daughter at the entrance to the circle.

Marilyn handed Cheryl a dozen roses with baby's breath and a wide beautiful smile. "Congratulations, Cheryl. You are about to be married."

Hal handed Max the zirconia. "I can't believe you're so cheap."

A mild applause and a few cat calls rose from the jumpers. The women shouted, "Go Cheryl!"

Marilyn escorted Cheryl and Hal escorted Max to the center of their new friends.

Several comments were made in the crowd.

"I can't believe she is going to marry that old fart with glasses."

"He will have heart failure before the day is over."

A shout from one of the ladies, "He is second hand, and slightly used, but he is a good one."

"Dearly Beloved, we are gathered here today to join Cheryl Pritchard, and Max Mason, in Holy Matrimony . . ."

" . . . to have and hold, for better or worse, to love and to cherish . . ."

" . . . I now pronounce you Man and Wife."

They turned and faced one another.

"I love you Cheryl."

"Seal it Max."

They kissed.

"Did you feel the transition?"

"With all my heart!"

THE END

EPILOGUE

"Max, when does our honeymoon start?"

"I guess it officially starts now or tonight or tomorrow."

"Max, do you know what day tomorrow is?"

"Yes, dear. Now that you mention it. Tomorrow is the Fourth of July."

"Max, that would be a great day for my sunrise load. Why don't we skip KOA and camp here tonight? Tomorrow we can get a hop and pop at sunrise, and then we can cruise to the nearest breakfast grille to order steak and eggs. I could fork feed you some greasy sausages. What do you think, Max?"

"Your greatest wish, my smallest desire."

PARACHUTE RIG

Container, harness, leg straps (pilot chute pouch on back of leg strap—white paper) locking loop and pull up cord (shoe string), open empty main canopy pack tray, closed reserve pack tray (with reserve),

Chrome reserve ripcord handle, red cutaway handle,

Chest strap, altimeter,

Two chrome three ring main canopy release points (at the bottom of each riser), Risers, steer and speed control toggles (red)

Suspension lines (four groups), slider (black square fabric with white border)

Main canopy partially stowed in black canopy bag,

Red pilot chute ribbon/bridal with chrome pin, Red and white pilot chute, small white plastic pilot chute handle

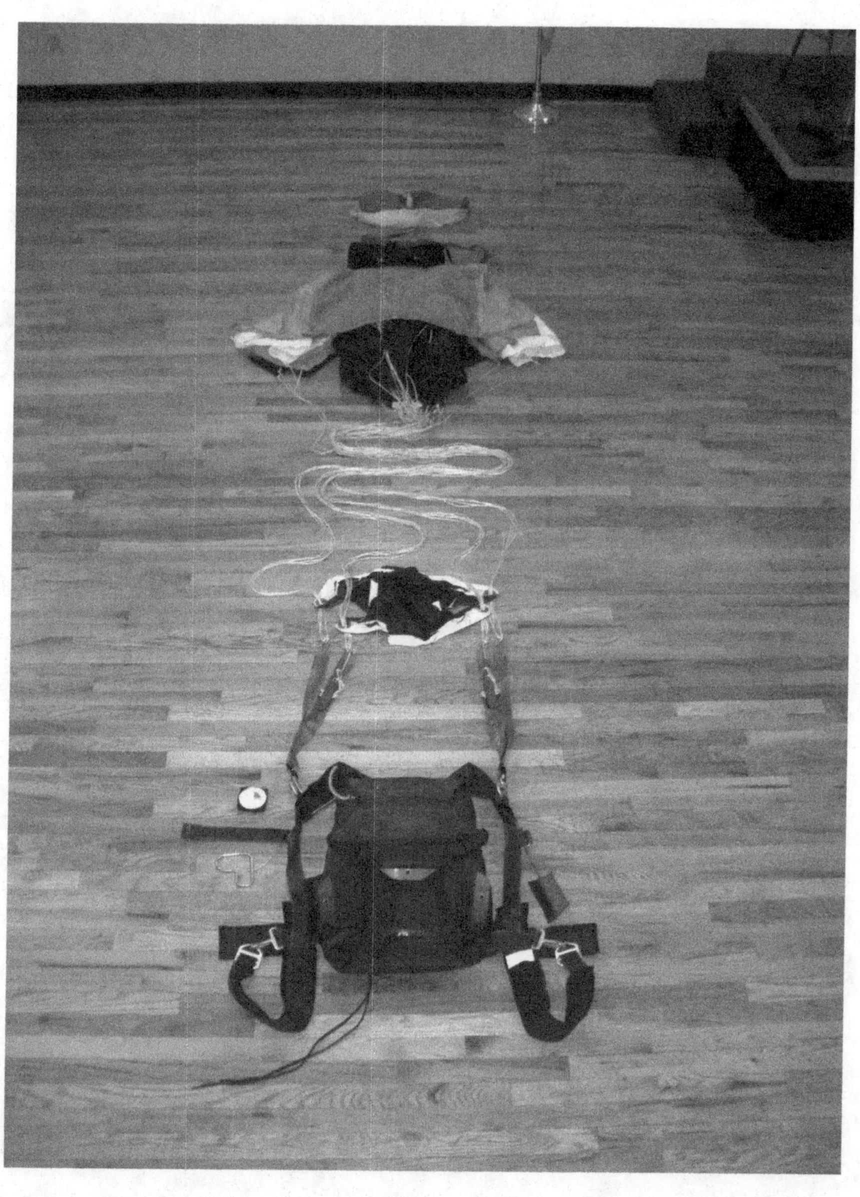

ABOUT THE AUTHOR

Bill Overmyer has made several skydives in Arizona and Colorado. He holds a D License proficiency rating and is a member of the United States Parachute Association. Bill lives in Colorado where he enjoys camping and skiing in the Rocky Mountains. Bill is the author of Your Stock Market Your IRA and the Dead Cat Bounce.